THE GIRL WHO TOLD THE TRUTH

BOOKS BY CATHERINE HOKIN

The Fortunate Ones

What Only We Know

The Lost Mother

The Secretary

The German Child

The Secret Hotel in Berlin

The Train That Took You Away

The Secret Locket

HANNI WINTER SERIES

The Commandant's Daughter

The Pilot's Girl

The Girl in the Photo

Her Last Promise

THE GIRL WHO TOLD THE TRUTH

CATHERINE HOKIN

Bookouture

Published by Bookouture in 2026

An imprint of Storyfire Ltd.
Carmelite House
50 Victoria Embankment
London EC4Y 0DZ

www.bookouture.com

The authorised representative in the EEA is Hachette Ireland
8 Castlecourt Centre
Dublin 15 D15 XTP3
Ireland
(email: info@hbgi.ie)

ISBN: 978-1-83618-669-4
eBook ISBN: 978-1-83618-667-0

For Clive,
whose light will never go out

PROLOGUE

MARCH 1936

Annie Kirson had never thought about death. She was barely a hand's breadth from childhood, her life balanced on the cusp between dolls and daydreams, between hopscotch and tea dances. Death was a game for the impossibly old. But now death had come to live in her world and she couldn't get out of its way.

'She could wake up – many do. Head injuries are strange things; often there's nothing to be done except wait, but you being here is a comfort. Talk to her, Annie, hold her hand. I know it's hard, pet, but be as strong for your mother as she's been for you.'

Strong. The nurse meant well, but the word was a knife. Her mother's strength hadn't been the problem; her father's had.

Annie slipped her hand round her mother's limp fingers. The bruises had faded from Peggy's soft cheeks. She looked more peaceful than she'd looked in months, despite the blue shadows beneath her closed eyes and the cast encasing her right leg.

'You're going to ruin our lives, Sid, and I don't want any more part in it. And I don't want our Annie messed up in your politics either, or anywhere near that German girl you'd be done with if you had any decency. I'll take her away from you first.'

A threat overheard from behind the banister's dark shadows. Her father's answering growl swallowed up in the smash of a glass hitting the floor and her mother's cut-off cry. A promise to remake their lives that had both terrified and thrilled Annie.

I would have gone with her if she'd asked me. I would have run from that house without a backward glance. I wish I'd told her that.

Annie twisted on the hard chair, her back aching from all the hours she'd spent willing her mother to open her eyes. The tiny room had become the centre of her universe. Spring had apparently arrived outside its thinly curtained window. One of the neighbours had brought Peggy a bunch of snowdrops; another had brought daffodils. The women who gathered round her bedside, bobbing to the doctors like nervous birds, could spend a whole visit discussing the weather and the new buds in the park. Annie ran between the home that wasn't a home without Peggy in it and school and the hospital and barely registered the shift.

'Is it Grete? Has she been writing to him again? Or is there going to be another march? Are you worried there's going to be trouble?'

All the questions she'd peppered her mother with once Sid had finally slammed out of the house because she couldn't ask the one that really mattered: 'Why does he bully you so, Mum? Why is he such a brute?'

Annie got up and climbed onto the bed, curling her body round her mother's as if she could fill Peggy with some of her restless energy. The stillness was the worst. Peggy was never still. She was a whirlwind of cleaning and cooking and tea with the neighbours, although there'd been less of those visits the more time Sid spent in his black-shirted uniform. Annie shifted around as her memories pricked. It was the silence that was worst, not the stillness. The house had been thick with it lately, and it thickened even more with each letter from Germany. Swallowing Peggy's laughter, stealing her voice. Especially after that last bitter row.

'Just keep away from Grete if she comes back – that's all I need you to do. Do you understand?'

Annie hadn't; she'd been under Grete's spell then too. But she'd have done anything to bring her mother's smile back, so she'd pretended not to see Peggy's purpling cheek and agreed.

And added another layer to the lies.

So much unsaid, so much that might stay lost forever. Annie's body started to shake.

'Wake up, Mum, please. Tell me what happened. It wasn't an accident, was it? She was there when you fell down the stairs. Did she push you, is that it? Did...'

Annie stopped. There wasn't a sound from the corridor. There was only her voice, which was too loud for the secrets it carried. She nestled closer to her mother and tucked her arms round her, looking for the anchor that had secured her through childhood; wishing she was the one wrapped safe inside the hug.

'Did Dad have something to do with it?'

It was said. The suspicion that had no real basis beyond a half-heard conversation, a half-seen look. The suspicion that filled her with fear.

Annie lay as still as Peggy and waited. For a movement, for a murmur. For a sense of her mother returning. The silence continued. Peggy's shell remained a shell, the truth locked away inside her as securely as a pearl in an oyster.

She got slowly up; gathered herself and her belongings. Home was the last place she wanted to go; Sid was the last person she wanted to see. But she owed her mother answers, and she owed her mother justice, so home was where she had to be.

PART ONE

CHAPTER ONE
DECEMBER 1934

'Annie, sit down and sit still for goodness' sake. And for the last time of telling, close the window. You'll crease your dress and get covered in soot. Do you want to arrive looking like a ragamuffin?'

Annie sat down, but she couldn't sit still. *Sit down* was all very well for her mother to say. Peggy was determined to play the lady and had turned impossibly prim. But Annie could barely contain her excitement into one carriage, never mind one seat. Left to herself, she would have gone running up and down the train, poking her nose into the other compartments, trying to spot the other party guests. Nothing about the day so far had made *sit still* a possibility, except her father's frown; everything else was too new.

Her parents were taking her out of London, something they never did. They were taking her to the countryside, which city-bred Annie, even at thirteen, remained partly convinced only existed in novels. They were going to a place whose name, Savehay Farm, sounded as if it belonged in a book. To a Christmas party where there would be dancing and a live band and champagne served in crystal glasses which all sounded impossibly romantic. Her father Sid had laid on a taxi to Marylebone Station; Sir Oswald Mosley, their host, was sending a chauffeur-driven limousine to collect them from Denham. That part alone was worth all the homework Sid had made Annie and her mother do in the past week.

'You need to read and memorise this. I won't have either of you making a show of me.'

This was *The Ten Points of Fascism* by Sir Oswald Mosley. Annie had never read anything so dull. Sid had presented the two of them with copies of the scarlet pamphlet as if they were priceless pieces of jewellery. He'd instructed them both to learn its key points, 'in the very unlikely event somebody at the party wants to know what you think'. Peggy had flicked through the first pages and put it aside with a sigh. But Annie – who still clung to the hope she could impress her father – persevered, reading and rereading the closely typed pages until she was able to regurgitate the phrases Sid had underlined, even if most of them meant nothing to her.

'It's about patriotism and putting Britain first. It's about achieving progress through teamwork and discipline, and getting rid of unemployment and poverty by looking after the national interest.'

Sid had clapped when she'd parroted her lesson, as if she was one of the performing monkeys dancing to a barrel organ in Shoreditch High Street.

'Very good. And what about the alien menace? What does Sir Oswald say about that?'

'No British jobs will go to aliens entering our country. And if the ones who are already here abuse our hospitality, they'll be sent back where they came from.'

Annie had no idea what was meant by *aliens* or where it was they'd come from, or why Peggy had frowned at the word. But she'd performed the memory trick again, and Sid had given her a penny and sent her to the sweetshop. His approval was so hard to come by, winning it had left her brimming with confidence. She was certain she could hold her own in the unlikely event anyone decided to test a girl on the workings of the British Union of Fascists – the organisation Sir Oswald ran and her father thought was the answer to all Britain's problems. Although everything she'd learned fell out of her head when they finally reached the farm that looked more like a mansion.

There were no barns or animals; there wasn't a thatched roof or a duck pond or a shiny big-wheeled tractor. Savehay was constructed from red bricks and a black-and-white timber frame and sat at the far end of a tree-lined avenue. It was the kind of rambling manor house where Queen Elizabeth I would have felt perfectly at home.

Annie was even more convinced she'd stepped back in time when Sid told her to stop gawping and chivvied her inside. The entrance hall had pictures painted directly onto the walls which, according to the date above them, were over three hundred years old. A minstrels' gallery ran round the vaulted great hall. A Christmas tree encrusted with silver baubles stretched up to the ceiling. When a stiff-backed butler appeared and announced that the dinner gong would sound at precisely seven o'clock, as if he was expecting the King to come and execute anyone who arrived a second late, it was all Annie could do not to giggle. Sid had disappeared into the depths of the house, so she tried to catch her mother's eye and share a smile. Unfortunately, Peggy didn't notice. She was completely mesmerised by the house and the poker-faced butler and was already trotting obediently after him up the stairs. Annie assumed she was supposed to follow her, until the day's next treat arrived.

'You must be Annie. I'm Vivien. I'm so glad you're here. Father never normally invites anyone my age, and Nicolas isn't down from Eton yet.'

The girl grinning down at her from the top of the thickly

carpeted stairs had the prettiest hair Annie had ever seen, a mass of dark curls that clustered round her pale face in a fluffy black cloud. She looked like the Blackberry Fairy from Annie's favourite childhood picture book. Annie's hand instantly flew to her own rather less exuberant strawberry blond waves, wishing she'd taken her mother's advice and given in to the discomfort of curling rags. Not that Vivien appeared to care.

'Come on – hurry up. I want to show you round. We're going to share a room, and we're allowed to watch the dancing after supper, which we're going to have in the kitchen tonight and not in the stuffy dining room.'

Vivien talked as quickly as she moved. She flew Annie through the house, keeping up a constant commentary as she flitted between the floors.

'That's the main upstairs corridor where the house guests will sleep; our room's round the corner at the back. That way goes to the top floor. My father's room's up there and we're not really meant to go near it. This is the back staircase. It's supposed to be for the servants, but I use it all the time to get round without being bothered, especially when Lady D's on the prowl.'

It took three times of asking before Vivien told her who Lady D was. By the time Vivien whisked her back to her flower-sprigged bedroom, Annie had worked out that the girl was a whirlwind because no one cared enough to calm her down.

'Lady D is Diana Mitford, the one with her claws sunk into my father. I expect she'll be my new mother soon enough.'

There was a bleakness in her tone when she said that which was deeply at odds with Vivien's lively manner and reminded Annie to tread carefully. In all the excitement of the arrival, she'd forgotten what Peggy had warned her to remember if Sir Oswald's children were at home – that their mother had died the previous year and was buried in Savehay's grounds. Annie had to supress a shudder as that story came back. The thought of her own mother dying was unthinkable; the idea of having someone buried in the back garden was bizarre. Luckily, Vivien didn't notice – she was too busy talking.

'Don't mind me. Everyone says Father has to marry again and can't keep having a string of girlfriends. And everyone else loves Diana, especially the men, because she's very beautiful, so I expect that's why he chose her. But she won't take any notice of us – she's not a big fan of children, including her own babies if you believe the papers. Not that it matters because we've got Grete to ourselves for the next few hours, and Grete is the best.'

She really was. Annie decided that within five minutes of meeting the seventeen-year-old German girl who was spending a few months at the farm to help with the children. Her life was a series of thrilling stories. Skiing in the Bavarian Alps where her family had a holiday house. Swimming in the lakes near their main home in Berlin. Hand-feeding a baby hippopotamus that had recently been born in the city's zoo. Her fluency in English was a source of wonder to Annie, who was still jabbing at her schoolgirl's German lessons like a babbling toddler. And her outfit was everything Annie had dreamed of wearing and never could. Sid had very strict opinions on the subject of women's clothing. He would have been outraged by Grete's flowing tweed trousers, never mind the heavy gold ring which dangled from her slim finger like a misplaced bracelet. He would have labelled her *mannish* and unfit company for a young girl. Annie thought she looked like Carole Lombard and worshipped her accordingly. She would have happily spent the whole evening with Grete, but the au pair clearly had other things on her mind. She grew increasingly preoccupied as the hours ticked past and put an end to their chatter with an abrupt, 'I have matters to deal with,' that left Annie feeling uncomfortably dismissed.

Vivien either didn't notice Grete's failing interest in them or had decided it was politer not to say. She kept up a stream of chatter as she led Annie back to the bedroom, which quickly disappeared under a sea of clothes and hair ornaments. Vivien discarded three dresses before she settled on an ankle-skimming green velvet with a square neck and ruffled sleeves that made her look far older than her years. Annie's transformation was far quicker. She had only one choice: a navy dress chosen to highlight her indigo blue eyes which had cost her parents considerably more than the simple skirts and sweaters she normally wore. The dark blue satin with its lace-edged Peter Pan collar had looked crisp in the shop. Now its colour and knee-length skirt made her feel like a child dressed up as a waitress. She half expected to be asked to carry a serving platter when they went down to the ballroom.

'Look at Diana and Grete. They could have flown in from Hollywood.'

Vivien didn't argue with Annie's open-mouthed admiration. Nobody could. All the women – including Peggy – were dressed very prettily in a rainbow of colours and rhinestones, but there was no doubting who shone the brightest.

'Maybe he'll change his mind and pick Grete to marry instead. Although I overheard the maid say she keeps a picture of Hitler by her bed, so maybe she's set her sights a bit higher than us.'

Annie didn't know how to respond to the strangeness of that image or to Vivien's wistful tone. As far as she could see, both Grete and Diana – who, according to Vivien, was the elder of the two at twenty-four – were far too young for the considerably older Sir Oswald, no matter how handsome he was. Not that he seemed to agree.

He looks like he'd own them both if he could. He looks as if he wants to devour them. And Diana can see it as clearly as I can.

There was a fluidity to Diana, as she moved round her guests with her silver lamé gown rippling like iced water, that was at odds with her marble face. She kept her distance from Grete and everyone else. She ignored the hands stretched out to take hers. Her pale blue eyes drifted over shoulders and away. There was a marked arrogance to her manner, but nobody seemed offended. Everyone she stopped beside, men and women, turned a little pinker, a little breathless. Diana was stunning and ethereal, but she was cold. Annie wasn't surprised Vivien didn't like her. Whatever fire the woman possessed was reserved solely for Mosley – as soon as he appeared at her elbow, a glow lit up her sharp face, and her fingers went searching for his.

And Grete's watching that with as much interest as me.

It took a moment for Annie to realise that – for all the warmth of her rose-gold sequinned dress and caramel-coloured hair – Grete's face was as frozen as Diana's when no one was looking her way.

They're both as metallic as their dresses. They're not women you'd want to cross.

Annie shivered. She had a sudden urge to be near her mother, a peculiar feeling that she was out of her depth, but Peggy was having fun and that was too rare to spoil. She stayed on the sidelines instead as the music grew louder and the dancers swirled faster. As the mingled scent of perfumes and pine prickled her nose and the champagne Vivien made her try puckered her mouth. As Grete, who'd been so friendly before in the kitchen, became a stranger. She ignored Annie's wave. When she wasn't spinning round the dance floor, she was prowling its edges, checking her watch and the windows. Annie wasn't sorry when ten o'clock came and Sir Oswald – who hadn't acknowledged his daughter all night – sent a servant over to escort them to bed. The party had not lived up to its magical promise, and the adults were welcome to it.

Vivien fell straight to sleep, but Annie kept picking at the undercurrents in the ballroom as if they might eventually make sense to her and couldn't settle. The sudden crunch of tyres across the gravel below the bedroom window as midnight approached, and the car headlights raking the room, was a welcome distraction. She assumed the non-staying guests must be leaving.

Which might mean a parade of glamorous fur coats and hats.

That pulled her out from under the covers. She wrapped herself in her dressing gown and slippers against the bedroom's cold bite, and crossed to the window, slipping inside the heavy curtains rather than opening them and waking Vivien. But there was no fashion show waiting; guests weren't leaving. Someone had arrived instead and, from the reception committee formed up by the car, whoever had come was expected. Annie forgot about the draught nipping at her ankles; she was too curious about the new arrival to feel it. She didn't understand why anybody would come to a party so late. Or why her father was standing outside in the cold beside Sir Oswald, his chest all puffed up like one of the East End's grubby pigeons.

The strange pantomime continued as a uniformed chauffeur opened the car door. Sir Oswald bowed when the first man got out. Annie had to bite her lip not to laugh when her father did the same. He looked ridiculous with his head bobbing about above his round stomach. He looked even stranger when a second man joined the first and his arm shot up in the air, almost poking Sir Oswald's eye out. Both the new arrivals looked far too ordinary for such a grand welcome. Annie's teeth started to chatter as the cold finally found her, she was about to let the curtain drop. Until the taller of the two men suddenly looked up at the sky as the clouds shivered away from the moon and his face became visible in the silvery light.

I know him.

The sideswept fringe and stubby moustache were achingly familiar, although it took her a minute or two to place the features onto the front page of a newspaper. Adolf Hitler. Annie clutched harder at the curtain. Adolf Hitler, the Chancellor of Germany – and the bizarre object of Grete's affections – was nodding to her father and following him and Sir Oswald through Savehay Farm's back door. The idea was preposterous, but it was happening. And the air of secrecy around the visit made it too intriguing to miss.

Annie was outside in the corridor before she considered that spying on a secret might not be her best plan. The music had stopped. More cars came crunching across the gravel with their headlights beaming, but they were arriving at the front entrance this time. The hall was suddenly full of chatter as guests said their goodbyes and left, or began heading for their bedrooms. Annie could hear Diana directing the leavers and cutting their farewells short. She could hear Grete ushering the house guests up the main stairs in an equally efficient manner.

Common sense finally kicked in, and Annie ducked back inside the bedroom. Sleep was an impossibility, but getting caught wasn't. Peggy's voice ran through her head in its familiar litany: *curiosity will kill you one day, Annie Kirson, never mind the cat.* It was a sensible warning, but she'd heard it too often to listen, and eavesdropping – which she regularly did at home when her father held his political meetings – had never tripped her up yet. So Annie didn't go to bed; she waited what felt like hours for the house to settle, and then she tiptoed down the back stairs.

It didn't take long to find the right door – it was the only one showing a rectangle of light. Annie crept towards it, almost jumping out of her skin when it suddenly swung open. She fell back into the shadows as Grete appeared, clutching the elbow of a man who was obviously drunk.

'You're a disgrace to the Party and to yourself. Banks will pack your things. Don't show your face here again.'

Her accent wasn't soft anymore; it was guttural. She

handed the man – who was calling Grete names that made Annie blush – over to the butler and turned back into the room. But something, perhaps the last insult that was fired her way, made her fumble with the door so it didn't close properly. Annie gave the girl a chance to correct her mistake, but she didn't come back and the door stayed ajar. Annie decided to read that as an invitation. She sidestepped the light falling like a sliver of sunshine across the darkened hallway and pressed herself behind a cupboard from where – when she screwed up her courage and pushed the door a fraction more open – she had a clearer view of the room. She could hear Grete talking in German. Whatever she was saying sounded like an apology.

Other sounds began to separate themselves out as Annie concentrated. Diana's laugh, a peal of bells which was far warmer than she was. Mosley's velvet-rich tones. Her father's cockney twang. And a constant murmur of German – sometimes from Grete, sometimes from an unseen voice – which Annie guessed was the English conversation being translated. She pressed closer to the doorframe, until shapes solidified into people. Grete sitting on the arm of a chair opposite Diana. Mosley and her father standing next to a group of well-polished men who'd been at the party. Hitler at the centre, seated next to the other visitor. Annie knew his thin face too – he was frequently in the same photographs as Hitler – but she couldn't remember his name. The conversation, however, was wrapped round familiar themes. *Discipline. Teamwork. National interest. No place for aliens.* The words from the pamphlet, and from the BUF meetings Sid held in the parlour at home. They grew darker very quickly at Savehay too. *Purges. Enemies who must be removed. Ungrateful Jews who need to be taught a lesson.* Annie's skin itched, but she didn't dare scratch it.

'That's our warning to wrap things up. We need to move our guests back to the airfield before the village starts stirring.'

The clock chimed part way through what sounded like the

offer of a pledge of money from Hitler to Sir Oswald and the party instantly broke up. Annie leapt up too – getting caught where she shouldn't be at home would be bad enough, but Sid would murder her if he found her lurking here. Unfortunately, she'd moved too quickly for her cramped feet, and she lost her balance. The vase she hadn't noticed perched on the top of the cupboard toppled achingly slowly, as if it was tempting her to reach out and catch it. But it fell far too fast when it finally tipped over and crashed against the tiles with a smash that bounced round the hall. Grete moved first, her face twisting into sharp points. She was fast, but Annie was faster. She sped up the servants' stairs to Vivien's bedroom and leapt under the bedclothes, staying in the same frozen position until there were no more footsteps prowling the halls. Nobody came knocking on their door, but that didn't matter. She didn't dare close her eyes for the rest of the night.

It was early when Peggy came to get Annie for breakfast. Vivien rolled over and refused to wake up or say goodbye as Annie climbed into her clothes and slipped out of the room. Peggy was too exhausted herself to notice her daughter's smudged eyes. She reacted to Annie's tugging hand and, 'Mum, something happened last night I need to tell you about,' through a fog.

'Why? What's the matter?' She finally noticed Annie's pale face and sighed. 'Oh dear, was Vivien unkind to you? I did worry she might be, with her mother gone and the new... Well, that's as may be, but I'm not sure there's much I can do if she was.'

'No, that's not it. It's nothing to do with her.' Annie jumped in before Peggy could go down a whole road of how different to them the upper classes could be, which was one of her favourite subjects. 'This is going to sound completely mad, I know, but Adolf Hitler came here last night as the party was ending. I saw him. And Dad met with him – he was outside when the car arrived – and Grete was involved somehow too. I haven't been able to sleep a wink trying to make sense of it.'

The effect on Peggy was electric. She grabbed Annie's arm and pulled her into a small hallway off the main one, her eyes suddenly wide awake.

'Oh my goodness, Annie, when will you learn to mind your own business? This has nothing to do with you, and you're to forget it this instant. If your father finds out you were watching... If one word of this meeting gets out...' She shook her head as if she couldn't find a threat big enough, before settling on, 'Well, you'll both be in serious trouble.'

Annie stared at her mother, trying to adjust to the fact that she hadn't dreamed the Führer up, which she'd started to believe might have happened as the night stretched towards dawn. Her mother's face had lost all its pink softness.

'You knew he was here? But how? And what was he doing here? And why do you want me to keep secrets when you've always told me that's the worst thing to do?'

Annie's world was shifting, and she didn't like it. Peggy was supposed to offer her a sensible explanation for the night's events; she was supposed to make her feel better. She'd done the opposite instead. And nothing her mother said next was a comfort either.

'Because they normally are. Oh, sweetheart, how do I explain this? Some things are bigger than us, that's all; they're bigger than the normal rules. Herr Hitler...' Peggy lost her flow as she said the name and had to take a breath. 'It was a private visit, as I understand it, which means it could be an embarrassment for the government. They wouldn't like him being here without permission. And the people who don't understand what he or Sir Oswald are trying to do wouldn't like it either. So, like I said, it's best to forget about it. I'm serious, Annie. No good will come if you go asking questions.'

Her mother's tone as much as her words said that the conversation was over, but Annie wasn't ready for that. And she didn't mean to sound petulant – she wanted to be treated like an adult after all – but she was tired and confused, and so her words came out all wrong.

'But Grete knew all about it – she was there. And she's barely four years older than me. Why does she get to know what's going on and I don't?'

Peggy's expression got caught somewhere between a sigh and a smile. 'I know you're growing up, even if I don't always want to believe it. And I know someone like Grete could seem very glamorous, but she's not the sort of woman you should admire. She's not the kind you should want to be.'

Annie knew her mother was partially right – she'd seen Grete's cold side for herself. But she'd also seen how the men flocked round her, including her own father. And she wasn't ready to lose the point.

'Maybe she's not, but I bet she could tell me about the things you never talk about, couldn't she? I bet she knows who the *aliens* are and why everyone Dad mixes with hates the Jews. And I bet she knows why Hitler's sneaking round in the middle of the night promising to give Sir Oswald money.'

The slap was so sudden and unexpected, it shocked Annie into silence. She stared at her mother as her cheek, and her pride, burned, and Peggy's face crumpled.

'Oh dear God, I'm so sorry. I'm so sorry. You're right, Annie, there's things get said and accepted in our house that need explaining to you, that aren't right. But that girl isn't the one to do it. Keep away from her, please. And you don't mention the money to anyone. This is my fault – I've spent too long believing politics is men's business. And that because your father supports Sir Oswald and Hitler's views on the world, we have to fall in line. It's much easier that way, but I'm not sure it's right. I'll try to do something to change that, if you promise me you'll forget everything you saw last night. Can you do that for me?'

Annie promised she could because she didn't want her world to tip any further off its axis. She sat quietly beside her mother at breakfast, smiled at Grete and Diana, and pretended to eat the poached eggs Peggy placed in front of her. She told Sid how much she'd enjoyed the ball on the journey back to London and let him beam as broadly as if he'd arranged it himself. She didn't ask him his views on Hitler, or aliens, or anything else in the weeks afterwards; she waited for her mother to step in and explain things instead. But when Peggy didn't and the rows grew louder behind the flat's closed doors, she worked harder at understanding for herself.

She read and reread the pamphlet, although its messages grew no clearer. She mulled over the conversations she'd over-heard at Savehay, picking at the unpleasant words they were filled with and trying to make sense of them. She carried on eavesdropping on the BUF men who visited her home on Friday nights and heard the cruelty far more clearly in their laughter. She got no closer to what *Sir Oswald and Hitler's views on the world* might mean in practical terms. But the more she thought about the conversation with Peggy, the more she realised that her mother hadn't been angry with her; she'd been frightened. And the more she began to understand – with a creeping sense of dread for where it might take her – that the politics her father had chosen to follow and shape their lives with had something very dark at its heart.

CHAPTER TWO
FEBRUARY 1936

'Everything I do is for you and your mother. Don't question me, and don't forget that.'

Sid's mantra – his rule book for their home – had sat at the centre of their household for as long as Annie could remember, and it had developed multiple uses. He repeated it on the three nights a week when he was away from the flat attending BUF meetings. He repeated it on the Friday nights when the parlour was reserved for his friends. And on the evenings when he was at home, he used it to preface his favourite lecture, which began with, 'You've no idea how hard life used to be...' and continued on into a journey through the Pennyfields slums in Limehouse where he'd been raised.

Annie always enjoyed the first part of his monologue. It was the only time Sid talked about his childhood, which had ended at the age of eleven when he'd been apprenticed to the Henry Hermann Furniture Factory, and about the grandparents she'd never known. She was grateful he'd 'pulled himself up by his bootstraps' as he put it, so she didn't have to live in the same brutal conditions he'd endured.

The East End slums, some of which still existed, sounded

terrifying. Damp and decaying houses with forty-five people crammed into less than a dozen rooms, built round stinking courtyards where the rats outnumbered the people. She was grateful Sid's hard work meant they weren't poor and she lived where she did, in a flat in Arnold Circus, which was a magical place. Two minutes outside their building's front door and they were straight into the bustle and chaos of Shoreditch High Street. But the Circus itself was as cut off from that as if a spell had been cast around it. The loudest sounds inside its ring of tall red buildings were the birds singing in the bandstand at its centre, and the horses clopping in from the dairy with the day's milk. Annie was grateful too that she'd been able to use Sid's 'work hard and you'll never regret it' philosophy to persuade him to let her stay on at school until she was sixteen and complete her School Leaving Certificate, rather than joining the factory floor at fourteen as so many of her contemporaries had to do. But grateful wasn't the same as happy, or comfortable, or close.

'Don't talk to him about university. Mention going there and he'll have you in the workforce before you can whistle. It's not where decent girls go – you know that.'

Annie didn't know that, but she knew better than to ignore Peggy's advice when it came to how best to deal with her father. Sid believed a woman's role was to find a husband and that her place was very firmly in the home, so the conversation about university never happened. He controlled that conversation the way he controlled them all, including how he spoke about his childhood. His lectures always followed the same pattern: from his family's struggles into a diatribe against the Chinese families he'd lived alongside in Pennyfields. Into a rant against their 'peculiar' food shops and 'ungodly' restaurants and how none of that was British. Into a rant about how many jobs Chinese men had stolen on the docks from 'honest working ones'. Annie hated that part – she couldn't bear how angry and unpleasant

Sid's language grew then. Or how close it was to the words he used on a Friday night.

But when Peggy asked him to have a heart for his daughter and leave those memories out, he'd raged at her for so long, Annie thought his scarlet neck would explode. She learned to listen with a blank face, the same way her mother did. She took some comfort in Peggy's, 'I wish I could change him; I swear he wasn't this bad before the war,' but she was too wary of Sid's temper to want the fights that followed when Peggy plucked up her courage and tried. She would have consoled herself with the fact that his hatreds were in the past if his present ones hadn't been so obvious.

Outside his work as a manager in a furniture factory – where he wore a brown overall which smelled of sawdust and beeswax – Sid wore a uniform. A black shirt that fastened high on his shoulder. Black trousers tucked into black boots. A blue badge with a white lightning flash pinned to his chest and a heavily buckled leather belt round his waist. Annie loathed the sight of him in that more than she loathed his ranting. The uniform made him stride around and flex his knuckles as if he was looking for a fight. It made him nasty. And it made the many Jewish families who lived in the Circus and sent their children to the secondary school there – the same one Annie attended – turn away and slam their doors, and refuse to speak to Sid or his wife and daughter. Not that Sid cared.

'This uniform is who I am; it's who we are. It's our right to follow whatever beliefs we choose. They can get used to it, or they can go somewhere else and leave us in peace with better neighbours.'

He never noticed how Annie winced at *we* and *our* and *us*, and she didn't dare question *choose*. She was his daughter: he couldn't imagine a world in which she disagreed with his views, any more that he would accept criticism from his wife. Sid believed women thought what they were told to think. He had no idea that the more she learned about his hate-tinged view of the world, the more upset Annie became because she didn't know how to tell him. And because her mother begged her not to try.

'Go along with it, Annie, and leave him to me to manage. You know what he's like if he's crossed. He'll fling his temper round the flat for weeks. Please God if you have a husband of your own one day, you'll make better choices.'

As far as Annie could see, no married woman ever made her own choices – Peggy hadn't been allowed to make a decision of her own since her wedding day, like most of the women she'd grown up with. She didn't say it: the last thing she ever wanted to do was hurt Peggy. Her father had proved, in multiple ways, that he was more than capable of doing that on his own. It wasn't just his temper that had worn lines across Peggy's face. A shadow called Grete had taken root in the flat after Sir Oswald's Christmas party; the slightest mention of her name led to slammed doors and shouting, although Peggy's side of the argument was quickly stilled. And Annie wasn't allowed a voice in the conversation at all.

'There's a postcard from Germany, look! Grete's been skiing in the Alps, like she told us she loved to do. Isn't it a gorgeous picture?'

The first time a card arrived, Annie had been too excited to notice it was addressed to her father and not to her, or to the whole family. When she did eventually point that out as seeming a little odd, Sid ignored her and Peggy's forehead gained another groove. No more postcards came after that, but letters did, with Sid's name and their address written on the envelope in the same slanting hand. He never left those lying around. He never let Peggy, or Annie, read them. And when Peggy eventually broke down and not only made the mistake of objecting to their arrival but questioned what Grete wanted with him, his roar at her to mind her own business echoed through Annie's bones.

The day that split Peggy's life in two started, as too many other days had started, with Sid throwing his weight around and a fight she couldn't win. Doors slamming, plates breaking. Sounds that were too familiar to warn Annie that this row was worse than the others, that this one was set on a far more dangerous path. Sounds Annie would replay over and over once the day was done, blaming herself for hiding, for letting Peggy stand on her own; for being too frightened of her father to challenge his rule.

'I don't want Annie to go there today. Not if she's coming. I don't want—'

'I'm sick of hearing what you don't want. I'm sick of you. You're holding me back, you're a dead weight on me...'

The rest of the fight, and Sid's savage insults, was lost behind a slammed door. When Annie finally stopped shaking and emerged from her bedroom, her mother was nowhere to be seen and her father was wearing the uniform she hated. And a smile that wasn't warm enough to break the flat's brittle mood.

'Get your things. I'm taking you to headquarters with me for the day.'

Annie's heart instantly sank even further. She wanted to be with Peggy, not Sid. She hated visiting the BUF's headquarters on the King's Road, the Black House as it was known after the shirt all Mosley's supporters wore. She'd hated it from the first day Sid had taken her there. Entering the premises required walking past two guards who greeted her father by raising their arms in a Hitler salute, prompting loud tuts and catcalls from passers-by. The walls inside were plastered with posters bearing slogans Annie could hardly bear to look at. Every time she saw the hateful words, *Perish Judah,* she wanted to run and apologise to the Kleinmanns and the Solomons and the rest of the perfectly decent Jewish families she wished she was allowed to know better in Arnold Circus.

Everything that Sid loved about the Black House, or 'the nerve centre' as he called it, made Annie want to curl up and pretend she didn't know him. It operated on military and – as he'd explained to her – German National Socialist lines, in keeping with Sir Oswald's allegiance to Adolf Hitler. The students training there marched to and from their lessons and flung up their right arms every time a senior official walked past; bugles announced lessons and lunchtimes. On her first visit, Annie had been escorted to a lecture extolling the merits of the Nuremberg Laws which Hitler's government had passed in 1935 to remove citizenship rights from German Jews. The more she'd listened to the lecturer praising Hitler's 'commitment to protecting his people's pure blood', the more she'd known there was no place for her at the Black House. And she especially hated visiting it when there'd been fighting at home, because Sid's mood was even more unpredictable then.

'Where's Mum? Is she getting ready? Shouldn't we wait for her to come with us?'

The flat was too quiet. There wasn't a sound from her parents' bedroom. Annie's heart lurched. It was barely a month since Sid had bruised Peggy's face so badly she'd had to stay at home for a week and then send Annie for a bottle of the make-up she never normally wore.

What if he's done worse this time? What if she's unconscious?

Annie took a step back, wondering if she should knock on the bedroom door or burst in. But Sid stopped her before she could try.

'She's gone out. You'll see her when you get home.'

He began shepherding her towards the coat rack beside the front door. Peggy's tweed coat wasn't hanging from it, but her soft green hat was still there. When Annie pointed out how odd that was, because the weather was cold and Peggy had rigid standards when it came to her appearance, Sid shrugged.

'She won't have gone far then, will she? She'll be with a neighbour, no doubt, swapping recipes, or whatever it is she does all day.'

It was a ridiculous answer, but Sid had a light in his eye that suggested no good would come from questioning it. Annie let him lead her out of the flat and towards the bus stop instead, peering through every window on the way. But there was no sign of Peggy.

Sid ignored Annie on the bus, which was a relief. She spent the journey pretending that sitting next to him was a coincidence. That the muttered and not so muttered comments about his uniform had nothing to do with her. It wasn't until they got off on the King's Road that he turned to her with his overly bright smile again.

'This is a special day for you. I've got a surprise. Someone I think you'll be thrilled to see.'

He wouldn't be drawn further. He bounced her through the door as the welcoming arms snapped up and into the foyer where he stopped, waiting as he always did for the reception committee which was primed to instantly flock at his appearance.

'Sir Oswald picked me out from the start, at the first meeting I ever attended. He didn't care that I'd come from the factory floor, that I didn't have money or position. He recognised my loyalty straight away, and I've been one of his most trusted lieutenants ever since. That's the glory of the movement: it's the part you can play that matters, not where you started from.'

That was another of Sid's favourite lectures. He'd delivered it on so many trips to the Black House that Annie no longer listened to it. But there was no welcoming committee today;

there was no entourage waiting to hang on his words. Instead, there was an argument raging at the top of the central staircase that had stolen everybody's attention.

'You're to keep away from my daughter, do you hear me? I've had to tell my girl to stay quiet once because of your carryings on. It won't happen again. I know Sid's plan, I know he wants you to turn Annie into some kind of poster girl for the Party but I'm not having it. You're not fit company for her, and you're certainly no role model. I'd rather see you handed in to the authorities myself.'

The twist in the staircase made it impossible to see who was fighting. It took Annie a moment to recognise the shrill voice as Peggy's: the threats and the fury held nothing of her gentle mother. It took Sid another moment before he realised the shouting woman was his wife and turned white. As for whoever she was arguing with... Annie couldn't hear what Peggy's opponent was saying, and she had nothing solid to base her suspicions on, but she couldn't shake one face from her head.

I don't want Annie to go there today. Not if she's coming.

There was only one unnamed *she* in their lives. There was only one *she* whose letters and – from the quickly silenced arguments Annie had pieced haphazardly together – whose visits could whip Peggy up into an anger that had no thought for the consequences. Annie turned to Sid in time to see the same conclusion burn two bright spots across his rough cheeks.

'Grete's here, isn't she? That's my "surprise". That's who you and Mum were fighting about. Mum isn't at a neighbour's; she came here to tell Grete to keep away from me. But why would she do that?'

Annie never found out if Sid had an answer. She had no way of knowing if it really was a stumble that tipped Peggy off the top step, as Grete instantly claimed when she came running down the stairs, her hands clasped as prettily to her mouth as if she was playing a scene. She had no way of knowing what had sent her mother tumbling backward too slowly and too fast and crumpled her on the marble floor as if she no longer had bones. The shutters came down around Peggy that day.

Time stood still for a second. Nobody moved except Grete. Nobody cried out except Grete.

She's not shocked. She has us all under a spell. Whatever's happening here, she knows every line of it.

That realisation snapped Annie out of her trance. She leapt to Peggy's side, screaming at Grete to explain herself, screaming for someone to help.

Sid finally moved then. But he didn't go to Peggy and he didn't grab Grete the way Annie was begging him to do. He left the Blackshirts to tend to his wife and ring for an ambulance. He grabbed Annie instead and bundled her out of the door, but not before she caught the look that passed between him and Grete. The one that was full of anger but not shock on his part. The one that looked like triumph on hers.

'It wasn't an accident – it wasn't.'

Sid bundled Annie into a taxi and told her to shut up; he led her into the flat as if she was a prisoner. And later he brought the doctor who administered a sedative when Annie wouldn't stop insisting that Peggy's fall was Grete's doing. That Grete had tried to murder her mother.

CHAPTER THREE

MAY 1936

It took Peggy almost a month to emerge from her coma. She came back to the world with her memories clouded, the day of her fall and the days around it submerged in a subterranean haze. After that, the accident – as everyone, including Peggy, quickly learned to call what had happened – rewrote the rules of the house. There were no more arguments; there were no more raised voices. Peggy returned from hospital with a limp from a broken leg that hadn't properly set and an utterly broken spirit.

There was no more mention of Grete either, or her letters. There was no discussion about what had happened at headquarters or why Peggy hadn't wanted Annie anywhere near the German girl. Instead, Sid grew stronger as Peggy diminished, and Annie – who couldn't shake the feeling that her father was a far more dangerous man than the quick-fisted bully she already knew – was too afraid to risk his temper and ask questions. His friends took over the parlour every other night and held their meetings there. He ordered Annie around as if she was one of his foot soldiers and praised her quiet obedience. But he had no idea that her silence was hard won and kept only for

Peggy's sake. He had no idea what went on in her head. He had no idea that Grete was lodged like an ice chip in her heart. He didn't know his well-behaved daughter would have burned the Black House to the ground if she could. Or that her sudden interest in attending rallies was born not from passion for the movement in the way he chose to see it, but from a desperate desire to find a way out.

'We'll make a proper day of it. It'll be a treat for you to hear Sir Oswald speak, and there'll be a nice little gathering at The Crown afterwards. They always do us a good spread.'

Sid had presented the outing to the May Day Rally in Victoria Park as if he was offering his daughter a visit to Buckingham Palace. Annie had accepted it not only because her attendance allowed Peggy – whose injuries had left her increasingly nervous of the outside world – to stay at home, but because she had her own business there. She longed more than anything to confront Grete, although she had no idea if the girl was still in London. And she was desperate to find people from the opposite side of the political street than the one she'd been forced to live in. People who might be willing to help her get justice for her mother or explain if such a thing was even possible; who might be able to offer her a glimpse of an alternative world. There was no one else she could take her questions to. The non-Jewish girls at her school thought the Blackshirts were glamorous and envied her proximity to them. The Jewish ones turned their backs if she tried to engage in their conversations. She'd seen posters in Stepney and Bethnal Green advertising anti-Mosley and anti-fascist protest meetings, but she had no idea how to go about attending one. So a rally where there would be dissenting voices seemed like the obvious solution. In reality, it was anything but; it was another prison.

The BUF families were corralled into a tiny square of the

park, inside a security cordon of stewards as tight as a steel belt. When Annie had asked if she could walk around outside it, she was told not to be ridiculous. There was no way to get close to the protesters. There was no sign of Grete. And Mosley's speech – which she couldn't escape from and was all she could hear – made her stomach curdle far worse than his pamphlet.

'We will protect good British people from racial contamination. We will protect them from racial impurity. We will build a better Britain free of Jewish control over our factories and our banks. We will build a better Britain without them.'

Each promise had contorted his face with hate. His supporters had greeted them by cheering, flinging up their arms and flinging back their heads and promising vengeance on the 'Yids'. They'd bayed for blood until Annie felt sick. Sid had howled along with the best of them. But the protestors and their banners and their chants were blocked from view by a row of snorting police horses. And by the time Annie was led away – in a car surrounded by a fleet of motorbikes – they'd been cleared from the park.

There'd been no escaping the victory party afterwards either. Annie had gone to the reception at The Crown because she had no other choice. She'd sat beside Sid while he held court. She'd stopped fighting the realisation that, *He's my father but I don't like him and I don't trust him*, which lived permanently now in her brain. She'd sat in silence, unable to eat, choking on the questions her fellow diners would spit at. That boiled down to: *Why is there so much hatred? What have these poor people you treat as less than human done to deserve it?* Determined to find a way into the meetings where Mosley wasn't regarded as a hero. To find a way to separate herself from a *we* and an *us* she hadn't asked for and didn't want to be part of. And to find a side of the story where innocent women weren't pushed down the stairs and their husbands weren't so at ease with the lie baked into *accident*.

CHAPTER FOUR
OCTOBER 1936

The flat had become a place of secrets and silences. Of letters that were snatched from the postman's hand before Annie or Peggy could get to the door. Of late-night muffled phone calls whose snippets – 'But why there and why then...? Why couldn't she have just disappeared...?' – filled Annie with a dread she had no one to confide in. And a determination not to let her father – or his henchmen – out of her sight.

'May Day was one thing, but that'll be no place for a girl.'

Sid dismissed Annie's request to go with him to the Cable Street parade on the fourth of October as if it was a ridiculous idea, although he'd been calling it the movement's most important event of the year for months. Or 'the day the whole East End unites behind Sir Oswald and takes a stand against the Jews who've stolen our city', to be more precise. When she tried again – repeating his words back to him – he wouldn't be pushed.

'No, Annie, you can't. This is men's work. If you want to get involved, volunteer at headquarters. There's plenty of jobs for girls there – making banners, writing leaflets. But you're not going on the march. There'll be too many protesters, and I haven't got time to waste worrying about your safety.'

Annie didn't believe Sid cared any more about her safety than he had about Peggy's. As far as she could make out, nobody at the Black House had asked Grete any questions about why she'd been arguing with her mother or about the consequences of that row. Nobody had informed the police or stopped the girl returning to Germany. One of the reasons Annie wanted to attend the march was to try and gather any information she could about what Grete meant to the movement, and to her father. Not that Sid had any idea about that. Or that *too many protesters* was the other reason she wanted to go.

Annie didn't believe the East End was about to unite behind Mosley: if they were going to do that, why would there be protests at all? And why would the BUF marchers need the stockpile of clubs and knuckledusters she'd glimpsed in the Black House, or the combat training she knew went on there? She might have taken Sid's advice and gone back to headquarters if she'd thought she might learn anything of use there, which she wouldn't. The whole place was riddled with paranoia about infiltrators, and all information about where and when public meetings would take place was shared strictly on a need-to-know basis. But if she wanted to attend the parade – which she did – she would have to find out more details than simply the date. Which meant she had to rely on her old habits and eavesdrop.

'We've got the police in our pocket. There'll be about seven thousand of them in attendance, with at least a third of that number on horseback. If the commies and the Yids try to disrupt things, they'll get a very tough welcome.'

The round of applause that greeted Sid's words snapped through the door like gunfire. His meetings never changed their pattern, whatever night they were held. Peggy and Annie were barred from the parlour as soon as the first man arrived. Peggy went to bed. Annie waited until her mother was asleep – which never took long now the doctor, who was as devoted as Sid to the movement, regularly prescribed sleeping tablets for her – and then sneaked back downstairs once the last visitor was inside. Nobody ever heard her, but the door was thin and they were loud, and she always heard them. The laughter at the damage the horses' hooves could inflict on the protesters could probably be heard in the street.

Annie waited for that to die down and for the clink of beer bottles as yet another toast was raised to finish. She waited for the rustle that told her Sid was handing out leaflets.

'These are the sites for the four public meetings that Sir Oswald will address tomorrow: Limehouse, Bow, Bethnal Green and Hoxton. And these are the routes the four marching columns of our supporters will take into the East End.' There was a short pause – Annie assumed Sid's audience was consulting the map – and then he resumed speaking. 'I'll be leading the one leaving from Whitechapel High Street and heading down towards Commercial Road. I expect to be on the move by two thirty. Study your routes carefully, tell the details only to those who need to know and don't let the maps out of your sight.'

The men dispersed soon after that, although Sid went back to the parlour and his beer. Annie had to wait until morning before she could check the room. She got up at dawn and searched through every inch of it – and her father's coat pockets – but there wasn't a stray leaflet to be found. That was a setback, but not a huge one. Annie knew the way down Commercial Street to Commercial Road well enough – she'd walked the route with Sid during her school holidays to visit the suppliers and smaller companies he dealt with there. She was confident she could find the place where his column would appear on the main road by herself. And perhaps that meant she wouldn't be able to join in and ferret any information out of the Blackshirts, but it would bring her closer to the protestors.

And then maybe I can find someone who'll believe me about how dangerous Mosley's men really are and help me help my mother.

It sounded like such a sensible plan. It never occurred to her that her father might have been right this time, and the danger she was about to walk into was real.

Sunday the fourth dawned cool and windy and ready for autumn. By the time Annie came down for breakfast, Sid was gone and her mother was still in a tablet-induced haze. Her mother's increasing withdrawal from even the smallest pleasures of her life normally broke Annie's heart. Today it was a blessing. She left a book by Peggy's chair, next to a box of the chewy toffees her mother had once loved. She doubted either would be touched, but the thought of not trying to at least tempt Peggy back into the world would break her heart too.

Annie reached Commercial Road without mishap. She'd expected the walk to be a quiet one; it was anything but. The sprawling Spitalfields fruit and vegetable market was closed to the public for the day, but that didn't stop the delivery carts getting ready for Monday, and competing for road space with the horse-drawn wagons clattering in and out of Truman's Brewery. Or traders with unofficial pitches from congregating along the litter-strewn pavements. There were hours yet before Sid's column was due to reach the junction with Sidney Street, which was where she assumed they'd come out. On any other day, Annie – who was rarely allowed to wander anywhere alone – would have lingered to watch the huge dray horses and the women haggling over bruised fruit. But today she had a destination, and today the streets weren't particularly welcoming. Men without black shirts or other recognisable insignia had already begun gathering in large groups outside the pubs and on the street corners. The closer Annie got to Sidney Street, the more she realised she'd never needed to shadow her father to find the march because the whole of East London was apparently already there. And they all understood the danger far better than she did.

Although it was only one o'clock, long before the parade and the speeches were set to begin, the area was packed. Men and women, and quite a few children, spilled off the pavements and into the road outside Aldgate Station. The air was as thick with static as the hours before a thunderstorm. Horns blared as cars veered down the road, packed with protesters hanging out of the windows yelling, 'Mosley will not pass – keep the fascist out!' at the tops of their voices.

Annie had never been alone in the middle of so many people. The noise and the press of their bodies against hers was a shock. She tried to back away as the pavements disappeared and the masses swarmed, twisting and turning as if they were caught in the wake of invisible currents. She pressed herself against a graffitied and shuttered shop window and tried to find a landmark, not that there were many she knew, but the crowds swept her back up in an instant.

'Down with Mosley! Down with the Fascists!'

The roar came from every side. Any sense of time or direction disappeared. Annie fought to stay on the edge of the chaos and not get sucked into the middle, looking for a gap and a safe place to perch. That appeared in the shape of a low wall, but the second she climbed onto it – and realised from the sign above her head that she'd been pushed along as far as Cable Street – someone yelled at her to get down. Seconds later, the wall was dismantled, its bricks disappearing into fists and pockets. She tried to crane round to see the size of the crowd, but she couldn't get a sense of the numbers. She couldn't stop anyone to speak to. The mass of people kept on moving, changing formation, surging without warning.

They're filling in spaces; they're blocking the road.

She'd thought the crowd had no purpose, but that wasn't true. Annie leapt to the side as a new cry flew up, 'Get them ready!' and a blockade immediately followed it – mattresses and bricks and pallets piled up in a toppling mass. She got knocked and turned round; she came close to falling. There was a crash from in front of her, another from behind. A searing sound of metal hitting stone and glass snapping. A shout rose up on gales of laughter: 'It's the drivers – they're tipping their trams over!'

Another gap opened up and closed as quickly as a pile of paving stones leapt onto the pallets. All around her, arms flew round shoulders and hands clasped other waving hands, and the voices kept rising and rising.

'One, two, three, four, five: we want Mosley dead or alive!'

The chant grew stronger, louder. It carried a force that promised a reckoning. But then it fell away and the sudden silence, and then what filled it, was terrifying. Drums. A thumping, pounding heartbeat that poured down the streets as if they were veins. That crashed through Annie's bruised body as if someone was beating their fists on her skin. And behind that a sharper clashing rhythm Annie didn't recognise but the protesters did.

'Horses. The bastards are coming on horses. Can't you hear their hooves on the cobbles?'

The cry ran up and down the crowd, followed by a roaring, 'They shall not pass!'

Someone yelled for marbles, and seconds later the ground was awash with the tiny glass spheres that were intended to topple the horses. Annie stopped thinking; she stopped trying to make sense of what was happening. She slid across the slippery ground, trying to propel herself behind the relative safety of the barricade. She couldn't see what was coming, but she could feel it. The marching feet striking time like an army. The horses' hooves breaking into a charge the narrow streets weren't built to contain. She was barely a dozen yards down the road, and nowhere near safety, when the horses came wheeling round the corner. These weren't the brewery's gentle drays – there was nothing soft about them. Their eyes rolled, their nostrils flared. Their hooves flashed as dangerously as the truncheons that followed them.

The police poured into Cable Street, tearing down the barricades, the Blackshirts marching behind them. The crowd gave up its slogans and resorted to bottles and fists and feet. Annie flattened herself against a wall as boiling water splashed down from a window above her and a horse reared up and kicked out, sending bodies diving for cover. She couldn't find a bolthole; she couldn't find a safe footing. She pushed and squirmed and tried not to panic as the street became a river of bricks and blows, and a hatred so visceral she could taste the blood it was soaked in.

My father's a liar. So's Mosley. They're not wanted here. There's no unity building behind him and his men. All they've done here is start a war.

A brick raced past her head. She ducked and faltered and barely managed to stop herself falling. But the arm she'd reached for to steady herself slipped away from her grasp instead and caught her a glancing blow across the shoulder that spun her around and stole what little bearings she had left.

Don't go down. Don't go down.

The order screaming through her head made sense, but her body couldn't find a way to obey it.

'Don't go down, do you hear me? You have to stay on your feet.'

The words weren't hers, they weren't in her head; they'd come from someone behind her. Hands came from nowhere, under her arms, across her chest. She was suddenly off the ground, moving up and away and thankfully not down, with the speed of a cork shooting out of a bottle.

'What in God's name were you doing in there? Trying to be our first martyr?'

The man – or maybe boy because he was somewhere in between – who'd pulled her out barrelled her into the open doorway of a pub Annie would never have spotted on her own. He had a red scarf tied round his neck and a vivid purple bruise on his cheek. His frown said he had no idea what to make of her. And Annie wasn't about to give him any clues.

'Maybe I am. If that's what it takes to get Mosley out of here and stop this carnage.'

It wasn't a deliberate lie; it was how she felt in that moment. A grin instantly spread across his freckled face and crinkled his brown eyes. Annie found herself biting her lip and hoping he wouldn't immediately run away again.

'All right, Miss Firebrand, but I'm not sure we need anything quite so dramatic. Which branch are you here with?'

She didn't know what he meant by that, and she didn't have another quick answer. Luckily, the need to find one disappeared in another roar and another avalanche of bricks. He pushed her further into the pub as the crowd surged again.

'If you want to help, and stay in one piece, get yourself in there. They need as many hands as they can get to help with the wounded. Tell them Harry from the Bethnal Green Labour Party sent you.' He stopped and looked at her properly again. 'And I'll come and find you when this is done. I'll bring you a progress report on how many heads we've smashed, if you'll give me your name in return.'

She kept that to Annie – she had no idea if her father's surname and loyalties were widely known, but it wasn't a risk she was prepared to take, especially not if it stopped him coming back. Harry grinned at her again and plunged into the crowd with a wave that disappeared within seconds. Annie went into the dark pub, thinking she'd be of no use to anyone, but Harry was right. They needed every spare hand and nobody cared whether she knew her way around a wound, not as long as she could hold on to her stomach at the sight of blood and tie a knot in a bandage.

The battle outside continued until the shadows started to lengthen. Harry didn't reappear, which disappointed Annie more than she'd expected. She gave nothing away about herself, but she finally got to ask some of her questions. And she learned very quickly what she'd suspected – that the East End was indeed united, but in its loathing not its love for Mosley. Every scrap of conversation she overheard made that very clear.

'He thinks he can split us apart and set us against each other... He thinks he can do what they're doing in Germany and turn people into *us* and *them*... He thinks he can demonise hard-working people and turn decent Jewish families into the scapegoats for what greedy governments have done... Well, not here. We won't be told what to do by men who peddle hatred, not on these streets.'

Annie drank in the words and the kindness. The offers of money to get her home safely, or a bed for the night. The different accents and backgrounds that had met together for one purpose: to say *no, this cruelty is not us*. She didn't ask the harder questions; she didn't ask, *Why the Jews?* People were too tired to deal with what she sensed was the impossibility of answering that question. She didn't share what had happened to Peggy – it wasn't the right time or place. But for the first time in the two years since her eyes had started to open, she felt that she wasn't alone. The other voices she'd finally found had confirmed what she already knew: that everything she'd felt was cruel and wrong about her father was indeed cruel and wrong. And that the path he'd chosen for himself could never be the right one for her. She only wished there was more comfort than danger in that.

CHAPTER FIVE
OCTOBER 1936

This is what beautiful women do, Margarete my dear. We manage men. And I sense you have something of a talent for that.

Magda Goebbels had, in Margarete's opinion, never spoken a truer word. And both Diana and Oswald Mosley would agree with her.

It won't last; she won't keep him.

A shiny new wedding ring hadn't changed a thing. Diana still clung to Mosley's arm like a child desperately hanging on to an escaping balloon, exactly as she'd done at the Savehay Christmas party. Mosley still accepted Diana's adoration as his due. And his wandering eye – which filled as many column inches in the British press as the exploits of his Blackshirts on the streets of East London – had continued to wander. When it landed – as Margarete knew it would – on her, she was tempted to point out his indiscretion to the rest of the room. She raised her eyebrows at him as if she might – it was amusing to watch him trying to stifle a laugh.

Five minutes married and he's already forgotten his vows. He really is playing to type. Not that anyone here expects any better. I'm surprised Goebbels can keep his face straight.

'Diana Mitford, the latest girlfriend, is certainly a beauty, but Mosley continues to concern me. His politics aren't in doubt, but the man's reputation as a playboy could be a problem.'

Joseph Goebbels, the Reich's Propaganda Minister, had already made his views about Mosley's suitability as a German ally very clear, although his assessment was somewhat hypocritical. The Propaganda Minister's appetite for pretty women was as legendary as Mosley's. Margarete – which was the name she reverted to as soon as she returned to Germany because she preferred its gravitas to the childish Grete – had overheard her father telling her mother Goebbels had planned to seduce Diana himself. The only thing which had stopped him was that the Nuremberg Rally – where he'd met her in 1933 – lacked the hiding places he preferred for his conquests.

That was the year Mosley had come to Hitler's attention, when the British press had dubbed him 'England's Führer'. Unfortunately, the same papers had followed that title up with an attack on the man's morals that had left Hitler raging at the comparison. The German Führer was in favour of Mosley's National Socialist views, but he was less impressed by the stories about the affairs Mosley had continued to have throughout his first marriage. Or the snide comments about the fourteen-year age gap between him and the dazzling Diana. Hitler's, 'I won't publicly endorse the man, or financially support his campaign, until I've got a better measure of him,' hadn't surprised anyone in his inner circle. But its solution had thrilled Margarete.

'Goebbels is arranging for you to stay at Mosley's house in England for six months. You'll act as an au pair for him and a communication channel for us, and you'll provide a detailed report on the man before the Führer takes any further steps. It's perfect. Nobody will suspect that you are there to do anything but improve your English.'

Her father Philip – who collected every honour and scrap of praise his daughter received the way some men collected paintings or wine and yet still publicly longed for a son – had treated Hitler's decision as if it was Margarete's right. Margarete had accepted it in the same way. She was after all the jewel in the family's crown – everyone said so. And she had talents, as Magda had pointed out, that even her father didn't suspect.

Margarete glanced over at Magda Goebbels. The bride in her gold dress was meant to be the centre of attention, but the Propaganda Minister's wife – who'd graciously allowed the Mosley wedding to take place in the drawing room of her Berlin villa – commanded the room. Margarete watched her smiling graciously as Diana butchered a sentence in her terrible German and tilted her head in the same elegant manner.

How on earth can she be such good friends with my mother?

Margarete had the same thought every time the two women were in the same place together. Magda was the Führer's confidante; she was to all intents and purposes the Third Reich's First Lady. And Sissi was...

An utter embarrassment.

Margarete sighed. Sissi and Magda had become close when they were schoolgirls, and that bond had bound their families together. Margarete had profited from its ties, but that didn't mean she understood why Magda kept it going. Margarete would never have chosen to keep company with her mother if she was in Magda's position. Sissi was an airhead and a fashion-plate, and an ageing one in Margarete's eyes – her peacock-blue dress was too young and too tight and lacked the elegance of Magda's draped burgundy brocade, a style Margarete had copied. She also couldn't resist dragging the spotlight her way, no matter how inappropriate that was. Margarete had to avert her eyes as Sissi started clapping before the registrar had finished the formalities and then burst into irritating giggles. It was little wonder her father took mistresses he could dispose of with far more ease when they bored him.

'Congratulations – well done! What a wonderful couple you make.'

Margarete pulled her displeasure away from her mother as the ceremony finally ended and joined the small queue waiting behind Hitler to offer their good wishes. She was amused not surprised when Diana acted as if they'd barely met: she knew exactly how clearly Diana remembered her.

'I'm sick of you mooning over that girl. I don't care who her father is or how important his business and his money are to the Führer, it's time she went back to Berlin.'

Margarete kissed Diana's cold cheek, certain she remembered the row that had spilled out of the bedroom Diana shared with Mosley at Savehay as clearly as Margarete did. And the sting of Mosley's response.

'Jealousy's not a good look on you, my dear. Do stop wearing it.'

Margarete would never have married a man who'd spoken to her like that; she would have walked out on him at once. Mosley had made no secret of his interest in her, not that Margarete had been tempted to give in to his relentless flirting. She'd been no more attracted to the man in 1934 than she was now. He was handsome enough, but he'd been thirty-eight to her seventeen. It was a horrible idea – but she'd enjoyed the power she held over him. She'd planned her rose-gold ball dress to be the complete opposite of Diana's silver number solely for the pleasure of watching his head swivel.

Everything I did that night was a triumph.

It could have gone so wrong. Everybody else involved in co-ordinating the meeting she'd pulled off with such style was convinced that it would. Mosley and Sid Kirson, his common little sidekick, had been so consumed by worry she'd been surprised they hadn't spun themselves into the ground.

'What if the Führer's coming here leaks to the press? What if the intelligence services have got wind of it? What if the weather turns bad and there's so much snow the plane can't land?'

The last question had been the only one that had really concerned her. The weather was the one thing outside her control, but a heavy snowfall would still count as a failure she'd struggle to shake off. As for the rest? Margarete had vetted every guest and supplier and servant and locked the house down behind a cordon no stranger could get past. She'd presented her report endorsing Mosley by telephone as instructed. She'd done the same when she checked the details of the visit with Goebbels, who would accompany the Führer. Nothing was written down; there was no evidence. Everything had gone exactly to plan, apart from the BUF member who'd drunk too much brandy, but he'd been, in Kirson's words 'properly dealt with'. Margarete rarely warmed to anyone, and she'd definitely not warmed to Sid Kirson. The man was a thug, no matter how much he'd played at happy families over breakfast. He'd proved that with the way he'd handled his problem of a wife.

'She's getting out of control. She wants me to leave the Party. She says my beliefs are evil. She thinks Mosley's a danger to the country. I can't be doing with it, Grete. If only Mosley wasn't so stuffy about divorce, I'd do it. I'd get her out of the way and find a more suitable wife.'

The way he'd said that a few months after the party with too much beer in him had been utterly revolting. His eyes lingering over her body, as if he thought she'd fall backward with delight at his slobbering attentions. The man was odious. But she'd played him. Mosley's attitude given his new wife's first marriage was as hypocritical as Goebbels' views on adultery, but he was adamant: he didn't have room for divorced men in his inner circle. When she'd suggested to Sid that there might be a more permanent way of dealing with Peggy, she'd been playing with him. She hadn't been serious. She hadn't expected him to look quite so eager, or to start spinning plans that could have had him executed and her potentially in the frame as an accessory if anyone outside the faith was listening. He should have known better than to insult her intelligence like that.

Well, he's got the worst of all worlds now: a wife who's an invalid that he can never leave. And I've got the best of them: I own him.

She'd proved herself perfectly; she'd honed her talents. She'd gone to England as one of Hitler's favourite 'nieces', as a useful little girl happy to serve 'Uncle Wolfie'. She'd come back with his respect and his trust.

'You're an asset to your family; and one day you'll be an even bigger asset to the Party and our Führer. I see a great future for you, Margarete dear, truly I do.'

Margarete was an important part of the machinery. Magda had been quick to acknowledge that when she came home, and so had her husband when he debriefed her.

'We'll leave the relationship with Mosley and Kirson in your hands. That will keep any hint of our ties to the BUF away from the British press. I'll tell you what to share with them in your letters; you pass on what they tell you about their activities to me. And we'll make sure you visit them in London every now and again, to remind them who holds the strings.'

He couldn't have been clearer. She mattered to the Führer and to the Party. Now she wanted to matter more; she just had to get somebody to listen.

The Nazi philosophy about where women fitted into the Third Reich limited their prospects to marriage and motherhood, and that wasn't a philosophy Margarete could live by. It didn't help that the expectations set by her family and her class were no different. Margarete didn't like limits; they didn't exist anywhere else in her life. Why would they?

She'd been born into wealth. Her father had taken over the

family steel business in 1913 and turned it into one of the country's success stories during the Great War. He'd made Fleiss Steel a key part of the country's war machine, doubled his money while his competitors fell apart during the years of economic chaos and hyperinflation that followed and then put himself firmly at the forefront of Hitler's plans for rearmament. As his only child, Margarete was the sole heir. A chauffeured car had swept her past the long lines of the unemployed as a young girl, past dirty-looking men she turned away from once her father informed her they were communists and Jews and not worthy of employment. A chauffeured car swept her to the parties she frequented now as a nineteen-year-old, where she was forced to fend off marriage proposals from men who both adored and bored her. It was a life full of privilege, but it wasn't enough. Margarete wanted a career. But not even her overindulgent father would listen to that.

In the end, the only thing he would allow her to do, because Magda suggested it, was to take a secretarial course, although he drew the line at paid employment. Margarete had been left with no option except to volunteer for the Party, where she spend her days passing on her secretarial skills to other privileged young girls who would never use them and driving herself to tears with boredom. Her days were filled, but her days were dull. Until she was assigned to assist with compiling instruction manuals for new mothers in the offices of the Reich's Women's Bureau and – in the last place she expected to find it – she rediscovered her purpose.

'I want to do what Gertrud Scholtz-Klink does. I'd be so much better at it.'

It wasn't easy to catch Phillip these days – he spent more time with the Party grandees than he did with his family. She'd had to loiter in his library on three separate evenings before she had a chance to deliver her proposal. Which, to her irritation, he hadn't instantly jumped at.

'Klink, the head of the Women's Bureau? Why? She's a dreadful woman, all plaits and dirndls and shouting. What do you want to be like her for?'

He hadn't listened properly, and he'd trotted out the same prejudices all the men shared. Margarete had been forced to bite her tongue and tell herself he was tired, not old and narrow-minded. She'd taken a deep breath and started again.

'Not like *her*. I want a job like the one she has. She's the only woman who's allowed to represent the Party. And she doesn't shout – she makes really good speeches, even if they are mostly about the joys of motherhood. Which is my point. Gertrud appears on the radio, and Goebbels has sent her to Rome and to London to speak about the role of women in fascism. She's allowed to have a voice. I could do that. I've already proved myself in England. I'm clever, I'm very persuasive. I want to be out in the world, telling our story too.'

Philip had burst out laughing, luckily at her daring, not at the idea. He'd promised to speak to Goebbels on her behalf. He'd sent her away with a 'You never know.'

Except I do.

Margarete caught Mosley watching her again. This time, she blew him a kiss and thoroughly enjoyed his subsequent coughing fit. Diana instantly whirled round, but Margarete had already moved on. Perhaps Mosley would figure in her future, perhaps he wouldn't. That wasn't for her to decide. Whatever else happened, he wouldn't forget her, and that was the point. She stood back with the rest of the wedding party as Hitler made his way to the first waiting car.

That's where my destiny lies. With the Party and with him.

She knew that as instinctively as she knew Sissi would drink too much champagne at the reception and make a fool of herself.

'I'm going to work for the Führer one day. I'm going to be the one person he can always trust.'

Philip patted her hand as she climbed into his beloved black Horch and fed her dreams as he always did by saying what she wanted to hear. 'I'm sure you already are, my sweet. Who wouldn't trust a girl as lovely as you?'

Margarete gazed out of the window as the car made its stately way out of the city, shutting out her mother's incessant chatter with a blank smile that was a mirror of her father's. Leaves fell from the trees like golden offerings as the convoy headed down Göring Straße. There wasn't a cloud in the crisp cornflower-blue sky. Margarete watched the grey people scurrying past and imagined them turning towards the car, pointing at her and waving. Their drab lives brightened by a glimpse of the Reich's youngest and most glamorous leading lady. Because that's what she would be, Margarete had no doubt about that. She'd been born to the role, and she wouldn't need a husband to secure it. Her life hadn't fully started yet, but its triumphs were coming.

And when they do, everybody across Europe, never mind Germany, will know Margarete Fleiss's name.

She wound down the window and waved in a gesture that was positively regal. She was convinced she saw someone bow.

CHAPTER SIX

JULY 1939

Nothing changed that day, despite the bricks and the barricades, or I wouldn't be standing here now, three years later. Watching the troops rally for Mosley again.

Annie had trudged her way back through the battle-scarred streets in 1936 with no idea which side would claim victory. She'd readied herself for a row with her father over her lateness, but she'd arrived to find Peggy already returned to bed and nobody fretting over her disappearance. It was the next morning before she realised that Sid hadn't actually returned home. It took a day combing the local hospitals before she found him.

'I was jumped on by a mob on my way to a peaceful parade. I don't know what the world's coming to.'

The story he'd told the nurses was a lie, but the broken arm and broken rib and the cuts and bruises he'd sustained were enough to keep him in hospital for a week. Annie didn't waste time taking issue with his interpretation of the facts then, or on the next day when the *Daily Mail* he asked her to bring him told a similar story. The 'deeply horrified' journalist at the scene reported that there'd been thousands of demonstrators involved. He described the torn-up paving stones and the overturned trams in dramatic detail, but he put the blame for the disorder squarely on the 'Reds' and the 'communities who may live on our streets but aren't truly part of Britain'. The *Hackney Gazette* did a more honest job. It interviewed the terrified Jewish shop-keepers who'd witnessed a little girl being thrown through a shop window and noted that Mosley had been stopped from making any of the speeches he'd planned. But its circulation was a fraction of the *Mail*'s, and Mosley's *Blackshirt* – copies of which were distributed all over the East End for weeks after the battle – also claimed the victory as his. And altered the protesters' furiously chanted slogan from 'They Shall Not Pass' to 'They Shall'.

And the fools have been fighting for the liars ever since.

The hall was packed wall to wall with those fools now, including her father. Sid had already disappeared into the throng. The last time Annie saw him, he'd been gladhanding his way round Earl's Court's giant auditorium, clapping shoulders and trading war stories with the rest of Mosley's merry men. She couldn't spot him now; she was glad he wasn't close by. She could hardly bear to be near him anymore. Annie had hoped the reality of the Cable Street riots and the East End's rejection of the fascists who'd tried to consume it might have broken his loyalty as well as his bones. That the family's involvement with Mosley might fade to a distant memory along with his bruises. But Sid had emerged from hospital bandaged and bitter and determined to let everyone see whose flag he followed. Which was now the red, blue and white badge of the British Union. A new name for the reorganised BUF and a worse flavour of it.

Annie stared at the uniforms packed into the seats around her. The black shirts and trousers had been joined by a peaked cap and a belt buckle bearing an engraved axe next to a bunch of sticks which Sid said represented the rule of law. They were topped off with jackboots and a red armband bearing a white lightning flash inside a dark blue circle. The finished outfit looked like something designed for the German SS. Nobody was even supposed to be wearing it – when the dust had finally settled and some of the truth came out, the Cable Street riots had led to a ban on civilians wearing military-style uniforms in public places and at public meetings. Nobody took any notice. Sid wore his every time he went to the Black House and no one challenged him, or anyone else flocking on and off public transport and in and out of headquarters dressed in the same confrontational way. Nobody had been challenged entering Earl's Court either.

Because the police are still in Mosley's pocket. And, if my father's to be believed, the Germans are funding the bribes it takes to keep them there.

Annie wholeheartedly believed that. She also suspected that was why Grete had come back to England. She'd stopped doubting anything Sid said about how successfully the movement was growing, even if she refused to believe any of the hatred and bile that came out of his mouth. What she hadn't managed to do yet was get any nearer to the truth of what had happened to Peggy, or get her or her mother away from him, because Sid's star was on the rise.

He'd stood as a BU councillor, albeit unsuccessfully, and had begun talking about running for a parliamentary seat. He spent every weekend at Mosley's side, whipping up violence on the streets of Bethnal Green and Stepney. He'd given a speech of his own in 1938 on the day after Kristallnacht – when the Nazis had unleashed a wave of violence against Jewish people and property and burned down hundreds of synagogues all over Germany – calling the destruction and the round-ups 'a blueprint for Britain'. And the higher he rose, the more he demanded his family fell into line. Peggy was no longer expected to attend fundraising dinners or rallies on a regular basis. Her body had recovered, but her mind was still fogged, and she tired easily and couldn't always remember who people were, a weakness she couldn't help but Sid had no pity for. Which meant Annie was expected to stand in for her as well as volunteering at the Black House. Refusing was an impossibility. Sid's temper was as mean as ever although he'd stopped the physical if not the verbal attacks on his wife and hadn't, as yet, switched his fists onto Annie. That didn't mean the threat of worse than a tongue-lashing wasn't permanently there, hanging round the flat like creeping damp. And it meant Annie was stuck. She couldn't tell her father how much she loathed his politics. She couldn't leave her mother alone with him at Arnold Circus, not that she had anywhere else to go. She was as trapped inside his orbit as she'd always been.

If it wasn't for my job, I think I'd go mad. Although God knows how long that will last if anyone finds out I was here today. I doubt I've another life left there.

Her job as a junior typist at the Edelstein Clothing Factory – where her mother had worked as a machinist before Sid told her she was mocking him by earning money he could provide – was the one bright spot in Annie's life. She'd talked her way into it two years earlier, when she'd refused to give in and take the sewing job Sid expected her to work at until some boy turned her into a wife. She'd arrived at the factory clutching her School Leaving Certificate with its bunch of distinctions instead, and the shorthand and typing qualification she'd taken when Sid had closed the door to any possibility of university. She'd talked her way past her age and her inexperience, until the owner gave in and said yes.

The owner, Mr Edelstein, who liked 'a girl with gumption' and remembered Peggy as one of his best workers, had made a pet of Annie. He'd paid for her to improve her secretarial skills at evening classes at the nearby East London Technical College. He'd even paid for her to continue with the German there that she'd finally done well with and enjoyed at school. He some-times spoke the language with her himself, when he was in a nostalgic mood for the country he'd left as a child and could no longer safely return to. The work, and the classes and the chance to mingle freely with people Sid couldn't vet were a lifeline to Annie. But the father she never spoke about to anyone she wanted to befriend had still almost cost her it all.

All it had taken was one jealous typist who chose to throw her poison while Mr Edelstein was in the room and Annie's carefully held-together world ripped apart.

'It's no wonder she loves learning German. She's Sid Kirson's daughter, and my dad says he's one of Mosley's top men. I've seen her going in and out of the Black House on my way home.'

Mr Edelstein had dragged her into his office with a horrified, 'You've got five minutes to explain yourself,' and an even more shocked, 'Is that true about your father?' When she'd nodded, he'd gone instantly on the attack.

'Dear God. As if it's not bad enough having to tangle with you people on the streets, now you're here in my factory. Are you spying on me, is that it? Trying to find dirt on a successful Jew? Are you using my money to learn German because you're a Nazi? Do you think I'm not British enough, that my family shouldn't have rights?'

He only stopped shouting at her because she burst into tears.

'No, of course not – none of that's me. I'm not a Nazi; I couldn't be. But my father is, and I hate him.'

That declaration shocked them both into silence. Mr Edelstein had huffed and puffed and found her a handkerchief. And then, with a visible effort, he'd put his fear and his suspicion to one side and said, 'Talk to me.' So Annie did. Starting with the day Sid had given her Mosley's pamphlet and finishing with the march at Cable Street where she'd almost ended up under a horse. She was as honest with her boss as she could be, although she skipped over the events at Savehay and what had happened to Peggy. She didn't think either of them were ready for those.

'I know everything my father believes is wrong, but I don't know why he believes it, and I've never known who to ask. I've tried. I've been to marches, but they were too chaotic to speak properly to anyone. I've read different newspapers to the ones we're allowed at home, but they're not much help. Most of them seem to hate communists more than fascists, and none of them are exactly friendly towards—' She stopped. She didn't know how to say the word without it sounding as if she also boxed people into *us* and *them*.

Mr Edelstein said it for her.

'Jews?' He shook his head. 'No, they're not, and I'm glad you can see it. I imagine you found plenty of stories about swindling Jewish chemists who substitute cheap drugs for real medicine? And corrupt Jewish landlords ruining honest tenants' lives?' He grimaced as she nodded. 'But not so much about the old men who get beaten up by black-shirted thugs as they leave the synagogue on a Friday night. Or the Jewish shops that get looted while the police look the other way.'

'There's none of that side of the story at all.' Annie took a deep breath and asked the question she'd wanted to ask in the pub on the night she'd bandaged battered heads and hands. 'But why is it like that? Why is everything that's bad blamed on the Jews?'

Mr Edelstein sighed and rubbed his eyes. It took him a while to find the words he wanted.

'That's a question as old as time and an answer I don't have for you. And a pattern that repeats itself over and over until it breaks our tired hearts.' He shook himself as Annie frowned, as if to remind himself of her age. 'Oh, Annie, what can I tell you? All I know is that when times are hard and money is tight and living conditions leave a lot to be desired, people like Mosley – who feed off uncertainty so they can build their own power – are clever at finding a scapegoat for the masses to blame. And the masses feel better for having that. But as to why that scapegoat is us?' He fell silent again. His anger was still there, but it was no longer directed at Annie. 'I wish I knew, but the fear and the hatred and the roots of it go so far back no one seems willing to unpick it. Mosley frightens me, I can tell you that much. And Hitler frightens me too. And the idea that they might be working together... Rumour has it that Mosley's wife runs backward and forward to Berlin all the time, and is some kind of favourite of the Führer. God help us all if the monsters have gone and joined up.'

It was on the tip of Annie's tongue then to tell him about the Christmas party at Savehay. About what she'd overheard since then about meetings between English and German fascists in Berlin and London, and the German money finding its way into the BU coffers. She started to speak, although she wasn't sure that sharing her knowledge would help either of them. Mr Edelstein seemed to sense that too. He stopped her before she got further than, 'I think maybe—'

'And you're just a girl, and none of this is your fault. Go back to work. Let's say no more about it. But my office door is always open to you if things at home get overwhelming. If you need a friend.'

He gave me an education and a safe haven that day, but I'm as stuck now as I ever was.

Mr Edelstein senior was no longer at the factory: he'd been taken ill a few months after their conversation and retired. His son had no interest in the personal problems of junior typists. He would sack her in an instant if he knew she was at the Earl's Court rally.

Watching the Third Reich make a grab for Britain that would take his whole world from him.

She forced herself to breathe deeply to stop her body from shaking. Mosley was riding high on a worse kind of fear than rising living costs and rising unemployment. War was creeping closer again. Hitler had annexed Austria; he'd successfully grabbed Czechoslovakia. His arm was sweeping further and further around Eastern Europe. Some of the newspapers predicted that he'd soon start looking to the west. And Mosley was standing in the wings watching Hitler's every step, wearing a very clever disguise.

This Is Not Our War

Germany Is Not the Enemy

The Only Way Forward Is Peace

The slogans were repeated all over the East End, next to stencilled outlines of Mosley's face, and they reappeared as fast as they were scrubbed out. Mosley had grabbed on to the fears of the thousands who remembered the all-too-recent horrors of the Great War and were still mourning its dead. He'd drawn them to his side by vigorously campaigning against a second one. 'Britain is not under attack... Aliens in our country are trying to drag us into a quarrel that isn't ours.'

People were listening. Membership numbers were on the rise. Mothers frightened for their sons flocked to him, so did ex-servicemen who'd already been to hell on a battlefield. Nobody realised the truth that Sid and his cronies understood all too well: that Mosley seizing power and preventing a war wouldn't mean safety and life in Britain carrying on as normal. That it would mean a pact with Hitler and the country becoming part of the Third Reich.

He's fooled them completely, and this is the proof.

Thirty thousand supporters crammed into Earl's Court Arena. A huge security cordon of Blackshirts and police outside to make sure nobody without a carefully vetted ticket came in. A gigantic podium that resembled the keep of a medieval castle, flanked by lightning flashes and a huge Union Jack. Balconies encircled by banners proclaiming *Unite for Peace and for British People* and *Britons Fight for Britain Alone.* And a walkway that ran along the entire length of the ground floor, which had suddenly gone dark.

'He's coming! He's coming!'

Trumpets blared out in a fanfare that flooded the hall. Drums pulled the crowd to its feet. The audience began cheering and clapping as the lights snapped back on and the musicians and the flag-bearers marched through their middle.

'Mosley! Mosley! Mosley!'

The chant fell into time with the drums, building a tidal wave of noise that swept up over the balconies. Annie had to clasp her hands tight to stop herself covering her ears. The advance party lined up beside the podium. The lights dimmed again. Silence fell. The hall held its breath as if every heartbeat was dancing to Mosley's tune. And then a searchlight swept down the central aisle, and there he was, the prize they'd been waiting for. Mosley, with a small group of men – Sid among them – marching in step behind him. The roar that greeted him was primal. Arms snapped up and stayed high as Mosley marched past. Annie had to grip the chair in front of her to stop herself shaking. She waited for the cry to switch from 'Mosley' to 'Hitler'. She waited for the woman beside her to start speaking in German. Earl's Court dissolved and was replaced by Berlin's Sportpalast, the heavily photographed arena where the Führer addressed his adoring audiences. She stared round the crowd as Mosley ascended the podium. They'd turned into one body. Falling silent because Mosley had gestured to them to do so; sitting because he'd lowered his hand.

They'd run out into the street and tear down every Jewish shop and home and synagogue if he told them to. They wouldn't think twice.

The audience settled into an expectant hush. The speech began.

'We will smash Jewish money's power... We will not take part in Jewish quarrels... A million Britons will not be dragged by those jackals to their deaths...'

How can you say these things when Hitler is cutting Jews out of their lives all over Germany? How can you be so free from compassion?

The same hatreds, the same lies filled the auditorium. Annie bit her lip, but her tongue was desperate to be heard. She imagined letting it loose. She imagined standing up and yelling her disgust back at the stage. She wondered how quickly some-one's fist would lash out to silence her and reckoned it as seconds.

I don't want to be here. I hate him for making me party to this.

'I'll be back in a minute; I need to find a bathroom.'

She couldn't stay, and she wasn't going to return whatever the consequences, but she made an excuse to the woman sitting next to her in case Sid had planted her there. Her absence was a poor protest, but it was the best she could offer. If her father lost his temper, this time she'd lose hers back. Whatever chaos that led to had to be better than condoning this monstrosity by her presence.

Annie slipped out of her seat, ignoring the steward who tried to wave her back into it. The corridors outside were empty. Annie plunged through the gloom towards the doors they'd been escorted through what felt like hours before. One sharp push and she was outside in the lingering heat of a July evening, sucking in air that was laced with petrol, not flowers, but still tasted sweet. She hurled herself through the police horses, holding herself well away from their vicious hooves. She hurled herself onto the pavement, her eyes dazzled by the lowering sun, her feet tripping over themselves. Somebody shouted after her, but she kept on running. Somebody grabbed her arm, and she whirled round like a wildcat, expecting to see a black sleeve.

'Get off me! Get off!'

'I'm sorry, I'm sorry. But you were about to run into the road.'

The man who'd pulled at her arm jumped back with his hands up, stuttering apologies. Annie retracted her claws when she saw his white shirt. A policeman was watching – the last thing she needed was a scene. She muttered a 'thank you', and was about to run on and put as much space as she could between herself and the rally, until the man frowned and said, 'Don't I know you?'

Annie instinctively shook her head, in case he was a BU member despite his civilian clothes. 'No, I don't think so.' She stopped. There was something familiar about the hazel eyes and the freckles, and the grin spreading across his face. She was still searching for the connection when he made it.

'I've done it again, haven't I? I've come to your rescue. You're the girl with the death wish from Cable Street.' He paused for a second, his eyes flicking as if he was searching through files in his head. 'It's Annie, isn't it? I'm Harry – do you remember? I'm the one who pulled you out of the riot and into the pub.'

She did remember, although *rescue* felt like a strong word for today. She would have nodded and moved on, except his next words brought back the rest of her memories.

'I came back to find you when the fighting finally ended, but you'd gone. I thought then what a shame that was.'

I thought the same thing too.

And there it was, that moment of disappointment when he hadn't returned, slipping back into her head. A hole in the middle of a crowded pub, a flash of delight when she glimpsed a curly head that had faded when the face wasn't his. She'd assumed he'd forgotten her, which wasn't surprising given the circumstances. But he hadn't forgotten her at all. Her heart fluttered in a very unexpected way, until she realised he was looking at her as curiously now as he'd looked at her in Cable Street and the last thing her thin skin needed was his scrutiny.

'The way you were running, as if there were dogs after you... Did you come out of there?' He nodded at Earl's Court. 'Were you at Mosley's rally? Was someone chasing you?'

Annie couldn't think of a truthful answer that wouldn't end in him walking away. She didn't want that. She didn't want to tell him her full name either when he asked for it as he was sure to do, in case he knew Sid's. She didn't want to tell him why she'd been in the hall, but what else could she do? If she lied to him, that would be the end of this strange new meeting too.

'He's a good one that Harry, one of the best. He's going to be a journalist one day, or so he says. You'd do worse than set your cap at him.'

They'd teased her about Harry in the pub – she'd forgotten that. And they'd all spoken highly of him. Maybe he was someone she could confide in; maybe he was worth the risk.

Or he is a journalist now, and he'll splash my name all over the papers for my father to see.

The day suddenly caught up with her and wobbled her knees. A few moments later, she was tucked into the dark corner of a nearby pub with something called a port and lemon sitting on the grimy table in front of her.

'I didn't know what else to get you. It's my mother's favourite, so it's probably very old-fashioned. But you look like you'd had a shock, and the brandy in here smells like lighter fluid.'

His honesty made her laugh and brought down her shoulders. She took a sip of the drink which was both tangy and sweet and not at all unpleasant. Harry gave her a minute to catch her breath, and then he put down his pint.

'I'm a journalist, Annie, I work for the *Hackney Gazette*. I might as well tell you that from the start. It's why I was hanging round Earl's Court. And I can sense there's a story here, with you somewhere in it. Do you want to tell it to me?'

She did as much as she didn't. His face was as kind as it was handsome, and she was too exhausted from all the lies she lived with to add more to the pile. So she took a deep breath and she told him her surname, and watched his brain make the connection. And when he didn't get up and walk away, when his expression barely flickered, she decided to trust in his kindness and told him the rest.

'I can't get a hold of my own life. I loathe my father, but I can't get away from him. I loathe the Blackshirts and Mosley, but they're all over my world. And what that's led to...' She stopped. She wasn't ready yet to tell him about the attack on Peggy, although she sensed that one day she might. She shook her head. 'I'd do anything to stop them if I could, but I haven't a clue what that means.'

Harry's fingers were tapping by the time she finished, as if he wished he had a typewriter. Annie stopped talking and took a sip of her drink, which had turned sticky. The sky outside the tiny circles which made up the window had grown as dark as the pub's dingy interior. She waited again for his judgement. And again it didn't come.

'That's quite a story, and a miserable place to be stuck in. And I agree, I thought Cable Street would finish them too. But you're right about why it didn't: Mosley's tapped into a rich seam by shouting for peace, and it's making him stronger. The *Gazette* keeps getting letters from all sorts of people, from all walks of life, who agree with what he says and get cross when we publish anything negative about him.'

'They shouldn't believe any of it.' Annie closed her eyes briefly as the image of Mosley banging the podium and aping Hitler rushed back. 'He doesn't care what happens to anyone but himself, and all this shouting for peace is purely for his own ends. He imagines himself ruling side by side with Hitler, running Britain along National Socialist lines. And God help anyone he decides isn't *one of us* if that happens. If he gets into a position of power – and he's determined to bring the government down somehow and do that – there'll be a repeat of Kristallnacht here the second he takes hold of the reins. The people around him are ruthless enough.'

They both fell silent, remembering the frightening reports and photographs that had emerged from Germany the previous November. The ones filled with synagogues covered in flames and terrified people being attacked and turned out of their homes.

'Are you certain about the financial connections between the BU and the Nazi Party?'

Annie nodded. 'As certain as I can be given how secretive they are. A German girl called Grete is one of the conduits as far as I can make out.' She paused. 'I met her in 1934. She's been in contact with my father by letter since then, and she's been back to London and to the Black House. She's dangerous, and one day I'll prove it. And she's involved with the Party at a high level – she was there when Hitler came to Mosley's house – she was part of that night's meeting.'

'Wait a minute, when who did what?'

Harry slammed his pint down so hard, the brown liquid seeped over the sides and into the cracks that made up the table. Annie ran through the bones of that story while he ran his hands through his hair until it stood virtually upright.

'Have you ever told anyone about that?'

She shook her head. 'I was thirteen years old – I had no proof. Who would have believed me?'

'Proof's always the problem with him.' Harry sighed and swallowed the rest of his drink. 'Everyone suspects Mosley is in Hitler's pocket, but trying to get any evidence about the BU's financial dealings is as impossible as it was to get a photograph of his wedding to Diana Mitford in Berlin. Mosley's got more layers of protection round him than the King.'

'What if I could get the evidence for you?'

She said it without thinking through what the offer meant but knowing it was the right thing to do. Harry's head snapped up. Annie's blood began to fizz as all the disjointed pieces of the last five years finally started to knit together.

Slow down, take a beat. This could be dangerous; this could be impossible.

She picked up her drink and drained the last treacly drops as the more sensible part of her brain tried to backtrack. But she didn't want to slow down or go back, and she didn't want to believe in *impossible*.

'Think about it, Harry. The Blackshirts are paranoid about infiltrators, but I've got a foot in their camp – I've been part of their circle for years. And I'm Sid Kirson's daughter, the good girl who volunteers at headquarters and goes to rallies with her dad. Nobody thinks I'm anything but loyal – why would they? Nobody could get closer than me. And if I could find a way to prove that Mosley isn't putting Britain's interests first, that he'd put them second to Germany's in a heartbeat... If you could use that in the paper and bring his ambitions down, and I could use it to prove Grete is—' She stopped. She wasn't ready to say 'capable of murder' and then have to explain herself. Luckily Harry had already picked up his glass.

'It would be incredible. It would be a hell of a story.'

He grinned at her over the top of the glass as he clinked it against hers and the future suddenly rang with possibilities.

A hell of a story.

It was a way to bring Mosley down. It was a way to break Sid's shackles. It was the best toast Annie had ever heard.

'Time to go home – last orders were called long since.'

The barman's sudden appearance at Harry's elbow made Annie jump. She got up in a hurry, blushing as she realised that the rest of the bar had emptied while she and Harry were locked in their own world.

'I'll walk you to the Underground – come on.'

Harry hooked his arm through hers as they tumbled out into the still-warm night air. They fitted together perfectly. The port had made her light-headed, or that was what Annie blamed the streets' softened edges on. Moonlight cast its silver glow across the giant arena and turned it into the elegant liner its architect had imagined when he'd traced its first outlines. Once she'd seen that, it didn't take much effort to recast the salty tang from a nearby fish shop as the scent of the ocean, or the black-and-white-striped traffic lights as a species of exotic palm tree.

'Shall we sail away? Shall we keep going until we find an island nobody's spoiled?'

Harry's whisper shivered against her cheek. He'd felt the magic too. Annie turned to him. She didn't think twice about stepping into his arms, or about raising her lips to his, or about sinking into a kiss that was as gentle and all-consuming as the waves they could both hear dancing around them.

His eyes were dark when she finally surfaced and stared into them, mirrors of the inky black sky. Her name on his lips sounded lovelier than any nightingale singing its song in a secluded London square. She smiled and touched his cheek and kept her hand in his until the guard came to close the gates and hurry the last passengers towards the last train. And she carried his kiss as carefully as a diamond all the way home.

CHAPTER SEVEN

MAY 1941

All the plans we made, as if we thought we had any say in the world. And now she's miles and months away from me and I can't bear it.

Harry stared at the envelope addressed in Annie's unmistakably neat writing. He lived for her letters and he dreaded them. They were part of a life he could no longer imagine himself returning to.

'We'll ruin him. We'll be national heroes. Special Branch and MI5 will be falling over themselves to offer us jobs once we pull Mosley down.'

Memories of that first night in the pub with Annie could still make him giddy. She'd been so brave, telling him the truth of who she was and who she wanted to be. She was utterly fearless about everything.

'I'll get your proof and your story for you. They'll never suspect me – it's perfect.'

He hadn't doubted for a second that she had the ability to do it. And that first kiss when he'd walked her to the Tube station... He'd never kissed a girl so quickly after meeting her before, but Annie's eyes had sparkled at him under the streetlight, and her smile had stripped him bare, and Earl's Court's scruffy streets had suddenly turned through some trick of the moon into a Hollywood backdrop filled with palm trees and an ocean-going liner and the soft, sweet scent of the sea. He'd lost any sense of himself then. Her laugh when he finally let go of her had become his favourite music. Unfortunately, not everything after that had worked out so well.

For all Annie's efforts to unpick the Black House's secrets, the story had got lost two months later when Hitler – who clearly hadn't taken Mosley into his confidence for all the man's boasting – invaded Poland and wiped any notion of peace off the table. The King's Road headquarters double-locked its doors and its filing cabinets, and nobody could get inside except Special Branch, who kicked their way in rather than waiting for keys. There was nothing for Annie to bring him; there was no front page to write. But that first kiss had bound them together, and they kept on meeting anyway.

'I envy you your job. I envy the voice and the chance to do good it gives you.'

She'd meant it, and Harry had meant it when he said he thought she'd be good at it too, if only newspapers dared to employ women. And now two years after being forced to walk away from it, he still missed the job that had turned him into a man almost as much as he missed Annie. Harry had joined the *Hackney Gazette* in 1933 as a wet-behind-the-ears boy of sixteen, clutching his School Leaving Certificate as if it was a passport to a new life. Which it was. He'd started as the lowliest cub reporter, barely entrusted with collecting the information for birth and death announcements and rarely allowed to write even those up. He'd had his first byline three years later when he'd been the only *Gazette* journalist brave or foolish enough to throw himself into the middle of the Cable Street riots. By the time his path crossed with Annie's again, he'd begun to make his mark on the paper's admittedly limited politics desk. He'd also started studying for the University of London's new Diploma in Journalism – his mother who, like his father, had left school at fourteen, had cried with pride for a week when he brought that news home. He'd thought he was riding high, but he'd soared when he kissed Annie.

Harry picked up the envelope again and held it close to his face, searching for even the barest trace of her violet perfume. It was a hopeless task: the paper had sat far too long in a mail bag to smell anything but musty. He closed his eyes tight instead and conjured up the long evenings they'd made theirs in that magical summer before the war, when they'd believed they were going to change the world. When they'd lain wrapped in each other's arms in Victoria Park, hidden from the world by the long grass, trading kisses that melted their bodies. When each day had felt like a promise. His Annie had been so full of dreams then they'd made her eyes dance. For a life away from her father, unpolluted by his beliefs. And for a braver way of living that Harry had also wanted for himself. One that wasn't lived looking backward the way their parents did, fearful that the poverty they'd escaped would reach up and reclaim them. One filled with possibilities and adventures instead, and not the narrow road towards marriage and children and nothing real outside the home that tradition and family intended for her.

An old-fashioned life, that was what she called the one she didn't want, and so did I then. But I'd give a king's ransom to be living that life with her now.

The war had taken Annie and his job and the East End from him and – like the rest of his shipmates, who no longer trusted that one day would automatically lead into another – he wanted those familiar places back.

'I have to do my bit, so I'm enlisting with the Merchant Navy. I come from a family of dockers after all – it seems like the best fit.'

Harry couldn't see himself as a soldier aiming a gun at other men his own age, so he'd made his choice and carried it out on the day full conscription was announced, with as much bravado as he could muster. His boss patted him on the back and promised him his job would stay open. His father shook his hand and told his mother to be proud and not fuss. He'd passed his pre-sea training course with flying colours and been assigned his first voyage on a refrigerated ship sailing from Tilbury to Buenos Aires, where it was destined to be filled up with beef. Annie had waved him off looking twice as pretty as any of the other women standing on the dockside, and putting on a brave face too.

But she wouldn't marry me before I went. She wouldn't see me off as a wife.

He couldn't keep that thought at bay when loneliness and fear hit him. He couldn't make peace with the hurt he knew she'd never intended to inflict.

'I love you, Harry, I do. But I'm eighteen; I'm too young for marriage. We both are – you know that. We hardly know each other yet. I don't want to speed my life up because of the war, and I don't believe you do either. Let's be sensible and wait it out, give ourselves time to grow into this. Because we will. We'll be together when it's done, I truly believe that.'

Except it wasn't done. It wasn't close to being done. Two years had gone by since that first leave-taking with no sign of an end, and everything was getting worse. He was barely twenty-four, but he felt like an old man whose life had passed him by.

We've turned into cave dwellers, forever running between bunkers and tunnels and shelters to get away from the bombs. I swear I could beat a mole in an under-ground race.

God knows where you'll dock when you come home next – the riverfront is such a mess. The last raid hit the flour and the sugar mills. Everything melted and burned until the air was as sweet and sticky as a bowl of cake mixture. It drove the dogs and the children wild!

Annie kept her letters light-hearted. She turned the Blitz into an adventure and the typing job she'd taken at one of the war ministries into a series of anecdotes about the fearsome Miss Carter who ruled there and could make a general quake with a look. Some of Harry's shipmates had more forthcoming families. They read out accounts of overcrowded and flimsy shelters whose walls shook with every explosion. Of the constant barrage of noise from sirens and falling bombs and tumbling roofs that had made sleep a memory. Of fires that burned a scarlet path to the river and billowing smoke that blacked out the day. Those letters rendered the men mute and powerless. Desperate to be away from the merchant shipping convoys that sat in the water like sitting ducks and the German U-boats that stalked them. To get back home to where their loved ones were crying out for help. Harry was no different, for all Annie's bravado.

I miss her. We could be snatched away from each other for good at any moment, and I want to tell her that I love her and I miss her.

The months they'd spent apart crowded into his narrow bunk. His scant weeks of leave came without warning and never seemed to properly align with her job. Once Hitler had rolled over France in 1940 and the war really shifted into gear, all they'd had were snatched days.

And every one we get, as precious as it is, is haunted by the goodbyes that come with it.

The need for her smile and her touch suddenly overwhelmed him. He ripped open the envelope, desperate for anything that would bring her closer to him. He had no idea if his last letter had reached her. He was somewhere in the middle of the Indian Ocean, sailing above a nest of submarines. It was a miracle the latest supply drop had reached them and there was any letter from her at all.

Marry me, Annie. I can't live with uncertainty anymore.

He'd begun his last frantic scribble to her with the words he wasn't supposed to say, but what else could he do? The middle of an ocean was a desolate, friendless place. It was easy there to lose sight of the world, to imagine himself forgotten. All the men needed surety, a promise that there was a fixed point to return to. She had to forgive him for craving that. Surely by now she had to want the same thing?

My darling Harry,

How far away are you now? I've been staring at maps, trying to imagine where your ship is sailing. Shall I play a guessing game?

She hadn't received his desperate proposal. He closed his eyes, needing a moment before he tackled the rest. Needing a moment to let go of the happy *Yes of course I'll marry you, I'm sick of waiting too* that he'd been longing for. But he didn't even get the respite of that. What he got instead was a series of explosions that tipped the ship off its steady course and flung him out of his bunk. What he got was a sheet of flame and a suffocating wave of smoke as he wrenched open the cabin door.

'Run!'

He didn't need the instruction; he couldn't tell where the voice was coming from. It could have come from inside his own head. He plunged through the smoke, his eyes streaming, the fire chasing him like a maddened dog. He hurtled up a stairwell, burning his palms on the metal handrail, crying out as his eyes filled with soot and his heart filled with fear. Another leap and he was on the pitching deck. Another and he was somehow in a lifeboat, its bulk swinging and banging into the side of the straining ship as the ropes unravelled, until it landed on the black water with a thump that threw at least one man out.

'Row! Come on. She's going down – we need to get away from the wake.'

He grabbed an oar and pulled on it until his shoulders screamed. Until all they could hear was the creaking and groaning as the ship tossed on the water like a fish caught on a line, leaping and bucking as the last explosions ran through it. And finally surrendered to the water as the roaring waves smashed relentlessly through its spine.

CHAPTER EIGHT
DECEMBER 1941

'It's not very conventional, I suppose, that you can't speak to her father first. But that's probably for the best.'

Harry's mother Dolly tailed off and began fiddling with a plate of thinly filled sausage rolls that didn't need fiddling with. Harry didn't know what to say. His nerves were already stretched as tight as piano strings without worrying about the lack of Sid Kirson's approval. It wasn't as if either of his parents wanted to mix with the man any more than he did. In the early days, before they'd properly known Annie, they'd been so concerned at the family she'd come from, they'd been equally as wary of her.

So I can't be sorry he's locked up, and it's got to be better for Annie.

Sid had been arrested in May 1940 along with Mosley and his other supporters. There'd been no trial then, and there wouldn't be in the future: he'd been indefinitely interned under the new 18B regulation that enabled the detention of anyone suspected of being actively opposed to the war. Harry – who'd been on shore leave when it happened – had been worried Annie might want to visit her father in Brixton Prison. But once the shock of the fists pounding on the front door had worn off, Annie had confessed she was glad he was gone and had refused the visitor's permit. And now Sid had been transferred to a camp on the Isle of Man where he apparently remained a disruptive threat and was no longer allowed to receive letters, let alone visitors. Which his mother had consigned to her mental basket of 'good things'.

'I wouldn't wish him ill, but it's best he's not here. Annie's a darling now that we know her, and her mother's as lovely as she is, but that father of hers isn't the right sort of person for us. We'll all do very well without him, I'm sure.'

Harry pulled his mother into a hug as she echoed his thoughts and did what she always did: looked on the bright side and smoothed troubles over. There were days when Dolly felt like his only solid fixture in an increasingly shaky world. She'd been trying to make that world normal when it was anything but since he'd stumbled ashore after five long months away from home, three of those listed as shipwrecked and missing. She'd never once cried in his presence over that long time of waiting, although her eyes were frequently red in the first weeks when he came down in the morning. He kissed the top of her head and offered to make himself useful in the kitchen, which sent her into peals of laughter at the idea of it.

I don't make her – or anyone else – laugh enough these days. I need to try harder for all of them. They're trying their hardest for me.

It was easier thought about than done. He groped his way into a chair as his body betrayed him yet again. There was nothing physically wrong with him now the burns from the wreck and the ferocious sun on the lifeboat had healed, but sometimes his legs fluttered as if they were trying to break free from his body. And as for his nightmares...

'They will stop. Give yourself a chance, lad. Your ship went down with too many hands; you were almost drowned yourself. A bit of time's what you need and you'll soon be right as rain.'

The doctor had meant well when Harry finally dragged himself – at Annie's insistence – into the surgery, but he hadn't a clue. He'd despatched Harry's night terrors in a couple of sentences that Harry heard as, 'Buck yourself up.' Harry had hated the doctor for that. He'd stumbled out of his office filled with an anger he couldn't share, although the words he longed to shout back at the man ran like drumbeats through his head.

You weren't the one drifting in a lifeboat under a piercing sun, counting the drops of water left and trying to divide them between too many men. Straining to see a rescue ship that took too long to come. You weren't the one listening to the screams the broken boat made when it went down, or the screams of your drowning shipmates. And you're not the one who wakes up in the dark feeling hands stretching up through the water, and cries out like a lost child for his mother.

So much unsaid, not to the doctor, not to Annie. Not to the mother who came without fail to calm him when he cried.

Who's built the kind of loving, gentle life round her family I want for my children.

Harry had changed, he knew that, even if he couldn't express what that change meant any better than he could discuss his bad dreams. He knew that he'd left the Harry who craved adventure and excitement behind in the pitiless expanses of the Indian Ocean. That what he longed for now was for the war to end and let him live a quiet, steady life built round hard work and the strong working-class values he'd been brought up with. A safe job, a family and a wife to come home to. The things that had seemed mundane in 1939 sparkled with security now.

'Harry, for goodness' sake, have you gone deaf? Look lively and fetch your father. They're here and I'm still in my pinny.'

Harry jumped to his feet as his mother came flapping in, chiding him for being oblivious to the doorbell.

'Hello, beautiful.'

Peggy turned bright pink as Harry pretended the greeting was intended for her. She was, as Dolly had said, a lovely woman. What had happened to her broke Harry's heart, although he hadn't told his parents the full story. All they knew was that she'd had a fall down some stairs which had left her delicate and forgetful. It wasn't exactly a lie; it was, after all, the version Peggy had been told constantly by Sid, and the version Annie had decided it was kinder to let her believe in. He hurried the two women in out of the snow which had begun falling in time to ensure a white Christmas, and let his father fuss gently round Peggy. Annie bounded out of his arms and into Dolly's, before pouncing on his father who pretended that wasn't exactly what he'd wanted her to do. Jim was as smitten as Dolly now. Annie had turned him into a man who was happy being kissed on the cheek without warning and thoroughly teased.

'She came here every Saturday while you were missing. She wouldn't let us give up hope, and she wouldn't give up on you either. You'll not do better than her, lad, whatever we might have thought at first. She's the genuine article.'

That blessing, from the one father who mattered, was the only one Harry needed.

The Christmas Eve celebration was soon a happy mixture of sherry and fruit cake and swapped stories about the bargaining Dolly had to endure to create the treasured 'proper Christmas' she was determined everybody should have. Nobody mentioned Sid. Annie was at the heart of every conversation, but she kept looking over at Harry. He loved that connection, the pull running between them. She'd wrapped herself round him like a vine when he'd finally come home after the shipwreck; she'd refused to let go until she'd assured herself he was in one piece. When she'd held his face, when she'd poured her heart through, 'The day I thought I'd lost you, I couldn't see colour anymore,' it was the first time since the sinking that he'd cried. And she looked as beautiful tonight in her blue velvet dress as Harry had said she did when he'd opened the door. But she also looked tired – the job she'd taken on at the ministry was clearly too much for her, whatever she said to the contrary.

'I love it. I can't tell you much about what I do, not now I work in intelligence, but if I could? Harry would have enough stories to fill his paper for a year.'

Harry smiled as Jim laughed. He was pleased she'd found something to do that made her feel part of the war effort and was more interesting than typing invoices at the clothes factory. But he didn't want her to be exhausted by a hard job. He wanted her to be looked after and cared for. He was prepared to spend his whole life doing that.

'Can I have a bit of hush for a second?'

Harry stood up and moved over to the Christmas tree, his hand firmly clasped round the little box in his pocket. The ring inside was a pretty half-hoop of diamonds that had belonged to Dolly's mother. A piece of family history for the newest family member.

'Annie, could you stand up and come over here please?'

Dolly and Peggy gave the game away by gasping and clutching each other's hands. Harry didn't mind. He knew how desperate they were to join the two families. He wanted to honour that. He wanted to honour the values they'd built.

'What are you doing?'

There was an odd note in Annie's voice – she didn't sound as excited as he'd hoped. She did get up from the sofa, which was a relief, but she came towards him as slowly as if the carpet had sucked up the Christmas cake's treacle.

'You know. You must know.'

He held out his hand, praying Annie wouldn't hesitate. Choking back a sob of relief when she took it. Holding on tight as she glanced round. As her bitten lip told him what he'd feared might be true: that this wasn't the right time or place.

Maybe a more intimate setting would have been better. Maybe she's still not ready.

Harry closed that voice down before it took hold of his head. They had to be ready – this could be their last chance. He'd been pronounced fit for duty again; he only had a few days of leave left. God knows where he'd be sent next. The only certainty was that there'd be U-boats circling. And besides, what better setting could there be than this? The Christmas-tree lights twinkling like stars round Annie's head. The people who loved them most in the world watching their story progress to its only conclusion.

She shook her head at him as he went down on one knee. She shook her head, but she was smiling. He took a deep breath and opened the box. He asked the question that, in his head, felt already asked and answered. He kept his eyes locked on hers as the seconds ticked past. One, two, three and each second that went by cancelling out a beat of his heart.

'Yes. I'll marry you, yes.'

She said something else too, something that sounded very like, *but just not yet.* But Harry pretended not to hear, and anyway her words were lost in the cheering. She'd said yes – that was all he needed. She was smiling. She was his. And the few seconds when his heart had almost stopped were completely forgotten because Harry's world was finally healed and complete.

CHAPTER NINE
NOVEMBER 1944

'I needed a wife, Margarete. It was expected of me, and you've been very clear that wife wouldn't be you. I don't see that anything has to change between us because of Ursula.'

Margarete rolled out of bed, leaving Hans lost to sleep, wishing his announcement the previous night would stop irritating her. He'd been right. She'd never had any intention of marrying him, or anyone else. Her parents' transactional marriage had closed the door to that, whatever the Party might believe was appropriate for women. She had no interest in keeping house for a man she didn't love and who didn't love her – there wasn't enough expensive jewellery in the world to make her settle for that. She had her own ambitions to feed. And she didn't know or care about Ursula, so he was right about that too: nothing about their relationship had to change. But she didn't like the fact that he'd chosen someone else to be part of his life. She preferred the men she chose to remain her property; she'd never liked to share.

Margarete wrapped one of the coverlets from the bed around her shoulders and crossed to the tiny window. It was almost impossible to see out – the branches that camouflaged the compound's buildings hung over the glass in a thick green fringe – but the act of doing it felt normal. And anything that felt normal these days was a relief.

She shivered despite her warm covering. She'd have to leave the hut she'd turned into her sanctuary soon and go into the main bunker to start her day. As proud as she was of her job, she'd never got used to going down inside the Wolf's Lair, Hitler's Eastern Front headquarters that lay deep inside Poland's occupied Masurian Forest and deep under the ground.

It wasn't a welcoming place. Daylight disappeared with the first heavily barred door. Air had to be circulated through ventilators embedded in the ceilings, and the temperature they produced was stifling. The walls were made from reinforced concrete that was as cold to the touch as the air was hot. The offices were connected by a maze of corridors that could still confuse her after three years walking them. And since the assassination attempt on the Führer the previous July – by a traitorous group of German officers Margarete would have happily shot herself – the security on site had made prisoners of them all. When they'd first arrived in 1941, there'd been bike rides and hikes through the forest to balance the days spent underground. Now there were three heavily patrolled and guarded security zones outside instead, and the area left for walking had been reduced to a narrow patch of scrubland.

It's little wonder the poor Führer sometimes loses heart when he's so isolated, and so far away from the mountains he loves.

No one was allowed to refer to Hitler's darkening moods, but Margarete – who was one of the few people who could snap him back into being her dear Uncle Wolf – felt every moment of them. She worried about his health and his state of mind far more than she worried about Hans, despite the fact they'd been sharing a bed and a small part of their hearts since they'd met at a party almost four years ago. Despite the fact that his job as a Stuka bomber pilot put his life in danger on an almost daily basis. As well as his apparent inability to comprehend fear – as attested to by the new medals that had to be devised for him every time he broke another record for bravery. She was as fond as she could be of Hans, but he was simply part of the machinery, there to serve the Führer, the same as they all were. His life, and hers, took second place.

Margarete had understood that her destiny lay with the Party in 1936, when she was nineteen. She was twenty-seven now and that certainty hadn't changed. Even if the rest of the world had turned upside down since the first heady days she'd spent working at the heart of the government.

'Your six-month probation is a formality for the paperwork of course, given that you've been recommended by Frau Goebbels, and with your family connections. You'll be based here in the Reich Chancellery, but you'll also liaise with Chief of Staff Bormann's office which is on the other side of Wilhelmstraße. You are also entitled – with your parents' permission – to move into your own apartment in one of the houses in the Chancellery's park. That is what we'd prefer you to do if you can – the war means everyone needs to be available at all hours...'

Margarete let the secretarial administrator – whose name she'd already forgotten – ramble on. The woman had stumbled over *Frau Goebbels* and *family connections*. She'd caught her breath at Margarete's belted polka-dot skirt and matching bolero jacket, an outfit that would have made a mockery of her thick waist and short body if she'd tried to copy it. She was overawed by Margarete, and Margarete wasn't interested in her, but she was delighted with her new position, and she was fascinated by the building that would house her ambitions.

The Chancellery had the size and feel of a museum or a Renaissance palace with its long, wide corridors and love of marble and mosaics. It was effortlessly grand, but it wasn't as cold and deliberately intimidating as those places could be. It was intended to be a home as well as a showcase. Each room Margarete walked through was lined with huge cream and blue porcelain vases filled with a florist's worth of flowers whose colours had been matched to the paintings above them. The Ladies' Salon was a pale pink and lemon confection. The Winter Garden Room bloomed with chintz-covered armchairs and views of the park that were delightful all year round. Even the offices had crystal bowls crammed with fruit and deep-cushioned sofas to soften their functional edges.

It's the most elegant place in Berlin. It's a palace fit for a king, as it should be.

'It's perfect.' She used the compliment as a full-stop to halt yet another rambling sentence. 'It's exactly the way our Führer should live.'

Her words lit up the woman's lined face. They were repeated around the whole building by the end of Margarete's first day. And when she was summoned into Hitler's personal office three days later to share his afternoon tea and cream cakes, the rest of the secretarial team reshuffled itself and let Margarete take her rightful place.

The war was good for me when it started. It was good for us all.

Margarete turned away from the window. Hans was still sleeping. She would need to wake him up soon and hustle him out of her private quarters before the compound came to life. Nobody had commented publicly on their affair yet – there were far less prickly targets for gossip than Margarete, who never let the smallest slight go unnoticed – and that was how she intended to keep it, especially now that Hans was married. The thought of Uncle Wolf being disappointed in her conduct was unbearable.

She went to the small bathroom to get ready, gritting her

teeth as the taps trickled once again with nothing but freezing-cold water. The start of the war had been a personal and political success story, so had its early years, but now? Margarete shimmied into her warmest skirt and jumper and pulled her suitcase down from the top of the cupboard, trying not to think about *now*. It wasn't easy. The questions nobody was meant to ask always refused to stay quiet in the morning's early hours.

Why did his own officers turn against him and plant a bomb? How did we lose at Stalingrad when our armies are supposed to be the best in the world? How did the British not only survive the Blitz, but also come back strong enough to liberate France?

She didn't have the answers. Nobody did. They all clung instead to what had become the Wolf Lair's most repeated promise: 'Nothing's lost yet; it's all still to win.' Margarete believed that with every breath she was made of. She also believed every victory-filled speech she was asked to type, and sometimes to contribute a line or two of her own to. Especially now typing those had become her personal domain.

'Party Chief Bormann has requested that you join his team, reporting directly to him. It's a great honour, Fräulein Fleiss, well done.'

Whether it had been an honour or her due, as Margarete chose to believe, working for Bormann had been the perfect placement. Once she'd got the man's delusional expectations regarding a more personal relationship under control, it had become even better. The year 1941 – when Bormann had achieved the first of the promotions which had resulted in him becoming Hitler's private secretary, and had taken Margarete up the ladder with him – had been a good one for her and a good one for Germany. Britain had been broken by nightly bombing raids and was on the brink of surrender. Hitler had successfully invaded Russia and brought Stalin to heel. France, and much of western Europe as well as large swathes of the east, had been swallowed into the Reich. The camps intended to take care of the Jewish problem were established and expanding. There'd been a great deal to celebrate that year, and they'd celebrated in style.

The Führer – who wasn't a dancer but loved to watch a pretty spectacle – had held regular balls in the Reich Chancellery, filled with women dressed in shimmering satin and men who clamoured to dance with Margarete. He'd taken his entourage to his beloved Berghof retreat in Bavaria for the summer. They'd spent hours wandering among flower-filled alpine meadows and eating apple-stuffed pastries in the little teahouse perched on a plateau above the River Ach, dazzled by the beautiful views across the mountains to Salzburg. Margarete had deliberately made a friend of Hitler's girlfriend, Eva Braun, even though the woman was as empty-headed as Sissi and had few interests beyond fashion and the two irritating Scottish terriers Hitler had christened 'the dust brushes'. She'd been so at home at the Berghof, her father had almost doubled in size when he saw his daughter holding court at the Führer's dining table. So 1941 had been a perfect year, and the ones following should have matched it, especially as she mirrored Bormann's rise and Hitler's private office became permanently open to her. Instead...

Margarete stopped folding jumpers as *now* forced its way back into her head. Her personal star was glowing – that wasn't a concern. Ever since they'd arrived in the Wolf's Lair – for a stay that had only been meant to last a few months but had dragged on for years as the war's successes reversed – she'd been entrusted with the task of typing up the bulk of Hitler's speeches. The Führer's two main secretaries – Christa and Traudl – had made no objection to that, which had surprised Margarete until she was given her first assignment. Even she had had to admit then, if only to herself, that he wasn't an easy man to work with. He dictated his speeches from notes he never gave Margarete to look at. His speaking pace varied from laboured to fast without warning. His voice frequently dipped and became lost in the cavernous underground office, and he didn't always complete one sentence before ploughing into the next. It was a challenge to capture his words the way he wanted them captured, but Margarete rose to it, retyping the drafts over and over until they flowed. Even Goebbels – the master of rhetoric – was impressed.

I'm going to be the one person he can always trust.

Her promise to her father and herself had come true, but the rest of the sky had dimmed round her. The war had changed course, the road to victory had grown longer, and trust had become a moveable feast. Some officers raised their eyebrows when they heard Hitler delivering her passionately constructed speeches. Some pored over the devastating photographs of what had been done to Hamburg and Frankfurt by the Allied bombers and questioned the cost of the war. Margarete had reported them of course: nobody needed another conspiracy or a repetition of the bomb plot. Everyone she'd named had been dealt with.

'You have to get up and get going. Today's starting early.'

Hans was out of the bed as soon as she shook him. He knew the drill by now: a quick exit and no promises for their next meeting. Neither of their lives had space for that. He would reappear whenever Hitler requested his presence at a medal ceremony or a photograph opportunity. Margarete would fit him into her schedule if she could.

And if this next mission becomes his last?

Margarete folded that thought away with her sweaters as Hans silently closed the door. There was no point in dwelling on the danger he lived with. Someone would tell her the news if his luck failed. She assumed she would grieve when that happened; she had no sense of what that grief would look like, or how deep a hole he might leave in her life. She had no time or inclination to worry about it, not when the Führer required all her focus.

The Russians were closing in – Margarete could hear their guns in the distance as she packed. Not even her wordsmithing skills could put a positive spin on that calamity. Terrible reports had arrived from the towns and villages the Red Army had already swept through, but there was nothing to be done. Hitler no longer had the forces at his command to hold them back, and he'd finally accepted that and stopped refusing to abandon the front. So now they were leaving the Lair and returning to Berlin, a city she'd only seen in snatches since 1941. Everyone had been instructed not to call it a retreat.

Margarete fastened her suitcase and left it outside her door, ready to be collected and stowed on the Führer's private train. The first time she'd travelled on that, on her way into Poland, the experience had been a delight. Her cabin had been as pretty and as personal as the decorations she'd requested for her Chancellery apartment. The sofa covered in embroidered satin cushions transformed into a very comfortable bed at night. The silk coverlet and all the other trimmings had been worked in her favourite shades of violet and rose gold. The walls were wood-panelled, the carpet was velvet-soft. The shrimp vol-au-vents she'd eaten in the train's dining carriage had been as good as any they served in Berlin's famous Horcher's restaurant. Unfortunately, that wouldn't be the case today. The best she could hope for was a comfortable seat for the fourteen-hour journey and an edible sandwich. There was no room anymore for a dining carriage or personal cabins. Today's train was set to be packed with boxes and people; nothing could be left in the Lair.

He'll need to have something ready to say when we leave, or perhaps for when we arrive. He'll need to keep everyone's spirits up, as well as his own.

Margarete knew the Führer would be downhearted, but if

anyone could help him overcome that, she could. This was a regrouping after all, not a rout.

We are home in Berlin; we are back in the heart of Germany. We are ready to confidently turn the next page.

The words leapt into her head as she hurried towards the bunker. It didn't matter that Hitler's heart belonged to Bavaria, or that he hated Berlin, which he thought was too bohemian and would never think of as home. What mattered was the sentiment, the rallying call, and who better to craft that than her? She could almost see the Führer's shoulders relaxing as she ran towards the steps.

'Has anyone seen Secretary Bormann?'

The overstretched typists and soldiers tasked with emptying the offices stepped aside as Margarete rushed in. She didn't notice; she expected no less. Margarete never looked at the waiters who brought her coffee, or the cleaners who straightened her rooms. She never looked at the typists who had to stay on duty no matter how late she chose to work. Those people didn't matter – she had no need to see them. But she saw Bormann when he emerged from his office wondering who had the temerity to call out his name. She saw Hitler when he waved her into his private room and pronounced himself delighted with her plan. She always made sure they saw her. It never crossed her mind to look down at the people she considered beneath her. Why would it? The only direction Margarete was interested in looking, or going, was up.

CHAPTER TEN

FEBRUARY 1945

'Here you are, Sylvie, a nice cup of tea. I've stuck some of the major's sugar in it – don't go telling on me.'

A nice cup of tea. The medicine for all ills. The shorthand for *I know you're having a rough time; let's try our best to get through it,* which could be thought but not said. Sylvie was a widow; her husband had died at Dunkirk. She had elderly parents living in her small house and three children to look after. It was hardly surprising she'd fallen asleep at her desk. Annie patted her shoulder and moved on, all too aware that the whole office was filled with women juggling lives as difficult as Sylvie's, making sure the workload on each desk was evenly distributed. Trying to remember if it was her turn to stand in the butcher's queue after work or Peggy's.

The war that was meant to last six months was in its sixth year. Life before it began was a memory; what life would be after it ended had no discernible shape. Rationing and shortages and make-do-and-mend were a daily and exhausting reality. The world had become a grey place, ruled by casualty lists and telegrams that only ever brought bad news and headlines full of atrocities. It wasn't easy to find a moment full of light, although Annie had found one at least she could rejoice in.

'He's not here to make the rules, Mum, so maybe it's time we changed them. They don't have to be our people anymore.'

Peggy had handed the first letter to Annie without really understanding what it meant. It was a request from an ex-comrade of her father's for help with a campaign to release the 18B detainees and arrived the year after Sid was arrested. Annie had taken great delight in tearing it up. A year without Sid had given Annie room to breathe and Peggy the quiet she needed to heal. He wasn't missed. The apartment was a lighter place without his fury and his complaints. Peggy began to read her beloved novels again; she rediscovered a favourite bench in the park. But she wouldn't talk about her fall. She'd pushed that into a box she kept firmly shut, and any mention of it, or Grete, caused her so much distress, Annie stopped trying to bring the subject up, but she couldn't forget it. Peggy's recovery was painfully slow; there were days when she was more like the child than the parent. That frailty tore through Annie and kept her hatred of Grete alive. The war was terrible and heart-breaking for so many reasons. That it had put Grete out of reach was an added, private misery. And the wedding that Peggy forgot about as often as she remembered it had become a thorn in Annie's side.

Harry had run too fast and too public with his proposal. Once the Christmas glitter fell from their eyes, his mother – and Harry – knew it. Annie had said yes to him because she was always going to say yes to him. Loving Harry had become part of her being. The lust for life she'd seen in him spoke to her soul: she'd learned that in the kiss that had taken her breath away while passers-by whistled outside Earl's Court Tube station. She'd explored its depths in the long summer evenings they'd spent sharing their dreams. Their love had come quickly, and the thought of a life that might have to be lived without him had crystallised it. The telegram marked *missing* that she'd taken from Dolly's shaking hand had split Annie's life into a before and an after that could still catch at her throat. She'd told herself he would come home through all the long months of waiting. She'd forced herself to stay positive for Jim and Dolly. But there'd been more lonely nights than she ever wanted to live through again when she lay sleepless in the dark, hopelessly convinced he was gone. So saying *no* had never been a possibility, especially once she realised how deep the scars from the shipwreck ran. She would do anything in her power to soften those.

Unfortunately, as happy as it made her to be promised to Harry, the engagement had backed her other dreams into a corner. Which was why she'd refused to make plans for the wedding until after the war. And why the ring had left her finger for a chain round her neck the instant she went back to the office. The sad truth was that becoming a married woman came with more trappings than a dress and a cake.

'Everything will be different after this. We've proved ourselves now – they can't expect us to simply pack up and go home again.'

Annie wasn't the only woman who'd found a sense of freedom and purpose waiting inside the war's ministries. All the women she worked with felt as if they'd stepped out of a cage. The fighting was a terrible thing, only a fool would deny that, but it had opened doors to girls like her who'd had their wings clipped by family expectations and a shortened education. There were days when Annie still couldn't believe her luck. Especially as she'd expected the first door she'd walked through to instantly slam shut.

'Your references are excellent, Miss Kirson, and I'm delighted you want to involve yourself in "more meaningful work", as your application put it. I imagine Edelstein's will be sorry to let you go, but the war requires sacrifices of us all. Now is there anything else about you I need to know beyond what's in here?'

Annie assumed Miss Carter – who ran the junior typing pool at the War Office as if it was an elite infantry squad – meant an above-average shorthand speed or an inability to make tea. It was impossible to imagine how the stern-faced woman would react to, 'Not really, except my father is currently doing everything he can to subvert everyone else's sacrifices. Including, apparently, turning a blind eye to a nearly fatal attack on my mother by a Nazi, which I've never had the courage to ask him about.' Whatever she did or didn't say, she knew Sid would catch up with her at some point. She'd half expected to be screened out at the application stage. But *some point* didn't happen in Miss Carter's office when she chose silence, shook her head and was offered the job on the spot. Or for the first year in the typing pool where she worked long hours and volunteered for extra shifts and shone. It wasn't until some months after Sid had been transferred to the Isle of Man, and made a nuisance of himself there, that somebody put the pieces together.

'Do you share your father's beliefs? Is that why you attended British Union rallies and other fascist events?'

The man asking the questions had a nondescript face and a nondescript suit and an MI5 warrant card. There was no introduction, no preamble. Annie quickly understood that she had no power. If it hadn't been for Miss Carter's welcoming smile and nod as she entered the room where he was waiting, Annie would have simplified the process and resigned without a fuss.

'I don't share them, no, not in any way. I attended rallies, and visited the Black House, and was a guest at parties Sir Oswald Mosley attended because I was made to do so. It was never a choice. That wasn't how my father ran our family.'

She didn't expect him to believe her; she assumed she'd

already been judged. The surprise came courtesy of Miss Carter.

'Before you go any further, you should know that I am aware of Miss Kirson's background. Another girl who has since left us was very keen to apprise me of that. I, however, am not a believer in children paying for the sins of their fathers. I did not confront her; I decided to see what she was made of instead. And that, I can assure you, is honesty and hard work. If I'd had any concerns about her character, she wouldn't be here. Please don't doubt me when I tell you that.'

Miss Carter was so clearly built from patriotism and tweed and the best of British that the interview terminated there. The man left with a warning that he'd be keeping his eye on Annie, which Miss Carter dismissed as 'nonsense and face-saving' the instant he closed the door. She dismissed Annie's breathless thanks as efficiently.

'Is it also true that you speak German? Presumably out of choice because you enjoy the language and not the more unpleasant motives our little telltale suggested?'

Annie nodded instead of asking why – Miss Carter never did or said anything without a reason that she would come to in her own time.

'I'm not fluent by any means; I haven't had the practice, but I read and write it fairly well, and I've kept it up. Once the war came and my evening classes ended, I continued practising the grammar and reading German novels by myself.'

'Good girl.' Miss Carter reached into her desk drawer and pulled out a folder. 'Then it's time we rewarded your hard work and made proper use of your talents. If that's what you would like to happen of course.'

It was as simple as that. Miss Carter belonged to the net of female administrators the men with grander titles didn't understand were actually in charge of the War Office. She scooped Annie out of the typing pool and into MI19, the fledgling intelligence unit responsible for collecting and analysing the testimony of captured German prisoners and spies. Annie went from typing up orders for battledress jackets and requests for improved combat boots to accounts of how well a spy bargaining for his freedom really understood Hitler's war plans. And from the War Office's overcrowded offices to an elegant run of mansion houses in Kensington Palace Gardens when MI19 finally branched out on its own. Which was where its real work began.

Interrogation Number 215D. Major Karl Pöpel. Captured Roer Triangle, 21 January 1945.

Annie picked up the report she'd completed that morning and filed it away in the overfull cupboard, wondering what Harry would think if he saw it. *I can't tell you much about what I do* was the line she hid behind, not that she needed it. Harry wasn't interested enough in her job to ask for its specifics. He assumed they'd never deepened beyond a typing pool. He had no idea that his fiancée had signed the Official Secrets Act, or that she worked in an interrogation centre as an integral part of the team.

Or that I know what they do in the sessions where they ask me to wait outside.

Annie's hand strayed to the engagement ring hidden under her shirt. Sometimes it was as hard now to reconcile the secret and public parts of her life as it had been when she'd been dancing to her father's tune. Outside the Gardens, she was a daughter and a fiancée, and her main challenge was trying to avoid conversations about weddings. Inside...

I'm a witness to how badly we want to win the war. And to the methods that might help us get there that can't leave this place.

Annie couldn't picture herself telling Harry what she'd seen and heard in the windowless basement, either by letter or when he came home. Every conversation she'd run through in her head ended with him recoiling.

'The rooms are kept deliberately bare so there's nothing for the prisoner to focus on except us. It's my job to sit in on the interviews and write down anything a prisoner says in German, or to ask a question they might be struggling to understand or respond to in English. Sometimes, when the interviewee isn't co-operating, the officer in charge will ask me to step out into the corridor. That's when buckets of freezing water or wheel-barrows full of heavy logs get delivered. That's when I hear the commands from inside to *stand still, pick those up, jump,* or the splash of water against stone. Sometimes a gramophone will appear and the prisoner will be left alone with a cacophony of discordant sounds that drill into my head too. Sometimes there'll be the promise of a bullet. The only thing that remains consistent is that when I go back in – which could be twenty minutes or a day later – the detainee will be far more co-opera-tive. And when my conscience gets the better of me, I pretend that the prisoner is Grete and she's being forced to admit what she did to my mother.'

It was hardly dinner-time conversation. The intelligence the service gathered was invaluable, it saved lives, but the looking away it involved? And how easily she could imagine putting Grete into a cell and walking away? That wasn't for sharing. She was too afraid he might think she condoned what was done.

'Do you have a minute, Annie?'

She pulled herself back from the basement's challenges as Major Langley, her boss, appeared at his office door. And she forgot all about them as soon as he waved her into a seat.

'Have you given any thought to what happens after the war?'

The question was so unexpected, Annie found herself

repeating, 'After?' She couldn't remember the last time she'd thought about that, and she told him so, although she'd longed for its coming with every casualty report she was terrified would include Harry.

Langley wasn't surprised at her reaction. 'It's an odd notion, I agree, but it's close. You've seen the reports and heard what's been said in the last few interrogations. The prisoners who've come in lately have definitely lost their bravado.'

That was true. Annie wasn't blind to that, or to the shift in the war's course that had arrived with the New Year. Hitler had made one last push into Belgium and Holland at the start of January, but his offensive had been quickly defeated. The Red Army had liberated Poland and Lithuania from Nazi occupation and was firmly on the advance. According to the captured *Oberstleutnant* whose testimony she'd typed up that morning, the Germans no longer had the ability to push back the Soviet armies who had advanced within firing distance of Berlin, although they'd fight with every last breath to try. Neither that prisoner nor anybody else had suggested a surrender was imminent, but now Annie took a moment to properly consider it, Langley was right: there was a sense that the end might be getting nearer. The hard part was allowing herself to have hope and believe it.

'I know what you're thinking, Annie. We've let ourselves imagine this day before, after the German rout at Stalingrad, after the D-Day landings recaptured France, and yet the war keeps blundering on. But I've been asked to look at a scenario for when it stops, to put together a picture of what comes next, and that's what I want to talk to you about.'

Annie pulled herself back from the image of men cheering from the deck of a ship that would never see combat again and frowned. 'But won't we be disbanded? If the war ends, won't our role here end too?'

It was what she'd assumed when she'd first been assigned to

the division, when she'd also decided not to worry about that happening. But now the question was asked, it dawned on her that Langley might have called her in to tell her that her working life was about to end faster than she was ready for. The relief when he replied, 'No it won't,' turned into an, 'Oh, thank God,' which made him laugh.

'Well, there's my answer, I think. There's actually going to be more need for intelligence operatives like us when it's done, not less, but we'll have a new focus. Once the dust settles, the truth of the camps and the massacres the Nazis unleashed is going to finally come out; it has to. There'll be scores to settle then; there'll be people with blood all over their hands who have to be made to pay for their crimes. Now do you see where I'm going?'

She had an idea. She nodded as her head began buzzing. *Like us* and *we* had told her the first thing she needed to know: that there would still be a team and she would still be part of it. But it was the horror of *camps* and *massacres* that had struck home. Everyone in MI19 was obsessed with those; they had been since the unit's first days.

Rumours about systematic mass murders in Lithuania and Latvia and Ukraine had begun to emerge in the summer of 1941, overheard by British intelligence officers listening to German radio broadcasts. Things had begun to snowball after that first leak. American journalists stranded in Germany after their country joined the war had described what they called 'an open hunt' for Jews across the Reich and its occupied territories, although no one was sure what the hunt was intended to lead to. Not long after that, the existence of a deliberate plan to exterminate the entire Jewish population had reached Britain via a report filed by a Chilean diplomat who'd used the word *eradication*. That had been a shock which bounced round the basement.

The team had redoubled their efforts to get prisoners to talk.

Digging deeper into every interrogation. Trying to uncover information about the slaughterhouses the Nazis referred to as concentration camps; about what was happening in the ghettoes that appeared to have sprung up in most of eastern Europe's cities. Getting clear answers had been an uphill battle, but now the soldiers liberating large swathes of the formerly conquered countries were beginning to uncover physical evidence that rewrote the definition of horror. Auschwitz. Majdanek. Bergen-Belsen. The names were written on every one of MI19's bulletin boards. The photographs the team had had to force themselves to look at had been used to justify the more brutal interrogations that were unleashed in the basement. Annie knew that as well as anyone. She wanted answers too, but now Langley was talking about justice, and she wanted that more than anything. And to be part of pursuing it.

Wouldn't that right some of the wrongs my father's done? Wouldn't that help balance the scales? And if there was a way to find Grete and make her pay too...

That thought had been at the back of her mind since she joined the intelligence services, even though she knew the chance of finding, never mind confronting, Grete was less than slim. She took a deep breath and waited for her pulse to stop racing. She couldn't share that thought out loud; there were parts of her life that had to remain secret.

'Do you think some form of punishment will really happen? Are there plans actually in place?'

Langley pushed a folder towards her. 'Yes and yes. Take this away and have a read of it. Stalin, Roosevelt and Churchill have held a conference in the Crimea at Yalta; its findings will be announced soon. What matters to us is that they've agreed to establish an International Military Tribunal which is going to be used to prosecute war criminals – they're agreeing a framework now for what that will mean. Imagine it, Annie. Hitler, Göring, Goebbels and Himmler on trial before the whole world.

Add whoever you want to the list because the minute the war's over and we can safely get people over to Germany – where plenty want the trial to take place – we're coming for the lot of them. And the question I'm asking you – like I'm going to ask everyone out there with the right skills for the job – is do you want to go there too as one of the team?'

Annie could barely speak. This was a possibility to be involved in writing history, to be involved in a trial that would tell men like her father how deeply wrong their world view was. To bring the heartless face to face with their crimes. That would have been enough on its own, but he was also offering her the opportunity to travel when she'd barely been outside London before. Until the war, Annie had rarely left the East End; as for travelling overseas... nothing in her life had ever suggested there would be a chance of that, and now she was being offered the possibility of going to Germany. The end of the war and the start of a new life for herself and for Peggy too, if Sid could somehow be kept at bay. She'd never wanted anything more, which was why she couldn't put her thoughts into words. She managed a nod and a *yes* instead that came out in a squeak and made Langley grin.

'Excellent. That's exactly the response I was hoping for. There'll be a bit of preparation involved – you'll need to do a crash course in Polish to back up your German, as that's what a lot of the survivors will speak, but that shouldn't be a problem for you. I'll get that in motion while you go and get Mike for me – he's next on the list.'

Annie jumped up. She would have run out of the room clapping her hands if it hadn't been for Langley's parting shot.

'There's just one last thing, Annie, and I'm sorry if it's a bit personal. Don't go marrying that sailor of yours when he jumps off his ship all fired up to propose. The only restriction I've got on the team is the usual one: I can't take married women.'

CHAPTER ELEVEN
FEBRUARY–APRIL 1945

The Führer did his best to rise to Margarete's rallying words, but even she had to admit how hollow they'd sounded in the reality of their arrival in war-torn Berlin. There was no triumphant return to the Reich Chancellery; there was no possibility of family reunions. Instead, Hitler's staff moved from the Wolf's Lair straight into the Führerbunker which lay thirty feet below the Chancellery grounds and swapped one underground prison for another.

And I'd set up camp in a third if he asked me to.

Margarete moved through the Chancellery's shattered husk, trying to find a place for her memories. Nothing was as she remembered; the Allied planes targeting the city had seen to that. Everything was mildewed and blackened. The whole edifice appeared to be sinking back into the earth – another night's bombing and it could vanish, and no one would remember its beauty.

The Russian army was less than sixty kilometres from the city now, the roar of their guns a permanent soundtrack. Everyone was on edge, tipped into exhaustion by the Allied bombing raids, especially the last attack which had been particularly relentless. Its blasts had reverberated through the bunker. Its bombs had caused a fire which spread through the east of the city and burned for four days, reducing large swathes of Friedrichstadt and Luisenstadt to ashes. Margarete had feared for the Führer's health when that report came in. He'd raged like a man possessed, swearing to visit a vengeance on the Americans and the British which would destroy them down to their last soldier. He'd raged even more when his trembling generals had told him he no longer had the planes or the manpower to do it.

And Hans was as weak as the worst of them.

'He has to accept it's over. I'll fight for him as long as he asks me to; all his loyal officers will. But the war's lost, Margarete. The Allied leaders are already meeting, holding conferences, discussing how they're going to break up and rule Germany. Every day he refuses to accept our defeat is another day when men die pointless deaths.'

His defeatism had stunned her. Her immediate inclination had been to report him, German hero or not. She'd had to work hard to persuade herself that his disloyalty was the result of the pain of his amputation or the high doses of medication he was taking, not a newly baked streak of cowardice. She'd only held back from her duty because his betrayal, on top of his injuries, would have hurt Hitler too much. The bad luck Hans been dodging his entire career had finally caught up with him. His Stuka had been hit by a heavy barrage of anti-aircraft fire; he'd lost his leg below the knee as a result of his wounds. It had been a shock for Margarete to see him lying white-faced and bandaged in a hospital bed. Until he'd broken her trust and she'd regretted going to see him at all.

He was wrong. He has to be wrong.

Margarete picked her way through the smashed statues littering the muddy pathway between the Chancellery and the bunker, ignoring the evidence of how right Hans was. Defeat wasn't a word she used. It wasn't a concept she understood. And it couldn't be happening, not when they'd fought so hard for the cause. National Socialism was more than a political creed for Margarete: it was the only decent way of living. Blood purity. Homeland. Obedience to the Führer. Elimination of all enemies, inside the country and out. They were the pillars of her life. She couldn't imagine living in a world where those principles weren't sacred. She wouldn't.

They're what make life beautiful.

'Come back in, Margarete. He needs you.'

Margarete blinked as Traudl – who was leaning as far out of the bunker door as she dared – called and waved to her. The rubble and the ruins instantly disappeared. *He needs you.* Had there ever been happier words?

Traudl disappeared down the steps away from the black clouds where fighter planes might be lurking. Margarete followed her far more calmly. As long as she was needed, there was nothing to worry about, and defeat could stay at the door.

'We're going to have to start rationing the water soon – the supply system's becoming increasingly unreliable.'

'It's time to start destroying paperwork, especially orders and reports that have specific names attached to them.'

'We're running out of medicine and tinned food and cigarettes. We're down to our last communication line with the outside.'

Defeat hadn't listened to Margarete; it had seeped in everywhere. Every day, sometimes every hour, brought a new problem. The bunker was overcrowded and restless, alternating between despair and a wild optimism that had nothing to anchor it. Beds were at a premium. Sleeping quarters had been turned into makeshift hospital wards and operating theatres as Russian shells joined the bombs raining down on

Berlin. Margarete kept tripping over soldiers lying asleep, or drunk, on the ground. Eva Braun had found a gramophone player and a pile of discarded records in a forgotten corner of the Reich Chancellery and kept throwing parties only she enjoyed. And the Führer was... *Exhausted. Not beaten. Exhausted.*

Margarete gathered up the closely typed pages she'd prepared for his next speech. She didn't know who it was intended for; she didn't know when it would be delivered. Neither of those details mattered. The important thing was that Hitler had snapped out of the melancholy mood he too easily slipped into and wanted to work and to consider the needs of his people. She checked through the document as she walked down the dimly lit and sour-smelling corridor towards his office, checking she'd got the tone right.

'Every bridge and every building must be defended down to the last man and the last bullet... Every citizen must fight with whatever weapons they have... There will be no negotiations; there will be no surrender.'

She'd got his words down as best as she could, although Hitler's hand was so shaky now it had been hard to read his corrections. And his voice...

Needs time to recover its strength, that's all. Time and fresh air and good food, in the mountains not in a bunker.

Margarete smiled as she imagined her soothing words bringing the light back into his eyes. Positivity was what he needed most. He was surrounded by generals telling him what he couldn't do and acting as if the Soviets were already kings of the city. What he lacked was a confident voice in his ear, a gentle hand on his shoulder that said, 'Everything will come right.'

What he needs is his favourite niece.

Margarete was so lost in her thoughts and her importance, she almost fell over the lump blocking the stairs. She would have kicked the drunk out of the way, if it hadn't looked up in time and revealed a child, not a brandy-soaked soldier.

'What are you doing here?'

The lump sat up and revealed another one. Margarete squinted until her eyes adjusted to the stairwell's gloom, although that didn't make the situation any clearer. The Goebbels' six children were sitting on the stairs in two neat rows, as if they were about to lisp their way through a Christmas concert. Helga, the eldest and a poised and pretty twelve-year-old, tried to sound confident as she answered, but her lip suddenly trembled.

'Mother brought us here this morning, but we haven't seen her all day and the little ones are hungry. They don't like our bedroom either. It's cold and dark, and we're not used to being crammed in together.'

Margarete refused to acknowledge the shiver that ran up her spine. She dismissed the icy drops of sweat at her hairline as the result of the bunker's erratic heating system.

'You have a bedroom here? How long are you staying?'

Helga did her best to stop her face crumpling. She put her arm round her littlest sister. 'I don't know. I heard Father tell Mother that we wouldn't be going home again, but we've only been allowed to bring one personal item each, and one set of nightclothes.'

That was the moment Margarete knew. That defeat truly was in the bunker with them. That none of them could outrun it. That was the moment when the Führer's vow – which she'd closed her ears to – roared back and turned into a promise.

'I won't see another spring, but this was a lovely one.'

Hitler had gone up into the ruined gardens a week or so earlier, ignoring his generals' advice to stay underground. April had arrived in a burst of sunshine that wiped away the bitterly cold winter, and he was determined to see it. He'd returned carrying a bunch of daffodils and a spray of cherry blossom which he'd presented to Eva. She'd patted his arm when he'd referred to them as his final flowers; she hadn't appeared surprised. A day or two after that, he'd brought what must have been a private conversation between the two of them into the outer office and announced he would shoot himself before the Russians arrived to destroy his name and his legacy. Margarete had walked out at once. She'd refused to listen to him, or to discuss the announcement with a white-faced Bormann. She'd consigned the Führer's words to a depression brought on by the increasingly hard decisions about Berlin's defence he'd been forced to take.

But now the children are here, and they're not leaving.

Margarete sank down onto the stairs and didn't push away the child who immediately crawled into her lap. Magda Goebbels worshipped her sons and daughters, but she worshipped the Führer and the cause too, possibly more. Joseph Goebbels referred to his leader as his life. Margarete knew the couple's loyalty knew no bounds. That if the Führer truly was intent on killing himself, they would follow him. And she also knew that she mustn't let Helga – who her mother always referred to as a bright and observant girl – understand even the smallest hint of what every instinct told her was coming. The last thing the bunker's stretched nerves needed was a group of panicking children. She bent down to four-year-old Heidi, the one who had curled up on her lap, and tweaked the child's nose in the way she'd seen Goebbels play with her. She found a disarming grin for eight-year-old Holde.

'Well, that won't do, will it? Children aren't meant to be hungry. Come with me and let's see what surprises Uncle Wolf has hidden away for you in the pantry.'

Her jolly tone must have sounded less forced to the children than it did to her. They jumped up at once, formed into twos when she told them to pair up and look smart, and flocked giggling after her. Even Helga – who'd gone along with the game for the sake of her siblings but clearly not trusted it – was mollified by the sugar-soaked cherries and thickly buttered bread Margarete managed to cobble together. And when Magda eventually found them – sitting round a table hastily improvised from packing crates, sticky with syrup and finally sleepy – she greeted Margarete like a long-lost sister.

'We will talk about everything we must face in order to get through these dark days, but we will never speak about this.'

Margarete followed Magda away from the dark bedroom when the children were finally settled, more than happy to agree. She had no intention of going back into the stuffy room or discussing the children's fate. As much as Magda tried to lean on her in the remaining days, Margarete made sure to avoid the little ones. For the first time in her life, she was afraid that her face might betray her. And the children would see that they were already ghosts.

'He's chosen you, Margarete. To get past the Russians. To get these to England. To carry the torch when he can't. He's put all his faith in you.'

Margarete took the pouch from Bormann and tipped its contents out. And – for one brief beautiful moment as she stared at the diamonds tumbling like tiny stars across her palm – she forgot where she was. The cold and the chaos of the bunker dissolved as the jewels twinkled. She watched their light dancing, seeing necklaces and bracelets springing back to life; seeing the ballrooms she'd dazzled what felt like a lifetime ago. Margarete closed her eyes and let the dream take her. She let go of the frightened secretaries and bewildered soldiers crowding the corridors. She let women draped in shimmering satin dresses dance past her instead. She remembered what it was like to hold the world in her hands. She remembered what it was like before the world had been reduced to a glorified cellar.

The bunker had grown sleepless and silent as the shells and the gunfire drew close. It had become the whole world for the people left in it. Hitler's inner circle – Himmler, Göring, Albert Speer – had fled, but the Führer wouldn't leave, not even when the Russians encircled the city and the escape corridors narrowed to ribbons. And now even this tiny world was almost at its end. The last news had arrived from the outside on the twenty-ninth of April. The Russians had reached the Tiergarten, less than three kilometres from the bunker's main entrance. They couldn't be stopped. Margarete had taken down the clock in her office that day. There was nothing but waiting left, and she'd wanted to treasure not measure the last moments. And now the final mission was set, and the final mission was hers.

'But it won't be easy – he knows that too. There'd be no shame in it if you passed the task on.'

Bormann's greedy voice blinked her back into the present. She closed her fingers round the diamonds and slipped her other hand into the pocket of her jacket, searching for the ring sewn into the lining. Her father's gold signet ring. Passed down the family line from son to son until it had stalled in the empty space next to Margarete.

If I do this, I'll fill that space better than a boy ever could and Father will never need anyone but me.

The urge to run and tell her father what she'd been entrusted with was as overwhelming as it was pointless. Berlin was broken; he was too far away.

But I'll find him again when this is done. I'll build a future for us all.

'Are you all right, Margarete? This isn't an order; you don't have to obey. And it's not a job for the faint-hearted.'

If he thinks I can't do it, he'll take the job for himself. And then I'll be nothing; I won't count.

That was an outcome she wouldn't allow. Margarete snapped herself together and dismissed Bormann's doubts.

'Then it's a good job I don't have a faint heart.'

She tipped the diamonds back into their velvet pouch and stowed that safely inside her blouse. Bormann didn't avert his eyes as she re-ordered her clothing. She wasn't surprised, given that she'd been successfully fending off his attentions for years, although it was pitiful that he still had any thoughts in his head beyond survival. Not that he looked in any way capable of that. Margarete shifted away from Bormann's bulk as he spluttered into his hand-kerchief, which wasn't an easy manoeuvre – the man overcrowded every room he went into. That had been an irritant before, but now it was a real danger. The bunker was so packed with people, it had become a breeding place for disease. And Bormann was pale and perspiring, his usually florid face even more unappetising than usual. Margarete picked up the papers which were as important to her mission as the diamonds and tried to edge round him again.

'I'm not ill, if that's what's worrying you. Although a little concern wouldn't hurt if I was.' He sighed and shook his head. Margarete flinched as drops of sweat flew. 'You really do look after number one, don't you? No wonder he chose you for this. If anybody can get past the Russians in one piece, you can – you've certainly got enough tricks.'

He was angry, and afraid for all his bluster, and that made him unpredictable. Margarete ignored him and took another step towards the door. She was the hero in this story, not him. But Bormann wasn't finished with her yet. His hand landed like a damp cloth on her bare wrist.

'It's going to be tonight. That's the other thing I was ordered to tell you. He and Eva will say their goodbyes, close the door to their private quarters and that will be that.'

She pulled away from his touch, needing to take control of her body before it began shivering. *That will be that*. The words were too small for the enormity of the deed they contained. They couldn't hold the poison and the bullets, or the loss which ran through her like a heated blade. Of the Führer she idolised. Of the man she truly believed had only wanted the best for Germany.

The man who's entrusted me with keeping his dreams alive.

And that was what mattered, not her weakness, not her emotions. His dreams. Their future. She sucked in a deep breath, steadied herself. She was tired, that was all. She hadn't slept. She'd spent the night checking and rechecking the final documents Hitler had asked her to type, determined not to let the tiniest mistake mar them. Now she had to walk back into his office with them knowing she'd never see him again. And she had to do it with grace.

'Be your loyal self, Margarete – that's all he needs. Keep your grief for later.'

She didn't need Bormann's advice. She pushed past him, pushed her selfish fears away and knocked on the door to Hitler's private office. It was strange not to be met with barking, but Blondi – the Führer's beloved German shepherd – had been put down two days earlier. The final signal to anyone who needed it that the end was almost in sight.

'Margarete, how lovely. We've had such a happy day, so many visitors.'

Eva was sitting on the sofa beside her new husband, wearing the black dress with red roses round the neckline in which she'd been married the night before. Margarete had watched the registrar enter the sitting room while she was typing up Hitler's final instructions. She'd watched Bormann carry in a tray of champagne. And now it seemed Eva was determined to enjoy being a bride. She waved her gold ring at Margarete and trilled about how happy 'dear Adolf' had made her as if she was looking forward to a long marriage. It was a far cry from the feverish state she'd been in the previous morning, when she'd shown the secretaries her cyanide capsule that looked like a lipstick and insisted she'd make a beautiful corpse.

I don't want to be a witness to this. I don't want him to die.

But nothing she wanted mattered. Eva's overly bright eyes told her the die was cast; so did Hitler's barely there smile. They were already in death's grip; they were already half out of the world. She handed the manuscript over anyway, as if it was a normal working day.

'It's perfect. You've always captured my voice better than anyone could; you've never let me down.'

His blessing – because that's what Margarete heard – calmed her racing pulse. Her Hitler was there again, back in the room. The leader who would always command her.

'And you have the diamonds? You have what you need to continue my work?'

Margarete nodded. She wasn't stepping entirely into the unknown. Mosley had been imprisoned for much of the war, but he was free now, and the temporary house arrest he'd been placed under – which hadn't stopped their agents getting word to him – would keep him safe. He was still loyal to the cause; he'd assured them of that in the weeks before the bunker became detached from the world. So was Kirson too apparently, not that he figured in anyone's plans. The diamonds Bormann had given her would finance Mosley's ambitions for as long as he held them, or finance his successor if Margarete judged him no longer fit for the job. Hitler handed the pages back, patting her hand as he did so.

'You won't be alone. You'll have Hans, and the rest. You'll find each other when it's time.'

Margarete didn't need anyone else, and she wasn't sure she completely trusted Hans. If he'd repeated what he'd said in the hospital on his final visit to the bunker, she would have reported him there and then. But the man who'd defied his doctors when they told him his prosthetic leg meant he'd never fly again, who'd walked out of hospital and into his plane, had been back to his loyal self. Margarete had said nothing against him then, and she wouldn't say anything now. Her purpose was to carry out not question the plan.

'Then there is nothing more to say, my dearest niece, except goodbye.'

The impossible word was said. A nod gave her permission to leave. Margarete didn't flicker. She left the room with her head and her sense of destiny held high. If anyone could get past the Russian soldiers who were determined to devour Berlin, it was her. If anyone could get to England, where men like Mosley were waiting to take up Hitler's mantle, she'd be the one to do it.

The past is lost, the present is a tragedy, but we can't be broken by that. All that counts now is the loyalty we've sworn to our leader, whether he's with us in body or not.

They were brave words. She clung to them like a standard-bearer. But she didn't go back to her office. She went to the furthest corner of the bunker instead, to a stairwell close to a doorway where she could hear the shells pounding into the streets around the compound. Where she wouldn't hear the final gunshot.

PART TWO

CHAPTER TWELVE

MAY 1945

This could be the moment I lose her, and I can't let that happen. Not when we've made it this far.

Harry watched Annie searching for the words he was sure would end with her taking off her engagement ring and burying his hopes. Trying not to panic as what should have been the start of their future threatened to turn her into his past.

The war had finally ground to an end, in Europe anyway. Hitler was dead; Germany had surrendered. Almost six years of fighting and separation, of bombing and fear and loss was officially over. The papers had been awash with victory and excitement that morning. Their headlines promised a new day, a new world where turmoil and misery had vanished. It was a wonderful story, one the country had been waiting to read since the conflict began, but now it was written and its readers weren't so easily convinced. Harry had watched grey-faced men and women pick up the jubilant editions at the newsstand and congratulate each other on the arrival of better times. But he'd also noticed how they shook themselves before they spoke, as if they were about to perform awkward roles in a play. He'd seen how thin their smiles were, how hollow their eyes. He'd heard the worried notes floating through the words, 'Isn't it wonderful?' because he felt the same way.

The shift from war-footing to freedom wasn't seamless; it couldn't be, whatever the newspapers hoped. People who'd lost their homes and their loved ones, whose sons were still fighting in the Pacific, couldn't quite make sense of, 'It's over.' They needed more time to draw breath than the twenty-four hours they'd been given following Germany's surrender and the start of the official victory celebrations. And, as Dolly had indignantly pointed out, there'd been no sudden end to rationing to make a proper party even possible.

Harry – whose latest shore leave had accidentally coincided with VE Day – would have swerved the whole thing if he'd been left to himself, but Annie was too consumed by nerves to stay another minute in the house, and she'd pulled him into the street before he could refuse. Not that he would have done that, not when Annie so clearly needed him. The end of the war had brought shadows to Arnold Circus. Peggy had slipped further inside herself since the news of Germany's surrender, and Sid's likely release, broke. She'd barely spoken about him since his imprisonment, but now some memories of his fists or his cruel tongue she couldn't share had re-emerged with the possibility of his return, and she'd retreated into her fog. Annie's distress at that had been the spur Harry needed to stop fixating on his lost shipmates and the creeping despair of *What was it all for?* that he couldn't seem to shake. Annie had needed to laugh and feel hopeful, so he'd grabbed hold of the hand she offered him and followed her down to Shaftesbury Avenue, to where the country was trying on a new mood.

By the time they'd abandoned the overcrowded buses and finally reached Piccadilly, so many revellers had clambered on top of Eros, the winged statue was barely visible, and the crowds between that and Buckingham Palace were thousands deep. There'd been a far jollier air there than in the more sombre and bomb-torn East End. Most of the crowd had done what Annie had done and cobbled together patriotic outfits from whatever they could find in their cupboards. She'd wound the red scarf he'd worn long ago at Cable Street into the neck of his blue-and-white uniform and pinned a red cardigan over her navy striped summer dress. Clapping at each other's costumes had united the crowd. So had the first conga lines and the impromptu sing-songs.

Harry and Annie had flung themselves into the fun. They'd laughed at the extravagant paper hats which had become the day's favourite fashion accessory. They'd cheered at the bus bearing the slogan, *Hitler Missed this One* painted on its side. They'd clapped for the King and Queen, although the royal balcony never mind the royal family was invisible from where they were standing. As the evening wore on, they'd oohed and aahed with the rest as floodlights swept across Piccadilly and Trafalgar Square and the Palace, lighting up buildings that had been plunged into darkness for years. But it became harder to hold on to the excitement as the day rumbled on. There was a restlessness to the groups moving from one landmark to another. Cheers rose and fell as quickly, punctured by the unspoken *What now?* which refused to stop rearing its head. Smiles became fixed or forgotten. People kept looking round, searching faces, clutching at strangers and trotting out names they'd last seen on a telegram. Convinced someone would know where their missing ones were, that someone would have seen them alive. Ghosts loitered on every street corner demanding attention. And once the lights dimmed, the crowds petered out too.

'Shall I walk you home?'

Annie had nodded, but she'd also stuffed her hands in her pockets before Harry could take her arm. They'd walked away from the Palace as it shuffled back into the night and on into a much quieter London. There were bonfires here and there on patches of wasteland and the odd lively pub spilling party-goers out onto the pavement, but the streets grew darker the closer they came to Arnold Circus. Most of the windows they passed were still blacked out, as if nobody could quite believe the surrender would hold. Annie had sunk into herself and taken Harry's voice with her. An ocean he didn't understand how to cross stretched out between them. And all he could think about was loss.

'I don't know what it means yet, do you? I don't know what peace looks like in a country where so much has been broken.'

Annie didn't answer. Harry's eyes smarted yet again at the thought of all that had been lost and all that remained uncertain. The future he'd been living for since he'd put the ring on her finger still seemed so far out of reach it might as well have been on the moon. By the time they reached her home, his stomach was so knotted it was an effort to stand up straight. And still Annie said nothing.

'Talk to me, Annie, I'm begging you. I'm going out of my mind here. Tell me whatever it is that's got you distracted.'

His voice was too loud against the night's silence, and it made her jump. But at least she didn't pull away this time when he reached for her hand and led her up the grassy steps to the bandstand. He took that as a good sign.

There was no breeze. The trees were still; the Circus was silent under the inky black sky. Harry watched Annie stare up at the stars, twisting her diamond ring round and round on her finger. He longed to take her in his arms, but his body was stuck.

She's going to tell me we're over too. She's going to give me it back.

She turned towards him, her skin pale as silver in the moonlight. He didn't dare let her be the first one to speak.

'This would have been a better place for a proposal, wouldn't it? You and me and the stars, and no audience staring at us.' He paused and took a deep breath. Sometimes the unsayable had to be said, even if it led to the wrong answer. 'If

I'd done that, if you'd had a proper chance to think, what would you have said, Annie? Would you have still said yes?'

He waited for his heart to break in the snap of a simple *no*. She reached for his hand instead. Her touch took some of the sting from her words.

'Perhaps not then, Harry. I was barely twenty; you'd just survived a terrible shipwreck. There was so much love when you asked me, I know, but there was fear too, and I never wanted to start our life together that way. But I wouldn't have said no as bluntly as that. I would have told you to ask me again. I would have promised you there'd be a yes when the timing was right. I made my mind up about you and me when we swapped our dreams in Victoria Park. Nothing's changed about that.'

His heart, which had leapt with relief at *perhaps*, faltered at *that*. And stumbled as she went on.

'But I never wanted to rush us, war or not. I still don't. I thought we were going to do things differently. Have adventures, find our own path. Not be married and tied down while we're still young.'

He flinched at *tied down* – he couldn't help himself. But she'd been honest, and now it was his turn.

'What if I'm done with adventures? What if steady and sure sounds increasingly appealing to me?'

He didn't say, *What if the war's turned me old?* She seemed to hear it anyway. The light slipped from her eyes faster than a cloud hiding the moon. Harry wished he could take back what he'd said and promise her what he'd promised before he'd learned how fleeting life could be. He loved her too much to try, even when her voice shook.

'But what if I'm not? What if the *sure and steady* you seem to be hankering after closes the world down for me?' She shook her head at his confusion. 'Oh, Harry, I wish my life could be as simply laid out as yours, but it's not. That's why I've never agreed to set a date. Married women don't get to walk through the kind of doors I want to walk through.'

'What doors? What are you talking about?'

He had no idea what she meant. His mother had never fussed about doors, except to worry they weren't polished enough.

'My job. The one you don't ask about; the one you probably assume ends with the war.' Her sigh put her so many steps away from him, he finally realised why they were on separate paths. 'Since the ship went down, you've been trying to add me to the same box as Dolly. Good wife, good mother, bound up in the home.' She shook her head as he tried to speak. 'I'm not saying you did it on purpose. I'm not saying you've been trying to control me. You're too good a man for that. But you've been so fixed on the security that comes with marriage, you've forgotten it can have more than one shape.'

Harry stopped trying to argue; he stopped trying to explain himself. He forced himself to focus on *you're too good a man for that*, and he did what Annie needed him to do. He asked her what she meant.

'It's not to do with love. I love you, Harry, I do. It would be a very easy thing to be your wife. But when I marry you, I can't carry on working, or not in the kind of job I want to do anyway, where married women aren't allowed to stay. And that's not all: if I marry you now, I can't go to Germany, I can't do anything to atone for my father, or try and make things right for my mother. I can't make a difference at all.'

The words poured out of her and left Harry miles behind.

'Slow down, please; give me a chance to catch up with you.' She was going so fast, he couldn't pull all the strands together. 'What do you mean about going to Germany? What do you mean by *atone* and *make things right*?'

Annie paused long enough to take a deep breath, and then she sped on again.

'I mean what I could be doing next, if I stayed with the intelligence services like my boss has asked me to do. There's going to be a trial, in Germany – the Allies want to bring the Nazis to account. As a German speaker and somebody with experience of transcribing testimony, I've been asked to be a small part of it...'

Harry listened in stunned silence as Annie told him all the things he hadn't asked about her role at MI19 and about the proposed war crimes trials none of the newspapers had mentioned.

'I want to do it so badly. Because of my father and the terrible things he tried to make me believe, and has done, and for my mother. And for the chance to go overseas, even if that is the most selfish part. I never thought I'd have that opportunity – why would I? But now there's a chance of it? It's all I dream about.'

By the time she finished, there were so many new angles to her, he didn't know which way to look. And he was even more convinced he'd never keep her.

'How long will you be away, if you go?'

He wished he'd said *when* not *if* the instant her lips disappeared. He wished *It's all I dream about* hadn't hurt quite so much.

'A year. Perhaps a little more. Nothing's fixed yet, not even a start date. I imagine if I'm sent, I'll get leave, for Christmas and the like.'

He wanted to say, *Don't go.* He wanted to say, *I'll be back in the lifeboat without you, scared I've lost you for good.* Her face was as tight as her shoulders – he could see she was waiting for him to do exactly that. And that – no matter how much she said she loved him – she would walk away for good if he did.

'And then you'll come back?'

He managed to sound calm, to sound as if another year wasn't another lifetime. To make it a question, not an order.

'Of course I will!' Her eyes began glowing again;, her smile bounced back. 'And I'll marry you when I do, I promise. I'll come home and set a date.'

She was in his arms in a rush of laughter and curls and kisses. She was suddenly full of stories about her work and her colleagues that kept them wrapped round each other in the bandstand until the birds started singing and the sky turned pink with the dawn. Harry listened to her anecdotes with half an ear. He hadn't lost her, that was what mattered. She loved him. She'd promised to come home and to marry him. And if he concentrated on that part, on the anchor she'd offered, he'd be able to wipe away the image of Annie standing outside doors his love had slammed shut. And the misery she hadn't been able to hide in the way she'd said *tied down*.

CHAPTER THIRTEEN

MAY 1945

'They're bringing the children out. Stand back.'

Margarete pressed herself into the wall as the bunker's last living inhabitants formed up in a silent salute. A nurse and a white-coated doctor appeared from inside the children's small bedroom. Two wooden crates followed them – crates which were so light, they only required two soldiers to carry each one because the stairwells were twisty and narrow – and disappeared up the stairs.

'They injected the kiddies with morphine first, and then Magda Goebbels cracked cyanide capsules in their jaws. Apparently the older girl didn't fall deeply asleep enough – they must have got the dose wrong – and she fought back. None of this was their doing, but they got their futures snatched off them anyway. What kind of a mother does something like that to her own kids?'

'A brave one.'

Margarete rounded on the young soldier who'd thought he had the right to address her, and now had the good sense to hurry away. On any other day, she would have had him put on a charge that would have led to a firing squad, but this wasn't any other day, and there was nobody left to discipline him. There was also no sign of Magda or Joseph Goebbels. Nobody had set eyes on Magda since Hitler's suicide, although she'd clearly not stayed in hiding the whole night given the funeral procession her actions had led to. Nobody had set eyes on Goebbels since he'd helped carry Hitler's and Eva's bodies up to the surface for burning, and made a final broadcast to announce that the Führer had tragically fallen but had died with his people, as always, in mind. Margarete assumed they'd retired to their own quarters to avoid the last glimpse of their children and would shortly join the ranks of the dead. For a second, she considered going to see Magda, who must surely be drowning in grief, but there was no time for goodbyes today. Not if she wanted to stay alive herself.

'We're setting out in half an hour. Are you ready to go?'

Margarete nodded as Bormann lumbered past her. She'd been ready since she'd walked past the open door of Hitler's office what felt like a lifetime ago and seen the bloodstains blotting the sofa. Although it felt disloyal to admit it, his death had freed the rest of them to leave. And the children's deaths...

Margarete thrust the image of the wooden chests out of her head. It wasn't a 'terrible murder' the way some of the younger spineless soldiers kept whispering to each other. The deaths hadn't turned the bunker into a tomb, which was another nonsense she'd been forced to ignore. Margarete understood the truth, even if the others weren't brave enough to face it. The children were Goebbels' heirs; they were the jewels of the Third Reich. They couldn't have been left alive for the Russians to find any more than Hitler could. They couldn't have been left to try and navigate a world without National Socialism either. Their parents had done what they had to do. There was no point in shedding tears over the decision.

Margarete walked away from the open stairwell and the smell of petrol wafting down it. She was ready to leave now, never mind in half an hour; it was irritating to have to wait on Bormann's say-so. She'd packed away the skirts and dresses she'd worn until her last working day in her determination to keep up appearances. She'd changed into a pair of shapeless twill trousers and the man's jacket that she'd already sewn her more valuable possessions into; she'd scraped her long hair under a cap. She'd collected a pistol and packed her rucksack full of biscuits and chocolate from the depleted store cupboard before that was totally ransacked. And – whatever Bormann said about safety in numbers and staying together and listening to him – she'd memorised the route the first escape party would take out of the bunker because she wasn't going to trust her life to anyone's hands but her own. Bormann was slow; the other women were nervous. The men meant to guard them would look to their own safety first. And just because nobody had come to disturb Hitler's ashes yet didn't mean the Russians weren't already circling the bunker, ready to tell the world they'd claimed the war's greatest prize.

'Our only way out is to head for the north of the city. If you get separated, keep moving that way.'

Bormann had produced a roughly drawn map when he'd briefed his escape group earlier that morning. There were no compasses left, and there was no paper left to copy the plan onto, but Margarete had held the sketch for as long as she could before passing it on, fixing the details firmly into her brain. She ran through them again as Bormann gave the signal to move and led the small group through the bunker's still functioning operating theatre towards the one safe exit. Partly because remembering them could mean the difference between life and death when they reached the outside. Partly to divert her attention from the buckets filled with blood and amputated limbs which littered the slippery floor. North. That was the main thing to remember, and the only direction Margaret wanted to go. That route would take her towards where the British troops were said to be massing, and she would need to rely on them if she was going to continue her journey out of Germany and on to England. Besides – according to the final bulletin they'd received which was already at least two days out of date – they had no other choice except north. The Russians had blocked the key roads to the rest of the city, including south to Lichterfelde and her parents. Not that she'd considered going that way, or not seriously. Family ties couldn't be allowed to jeopardise the mission. Her father would never forgive her if she failed that by acting in a sentimental way.

'Watch your footing. If you fall and get injured, we can't wait for you.'

It was dark by the time Bormann led them out of the bunker into the rubble-strewn chaos of the Chancellery grounds. Margarete hadn't tasted fresh air in almost a month. The urge to stop and drink it in was overwhelming, although she forced herself to keep moving as she gulped at it. April had ended with Hitler's suicide; May had arrived while they were preparing to escape. She sniffed at the air as she picked her way over the fallen bricks, searching for the scents of lilac and spring roses. There was nothing but cordite and brick dust and the petrol that was sewn through the ground. Margarete instantly stopped imagining warm days and springtime. Mooning over them would be of no use to her if it meant she got caught. She wrapped her scarf tight round her mouth instead and moved to the front of the group, running as fast as she could down Voßstraße towards the entrance to the Kaiserhof U-Bahn station, more desperate than she ever thought she could be to get back underground.

'Watch yourselves, the steps have gone!'

She flung the warning down the line as she threw herself into the station. A bomb or a shell had taken the stairs away and turned the opening into a slide. Margarete scrambled her way down into the darkness, horribly aware how little use their map was likely to be, repeating the first instructions to herself anyway.

Go right towards Stadtmitte, then left and straight up the tunnel towards Friedrichstraße and out. Follow the signs.

Except there were no more signs left than there were steps. There was nothing but the memory of train journeys she'd taken so long ago and so rarely, they may as well have never happened.

'The stations are very close together – Stadmitte has to be the first exit.'

Nobody argued – nobody had any more idea of the tunnels' layout than she did.

The map had promised straight lines and short distances. The reality was a pitch-black maze. What would have been a fifteen-minute walk above ground on a regular day became a stumbling search that ate up more time than Margarete could count. The station was packed with people desperate for shelter. She weaved her way through them, Bormann panting at her shoulder, running her hand along the tunnel's filthy sides to keep her sense of direction. Refusing to let her imagination conjure up the roar of a train that was no longer running. Stepping over bodies and rats and fallen masonry. Stepping through pools that smelled like the inside of a butcher's van and filled her boots and socks with stinking black water. She stopped looking to see who if anyone was behind her. She ran blind, not speaking, trying not to take deep breaths because of the smell, even though her chest felt as if it was tied round with a band.

Incredibly, her luck held. Thankfully, there were steps at the end of the tunnel and they'd judged the distance correctly if not the time. Margarete burst out onto Friedrichstraße gulping at the air – and immediately began coughing as she inhaled a searing lungful of ash.

Why are we inside a furnace? Why is there so much smoke?

It was as hard to steady her head as her shaking legs. The

next stage of the route should have been a simple affair: a straight run down Friedrichstraße to the Weidendammer Bridge and over the Spree. But there was no such thing as a simple or straight run in the newly redrawn Berlin. What the reports hadn't made clear to the bunker's inhabitants was that the surface they'd kept well away from was a battleground where every inch was contested. The fight for Berlin was being fought as fiercely as Hitler had directed: street by street, house by house, down to the last bullet and the last drop of blood. Friedrichstraße was a sea of blazing barricades and overturned trams. Sniper fire flew in all directions, the bullets screeching over their heads like plagues of maddened mosquitos. Margarete took one look at the carnage and stopped thinking because thinking wouldn't help. There wasn't the time to do it.

She snapped on her senses. She ducked and zig-zagged and clambered across twisted metal and charred wood, kicking obstacles out of her way, ignoring the splinters that tore at her palms, leaping across smouldering ashes. She pushed her body past its limits because there was nothing else to be done. She couldn't tell if the shadowy figures she glimpsed running from one sheltering spot to the next were German soldiers, or Russian soldiers, or terrified civilians. She wasn't foolish enough to stop them and ask. She launched herself across the thankfully undamaged iron bridge with her body tucked as small as she could make it. She didn't look round or pause for breath until she was on the other side of the river from the worst of the fighting and inside the maze of dark courtyards that surrounded the Charité Hospital. When she did, she was completely alone.

There was no sign of Bormann. There was no sign of the half a dozen other men and women who'd left the bunker beside her. There was no clue as to what had happened to them. She hadn't heard a recognisable scream; no one had called out. She scanned the streets that fanned out from the water for as long as she dared, but nobody was coming, although she could have sworn Bormann had pounded after her towards the bridge.

I can't be the only one who escaped, surely?

But Margarete knew that she could.

She bent over and sucked in great lungfuls of air. She threw her head back and stretched every part of her aching body. The sky looked impossibly far away after months living under the bunker's low ceilings. The courtyards felt as big as Alpine meadows after its narrow corridors. She was filled with a sense of freedom she hadn't known in years, but that was a dangerous spell to fall under. What she'd seen so far proved that freedom was a forgotten concept in Berlin. The deserted courtyards were a moment's reprieve, nothing more. A battle as bitter as the one she'd run through had to have stretched its fires and roadblocks and tanks throughout the whole of the city. Which meant every part of the journey she'd planned to make out of Berlin would take double or triple the amount of time she'd estimated. That it would come loaded with danger. And it couldn't be easily completed in one night. She would have to find a place to rest in a cellar, or in one of the public shelters Bormann's map had identified, in the flak tower at Humboldthain or the giant brewery at Prinzenallee.

Except any one of those could deliver me into the hands of the Russians. If we knew huge groups of civilians had taken refuge in them, they will too. And that's where they'll go looking for escapees like us.

Bormann's information was out of date. It was based on a city that hadn't been so thoroughly invaded. She had no idea how far the fighting extended. And she didn't know how far the British armies had advanced towards Berlin. Nobody did. The only soldiers who'd been identified so far were Soviets. Going on alone should have been a frightening, hopeless prospect. Except Margarete wasn't afraid.

My mission will keep me safe.

She'd been holding that thought in her head along with the map's details from the first second she'd crawled out of the bunker.

'You've never let me down.'

Hitler's blessing was a shield none of the others possessed, which was why she was the only one who'd made it safely across the river. Bormann didn't have diamonds or a letter. His face was so well known, he had to be a target for the Russians. Goebbels was presumably dead by now. And as for the rest, Himmler and Göring and Speer, they'd proved at the end they were worthless and not fit to carry the flame.

'You won't be alone.'

There were other standard-bearers escaping the city – Margarete could sense them in the shadows streaming around her. She would no more let them down than she would let down the Führer.

She straightened up. She tightened the straps of her rucksack and checked that the papers and the diamonds were safely stowed inside her blouse. Other people might need shelter and rest, but not her. Other people might be afraid of the tanks and the guns, but not her. Margarete stopped thinking about snipers and stray bullets. She stopped considering the possibility of capture. She stopped wondering where Bormann and the rest of the escape party were. She was the only one of them who needed to survive. She was the only one who mattered.

It was a good feeling to acknowledge that. It was better than a meal or a night's sleep in a dirty cellar.

Margarete shook out her body, enjoying the strength running through it, certain she was a match for any soldier who might get in her way. She closed her eyes briefly, remembered her leader and his last words. Then she plunged into the darkness and marched on.

CHAPTER FOURTEEN
NOVEMBER 1945

'This is it, ladies and gentlemen. This is the place where a spotlight will shine on the worst of humanity, and where we will make sure that justice is done.'

As long as we can make the doubters listen.

Annie stared round Nuremberg's hastily refurbished court-room with its barely dried paint and newly mended windows and kept her thoughts to herself. Sir Hartley Shawcross, the chief British prosecutor who was leading the tour, wanted them to believe that the process would be a straightforward one. Annie wanted to believe it too, but she'd already spent enough time in Germany to understand that nothing about the country was straightforward. And she'd already heard too many dissenting voices.

'It's a joke, a waste of time and money based on a pack of Jewish lies.'

Annie thought she'd left her father behind in England, but his voice – and the voices of his rediscovered cronies – kept creeping back into her head.

Sid had finally reappeared without warning part way through June. His bulk had vanished. His skin was crumpled;

his hair was lank and grey. His eyes had shrunk inside baggy pouches that were the only soft thing about him. And his story was a litany of complaints. His war had been the hardest fought, the cruellest suffered.

'Locked away like a criminal... Transported from pillar to post... Treated as if I was the enemy, instead of the turncoat Germans and their Jews who wanted nothing more than to see Germany destroyed, who made my life hell on that godforsaken island...'

On and on he went, dripping his bitterness at his internment through the flat with barely a pause for sleep. The first week was bad; the second was worse. By midway through that, Sid had tracked down his old BU comrades, his fellow 18B internees, and they'd stirred the pot until the bitterness was stoked to fury.

'We were fools to go to war. To let so many good men die in a conflict that had nothing to do with us, and the rest come home to a country that's still saddled with rationing and shortages, where the women have stolen the jobs. Mosley was right about that. And we'll be fools if we believe the money that's going to be wasted on these trials has anything to do with peace.'

Mosley and how right he'd always been was all Sid talked about. The BU leader had been released earlier than the other detainees and was apparently suffering the effects of his imprisonment, which was another burning coal on Sid's fire.

'He's not a well man, but he'll take charge again soon – he promised me that. And he knows what's what. Those photographs from the camps? They've been faked – he can prove it. Those bodies? They were victims of disease. The Jews will do anything to win sympathy. Digging up a few graveyards and shouting murder is nothing to them.'

Sid had come back from his audience with Mosley as if he'd seen the face of God. Annie had wanted to be sick when he began holding court with his filthy nonsense. She'd wanted to tear him to shreds and salt his wounds with all her suspicions over Grete and Peggy. She'd started to – she would have threatened him with the police if she'd managed to get further than her first sentence. That heartfelt, 'Will you just stop it. We're done listening to your lies,' had plunged the flat into a momentary silence. His shock had fooled her into thinking she had the upper hand; it had given her a badly misplaced sense of courage. 'Those pictures aren't—' But that was as far as she got.

'Don't you dare talk back to me.'

His rage was contained, precise. A table overturned, a set of plates smashed. A fist as close to her face as a hair's breadth, only Peggy's horrified screams holding it back. He'd walked away that time. Annie had kept her mouth shut to keep the peace and keep her mother safe. She'd watched her mother disappear again and put away any thoughts of Nuremberg, until Harry told Dolly that Annie had given up on her dreams and Dolly stepped in for all of them.

'I know you're afraid for her, pet, but it's time to let someone else share the worrying. I'll visit every day. If he knows someone is watching, he'll keep his hands off her. This is such an incredible opportunity for you – even my daft lad has come round to that. And if Peggy thought you'd lost it because of her? It wouldn't help, I promise. All I ask is that you're careful how you manage your leaving, so he can't get in the way of that too.'

Dolly wasn't to be argued with, and neither was Peggy when Dolly explained the situation to her. It was her excitement at the thought of her daughter's importance that finally made Annie give in. And she continued to followed Dolly's advice: she told Sid her new posting was an order she couldn't avoid, and he had too much respect for the military to fight her. But his parting, 'Remember where you come from and make sure your bosses do right by good men,' had stung all the way to the station.

And there's plenty at home, and here, who'd cheer him for saying it.

Annie continued her orientation tour round Nuremberg's Palace of Justice with her head down and her thoughts in a whirl. She'd been in Germany for almost four months. She'd left England from RAF Northolt, strapped into a too-flimsy seat inside the cavernous body of a Douglas Dakota on a sticky day at the start of July. And not once in that time had she been able to get a proper hold on the country.

Heavy cloud – which Annie had later been told was comprised mostly of brick dust – had obscured her view of Hamburg, the British army's transiting hub, as they'd flown over it. There'd been no time to visit the city itself. She'd been taken by jeep as soon as they landed to the small town of Lemgo and her first posting, collecting testimony at the department for Prisoners of War and Displaced Persons. Which meant her first proper sight of Germany had been... *impossibly pretty and impossibly out of step with where I am now.*

Lemgo had made very little sense to Annie when she'd arrived there, and it made less sense now she was in Nuremberg. There'd been no sign of time passing at all in the small town, never mind the ending or the start of a ferocious war. The twelfth century continued to live on in its ancient market square and water wheel and timber-framed houses. For the first few days, Annie felt as if she'd stepped into a Grimms' fairy tale and was about to run into Hansel and Gretel. Until she'd started looking around her properly and realised that the storybook was deeply blotted.

'Don't forget who they are and what they've done. Don't waste your time or your pity or our resources on them.'

That order had underpinned every reluctant contact between the British occupying forces and the German civilian population. *Deceitful* and *manipulative* were some of the politer words used to describe the townspeople who'd been forcibly removed from their homes so the British Army could move into them. The air surrounding Lemgo's pretty buildings was steeped in as much resentment as Sid, and neither side had the will to change it. The British had been fed on a wartime diet stuffed full of German savagery and cruelty, thick with SS uniforms and dead bodies stacked up in concentration camps. The Germans knew that. They understood exactly how small they were meant to feel. They felt the hostility and the disgust in every look exactly as they were intended to.

Once Annie recognised how thin its surface was, Lemgo quickly lost its charms. She stopped delighting in the large and airy bedroom she'd been allocated once she realised the house's previous owners now lived crammed into the basement, turned into servants tasked with cooking food they'd never be allowed to eat. And when she asked one of the officers billeted with her why so many families had been stripped of their lives by the occupation, there wasn't an ounce of pity in his answer.

'Because none of them will admit they were a bunch of murdering Nazis, so it's best to assume they all were.'

The British and American politicians might talk about a peace which included reconciliation with former enemies, but their voices went unheard in Lemgo. The soldiers Annie ate and worked with were firm believers in a much harder path, one that was founded on punishment, the only treatment they deemed suitable for the 'heartless people' the men were determined to avoid. The town soon became a place where notions of justice rang hollow on both sides. And Nuremberg – where Annie arrived at the start of November to prepare for the trials which would begin on the twentieth – felt like a place where justice had no meaning at all.

It's not a city. It's a corpse.

Annie flew out of the British and into the American-occupied sector of Germany on a bitterly cold winter's day painted with vivid blue skies and – unlike Hamburg – no cloud cover.

The sunshine gave her arrival a strangely festive air. One blink and it could have been a different plane to hers casting its shadow across the city below. One blink and she could have been starring in the opening sequence of *Triumph of the Will*, Leni Reifenstahl's documentary about the 1934 Nuremberg Rally which had both enthralled and horrified her when Mosley had shown it at a private screening for BU supporters in 1938. If the city had still been the one Hitler had flown over in the film's opening reel – a forest of beautiful gothic spires, thick with medieval churches and frescoed gabled houses, wide cobbled streets and a great palace looking down from a hill. If that city had still been there, arriving in it would have felt like a triumph. But it had so spectacularly gone, the shock of what was left had snatched her breath away.

Annie had seen her share of serious bomb damage during the Blitz, especially around the docks, but the worst of that had been cleared away in the years after 1941. Nothing had been cleared away in Nuremberg. Nuremberg was an open wound, a city wracked with pain and still caught in its death throes. It was as ancient and obliterated as Pompeii. Annie had gazed down on it through eyes that felt seared by the broken land-scape, by the churches and houses that had been skinned, whose few standing walls rose like fossilised limbs from a sea of craters and rubble. There was no great palace or cathedral left; there was no discernible centre. There was nothing to map a city by. She hadn't wanted to land. She'd sat with ice seeping into her bones, willing the pilot to fly on and away. But he'd begun his descent instead, wheeling round a charcoal-black lake to land on a wide expanse of concrete flanked by mud which had clearly never been designed as a runway.

'It's the Zeppelin Field, the Nazis' parade ground. There's no functioning airport in Nuremberg, so this is the only place we can safely land. It's quite a sight to take in. Do you see that building over there?' Annie had followed her fellow passenger's pointing finger and caught a glimpse of the edge of a massive circular structure as the plane bumped its way down. 'That's the Congress Hall. Hitler based its design on the Colosseum in Rome. It would have been twice the size of that if they'd finished it.'

The rest of what he'd said about Hitler's ambitions had been drowned out by the taxiing engines and a bitter wind which battled against them as they disembarked and hurried along a vast boulevard, bordered by the remains of ruined tanks and a half-destroyed grandstand. Annie had climbed into the waiting jeep, wishing it was a solidly built Morris car whose sturdy roof and sides would keep the war's scars at bay. Those had been no easier to face on the ground. They'd driven into the city past a huge and devastated railway station which was as out of commission as the airport, while the American soldier driving her kept up a running commentary she hadn't known how to reply to.

'You should have seen the place in May, ma'am, when the battle for it ended. It was in a way worse state than this.'

Annie listened to his descriptions of the heavy fighting that had run from street to street for almost five days, unable to imagine *way worse* even with the details he supplied, while her head ran in circles.

How could buildings be more broken than this? How could the air smell worse? How could the people look more ragged and wretched and worn out than they do now?

She didn't want to know the answers, so she held her scarf over her face to block out the acrid mix of soot and plaster dust and raw earth and didn't ask. And she didn't smile back when he told her with a grin of his own not to expect the Grand Hotel where she was billeted to live up to its name. He meant no harm. She hadn't fought like he had, she wasn't still caught up in the relief of being alive and in victory's glow, and it wasn't her place to contradict him. She was simply grateful there was a room intact. It wasn't until the next morning – after a largely sleepless night on a mattress that was more lumps than comfort – that she realised how badly provisioned the hotel was. Most of the windows were filled with cardboard not glass. The damaged floors were held together with roughly hammered-in planks. There wasn't a drop of hot water. The hotel was as dilapidated as the rest of the wrecked city, and in no condition to hold the huge numbers of journalists and clerks and trial personnel billeted in it. Nowhere in the city was.

When Major Langley had announced – from behind a cup of tea in the comfort of his office – that Nuremberg had been chosen as the venue for the trials, the location had made sense. There was a symbolic aspect to the city not even Berlin shared. Nuremberg had been close to Hitler's heart; it was the cradle of fascism. It was the place where he had held his huge rallies and announced his life-altering laws. It was where he'd laid out his plans for the Thousand Year Reich.

But this courthouse has nothing to do with what's happening out there now, and that could be its downfall.

Courtroom 600 – where the prosecutors and defendants would shortly begin debating the nuances of the newly minted charge 'Crimes Against Humanity' and apportioning blame – wasn't a ruin were people grubbed through their days. Unlike the rest of the city, this room was needed by the Allies and had therefore been restored. Every inch off it was pristine. There were no burn marks to mar the highly polished panelling. The glass panes in the long windows were perfectly intact and gleaming; the drapes were thick and clean and newly hung. There was a sense of quiet order inside the chamber that was totally absent from the chaotic streets beyond its scrubbed walls.

Which must be hard enough for any local who sees it. But none of the main players will sit in the dock, and there's not one German judge on the bench, and that's worse.

The courtroom could be prettied up, but the roster of who

would sit in it couldn't be changed. Despite all the high hopes when the trials had first been mooted in February, the list of the prisoners was not the one anybody wanted. There was no Hitler, no Goebbels, no Himmler or Bormann, no Hess or Mengele or Eichmann. Whether anybody had called for things to be more balanced or not – which was information Annie wasn't privy to – no accusations would be levelled against the Allied bombing raids which had obliterated Hamburg and Dresden and countless other German cities and cost thousands of innocent lives. And there was a Russian judge presiding along with the Americans and the British and the French, despite the terrible acts Russia and Germany had unleashed on each other. She could already hear the slurs she dreaded whispering through the empty galleries, waiting to make themselves heard. The ones Sid would echo that called the proceedings pointless and vengeful and unfair.

Annie kept her thoughts to herself as Shawcross finished his welcoming speech and one of the clerks began to outline how the trials would unfold. But she wasn't the only one aware of the gaps and the stories hiding inside them. The journalists who gathered in the Grand Hotel's gloomy bar each night talked about little else.

'The Germans keep saying the trial's been imposed on them – they're calling it victor's vengeance. Is that a valid viewpoint? Can we report it?'

'Will anyone care what happens, given the main criminals are dead or have escaped? Is Göring enough of a prize?'

'How can this work without a German judge sitting on the bench? How can this work with a Russian one?'

How can this work? was every night's theme, and nobody had an answer. All Annie knew – and had said multiple times – was that it had to. She thanked Shawcross with the rest, and she noted down the clerk's detailed instructions. But she came away from her first day at the trials she'd had so many hopes for feeling the way she'd felt on VE Day. That nothing was solid, that nothing was backed up with certainties.

Which might be true, but it can't matter.

Annie stopped in the courtyard, oblivious to the ice in the wind and the scent of snow in the air. She closed her eyes tight, blocking out the ruined state of the city and the problems already besetting them. She imagined the charges instead. She imagined the testimony; she imagined the world listening and believing the witnesses whose suffering no one should doubt.

But will it be enough? Will all the words that are about to flood this place have the strength to stop the poison?

It had to be – there was no other answer. Because the world had to believe. For the victims with voices, and the far more without, who couldn't be allowed to live with the alternative: the silence that would let men like her father and Mosley carry on twisting the truth and spreading their lies.

CHAPTER FIFTEEN

FEBRUARY 1946

'Don't tell them I'm coming home. Let's make this about you and me.'

Annie stopped what she was doing, her fingers all thumbs, remembering the last time she'd stood in this office, clutching the telephone, waiting too long for an answer.

'Come away with me. Let's have an adventure; let's have a stolen weekend.'

He hadn't said a word in reply. For a horrible moment, she'd thought she'd shocked him. She'd thought that her Harry, whose kisses had once set her on fire, truly had lost all his passion for life and become a man utterly wedded to tradition. She'd stared at the receiver second-guessing herself, wondering if the impulse that had led her to ask him was no longer the kind of impulse he craved. Waiting for him to break a silence that had grown as heavy as lead.

Annie had placed the call to Harry's new desk at the *Evening Standard* newspaper two weeks earlier, on the same Friday morning she'd been told she had a long weekend's leave and a seat on a plane to RAF Northolt waiting if she wanted it. The empty office had been too good an opportunity to miss.

There were over 160 typists and translators and support staff working in the Palace of Justice. They were crammed into the maze of rooms that ran under the courts, working four to a small table in shifts that rarely let up. Finding a breath of solitude and a phone that wasn't constantly ringing was a luxury Annie had had no more intention of wasting than her first few days of freedom.

She separated another stack of folders into finished and not as the memories flooded back and her cheeks turned pink. She'd been so desperate to snatch a few days out of the world that would belong to nobody but them. To wrap herself in his arms and find the Harry from Victoria Park again. She'd thought she'd pushed them further apart instead. Until he'd filled the yawning gap with a deep-throated, 'Oh dear God, yes please,' that crackled through the phone and her body.

And I need to stop thinking about that, and what came after, before somebody asks why I'm blushing.

Annie fanned her face with a folder and gathered the next set of completed testimonies together. Langley would spot her raised colour in a heartbeat, and she had no interest in being questioned – or teased in his clumsy if well-meaning way. She was regarded by her colleagues as professional, reliable, private. She was definitely not a woman who blushed or made secret assignations. And with that thought, Harry and the weekend they'd managed to snatch from the world jumped back into her head, flaring her face like a bonfire.

She dropped her bundle onto a nearby desk and crossed to the room's tiny window, wrenching it open to let in a blast of ice-packed air. One winter in Nuremberg had cured Annie of complaining about the cold at home. England on its worst days was never as bad. The temperature had slipped below zero at the end of November and was only now beginning to inch its way slowly up as February arrived. Despite the wood packed into the fireplaces, the women she worked with came to the office dressed in layers so bulky they bounced between the crowded tables without feeling their edges and they'd learned to type with their gloves on. And they were the lucky ones.

Outside the trial's relatively well-insulated bubble, winter was a far crueller thing. The ordinary citizens of Nuremberg were still squatting in cellars and foraging for firewood. They were existing on an official calorie count that was not only far lower than the one allocated to Annie, it was completely devoid of the additional coffee and chocolate and pancakes doused in syrup the American army canteens never ran short of. Which was why Annie had stopped venturing into the heart of the city. It took a tougher hide than hers to face the shivering and ragged children scavenging round the rubble when she didn't have to worry where her next, or any, meal was coming from.

Then don't make yourself face it again. You don't have to stay out there. You could come home for good any time you choose.

Annie pulled the window shut as the next shift of secretaries crowded in behind her and instantly began complaining about the chill. Her face had finally cooled, not least because Harry's frustration had crawled back into her head and pushed out the better memories. There was so much she wanted to remember about their brief time together, but that wasn't it. Harry talking as if it would be easy for her to leave the trials part way through hadn't exactly endeared him to her.

What she wanted to remember instead was the way he'd looked at her on that first afternoon a fortnight ago, as she'd walked into the pretty little red-brick inn he'd found for them on the edge of the Colne Valley. As if she was the gift he'd been waiting for his whole life. Or the proud way he'd introduced her as 'my wife' while she kept her hands in her pockets, even though the manager had clearly played host to too many pilots from Northolt to worry about the lack of a ring. What she wanted to hold on to were their first moments in the low-ceilinged bedroom, the first time they'd been together in one. His arms round her waist. His mouth finding hers. The instant of knowing their kisses could last the whole night and have no stopping point. She wanted to hold on to the bed that had been their whole world in the moonlight, and to the days spent walking through early snowdrops by a glistening river waiting for the nights to begin. She wanted, more than anything, to hold on to that Harry. The one she'd repledged herself to in the bandstand, who'd looked at her as if she was priceless. The Harry who'd listened to her, who'd understood. Who'd helped her get away from Sid. That was the Harry she'd telephoned and rushed to meet, who she'd felt more married to in that little hotel than any church could make them. But that Harry had left again somewhere during the weekend, to be replaced by the version who turned the conversation away when she began talking about her job. Who seemed to have forgotten how important the trials were to her and relegated her part to an even smaller one than she had.

Who seems to have lost sight of all the values he once had.

Annie hated that thought when it came, and it came increasingly often. It had first reared its head at breakfast on their second day, when he'd cut across a story about her job with a story about his own. They'd come close to a row then. They'd come close to another when he'd informed her – without a scrap of indignation or surprise – that the *Standard* had stopped reporting on the trials because 'the reporter who sends copy to us is too preoccupied with the living conditions of people in Nuremberg and that's of no interest to our readers. And they find the legal stuff dull.'

He'd reacted to her horrified, 'How can you say that?' with an explanation that was more careless than she'd expected from him.

'Because it's true. The trial's been going on for too long. Without Hitler and the main Party leaders in the dock, it's hard to whip up interest. And as for how difficult it is for Germans to get food or housing... Nobody cares, Annie. People are living with too many shortages in Britain to worry about how hard it is to survive in Germany. They've no sympathy, and they're furious that the supplies we should be getting are being diverted there instead as part of the occupation deal. And perhaps I shouldn't say it, but I can't blame them. People are exhausted in England too.'

I should have stopped the conversation there and focused on us rather than spoiling our time together.

Annie pulled her cardigan tighter as she dodged the draughts in the law courts' corridors. It was an easy wish to have in hindsight, but it had been impossible to let the subject go at the time.

'I understand that. But exhaustion's not the same as starvation. If you could only see the hungry children for yourself, you'd feel differently, I know you would. If you could see the true extent of the damage and how broken the people really are, you'd never be able to call the trials dull.'

The argument had quickly spun out of control after that. She'd accused him of 'lacking compassion, something the old you always had'. He'd hit her with a, 'You do know your mother needs you at home,' which had churned up the reservoir of guilt she carried. If he'd refused to accept her tear-stricken, 'Don't you understand why I care about justice? Don't you get that this is about her?' she would have gone straight back to Northolt. But the Harry she loved had resurfaced then, full of love and apologies. They'd had a reconciliation of sorts in the bar; they'd had a more successful one in bed. But Annie had been the one turning the conversation away from her life after that, and she hadn't mentioned the trials again.

Because I didn't want to admit he was right.

Annie rubbed her hand across her cheek. There was no fire left in it – the good memories were all doused, lost in a fog of who was right and who was wrong she'd never wanted to find herself caught in. But if the importance of the trials was a competition between them – which Annie had increasingly worried that they were as the weekend continued – then Harry was definitely the winner. As much as she hated to face it, and as impossible as it was to believe, he was right: the proceedings had indeed become dull.

They hadn't started that way. For the first few weeks, Annie had been overawed by the prosecutors' eloquence, almost as much as by the gravity of the crimes. The silence that had gripped the packed rows in the courtroom as the indictments were read out held a cathedral's rapt attention inside it. When each defendant returned a truth-defying, 'Not guilty,' the anger from the galleries could have blistered the roof. As for the stifled sobs and the gasps as the witnesses began to recount the horrors that had rewritten their lives... Annie knew everybody who listened to those words and saw the pain it caused to express them would carry the testimonies inside their skin for the rest of their lives. But that had been four months ago, and – for all the prosecutors' determination to keep the victims' voices front and centre – the sheer weight of information had sunk the courtroom and blunted the outrage beyond an occasional horrified flare. Nobody had intended that to happen, but a courtroom wasn't a comfortable place for emotions. Too many days had been lost in complex legal arguments nobody but the lawyers could unravel. Somewhere along the line, the trials had lost sight of the brutality they were there to get justice for and had become impossibly mundane. There were few stirring headlines to be had; there were no shocking admissions of guilt. The defendants weren't the kind of men who could spark up a mob because too many of them were faceless.

Hermann Göring, the head of the Luftwaffe and Hitler's one-time successor, was admittedly well known to everyone. Rudolf Hess, who had once been Deputy Führer and had the kind of bushy eyebrows which were a cartoonist's dream, was instantly recognisable. Anyone familiar with the workings of the Third Reich would know its chief architect, Albert Speer. And possibly von Ribbentrop, who'd once been ambassador to Britain, or among those in the courtroom anyway. But outside it and outside Germany? Annie doubted that Julius Streicher or Baldur von Schirach were familiar names to the general public. She doubted it would be easy to stir up indignation in the *Evening Standard* when men nobody knew rolled their eyes and took off their headphones, the way the defendants did. When they refused to accept that they were accountable for anything except following orders they claimed not to have instigated. When they denied any awareness of the ghosts they'd brought into the courtroom. Even the worst details hit a brick wall against that level of disdain.

The defendants shrugged and looked blank as the evidence was brought out; they looked pointedly away. The shrunken heads collected by Ilse Koch, the wife of Buchenwald's commandant, and her lampshade made from human skin. The pictures of the ovens. The impossible numbers of the bodies. Each detail glanced off them. The journalists reacted; all the observers did. They recorded the facts and their horror; they filed their copy. But that wasn't picked up by the newspaper editors as quickly as it had been in previous months before the trials slowed and domestic considerations took over. And meanwhile Göring coughed and muttered that he didn't believe what he'd been shown, and the others took their dispassionate lead from him. Which was the story Annie feared would keep seeping out to find willing ears. And the story she was determined to fight with every scrap of testimony that crossed her desk.

Annie hugged the folders tighter as she knocked on Langley's door. Each one was precious. Each story she'd listened to or translated or typed up was unique, and yet it wasn't. The

Jewish man who'd survived the massacre of thousands when the ghetto in Vilna was liquidated, including his wife and baby, shared his suffering with the hollow-eyed survivors from Riga and Warsaw. The questions asked by the Jewish woman who'd been a prisoner in Auschwitz, who wanted to ask German mothers why her children had been murdered, were echoed in the cries of a woman who'd crawled out of Treblinka without her family. Each story had its own words and its own way of telling, but the tapestry they formed ran in repeating lines. Which was what she had told Harry.

'I can't leave until every voice has been heard. I can't leave until their stories have been told and retold across the world's stage and every last doubting defender of the Third Reich has been made to face up to them. You understand that, don't you? You understand that I'm here to stop men like my father?'

He'd rallied to her side then. He'd told her she was brave. He'd told her that yes, he understood. But then he'd brought up the wedding again as he was leaving, and her newly warmed feelings had stalled. 'I can't think about that now,' hadn't been the response he wanted, but it was the only one she had. There were far more important questions in the world than when Annie Kirson might want to get married. The testimonies she typed up every day were proof of that.

Langley's door was ajar. Annie knocked and pushed it open with her hip as she balanced the slippery pieces of onionskin paper in her arms.

How can something so light feel so heavy?

It was the same question she puzzled over every time she gathered the statements up. The only answer she could think of was, *From the pain.*

CHAPTER SIXTEEN

FEBRUARY 1946

'My name is Margarete Fleiss. I was personal secretary to Martin Bormann during the war, and, through him, I also worked closely with the Führer. And I was in the bunker with them both until the end.'

The shock on their faces was a joy to behold. The way they'd scrabbled for lists and stared from her to each other was proof that the British officers loitering in the dingy reception area knew her name, that they'd probably been looking for her since the war ended ten months earlier. Margarete allowed herself a small smile.

It's proof they're no match for me.

That was hardly a surprise. Margarete had outwitted everyone she'd encountered since she'd left the bunker. By relying on her instincts, not Bormann's hopelessly out-of-date map, she'd not only stayed one step ahead of the game, she'd written its rules to suit herself.

Avoiding the communal spaces where people might congregate and become sitting targets had been the first of her many good decisions. She'd sidled her way round Invalidenstraße after she left the Charité, carefully watching the run of cellars

Bormann had marked on the map there as a possible hiding place. Five minutes after she arrived, so did a Soviet patrol, who'd clearly been tipped off that the place would be full of German civilians. They didn't waste time checking. They'd thrown so many grenades down the stairwell, Margarete had felt the street lift under her feet. There'd been no mercy, not that she'd expected it. The Russians had mown down the few survivors who emerged screaming from their burns with a quickly mounted machine gun. Margarete moved on before the screams faded.

She'd skirted the flak tower too, assuming the tens of thousands hiding inside it would suffer a similar fate. She'd done the same at the brewery the instant she heard the rumbling tanks, distancing herself from the hordes of crying men and women trapped between the Russian troops determined to kill them and the trigger-happy and exhausted German soldiers firing blindly at anything that moved. If anyone from the bunker had made it as far as Prinzenallee, they wouldn't have survived long. Looking for them was a pointless exercise that would have only delayed her. Margarete hadn't tried.

It had proved remarkably easy in the end to be alone, to be responsible only for herself. After the close quarters of the bunkers she'd spent years living in, Margarete had quickly begun to enjoy it. She'd spent one night on the fringes of Wedding's flooded U-Bahn station, hovering around the displaced groups gathered there, sifting the information they traded. She pivoted west towards Spandau using what she'd gleaned. The British forces hadn't arrived at the citadel yet, but the rumours said they were only a matter of weeks away. The rumours also promised that there was a train line to Hamburg operating out of the town and spaces available on repatriation services to the British zone for foreign workers trying to find a way home. That had added spice to the game.

Margarete passed the hours it took her to walk to Spandau

resurrecting her schoolgirl French, reinventing herself as Marguerite Favré, a poor victim of the Nazis desperate to return to her native Normandy. She did it very well. She completely captivated the old and easily flattered official who nobody had smiled prettily at for years.

And it won't be any harder to captivate you.

Margarete accepted the chair the plain and awkward and definitely flustered captain offered her. She smoothed her skirt as she sat down and crossed her ankles as if she was in an elegant English drawing room, not a dusty wooden barracks. She assumed that was the kind of woman the captain was used to dealing with, if he was used to women at all. She sank into herself a little, making herself smaller than him, and glanced round the office as if it intimidated her. She let a moment's applause at her performance run through her head. She wasn't intimidated – why would she be? It wasn't an accident that she was there. It wasn't the first time she'd visited the British internment camp at Neuengamme since she'd settled in Hamburg, which was one of the long list of things the captain never needed to know.

Margarete had made the journey out of the city to the camp the previous summer on a train that – like everything else that was recovering far too slowly from the war for her liking – had taken three times as long as it should. She'd dressed very differently that day; she'd gone to survey the site, not to be seen there. The cotton dress she'd put on was faded and dull, like the scarf she'd wrapped round her hair. No one had noticed her as she walked round the perimeter of the camp which had housed twelve thousand prisoners during the war and worked them to death in a huge brickworks which served the nearby city. None of those prisoners were in the camp or in Hamburg now – the last of the survivors had been despatched to Bergen-Belsen in April 1945. Margarete had those facts at her fingertips because she'd heard the orders for the evacuation march being dictated in the bunker. Ten months on and the British had repurposed it, and nobody in Hamburg she'd spoken to apparently remembered its original existence.

Invisibility had been a useful tool on her first visit. She'd followed the fence at a careful distance, noting how lightly it was patrolled. She'd noted too the flowers planted round the dingy barracks and the child's swing hanging from a tree. She'd watched the displaced people who were now living there wandering round in the sunshine in their ragbag clothes, trying to create homes. She'd watched the German ex-soldiers wearing bits and pieces of their discredited uniforms mingling freely with them. Neuengamme was no longer a punishment facility; it wasn't securely run. That was all she'd needed to know. So invisibility was no longer the tool she needed today.

Margarete had built a carefully constructed life around herself in Hamburg. She'd remained French because that was easier than inventing a new German background or risking someone digging into her old one. Not that there was much to find there. She'd made careful enquiries about her parents' well-being once she reached the city, citing the Fleisses as her old employers. The response had been slow to come and bleak when it arrived. It seemed that Sissi had died in an air raid on Berlin and that Philip had disappeared at the end of the war into an internment camp run by the Russians. She'd left matters there. Her father was old, and the way he'd lived his life had made him rich but not healthy. There was little point in digging for more news and drawing attention to herself for the sake of a man who was most likely dead and could no longer be impressed by her. He wouldn't have thanked her for trying.

She'd focused on her own life after that. She'd talked her way into a typing job and a room in a house where nobody was interested in anyone else. And she'd taken full advantage of the desperate women plying their sewing skills in Hamburg for next to no pay. A couple of marks had paid for a fitted suit in a pretty shade of daffodil yellow that held the promise of spring. Another had paid for a matching flower-trimmed hat and an elegant shawl-collared blouse, and the woman who'd been careless enough to leave her new tweed coat unattended on a café chair didn't deserve to miss it. As for the nylons and the perfume and the lipstick that completed the oh-so-feminine picture, they'd come cheaply too. Courtesy of the men – including the factory owners who'd used Neuengamme's bricks to build their wealth and had deep pockets and short memories – who she'd promised favours to in Hamburg's nightclubs that they would never receive. Margarete had enjoyed collecting her spoils – she'd turned herself into a perfectly sprung trap. And the moment she looked up through her eyelashes, smiled a slightly wobbly smile and spoke in a halting and softly accented English, the unsuspecting captain was thoroughly snared too.

'You're right, it was unusual for me to come here, rather than surrender myself in Hamburg. I know I should have gone to a police station before now, but the men employed there…' She shivered and looked down as if they'd already laid hands on her. 'They can be rough, especially if you're a woman alone like I am. I'm sure you understand.' He did. She could see him already mentally saddling his charger and riding into battle on her behalf. 'But the truth is that I do want to talk now I've recovered from my experiences. There's things I know that could be useful to the war trials. And I'd like to be useful if I can. It might go some way to paying back…'

Margarete let her words trail away so the captain could turn them into the better intentions he'd filled her with. The truth was that she'd never considered handing herself in to the thugs masquerading as the German police. She couldn't risk bumping into an ex-Nazi with a score to settle with Bormann, who'd more than happily settle it with her. Or into one of the zealous new recruits she'd heard the British had employed, who were determined to distance themselves from the Reich by making an example of everyone else. She also had no interest in the trials and no wish to go to Nuremberg if she could avoid it. Her chief concern was finding herself a route to England. She'd only made the offer to win points. But her elastic concept of the truth was also something the captain didn't need to know about. She let her smile tremble again. She blinked as if she was holding back tears. Not that she needed to add any more gilding: she'd caught him in the little pauses after *experience* and before *useful*. But it never hurt to layer on the charm.

'The thing is though, it's all a bit frightening, reliving what I went through. And I really need someone like you to help me get it right.'

She had to cover her mouth with her hand to stop herself laughing as his chin shot up as if he had enough jawline to look manly and her flattery reeled him in.

Margarete pressed her fingernails into her palms to keep her temper in check as the argument raged on behind the closed door. Doug had turned out to be far less effectual than his captain's stripes had promised. If she'd known that from the start, she would have traded him in. Unfortunately, he'd jumped to her bidding in those first days and given her an overly confident idea of her ability to bend him. He'd given her his bedroom so she wouldn't have to sleep in one of the less than sanitary women's blocks. He'd handled her interrogation himself when she'd pleaded with him not to hand her over to someone who lacked his courteous manners. He'd asked his unimaginative questions as if he was worried about frightening her, exactly as she'd known he would.

'When did your employment with Adolf Hitler begin?'

'What was an average work day like in the bunker?'

'Did Hitler make military decisions in your presence? Were you asked to type those up?'

'What was his mood at the end? Was he depressed?'

Everything he asked was bland and boring and barely required any effort on her behalf. He'd accepted her short answers and her repeated, 'I was only a secretary; I wasn't required to understand anything about the war,' as if she'd been an innocent plucked from the typing pool. He'd accepted her tears and her, 'It's too awful to talk about,' as easily and stopped asking her about the last days. She'd danced rings round him, giving him nothing when she knew plenty, inventing details when it suited her. He'd treated her, 'I don't think that can be possible, not for a man of his character,' when he asked if Bormann might have survived the escape as if she'd handed him a casket of pearls. Margarete had only said it to make sure she wasn't called to speak at Nuremberg, where Bormann was being tried in his absence. Nobody had found any trace of him. She'd heard the rumours that he was alive and was hiding in Germany or Italy or South America, but she had no interest in speculating on those possibilities and opening herself up to questioning.

And yet here I am, in Nuremberg anyway, because Doug lacked the backbone to stand up to an order and keep me away. Wasting time, with no passport or confirmed sailing date to England. And if he makes a mess of this too and I get called to the stand...

She didn't want to think about the dangers in that. Nuremberg was crawling with men and women pretending they'd lived a different life in the war, hiding secrets they didn't want discovered. It had been hard enough to avoid them in the dreadful little villa she'd been sent to because Doug was incapable of explaining she deserved to be lodged in a decent hotel. Henny von Schirach – one of the other 'guests' who wasn't there by choice – would trade Margarete's life for her husband's in a heartbeat if she suspected what Margarete had been sent out of the bunker to do. Which someone might know. The bunker had been a crowded place – it was impossible to guarantee even the most private conversations had stayed private. Eavesdroppers could have heard Bormann's instructions to her through the office door, even if they hadn't fully understood them. And it was possible, if unlikely, one or two of the listeners might have survived.

But they won't be believed. Not without proof, and there's no one who has that except me.

Margarete pulled herself back into the corridor's shadows; pulled the veil attached to her hat a little lower, fighting to keep the doubts she was so seldom plagued with in check.

You won't be alone.

There'd been comfort in that when Hitler said it, the sense that she was part of a plan with deep roots. But here in Nuremberg? Where men with nothing to lose were fighting for their lives, and loyalty to the Reich was defined as a crime? Not being alone sounded rather like an unpleasant threat.

'This is ridiculous. She's given her testimony. She doesn't need to face any more questions; she doesn't know anything except what she's already said. Do you think I'd be marrying her if I thought she was a Nazi?'

Doug's voice squeaked on the rare occasions he shouted; it wasn't an attractive trait. He sounded like a mouse in a trap now. But he'd said *marry*, which was a good sign. He wasn't backing down. Margarete drew a calming breath and loosened her fingers, running what she knew to be true through her head, telling herself there was nothing to worry about. She'd kept herself to herself as much as she could in the house. She'd stayed very carefully on the fringes of the city and avoided the courtroom – nobody who mattered had seen her. Doug had sworn this trip was a formality, a rubber-stamping exercise. He'd promised they'd be in England and married in a matter of weeks. He'd even offered to give up his commission for her if necessary, as if that was an unthinkable sacrifice. As if she would still be around to care.

Margarete's spine uncurled. She stopped listening to whatever advice the major was flinging at Doug, safe in the certainty he wouldn't take it. She let her mind drift onto wedding dresses and whether she should wear gold like Diana Mosley had done. It would certainly be striking. She began to speculate about how long she would have to live with the charade of being Doug's wife. Not long, thankfully. There were enough diamonds in the bag to make that particular stage of the mission mercifully short. He'd already started making ridiculous assumptions about their life together and about children. She'd moved on to imagining the house she might buy once she'd found a discreet diamond dealer in London and the contacts she could cultivate there, when a shadow fell across her feet and she realised she was being watched.

'It's bad manners to spy – or to eavesdrop. Did nobody teach you that? Or warn you that, if you're going to do it, it's best not to stand under a light?'

She used the crisp tone that always terrified servants – it was better to take control than allow any element of surprise. It worked of course. The watcher instantly came forward into the dim glow of the overhead bulb, revealing a face Margarete hadn't seen in over twelve years. An ordinary face, pretty enough, not remarkable except perhaps for the dark blue eyes. But unforgettable for Margarete, who'd last seen its owner screaming out her anger and her pain across her mother's crumpled body.

It's Sid Kirson's daughter. What's she doing here? She's supposed to be one of us.

It was a shock to see the girl again, especially in such an unexpected place. It was on the tip of Margarete's tongue to ask her the question directly. But impulsive behaviour was the key to disaster, so she waited for a moment instead. And was grateful she did: the files the girl was holding were all stamped with the words, *Witness Testimony*.

So not one of us then. How disappointed her father must be.

Margarete sat back, checked her veil was in place and reached for a cigarette to hide behind. There was a time to attack and a time to withdraw, and this was definitely the latter. It was better to let the girl declare herself, if that's what she intended to do. Margarete would let her make the connection if she could; she would wait to see what the girl did with it and deal with the problem then. Next steps were, after all, always far too important to rush.

CHAPTER SEVENTEEN
FEBRUARY–MARCH 1946

'It's bad manners to spy – or to eavesdrop. Did nobody teach you that? Or warn you that, if you're going to do it, it's best not to stand under a light?'

The voice was soft, the English accented. There was a faint scent of a perfume which Annie – who hadn't owned a bottle of anything pretty for years – couldn't place. And there was an air of command in the woman's words which Annie automatically obeyed before she realised she'd done it. She stepped forward into the space where her shadow had fallen as the argument in the office raged on.

'Are you sure you know what you're doing? I appreciate we've moved on from the strict fraternisation ban, but marrying a German – especially one with a background like hers – and taking her back to England? That's a hell of a risk, Doug. Never mind what your family might think, it could cost you your career.'

Langley's voice raised in anger was as out of place as the woman. He was the calmest man Annie had ever met. She would have called him unflappable most days, which was no mean feat given the challenges they faced. But he was clearly upset now. And the man shouting back at him was furious.

'It's my decision, and it's none of your business. She's done her duty; she's given her evidence. And that past life you're so concerned about is behind her now. She wants to start fresh, and she wants to do that with me. If that's a risk to my career, then I'll happily find another one.'

'*That past life?*' Langley's sudden laugh ricocheted through the thin door. 'Are you serious? You make it sound like she was some hard-done-by Hausfrau. Get a grip on yourself. She was Martin Bormann's personal secretary; she was in the bunker with Hitler. And as for her evidence? If I had my way, she'd be going nowhere until we've drilled a lot deeper into her conveniently vague answers.'

It's her – it has to be. Martin Bormann's secretary, waiting for me to answer. What on earth do I say to her?

Annie blinked against the light which had dazzled her eyes as she stepped forward. She couldn't see the woman's face properly, which she suspected was deliberate. It would have been easy for her to lean forward or lift the spotted veil which clung to her black pillbox hat and make herself known, but she didn't do either of those things. And she didn't acknowledge Annie's awkward, 'I'm sorry, I wasn't being intentionally rude.' Instead, she shook a cigarette out of a smart gold case and slipped it between her red lips.

She's used to men lighting those for her. She's used to men doing her bidding.

It was partly the pause before the woman reached into the bag looped round her wrist for a lighter that suggested she was used to a coterie of admirers. It was mostly the woman's poise. Nothing about her manner suggested she was concerned by the raised voices or by the fact that the row was about her. She could have been waiting for a cocktail in an elegant hotel. And her clothes carried a quality and a sense of style Annie couldn't remember seeing for years.

Annie had never owned a handbag so small it suggested other people acted as sherpas on her behalf when she went out. She'd never owned such a frivolous hat. The window between wearing the practical garments her mother had chosen and earning a salary that might allow her to develop tastes of her own had been a tiny one that had disappeared with rationing. Annie's handbags – which had been built for carrying shopping and storing a gas mask – were remarkable only for their sturdiness, not their fashion sense. Her hats had been designed to keep out the cold or hide her lank hair when supplies of shampoo were scarce. Most of the clothes she'd bought in 1939 had had to last for six years and through so many rounds of mending and refashioning they'd lost anything beyond their function. She'd been left with a wardrobe that was serviceable if shabby, like most women she knew. But not this one. She was wearing a fitted suit that actually fitted her, and real nylons, not thick woollen stockings. And the coat draped over the chair beside her could have come from a Paris catwalk.

And she knows I'm registering every detail. She's playing with me; I bet she's playing with whoever that man is in there.

Annie was right: the woman's next words confirmed it.

'It's fascinating to hear men fighting over you, don't you think? No matter how old they are, there's always something of the playground about it.'

The tone was both amused and bored, and slightly familiar. Perhaps because its languid air reminded Annie of Diana Mosley's drawl. She shared the same coolness, the same sense that whatever was happening only mattered if she decided it did.

They're both as metallic as their dresses. They're not women you'd want to cross.

The memory came from nowhere, but Annie couldn't shake it. A long-ago ballroom. Two women vying for control.

I know her. I've met her before.

That thought made no sense, but she couldn't shake that one either, and neither could her body. Something in the woman's manner had stirred up a warning signal, a prickling in the back of her neck, a fingernail crawling over her skin. She was still combing through her memories, trying to dig deeper than Savehay, when the office door flew open with a force that threatened its hinges and a doughy man in a captain's uniform stormed out. His face was as tight as a drum, but it softened the instant he saw the woman he'd been fighting for and she held out her hand.

'He's not worth your time, my darling, old friend or not. We'll make new ones, you'll see. We'll make infinitely better ones.'

Her voice was a caress that wrapped round the captain. His shoulders loosened. He took her fingers in his and kissed them in a gesture that was both gallant and oddly subservient. And then she was up from her chair and gone, in a sweep of caramel-coloured hair and clicking heels and a devotion from the captain Annie could see in the woman's stiff back would never be shared.

'Dear God, save me from besotted men.'

Langley appeared in the doorway and waved Annie inside, grabbing the inevitable bunch of files from her as she sat down.

'How much of that did you hear?'

Annie didn't bother to pretend she'd heard nothing. They'd worked together for long enough to know that neither of them would walk away from listening to an interesting conversation.

'That the woman waiting outside was Bormann's secretary and your friend is planning to marry her, which doesn't sound like a great idea. And she's been released from giving further testimony, which sounds like a worse one.'

Langley sighed and dropped the new folders into the clutter on his desk. 'My thoughts exactly, on both counts. I've known Doug a long time, and he's a decent man, but he's forgotten all his basic training. Defendants will attempt to create a rapport with their interrogator. They'll attempt to make friends and build a personal relationship. It's essential to the outcome of every interview to avoid this scenario. It's page one of the manual. She's obviously got him in a right spin. He questioned her himself and signed off on her answers without anyone else seeing the paperwork until it hit my desk. He's never been Mr Dynamic, but I thought he was smarter than this.'

Annie picked up the file stamped with *Margarete Fleiss* and *Witness Released* he passed to her. It was remarkably thin for a woman who'd admitted she'd been in the Führerbunker.

'Do you think there's something to worry about?'

Langley rubbed his eyes and stared at the beige folders overcrowding his desk. 'Honestly? Probably not. She doesn't seem to have had a prominent role in the administration, or the bunker, and nobody else who's been interrogated from there – including the other secretaries Traudl Junge and Christa Schroeder, who were caught immediately after the war – mentioned her name. I'll get their files out anyway and maybe you could double-check "darling Grete's" account with theirs and see if there's anything new. What is it? What's the matter?'

Annie felt the blood rush from her head in the same second Langley saw it leave.

'What did you call her?'

He frowned. 'Darling Grete. Doug said it so often, it's got stuck in my head. Why are you asking, and why have you gone so pale?'

Poise. Caramel-coloured hair. Softly accented English. The heavy ring that slipped round her finger as she raised her cigarette. Grete.

The pieces fit perfectly together; they made sense of her

memories of the party. They made sense of her body's reaction. Margarete was Grete grown-up. The girl who'd cast the worst of shadows over Annie's life had been sat feet away from her. It was no wonder her skin had rebelled. Annie's chest tightened; her pulse stormed through her veins. But it was one thing to recognise the woman who'd tried to kill her mother, and another to know what should come next.

I'm not ready for this. I don't know how to tell the story.

But she had to say something better than the, 'Nothing, it doesn't matter,' which might help her get her scattered thoughts into some kind of order. Langley had already registered her hesitation.

'I'm not sure. A hunch maybe. A feeling that I know her, from before the war.'

The excuse bounced off him, which was no surprise. Langley's frown deepened. He shifted without a pause into interrogation mode. 'I'm sorry, Annie, but how? You came to us from a typing pool, didn't you, and virtually from school? And don't be offended by this, but not from an exactly monied or travelled background. Given that, how would you have known a German before the war?'

And there it was. The chasm that had stopped her speaking the truth. The chasm that would open up the moment she said, 'Because my father was a friend and a supporter of Oswald Mosley's. He still is. Which meant he had a lot of contact with Germans. And especially with her.' The hole Langley's respect and her career would fall into.

Except the connection between the girl and the woman was made. And that connection – which stretched out further into the Nazis' inner circle than Margarete's testimony had admitted and revealed a far more dangerous woman than she was pretending to be – could lead somewhere Langley would definitely want to go.

Never mind where finding Grete could take me.

Annie took a deep breath. She couldn't let this opportunity go. She had no choice except to tell Langley her story and hope that he would listen to it all, good and bad.

'There's some things you don't know—'

The telephone's shrill squawk cut her off before *those things* could take shape. Langley picked up the receiver and waved her away. But he was still frowning at her as she left, and she could see his well-trained wheels spinning.

But I've bought myself time, and that's not a bad thing.

Annie leaned on the door he'd told her to close and waited for her pulse to stop racing. Once Langley sensed a red flag, he would go digging faster than a terrier after a rabbit. Which meant she had to move faster than him and put some depth to her hunch – before she became the story and not Margarete.

The intention to act quickly was all very well, but it took Annie a week to get to Margarete's file. Everyone – which luckily included Langley – was working more hours than the day held. The prosecutors had begun working in relays, which put pressure on the typists and the translators. The work piled up so quickly, new cupboards had been added to the narrow corridors to hold the completed paperwork, not that they'd made much difference. Reports flowed over the desks and onto the floors in teetering pyramids while everyone obsessed over the idea of a final push, a sprint to the finish line which would put the trials back on the front pages again. Everyone except the defendants.

The men in the dock continued to behave as if the numbers and the photographs and the deepening catalogue of brutality were as much of a shock to them as they were to the gallery. Eyebrows jumped up and mouths fell open in a never-ending pantomime of surprise. Göring was overheard calling the pictures of the dead from the liberated camps a fabrication created by digging up graveyards in an aside Sid would have applauded. He laughed when a film showing fields thick with the bodies of Russian soldiers began with its images upside down. He picked up a book when the same film switched to the gas chambers and murdered children at Auschwitz and Majdanek. The whole court hated him for it, including Annie.

But the exhaustion with the process that had affected everyone had caught up with her too. As much as she wanted to see the defendants finally crack and accept their guilt, almost five months of a trial that the men had consistently mocked had also whittled away her patience. If there'd been a switch to speed up time and move straight to the verdicts, Annie would have pressed it in an instant. Instead, it was her days not the trial's that moved too fast. She worked so late and so often the military guards on the Palace's gates began to extend their sympathy instead of saying goodnight. And Margarete's file – when Annie finally opened it bleary-eyed after an already overextended day – did nothing to improve her frustration.

The file was so thin because her account was so sparse. There was no depth, no detail. Margarete's answers read like those of a disinterested bystander.

I was never required to type up military orders. In the last days, I was concerned solely with the Führer's personal correspondence.

I do not know the names of everyone who was present: personnel moved in and out of the bunker without warning.

I can confirm that the Führer died there. I can make no comment on the manner of that; it was a personal decision.

Her responses were clipped. There was none of the cruelty she knew the woman was capable of. There was no emotion at all, although the accounts given by the other female secretaries who'd been present in the run-up to the last days had been soaked in that. There was nothing offered to explain Margarete's successful escape from the bunker other than, *I managed to evade the Russians.* There was nothing relating to the way she'd eventually been apprehended beyond the name of the camp near Hamburg where she'd been detained by the mesmerised captain. At first reading, there was nothing but gaps. At the second, one answer in particular niggled.

> I can confirm Bormann left in the same group as me. As to whether he survived, I don't know, but I doubt it. He wasn't the cleverest of men when it came to the wider world; he wasn't used to fending for himself. Which may be answer enough as to what happened to him, given the state of Berlin at that time.

The only point at which Margarete's account became personal was when she was asked to comment on Bormann's fate. There was the cold and callous tone which made Annie shiver but didn't surprise her. There was the woman who'd been part of Hitler's inner circle since she was seventeen. There were the family ties and the heavily moulded upbringing Annie could partially understand. But that was where the similarities stopped: Grete had already proved that she was a woman whose beliefs had made her more than capable of violence. Which meant it was time to stop reading the answers Margarete had chosen to give and look for the answers she was hiding.

Annie went back to the beginning and went back again, until she found it. The response relating to Hitler's personal correspondence. Doug hadn't pushed her on what that meant – he hadn't pushed her on anything – but Annie couldn't stop picking at it. Had Margarete been responsible for typing up Hitler's last letters? His final thoughts to be sent to contacts outside the bunker? It wasn't impossible that such documents existed. Two typed copies of what were said to be Hitler's last will and testament had briefly surfaced in the American and British press at the turn of the year, before both governments supressed them. British intelligence agents had been told there might be others, that some might contain handwritten messages. Nobody had proved or disproved that theory yet.

But what if Margarete typed up some of those? What if she knew who the copies were intended to go to? What if she saw more personal messages?

By the early hours of the morning, as her brain fogged and scattered from lack of sleep, Annie had started to imagine a letter from Hitler to Mosley tucked inside Margarete's elegant coat and a very different explanation for her interest in Doug and England than the whirlwind love affair the hapless captain thought he'd been swept up in. She crawled back to her hotel room exhausted, thankful that the next day was a rare free one. But she didn't sleep well. Her dreams swam with parties presided over by Hitler, and men in black shirts laughing at the idea they might have lost. With Grete in the dock and Annie condemning her. She woke up to a grey morning with leaden eyes but her mind made up. Certain that the only way to get the answers she needed was to do what she'd wanted to do for years and finally challenge Margarete.

Nothing about her idea improved with the day. Annie kept telling herself that as she got dressed in trousers and shoes that were suitable for a long walk and ate the oddly dry powdered eggs the cook had scrambled for breakfast. She wasn't a trained interrogator, and Margarete had already proved she could run rings around those, never mind someone as untried as Annie. Even if she agreed to meet, Margarete had been discharged and would be within her rights to refuse to answer more detailed questions. Besides, she'd probably already left the city. Pursuing her was not only a waste of time, it could result in Annie getting into serious trouble if Langley found out she'd exceeded her authority before she had anything useful to tell him. Annie told herself all those things two or three times, and then she ignored every warning.

The only contact address she had for Margarete was the one they had on file for Party members and affiliates, including wives and witnesses, who needed a higher degree of protection, something Doug had presumably arranged for her, given her connection with Bormann. A villa in Erlenstegen on the eastern edge of the city, known to everyone at the Palace as the Guest House. The suburb was a long walk from the centre and far out of reach of the few trams which were finally operating. Luckily, a lorry transported supplies from the hotel's kitchen there twice a week, and although none of the journalists keen to breach its walls had the right credentials to request a lift there, Annie did.

It wasn't a comfortable journey. Returning to the city was a challenge. It was obvious that a clear-up had finally begun – miniature trains circled the worst of the ruins in an endless loop of rubble-filled and emptied wagons, and the twisted girders and jagged towers which had reached up towards her plane in November were gone – but there was no sign of any rebuilding, of any attempt at a return to normality. That was sad to see, but the coming confrontation filled Annie with dread. That Margarete might manage it so well that Annie would still be left without answers. And dread that it might not happen at all.

It was a relief at least to drive away from the city's sagging buildings with their peeling patches of colour, the only evidence left of what had – only six years earlier – been a highly decorated medieval city. The houses in Erlenstegen bore signs of neglect – most of them had tangles of dead vines running from window to window and gardens that were a forest of weeds – but at least they hadn't been bombed. And the Guest

House itself, with its red-gabled roof and sparkling windows, was storybook pretty. Not that her driver was impressed.

'Don't be deceived by the look of the place – they've put all kinds of scum in there. Hoffmann who was Hitler's official photographer, the one who introduced him to the dumb blonde he married. Baldur von Schirach's wife, who looks like butter wouldn't melt in her mouth but worships that husband of hers who turned little kids into Nazis. They're all as polite as you like, but I wouldn't give you a dollar for any of them. Including the Hungarian broad who runs the show and insists she's a countess. I'd take anything they tell you with a whole heap of salt.'

His advice was an echo of every *don't trust the Germans* speech Annie had heard since she'd arrived. But the names he'd mentioned sent shivers down her spine. Von Schirach had been the Party's youth leader and was one of the defendants currently mocking the authority of the court. Hoffmann was the man who, along with Goebbels, had created Hitler's image. He – unlike the photographers who'd entered the camps and scarred themselves for life – had made a fortune from his photos during the war. If rumour was believed, he was continuing to make a fortune from them now. She entered the house already biting her tongue, but the only person she encountered was the landlady.

'My guests are exactly that, Fräulein Kirson. We only use first names; we respect each other's privacy. We do not discuss why anyone is here. Some of them are vulnerable and it's my job to ensure they feel safe here. I'm sure you understand.'

Countess Kalnoky – who introduced herself with the emphasis on her title – set the rules as soon as she invited Annie to sit, and was very deliberate with her word choices. The GI might have baulked at *vulnerable*, but Annie understood its meaning perfectly well. Ever since Robert Ley – the head of Germany's wartime workforce, including its vast army of slave labourers – had strangled himself to death in his Nuremberg cell before the trials began, the court officials had become paranoid about any of the other prisoners choosing suicide over prosecution. It was hardly surprising that paranoia had extended to the Guest House, but the countess's attempt to portray the villa as a place of sanctuary rang hollow. It wasn't only the wooden panelling and the heavy drapes which made the place dark. Its air was thick with mistrust and suspicion, with betrayals and closely held secrets. It wasn't a place for lingering, so Annie got straight to the point.

'I'm looking for a woman called Margarete Fleiss. She's presented her testimony, but there's a number of gaps I'd like to go over with her.'

The countess wasn't a fool – she knew Annie's request was irregular. She had the grace not to mention that.

'And you've missed her, I'm afraid. Margarete has left us to be married, in England or so I believe. She didn't leave a forwarding address.'

Annie could hear footsteps above her. She could sense the villa's occupants waiting to reclaim their stage. She had no desire to stay and meet them, but she couldn't leave with such a vague answer.

'What did you think of her?'

The countess frowned and shook her head. Annie was convinced she was about to tell her to go. Instead, she glanced at the ceiling and lowered her voice.

'She was charming and clever and she had that captain of hers under a spell. I've never seen a man so lovestruck. But she was hiding something too.'

The countess paused. Annie stayed silent. She might not be trained, but she'd learned a few tricks. The woman was clearly bursting with a secret or a burden she'd get to in her own time. She swallowed a sigh of relief when the countess continued.

'Our guests are private people, as I've said, but she took that to extremes. It's understood that I have access to the bedrooms, but the one time I went into hers – after knocking of course – she screamed at me to get out as if I was a clumsy servant. She was packing, and there was something on the bed she didn't want me to see, a small bag which... Well, perhaps it was a trick of the light, but it looked to me like there was jewellery inside it, or possibly loose gems or coins. I wasn't foolish enough to ask her.'

She stopped a second time. Annie risked asking, 'Was there something special about her?'

The countess looked away and pulled at the diamonds circling her finger. When she looked back, the disinterested mask she'd been wearing since Annie arrived suddenly fell.

'Yes and no, which is the worst part. All I can say is that if you've got a hunch about her, follow it. I didn't ask for this job, and I didn't want it, but we take what we can get nowadays. I do what I'm asked, and I keep my *guests* alive, but I've no illusions about the people that are sent here. None of them are sorry for the crimes they or their families have committed. You have to know that. They believe the trials are a travesty. They continue to believe in the Reich. They're not alone in that, not by a long way.' She drew a deep breath, but it didn't calm the despair in her eyes. 'That's the thing nobody wants to admit. That Germany was beaten, but fascism? Oh no. That's as alive as you and me. It's simply gone to ground.'

'So let me get this straight because there's a lot here, never mind you attempting an unauthorised interrogation. It wasn't only that you knew a German. Your father was an active member of the British Union of Fascists and is still an associate of Oswald Mosley. And Hitler visited Mosley's house when you were staying there.'

Annie had never seen Langley dumbfounded before, and

she didn't like being the cause of it. Any more than she liked being the cause of his anger.

'Why the hell wasn't any of this in your file?'

'Because I wasn't judged to be a risk, and I'm not. My father is the fascist, not me.'

It was hard to stand her ground against his fury. And his fear, which he'd clearly expressed, that he'd had a spy in his unit for years. But Annie was prepared to put up with that if it meant he would listen to her. His irritated intake of breath suggested he was no more certain of that than she was.

'I hope that's true. I can certainly see why you took the countess seriously. It sounds like she's been pushed too far by her "guests". And I don't think you're wrong to flag your concerns about the Fleiss woman up. But beyond that?' He shook his head. 'There's nothing much I can do. Doug applied for early demobilisation, and his record was so good, he got it. He's no longer under military jurisdiction, and he didn't leave a personal address, so there's no easy way to look for him. And as for her? We've no evidence that she's planning to do anything in England except be a loyal wife. A half-glimpsed bag of what you think may or may not have been jewellery is not enough to go on.' He waved his hand as Annie started to argue. 'I'm not dismissing your suspicions. Write a report for MI6 and put everything you've told me in it, back to the party in 1934. But don't get your hopes up they'll read it any time soon – or act on it.'

Her brief moment of excitement disappeared, although she tried to hide it. 'Even if there's a direct link between Margarete and Mosley? And that's got something to do with Hitler's last wishes? Even if she could be dangerous?'

There was no turning back now. Annie rattled through the events at the Black House as quickly as she could, trying not to hear how hollow they sounded. A fall she was convinced was a push. Margarete's presence on the staircase. A hunch that Sid had invited her to be some kind of a mentor to Annie, that he was somehow involved with his wife's 'accident'. That he was somehow involved with Margarete. A list of suspicions and no evidence. It wasn't enough – they both knew it.

Langley sighed and began shuffling the papers that permanently covered his desk. 'I'm sorry. Because that's a horrible state of affairs, and because there's nothing I can do about it. Margarete's gone, and even if she wasn't...' He shook his head. 'I can't ask the police in London to put out a warrant for her or your father. There's no evidence of a case against them for being anything except Nazis. And no, Annie, you know as well as I do, issuing a warrant for that's impossible.'

He picked up a file and flicked through it; picked up another and did the same, his face growing older with every page. 'Here's the thing we're not meant to acknowledge. That all the people in these folders have done terrible things and that nothing will be done about it. This trial will be the last gasp against the Nazis, which brings me no pleasure. Once this is done, everything will be about building bridges with Germany so we can contain Russia's ambitions. You know how difficult denazification has been – nobody will admit to being a Party member. And once the Russians start flexing their muscles and trying to cement communism into their occupation zone? Everyone will forget about Nazis then.' He wiped his hand over his face and found her a smile, although it wasn't his old kind which had crinkled his eyes. 'I'm sure your report will be excellent – they always are – but it's not going to matter to anyone that this Margarete might be violent. It's not going to matter that she might be best pals with Mosley. His days are over. No one in England will have the stomach for fascism after what's been done in its name in the war. We're better people than that.'

He dismissed her then with an, 'I can't let the rest of what you've told me go, but I'll get to it later,' which sounded more exhausted than angry. Annie went away trying to take comfort in his certainty that fascism had had its day, but she couldn't.

'You can dig up graves in any cemetery you like. You can bulldoze the bodies into piles and call it murder. That doesn't make it true.'

Sid's words – and the echo they'd found in Göring's aside – were louder in her head than Langley's. Her father's hatred hadn't lessened with the war; it had festered. He'd fed it with the resentment carried by every BU member who'd crawled out of prison to find him, carrying some version of what it meant to be English that Jews and anyone else who didn't subscribe to their impossibly narrow definition didn't fit. Annie didn't believe they would let go of those prejudices. She didn't believe the men who'd designed the gas chambers and the camps and the slave labour programmes in Germany would easily give their hatreds up either. Ordinary German people had unleashed hell across Europe. Ordinary British people had donned black shirts and screamed *Perish Judah* outside synagogues, in the full knowledge of what had happened on Kristallnacht. Men and women like that, in Annie's experience, only believed their own truths. And that included Margarete.

Fascism? It's simply gone to ground.

The countess had been right, except in her use of *simply*. There was nothing simple about it. Things which went to ground lay dormant until the conditions that favoured them ripened. They flourished as soon as the cracks appeared that fed them and allowed them to breathe. If Nuremberg, with its broken landscape and unrepentant war criminals had taught Annie anything – if Margarete's and Sid's vicious way of looking at the world had taught her anything – it was that those cracks could appear anywhere. And nowhere was exempt from the poison that seeped out of them. Nowhere was better than that.

PART THREE

CHAPTER EIGHTEEN

DECEMBER 1946

Everybody knows who I am except me.

The feeling consumed her; it wouldn't go away. And the more solidly Harry inhabited his place in the world, the more flimsy Annie's place felt. Especially tonight at the Christmas party being held in the Cheshire Cheese, the rambling pub beloved by Fleet Street's journalists which Harry's editor-in-chief had hired for the night. Annie had gone along with high hopes for the evening. She'd lost one job, but that didn't mean she couldn't have hopes for another. And yes, the paper didn't employ women as journalists – it didn't employ married women at all – but she was hoping somebody there might have an idea how she could put her writing and language skills to good use. Unfortunately, nothing about her night had gone as planned. Instead of standing happily in the middle of a conversation that might move her life forward, she was standing alone. Abandoned beside a buffet table groaning with a ration-defying spread of cold salmon and thickly sliced ham and endless bowls of glacé cherry-studded trifle, as somebody wielding her name encouraged her to load up her plate like a child.

'Don't stand on ceremony, Mrs Garnet – nobody else will! Get yourself stuck in.'

Mrs Garnet. That's who she was. Harry's 'pretty little thing of a wife'. The subject of infuriating nods and winks from his leering colleagues who went pink at the thought of a newlywed. It didn't matter to them that she'd once been more than the sum of her wedding ring and Harry's job.

That hasn't mattered to anybody for months. Not since I blew my career up.

It had taken no time in Nuremberg for the details of Annie's earlier life to leak out; apparently, she hadn't been the only one who listened in corridors. Nobody had directly excluded her. Nobody had challenged her. But there'd been a general easing away, a withdrawal that had accelerated once discussions began about where the team might be deployed once the trials were done. Those petered out the instant she tried to join them in an echo of her schooldays.

Annie had done her best to ignore the silences. She'd buried herself in paperwork, taking on even more shifts, working twice as hard to prove she was an asset not a threat, waiting for the next chunk of gossip that would replace her. It had seemed to be working as winter gave way to a summer that was too hot and too dusty, and the trials staggered towards their end. Albert Speer was the last defendant called to the stand on the twenty-first of June. The final witness was summoned on the first of July; the prosecution rested its case three weeks later. And with that Annie's work was done. All that remained was the defence and the verdicts, and neither of those needed her. But she'd assumed something else would.

'I'm suggesting we release you from the clutches of the Grand Hotel and get you back to England.'

Langley had barely waited a day after the closing statements were done before he presented her with a 'suggestion' that contained no choice.

And I still didn't hear the bolts clanging.

Annie stared blankly at the buffet table as the memory flooded back, determined not to shed any more tears.

'Shall I report to the War Office when I get there?'

She must have sounded like such a fool. She hadn't even lost hope when Langley looked away and muttered, 'If you really want to.' She hadn't lost that until he coughed and, in his mind anyway, tried to help her stop wasting her time.

'I'm sorry, Annie. Your work's been excellent from day one, no one can dispute that. If things were different, I'd find a new role for you. But they're not. Your father's file does you no favours, I'm afraid. He carried on being a troublemaker right through his internment – attacking other inmates in the prison camp and attempting to start riots – and Special Branch have kept him on a watch list same as Mosley. Your connection to him might not have mattered so much in 1939 when we needed anyone and everyone we could get, but that's not the case now. We're already getting warnings about Russian spies infiltrating every level of the intelligence services. Nobody can work for us going forward without being checked and double-checked, and you won't get clearance.'

He hadn't allowed her an opportunity to speak. It took no time to get her final paperwork done. She was on a plane before she had time to write home and announce that she was coming, not that she'd wanted to do that. The thought of arriving at Arnold Circus and facing Sid while she was still burning from all the holes he'd ripped into her life was impossible.

Annie had gone straight from the air base to the War Office, determined to prove Langley wrong. The omens she'd looked for on the way had been promising. Harry's letters had mentioned concerns about rising unemployment as the demobbed soldiers continued to come home from Europe and Asia. Peggy's were full of complaints about the rationing she'd assumed would end with the war but still ruled everyone's lives.

About the constant shortages of identifiable meat and sugar and fresh fruit and the utter disgrace that was the newly introduced bread ration. Annie had expected to find a country plunged back into its greyest days, but London was a joy after Nuremberg. The streets were clean, and the worst of the remaining bomb damage was hidden behind brightly coloured advertising hoardings. Flowers filled front gardens. Children played in parks and proper playgrounds, not among broken tanks and piles of rubble. And although there were shortages and the shop windows were joyless, nobody was starving. Nobody's bones were too sharp for their face. Nobody's eyes were vacant.

Annie had presented herself at the War Office with her mood brightened by the sunshine, but peace had swept in a new guard and her old section had disappeared. Miss Carter was long gone, reassigned or resigned or pensioned-off. Wherever she'd gone, she was forgotten. And so was Annie. Without a letter of recommendation from Langley – which he'd refused before she'd finished asking for it – she was simply another girl asking for a position a demobbed soldier could fill. She left with a dismissive, 'We'll hold you on file,' she knew wasn't true – and would end her hopes in an instant if it was – and all paths suddenly closed to her but one.

I'll come home and set a date.

She'd made the promise. She'd meant the promise.

Did I?

Annie pushed the thought away. She wished it would stop coming. She loved Harry – she'd always loved Harry – and she'd owed him the certainty that her promise would be kept. None of what had happened was his fault. Besides, the deed was done now. Harry hadn't been the only one hanging on to her words. Peggy had been as eager to grab hold of a wedding as a child a hand's stretch away from a kitten, and Dolly was no better; it seemed they'd been making secret plans for months. Peggy's ivory silk dress had been refashioned in Annie's absence with a more modern sweetheart neckline and a ruched skirt. Dolly's pearls were polished and waiting in their velvet box. All anyone had needed from Annie was for her to agree to being patted and primped and walked the short distance from Arnold Circus to the church to be handed over. Everything was done. Everyone was ready for happy news. There was even a two-up, two-down terraced house waiting for her on the edge of London Fields, its deposit paid for with the nest egg Harry had built from his navy pay. He would have tied a bow round it if he could; his smile as he showed her around the tiny rooms could have powered the whole place for a year. She couldn't turn her back on so much joy. So the *one day I'll do it* which lived in Annie's head had arrived and swept her away before she'd summoned up the courage to say, *But I'm not sure it's that day yet.*

And I should be grateful for everything I've got, like I promised my mother I was on my wedding day.

'Excuse me, are you going to choose something? You've been holding up the queue for a while now.'

Annie jumped out of the past and hastily filled up her plate. She wasn't hungry – she was smarting too much from her memories to eat – but she didn't want to draw attention to herself again. She'd already done that enough for one evening, according to Harry anyway. She moved quickly away from the buffet, looking for a quiet corner without her husband in it. Their arrival at the party hadn't gone well, and she didn't have the energy to fight over another mistake. Not that she'd intended the first one. The spotlight had landed on her the second they'd walked in, which had been enjoyable for a minute or two. Unfortunately, Annie had mistaken the flurry of, 'Where's our Harry been hiding you then?' for genuine interest.

'I've been in Germany actually, for most of the last twelve months. I've been working at Nuremberg, at the trials.'

She hadn't known it was possible to alienate a room so

quickly. The men – and their largely overlooked wives – had stepped back and frowned in a way that prompted Annie to ask what the matter was. Once all the raised eyebrows had lowered, it had fallen to Angus – the head of the political desk Harry worked on – to tell her how much time she'd wasted.

'I'm not expecting you to know, my dear, but I'd dearly love someone to tell me what the point was. Eleven months and God knows how much money to try a handful of Nazis as if they were the only ones in the whole country with blood on their hands. I mean, it's so far from the truth it's laughable. Millions of people don't die unless thousands are involved in killing them. And what was the result? Göring swallows cyanide and escapes the rope. Half of them were given pathetically short prison sentences or acquitted. It would have been simpler to shoot them all on day one and be done with it.'

He'd finished his lecture with a nod to Annie that said, *Now it's your turn to thank me.* Which was apparently when, or so Harry hissed as the group shifted away from her, Annie had crossed the line.

'I won't take issue with your assessment that more Germans were involved in the atrocities than the men who were tried for them. There was a collective looking away at best, and complicity at worst, from the minute Hitler came to power that I don't think anyone knows how to deal with. But I can tell you what the point was. To shine a light on crimes that were so terrible we have to hold them up to the world and say *never again*. And to give a voice to the victims those crimes have silenced. Neither of which would have been served by back-street executions.'

She wasn't the one who'd muttered, 'Thank God for the marriage ban if it keeps irritating little hotheads like her out of the workforce.' She wasn't the one who stage-whispered, 'You've got to feel sorry for Harry – imagine being married to such a bossy young madam.' But she was the one who –

according to her husband – had been strident and rude. Which was why she'd been left by herself at the buffet table while Harry went off to 'paper over the damage' as he'd ungraciously put it, and the other wives observed her from a distance as if she was a grenade that had mislaid its pin. Annie was seriously considering leaving early and having the row she was determined to have with Harry in private. Until the crowd round the function room's doorway parted a little with the arrival of a new guest, and she caught the scent of a familiar perfume.

Blue Grass by Elizabeth Arden. She'd last smelled that in a dark corridor in Nuremberg. She hadn't been able to place it then, but she could place it now. A floral scent underpinned by spicy undertones that Peggy had dismissed as not fresh enough for a bride when Annie picked it up off the counter at Derry and Toms. When the woman wearing it came into view a moment later, Annie – who'd turned as numb as if she'd been caught in a snowdrift – wasn't surprised the crowd had stepped back. The new guest was – as she had been then – a fashion plate. The emerald brocade gown that reduced her waist to a hand's span turned the other wives – including Annie, who was wearing her now dyed and shortened wedding dress – into museum pieces. Her matching brocade evening cap was trimmed with another half veil. She was alone, which was a statement in itself, and she wasn't wearing a wedding band, which was another, although the heavy gold ring was still loosely in place. And if Annie had had any last doubts about who she was looking at, Margarete's next move – unclipping a cigarette from its case and waiting for the circle of flames which instantly flocked round her – confirmed it.

'What on earth is she doing here?'

She didn't know what to do. Charging at Margarete with her fingernails – which had been her first impulse once her body came back to her – clearly wasn't a sensible plan. A rose-taffeta-wrapped woman, whose name Annie hadn't been blessed with, heard her confused question and glanced round.

'Do you mean Countess Kalnoky?'

She frowned at Annie's, 'Who?'

'I'm sorry. From the way you spoke, I assumed you knew her. She's an Austrian widow, a friend of Lord Beaverbrook – who I assume you do know owns the newspaper – and one of the *Standard*'s patrons. She's very rich, as well as being considerably more charming than some of tonight's guests.'

The woman turned her back again. Her rudeness glanced off Annie. She only had eyes for Margarete, who was collecting up husbands and holding court. The reinvention was certainly a clever one. Margarete had borrowed a name and a nationality to account for her accent. She'd apparently already offloaded the hapless captain. And if Beaverbrook was any indication, she was making friends in high places who'd made no secret of their support for Mosley in the years before the war. What Annie wanted to know was why.

It looked to me like there was jewellery inside it, or possibly loose gems or coins.

The real countess had seen something more valuable in Margarete's room than a pretty necklace or bracelet, or a small amount of cash. Annie had suspected as much the moment she'd started playing with her diamond ring. And the outfit Margarete was wearing was the kind of couture only the very wealthiest women – or men – could afford. Every instinct was telling Annie that she – and her report that nobody at MI6 had responded to – was right. That there was a story here that had started but not ended with the war.

And I'm going to be the one who finds it. Not Harry or any of his horrible journalist friends. Me. The irritating little hothead with a deeply personal axe to grind.

The rush that ran through her was the same one that had fizzed her blood when Miss Carter decided Annie was wasting her time in the typing pool. The same one she'd felt when Langley had said *operatives like us*. The one Annie had lost when she'd walked unwanted out of Nuremberg and the War Office. It tasted even better than champagne, but she hadn't drunk enough of that to act on it. She couldn't afford to confront whatever new incarnation Margarete had adopted in public. She couldn't afford to make a mistake.

She began to skirt round the edges of the room instead, trying to get closer to her quarry. Margarete had barely moved; she hadn't needed to. Someone had brought her a well-filled glass; someone else had brought her a plate of food she hadn't touched. But now – although she'd barely been in the room for half an hour – she was beginning to say her goodbyes.

I'll follow her. If she's leaving this early, she's going on somewhere else, so let's see where that is.

It was cold outside, the air promising snow. Annie decided to head to the cloakroom, to get her coat before Margarete instructed one of her admirers to collect hers, and then wait outside where the dark would hide her.

She didn't even make it that far. Less than half a dozen steps outside the main room, a hand grabbed her wrist and bundled her through another of the pub's endless doors.

'Why are you here, and why are you watching me again? And intending to follow me, I assume from your less than subtle exit.'

The softened accent was gone. Margarete's voice was as guttural and terse as it had been when she'd thrown a drunk out of Hitler's presence.

Annie shook off her restraining hand and pretended to be equally as fierce. 'Why would you say *again*?'

The switch from hunter to boredom was instant.

'Really, is that the game we're going to play? How dull. Are we going to pretend it wasn't you loitering in the stairwell at Nuremberg? Fine. Although it would be good to know if hanging round like that is some strange hobby, or if someone is paying you to spy on me. Which is it?'

She wasn't afraid, that was obvious. Annie knew Margarete would laugh if she threatened to unmask her. The woman was used to being in command. But she also clearly wasn't used to being treated as an equal, so that was the path Annie – who was still full of adrenaline – took.

'Would that worry you? If I was spying? Because I could be. I remember you and not just from Nuremberg. Where you obviously remembered me.' Annie nodded as Margarete's eyes narrowed. 'And yet you didn't say anything then, and you haven't acknowledged who I am now. So I'm left wondering why.'

Annie held her nerve while Margarete's eyes raked over her. It was harder to hold it when she smiled.

'You learned a few things at the trial then, about evading questions anyway. All right, I'll play. Yes, I knew you were Sid Kirson's daughter. But I didn't know whose side you were on then, and I'm none the wiser now. Your father doesn't seem too sure either.'

That Sid no longer thought she believed his lies would ordinarily have been good news. But not tonight. Not if Margarete was reclaiming a relationship with her father and wielding it to take the upper hand. Not if Annie was going to follow her hunch and stop Margarete going to ground. Or find out the truth about what happened to Peggy. Which made her answer more carefully, avoiding the question *whose side* implied, and avoiding any mention of the Black House.

'Maybe we should start this again – it's all a little too cat and mouse. You're right, I am Sid's daughter, Annie. And as I'm sure you also remember, we met when you were an au pair here in 1934 when you called yourself Grete, the same name I've seen on the correspondence you kept up with my father before the war. But I'm confused now, I'll admit it. I heard the argument with Major Langley. I knew it was your intention to come to England with the captain and marry him. And yet here you are with yet another name and a different nationality and no wedding ring. It's quite the reinvention. I can't help but wonder why you've done it.'

She wasn't sure if it was a good thing when Margarete laughed.

'Oh, well done. I've a feeling you'd be a better interrogator than dear Doug, not that that would be difficult. Stating a guess as if it's a fact, not asking direct questions, waiting for me to over-fill the gaps. All right, this is fun. I'll keep playing. Let's start with him, why don't we? He's gone, which was always the plan. He was an excellent route to a passport but a dreadfully dull husband; I'm surprised I lasted a month. Being a widow is much simpler, believe me: dead husbands are far easier to manage than live ones.' She laughed again as Annie's eyebrows flew up. 'Don't be so dramatic. It's the fictional Count Kalnoky who died, not the captain. He's licking his wounds in the nasty little suburb he tried to flatten me into.' She stopped and cocked her head as Annie flinched and failed to hide it. 'That's an interesting reaction. So there's a story with you too, which I'm sure we'll get to in good time. Are you struggling at being a good wife?'

The barb was too close, too personal. Annie forgot she was trying to defuse the situation.

'That's none of your business. I'm more interested in whether this new persona means you've wiped Bormann away from your history too, or if you're still a faithful Party member.'

Margarete's face turned blank as she asked, 'Are you?' And stayed that way when Annie, who she'd wrong-footed, couldn't instantly come up with an answer and left the field open to Margarete.

'Not so keen on games anymore then, are you? No matter. I don't have time for this. I'm on my way to another event. I only popped up in here because it's helpful to have a few journalists dangling, ready to jump when I ask. Your husband's one of the pen-pushers here, isn't he? Doesn't he work on the political desk?'

Annie couldn't trust herself to do anything but nod. Margarete's smile when she asked about Harry had held a predatory edge it wasn't pleasant to look at. It didn't alter as the woman continued.

'I didn't get the chance to meet him tonight, which was a shame. But perhaps that will happen later. I'm going to the Royal Court next, to dear Sir Oswald's party. It's been such a delightful reunion, one that was long overdue. It's been such a joy to reconnect with him. And your father will be there too, as I'm sure you know. Can I assume you'll be joining him later, or are you on the other side now?'

It was a test Annie couldn't pass. She knew about the party – Sid had been full of it for weeks. There was going to be an 18B reunion at the hotel before the main dinner, and he'd bought a new suit, with the arms in the jacket carefully cut so he could make a proper salute. She had no intention of going, but she couldn't admit that and risk completely alienating Margarete. The woman would never trust her if she knew how much Annie hated all fascists. She had to leave some room for doubt.

'I hope so. But I might be very late. Harry can't leave before his boss – this is his work do after all.'

Margarete patted her arm. Annie managed not to recoil. 'And I assume you can't move without his say-so unless you want an unpleasant evening. What a nuisance husbands are. I'll try not to say that to him when we do eventually meet.'

The increasingly lively sound of the party flooded back as Margarete opened the door. She swept past Annie into the corridor and took the last words with her.

'It was good to see you again, Annie. I have a feeling we

could be useful to each other. As long as you didn't breathe in too deeply at Nuremberg. As long as your past loyalties still hold. I imagine you did some digging into me there; perhaps you've done more. But you've done enough now, don't you think? Sometimes it's best to leave the past in the past where it can't hurt anyone.'

Margarete's sudden glance at the roughly carpeted staircase was marked enough to be deliberate. Her, 'It's been quite a while since I saw your father, and I was so looking forward to meeting your mother again tonight, but I gather she's not well enough to come, such a shame,' was so unexpected it froze Annie to the spot.

She stood in the doorway of the dusty room, her whole body shaking, as Margarete turned and walked away. As her heels clicked down the stairs, the noise echoing as if a troop of SS men in black shirts and jackboots were marching in step behind her. Imagining tendrils that shouldn't have a place in the world unfurling around the woman's slim ankles with each footstep and pale shoots peeking up, waiting patiently for the light.

CHAPTER NINETEEN
JANUARY–FEBRUARY 1947

The argument started badly, and its aftershocks rumbled on long after the party.

'Why won't you take me seriously anymore? Why won't you listen to me?'

Annie had been far too rattled by her encounter with Margarete to hold her tongue. By the time Harry arrived home, overtired and steeped in cheap brandy and long after her, she was out of patience, and his inability to focus was the final spark.

'I can't keep telling you the same thing. The woman passing herself off tonight as a widowed Austrian countess was Grete, the German girl I told you about after Earl's Court. The one who was Oswald Mosley's au pair before the war and was present when Hitler came to his house. The one who attacked my mother and is far too close to my father. Her full name is Margarete Fleiss. She was Martin Bormann's secretary. She was in the bunker. I ran into her again at Nuremberg, and now she's here in England and she's up to something – I know it. If that doesn't add up to a front-page story, I don't know what does.'

She'd pressed the button that turned him pompous; the fight had nowhere to go but up.

'No, Annie, you don't, but I'm the journalist here, and I do. And ex-Nazis aren't it, not these days. It looks to me like you're trying to turn a personal vendetta into some kind of conspiracy that no one will believe. No one cares about her, except you, which MI6's lack of interest in your report should have made clear.'

Annie knew on an intellectual level that Harry didn't mean to dismiss what had happened to Peggy so callously. She knew that he didn't mean to use her failed report as a weapon. She assumed that he was still smarting from the way she'd spoken to his editor – and the dressing-down he'd apparently received because of it – and being hurt and feeling superior mattered more to him than listening. But it wasn't her intellect she was fighting him with. And his next attack did nothing to soothe her bruised heart.

'So she's reinvented herself, so what? She won't be the first German to do that – or the last. Which you should know, given how often you moaned about the impossibility of getting anyone to admit they'd been a Nazi when you were over there. And she's hooked up with Mosley again – what does that matter either? This isn't 1936; we're not fighting for the soul of the East End. Hitler is dead; the fascists were beaten. The only threat anyone's worried about these days is Russia.'

It was his dismissive tone as much as his words that got under her skin. That made her bring up the 'old Harry' again, as the version of him she preferred. The one who'd fought and written on behalf of the working man and the East End and would have leapt on anything involving Mosley. That made her deliver, 'You don't need to lecture me about Russia; monitoring them could have been my next intelligence assignment if I hadn't married you,' in a snarl that stunned them both.

I should take that back. It's not true.

But the silence stretched out too long and swallowed the moment when an apology would have mattered.

Harry slumped onto the sofa and dropped his head into his hands. 'Wow. Is that what this is really about? Because it sounded as if it's the married bit you regret most.'

Regret snapped Annie out of her anger. It was too strong a word for the confusion she felt, and she hadn't meant to throw that at him. But her, 'Of course it's not,' was too little and too late, and he shrugged it away.

'I'm not a fool, whatever you think of me. I know this house and this life isn't enough for you. I know you miss your job. But it wasn't my fault you lost that; it was your father's, and I won't take the blame. And I won't be made to feel like a villain for wanting to marry you, for offering you some kind of consolation prize that's already gone hollow.' He took a deep breath and stared up at her with eyes that were naked. 'Is that what this was for you, Annie? Because that's what it's beginning to sound like. Did you marry me because you'd run out of options?'

Yes would have been a lie, but *no* wasn't the complete truth. And the battle between those two positions ran too openly across her face.

'Oh God, you did. Or part of you did anyway. I don't know what I'm meant to do with that information.'

His head dropped again. His body crumpled as if she'd punctured him. His pain bit straight into her heart.

'I'm sorry. I'm so sorry.'

He didn't answer. He didn't look at her. He held himself as if he was ancient, as if his body was a collection of dust. Annie forgot all about Margarete. Her marriage was sitting on a fault line she could feel fatally shifting. And the only way to fix its foundations was with an honesty that could break it too. She sat down carefully next to him. She wanted to reach out and untangle his knotted fingers, but she kept her hands in her lap. Neither of them needed another rejection.

'Please let me try and explain. I was frozen when I came back from Nuremberg without the job I loved and with no chance of getting another one like it – that's the truth. But it wasn't your fault, and I'm sorry for saying it was. And you wanted me when they didn't, when I'd lost faith in myself. So perhaps marriage was the only, or the simplest, option I could see.' She took a deep breath and took his hand as he swore under his breath. She wouldn't let go of it when he tried to pull away. 'I do love you, Harry – that's a constant. I'd always imagined being your wife, but the reality of it? That's what I feared; that's what's making me sad.' She breathed a little easier as his hand stilled. 'It isn't about you; it's about the way being Mrs Garnet has closed my world down, exactly the way I was frightened it would. That's what I'm fighting against, not you. The way I'm nothing but a wedding ring to your colleagues.'

'"Married women don't get to walk through the kind of doors I want to walk through".' Harry looked away as he repeated her words back to her. 'I haven't forgotten. How can I when I live with your disappointment on a daily basis?'

He didn't say it in anger. He said the words wrapped round a hurt that allowed her to step out of her own.

'I'm so sorry for that, truly. You weren't supposed to pay for my confusion. But...' She paused, conscious she was about to step onto ever more fragile ground. 'I am disappointed in my life right now, that's true. I miss the work I was doing, but aren't you disappointed as well? The Harry I met...' She stopped as his hand started to withdraw under the threat of 'the old Harry' and started again with more care. 'Is working for the *Standard* really a good fit? Is it where you want to be? Beaverbrook has never been on the side of the working classes; if anything, he despises them. He certainly wouldn't support the kind of causes and crusades the *Hackney Gazette* would jump into, and he's a friend of Mosley's – and Margarete's. Maybe that's why you're not seeing the potential in taking another look at the fascists. He wouldn't exactly back it, would he? Maybe it's a story you could take somewhere else.'

It was a misstep, no matter how well intentioned; he read it as her trying to tell him his job. She reached for his hand again, but he shoved hers away and jumped to his feet as if she'd accused him of being the wrong Harry anyway.

'How many times do I have to tell you I'm not that man anymore? Don't you understand what the war did to me? Don't you listen? I don't care about pointless crusades, or stories that aren't stories, or righting old scores. I want to work for a paper that's solid and respected. I want a secure career. And a wife who doesn't look at me as if I constantly let her down. Thank God I at least got two out of the three.'

'Harry, come on—'

But the closing door slammed her voice shut.

No one in England will have the stomach for fascism.

Harry would have agreed with Langley's words, but Sid and the men who gathered in the parlour at Arnold Circus had already given the lie to them. So had Margarete's reappearance in Mosley's orbit. Now the first whispers of an early spring had begun to chase the bitter winter away, pulling people from their firesides and out into the open, and the lie was spreading. Not that anyone seemed to care except Annie, and she kept her fears to herself.

Harry had worked late and begun his shifts early for a week after their fight, while Annie rattled round a house that didn't need her and wondered what she was doing there. She'd packed a suitcase in the end, although leaving was the last thing she wanted to do. That was the night he came home unexpectedly early and they'd both ended up in tears. The precipice receded.

They hid away for a weekend and called it a second honeymoon. But there was no further discussion about the boundaries of Harry's new job, or about Margarete. And none at all about the shadows creeping back over the East End's streets, the ones Harry couldn't or wouldn't see.

'Your father can say what he likes about a *new and invigorated campaign*, or whatever he chooses to call it. A rebirth of fascism isn't going to happen outside his head. There's jobs again now the women are out of the workforce; some stuff is starting to come off ration. There's talk in the House of Commons about a new national health service which will mean free medical treatment for everyone. Conditions are improving – they're not ripe for a resurgence of Mosley's nonsense.'

According to her father – who Annie saw as rarely as she could – Mosley had finally beaten off the bad health which had dogged him since his days in prison. He was ready to take up the mantle of leadership again in a new bid for power at the ballot box. According to Harry, that was impossible. But it was Sid who Annie believed.

Harry worked in the city now, in the *Standard*'s office at Shoe Lane. He took the train from London Fields and the Underground from Liverpool Street to get there; he no longer walked round his old neighbourhood. But Annie did. She visited the library at Bethnal Green, and went shopping in the markets at Brick Lane and Ridley Road. She walked to Arnold Circus to visit Peggy on a regular basis. Which meant she saw the slogans and the graffiti Harry was too busy reporting on government matters to bother with.

It was the face that told her something was coming. A stencil of Mosley halfway down Commercial Road, an image she'd first seen dripping with whitewash in Cable Street in 1936, and again in 1939 when it was as untouched as it was now. This one was twice the size those had been, and it was repeated in an ugly pattern along the walls and shutters in the surrounding streets. A day or two after that, the first slogan appeared. *Hang the Jews.* A proclamation of hatred daubed in red across the front of a synagogue in Great Alie Street that took Annie's breath away. A week later, she saw another defaced in the same way in Fenton Street. By the time the first snowdrops peeked their heads through the grass in Victoria Park, there wasn't a synagogue from Commercial Road to Bethnal Green without pink stains marring its freshly scrubbed walls. And Annie – who'd wanted to believe that Sid was wrong and Harry was right despite all the evidence – was consumed with an outrage she could no longer swallow.

'How can this still be happening? Has everyone lost their memories? Does Auschwitz mean nothing? Are people really so stupid they actually want the Nazis to come back?'

Her rage came uncorked on a narrow pavement in Sander Street where two men were trying to scrub the words *Wir Kommen Wieder* off a synagogue wall using brushes that had seen too much use.

'There's a lot to unpick in that, not least why you can read German. A collective loss of memory sounds about right – or a refusal to remember or believe. As for who wants them to come back again?' The man who'd stopped rubbing at the paint to speak to her shrugged. 'The same lot who've wanted rid of us for as long as we've been here. Who'd rather have partnered with Hitler and become part of the Reich than gone to war against a leader they believed in.'

Annie watched the paint drip like blood down the wall as she tried to get a grip on her anger.

'I presume by the same lot, you mean Oswald Mosley?'

The man shrugged again. 'He's the main face of it, but there's dozen of others like him crawling round the East End and waving the fascist flag; there always have been. Whipping up another generation of idiots looking for someone to blame for their miserable lives.'

He was half Sid's age, but he was equally as bitter. And – despite what she'd said about the Nazis, which she assumed had put them on the same side – his face was filled with suspicion.

This would be a good time to go. Before he starts asking questions about me and why I'm upset, and I can't give him an answer that will improve his opinion.

That would have been the easier option. But Annie stood her ground and waited instead because that's what the woman she'd been in Nuremberg – the woman who'd sat and helped men and women find their voice and tell their pain-filled stories – would have done.

'Are you a member of the congregation here?'

The question he asked was as full of doubt as his face. He'd already taken in her blond waves and her deep blue eyes. He'd already decided she wasn't Jewish.

'No, I'm not part of a synagogue; I don't share your faith.' She answered his next question before he could ask it. 'But I'm angry this is happening, and I want to help stop it. I was there, at Nuremberg, at the trials. I collected and translated testimony from people who'd survived the camps, so that they could bear witness. I can't forget that, and I don't want anyone else to forget it happened either. And I've seen Mosley's members in action – I know how dangerous they are.'

The second man stopped working and turned around. They both drew in a tight breath that told Annie the testimonies she'd collated lived on in their blood. That the lies being told about faked photographs and dug-up graveyards, and the forgetting, were personal attacks on their lost ones.

And as soon as I tell them the truth, they could stop remembering that and hate me.

She sucked in a breath of her own and faced them with every scrap of courage she had.

'You're not going to like what I'm going to tell you next, but give me a chance, please; hear me out. I think I could be useful if you'll let me.'

It took all Annie's persuasive skills to convince Gerry and Morris – the two men who'd been cleaning the slogan off the wall – that she wasn't spying for Mosley or for the intelligence services, which amounted to the same thing in their eyes. It took all their persuasive skills to convince the rest of their group to give Annie a hearing. They managed that a fortnight after her first meeting with them in the street, although they weren't able to conjure up a warm welcome.

Beyond the fact that she was in a small, airless room behind a boxing gym, Annie had no clear idea where she was. Gerry had cloaked the whole enterprise in secrecy. He'd left her a message at the library and picked her up in his van next to a rubbish-strewn vegetable stall on the edges of Spitalfields Market. He'd driven her through a maze of back alleyways which rendered the East End's familiar landscape completely unknown. He'd said very little on the journey that wasn't an order, and his favourite word was *don't*.

'Don't ask anybody their names, or where they're from, or about their war. Anything they want you to know, they'll tell you. Don't repeat what you hear in the hall to anybody outside the meeting. Don't make the mistake of thinking we haven't been watching you since you came onto our radar, or that we'll stop.'

His manner should have been intimidating – Gerry was over six feet tall and heavy-set, and he towered over Annie. It wasn't. Annie was well aware of Gerry's bulk, but what resonated most were his hands on the steering wheel. They were spotlessly clean and perfectly manicured; they were an echo from Nuremberg. 'Survivor's hands', one of the witnesses had called them. A mark of men who'd known the dirt and degradation of the camps and couldn't stop washing it away. Gerry deserved her respect, not her fear. All the men, and the one woman, who met with her in the musty room deserved that, although they didn't seem to care if she gave it. Nobody spoke when Gerry led her into the room. Nobody smiled when Morris introduced her and invited her to speak.

'I'm here because I also have a personal story, a family that's been broken by cruelty, by men who hold evil beliefs. And because I don't believe fascism is beaten, whatever the papers and the politicians say about it dying in the bunker with Hitler. I know – same as you do – that's not true. I've seen the evidence at first hand. And I refuse to give up and give in and let the poison carry on spreading.'

Her voice sounded far thinner than it normally did, but Morris's promise that 'despite what I've told you about her father, she's worth listening to' had secured their attention, for a little while at least.

'The pain my family has suffered doesn't match your losses, I know that, but – as I imagine Morris has also told you – those losses are very real for me. I was at Nuremberg, and the shock of what I saw and heard there will never leave me. It was worse than anyone reported. When the charges were read out and the films and the photographs were shown to them, the men in the dock rolled their eyes. They weren't sorry; they weren't repentant. They didn't believe any of their actions were wrong.' She paused to let her audience absorb that.

'Göring dismissed everything as Allied propaganda. It won't surprise you to know that my father says the same thing. I've heard him and his cronies deny the camps and the murders. I've also heard him say that he wished the full extermination plan had worked and that Hitler had rid the whole world of its Jews. He's lying for public consumption when he talks about the camps not existing. He's not lying about what he wished had happened to you. People who think like him hold life very cheaply – I've seen that for myself too.' She paused again as jaws clenched and fingers curled. She'd been going to tell Peggy's story, but that was for another day.

She carried on, choosing her words carefully, grateful when tempers stayed quiet. 'Mosley is back and hungry for trouble again, even if the press is ignoring him. My father says his supporters are growing in number, and I believe that. And I think...'

She stopped, suddenly unsure of herself. What she was about to say was a hunch and no more. There was no evidence to support it. MI6 presumably thought it carried no weight. She'd barely articulated the idea to herself, never mind spoken it aloud.

'What? What do you think?' Morris was watching her as closely as any trained interrogator she'd worked with, scrutinising her face, weighing her up. 'You've got this far, which is further with us than most *shiksas* – especially one with a father like yours – would get. We're listening, so speak.'

Annie glanced around. The smiles caused by his use of *shiksas* had wiped years off her audience. Their faces might be lined and marked by the war, but nobody was much older than her. She held on to that as she nodded. They didn't mean her any harm. The worst thing they could do was dismiss her.

'Okay. Then what I think is that old ties are being reignited. There's a woman here in London passing herself off as Austrian, but she's actually a German, and she was close enough to Hitler to be in the bunker until the end. She knew Mosley before the war too, and she kept in contact with him and my father for years before it began. She's dangerous and capable of violence. And I've no concrete proof, but it's possible that she's brought funds with her to support Mosley's cause. She might also have brought orders for a new campaign. And if she's here, maybe there are others here too.'

It was said. Annie waited inside a silence that felt never-ending. Until the room erupted.

'What do you mean, orders? From Hitler? From out of the bunker?'

'What do you mean by funds? And what is she financing?'

'How well did she know him before 1939? Do you have any idea what they're planning?'

It took both Morris and Gerry to calm the group down. And all Annie could do when they did was admit she didn't have any answers.

'I don't know, I'm sorry. But the point is, I could try to find out. Margarete thinks – or she'd like to believe – I could be an ally, so I could pretend to be that. If they're planning another Cable Street, or something bigger that might set the scene for Mosley to get back into a position of power, I could try to find out what that is. And if you knew exactly what was coming, you could fight it a lot better.'

She hadn't won the room over. She could hear the muttered, 'Why should we trust her?' she was definitely meant to hear. She knew the only way to counter that was to stand up for herself.

'Morris told you about me, but I've done my homework too. I know who you are. You're the 43 Group. You formed last year when you realised the Blackshirts were a real threat again. When you realised the Jewish community here was in danger, but the government are blind to it and the police don't care. When it dawned on you that the terrible tragedies your people have suffered, that you fought a war to stop, don't seem to matter the way they should to the wider world.'

She had the room now. No one was muttering.

'And I know this because my father knows about you. The fascists have doubled their security round Mosley because they think you'll try to infiltrate their meetings in order to get to him.' She waited for the shouts of 'Good' and 'Let them worry' to die down. 'Don't misunderstand me. They're taking precautions, but they don't think you can do it – they don't think you're organised or brave enough to stand up to them. But I do. I've read the survivor accounts – I know how deep the scars run. And I'm on your side, but I can also pretend to be on theirs because they know me and I understand how they think. How many of your fighters can say that?'

'Why must we still have fighters at all? Why do we have to keep reminding everyone how dangerous fascism is? Why can't they face up to the truth for themselves?'

Annie couldn't see who spoke, but she heard the exhaustion and the anguish. Even if the questions had been directed at her and not at the room in general, she wouldn't have dared try to answer. She sat back and let Morris step in.

'You'd think it would be easy for people to do that, wouldn't you? You'd think one Auschwitz would be enough to convince the doubters, or the ones who don't seem to care. You'd think the details of one massacre – Babi Yar let's say – would do it. And yet there were hundreds and maybe thousands of camps and ghettoes – the trials told us that. There were undoubtedly more massacres and ravines packed with bodies than we currently know about. But the problem with the truth?' He paused as his face aged. 'It's everywhere and nowhere. There's as many people looking away as there are looking at it, same as they did the whole time Hitler was in power. There's as many twisting the facts to fit their own ends. Whatever the war achieved, it hasn't got rid of the divisions – there's still *us* and *them*. And now it's over? There's no world fit for heroes to come back to. That promise was built on sand. What we've got instead are broken cities packed with people who are tired and hungry, who've been tired and hungry for years. Who want a scapegoat. Who'll follow the men like Mosley who'll happily provide one as a stepping stone to take him to power. Sounds familiar, doesn't it?'

He paused again, his gaze sweeping the room. But this time his eyes were on fire.

'Well not this time. Not again. Let Mosley have his fools and his easily led. Let him build another thug-filled army. We've fought him before and we'll fight him again.' He glanced across at Annie and suddenly grinned. 'And we'll win by using every weapon.'

CHAPTER TWENTY

MARCH 1947

He's genuinely in love with his wife. What a novelty. Although it does make him a complete bore.

Margarete watched Harry staring moodily into his whisky and contemplated running a red lacquered fingernail across the back of his hand just for the fun of seeing him jump. She decided to let him languish for a while instead. He was clearly the type who responded better to a kind heart and a listening ear than the promise of a kiss – or more. The caring confidante wasn't her favourite role – especially if she had to listen to him talking endlessly about how besotted and confused he was by his wife – but it was a part she could play if she had to. Especially as she hadn't yet decided if it was Harry or Annie she wanted to pull further into her web, or whether it might be both. And he was so delighted to have an audience for his woes, it was very easy for Margarete to tune out and focus on the Annie she was interested in.

Annie hadn't appeared at Mosley's Christmas party, but what had interested Margarete more than her absence was Sid's reaction to it. He'd been deeply uncomfortable when their host – who'd become very eloquent on the importance of family now

Diana had presented him with another son – had pointed out that neither his daughter or his wife were present. What had been clear that night was that the Kirsons were broken, which didn't surprise Margarete. Sid had a hole where his heart should have been. The ease with which he'd decided to rid himself of his wife – the ease with which he would have replaced her with Margarete if she hadn't cured him of that foolish notion – had proved that. And now that he was even more trapped and bitter and twisted, he was even less of an attractive package.

Margarete presumed Mosley only kept Sid around because he enjoyed the slavish devotion, to him and to the cause. That hadn't flickered one jot, despite the spell of imprisonment the man talked about as if he'd been held starving in a rat-infested dungeon. His complaints had bored her almost as much as Harry. Most of the men at the Royal Court party – including Mosley – had referred to themselves that night as 'the 18B Boys' and they'd worn their internment as a badge of honour. They'd also been under the impression that Margarete would be as impressed with their bravery in surviving it as if they'd arrived wearing diamond-encrusted iron crosses. In truth, she'd been so sick of them all she would have happily locked them up for good and swallowed the key. But the daughter was a different matter.

According to Sid, Annie not only suspected that Peggy's 'unfortunate tumble', as he'd taken to calling it, had been deliberate, she blamed him and Margarete. Not that Margarete was apparently meant to be concerned at that. 'She's far too under my thumb to go throwing accusations about.' He'd revelled in the boast, but Margarete doubted it was true. She'd seen a spark in Annie that suggested a fire she kept carefully hidden from her father. That was why she'd made what turned out to be an appropriately pointed reference to the staircase and to Peggy at the pub. Annie needed to know who held the strings and the power, especially if Margarete decided to make use of her. Which was becoming a more interesting possibility, despite the red flags: Annie certainly had more potential as a conspirator, if she could be controlled, than clumsy, ignorant Sid. Which was why Margarete had thrown her little grenade at Mosley's dinner.

'I saw your daughter briefly in Nuremberg – did she tell you? I'd been dragged in by the British, who were trying to get information about dear Martin, who I truly hope escaped and is somewhere far sunnier than Berlin. I did wonder though, wasn't it difficult for you, knowing she was there? Listening to the Jews and collecting their lies? Mosley can't have been happy.'

That had hit home. Sid had shifted in his seat as if the chair was on fire. He'd looked positively ashen when Mosley referred to the absent Annie as 'one who needs to be returned to the fold'.

'She had her head turned there, I'll not deny it. She was overexcited at the prospect of travelling, and they bombarded her with propaganda she was too young to deal with. But that job's done with and she's home now, among decent people. And she's married, which will sort her out. We'll have her back in the family very soon.'

Sid had papered over the awkwardness with more skill than Margarete thought he possessed. His reference to *family* – which he'd made with a sweeping gesture round the room while ignoring the fact his wasn't present – had won him a round of applause. But he clearly didn't know his daughter. Margarete had managed not to laugh at the idea of Annie being sorted out by a husband, and had bombarded Sid with flattery instead. He'd latched on to her suggestion that she might be able to help Annie to see clearly again, like a child being patted not punished for breaking a toy. Three brandies later, Sid had confided in her that Mosley regarded Annie's defection to the intelligence services as a blot on his copybook, and that pushed him even deeper into her pocket. Which was where Margarete liked everybody to be. Including Mosley.

He'd greeted her reappearance bearing Hitler's final words and – some of – the diamonds as if she'd brought him the Holy Grail. He would have fallen into her arms and her bed if Diana hadn't snapped tight on his leash. Not that Margarete had particularly wanted him there. She knew exactly how to control him.

'I have no interest in being in the public eye, which is why – outside these circles – I've refashioned myself as Austrian and a widow. It's much easier to fade into the background that way.'

It would also stop Doug trying to follow her, which he sworn he'd do to the ends of the earth in a particularly unattractive and melodramatic moment when she'd told him she was leaving. Not that Mosley or anyone else would ever know about Doug. No one was allowed to have levers over her.

'I'll pull what strings I can from the sidelines of course – Beaverbrook is proving very malleable as a start, and I'm sure we can both identify other targets with suitably generous cheque books and platforms. I'll be as useful to you as I can. But the cause is what matters, not me, and the stage has always been – and always will be – yours.'

Mosley had loved that almost as much as the recognition from his dead leader. A woman specifically there to do his bidding without stealing the limelight, which Diana had a tendency to do, was his dream. He was fascinated by the way Margarete had reinvented herself, and by her talent for plundering wealthy bank balances. And Margarete was thoroughly enjoying herself too. She didn't mind Mosley thinking he was in charge. Being a woman who was elusive and unavailable once the donation was secured or the favourable write-up was published suited her very well. Although it was nice to have a new challenge, which Harry was proving to be. He'd been simple to snare, but he hadn't fallen blindly into her hands.

Although he will if I want him to, and he'll feel terrible for doing it too, so that adds a layer of fun.

'I've spoiled everything for Annie. I've stuck her in a home I'm not even sure she likes and turned her into a housewife, which was the last thing she wanted to be.'

Margarete stopped congratulating herself on her conquests and slipped on her sweetest smile as Harry's repeated mentions of Annie finally caught her attention and Harry grew increasingly morose. He hadn't been an interesting study; she was hardly surprised his company was dull. She'd spent a fortnight learning his habits – which had turned out to be very predictable – before she selected the most promising of his after-work drinking haunts to let him discover her in. The Crown in Hanging Sword Alley was a midweek favourite. The pub was tucked into one of the tiny roads London specialised in: a narrow lane overcrowded with peeling, ancient buildings Margarete thought would have benefited from a direct hit. It was as dark inside as out and divided into cubby-like booths into which journalists and lovers could disappear with their secrets. And run by a landlady who didn't care what trade Margarete was plying as long as she ordered enough gin and lime.

Harry had appeared on his own at exactly the same time as he'd wandered in on three other evenings, completely unaware that Margarete had slipped into the corner of a booth and was waiting for him. It hadn't been difficult to catch his attention – Margarete had never met a man who could resist a woman holding an unlit cigarette to her red lips. It hadn't been difficult to persuade him to sit down and keep her company either: she'd used the tried and tested trick of a faithless companion who hadn't appeared and waited for it to ignite his chivalry. But trying not to yawn while he talked had proved far more of a challenge.

'I don't think she wants the same life as I do.'

Margarete shook herself and managed not to roll her eyes as Harry trotted out yet another unhappy husband cliché. At least he wasn't a drunk, which she'd assumed might be the case, given how often he visited different pubs and her experience of journalists in general. Instead, Harry was wracked with guilt and misery and even lonelier at home than he looked in The Crown. And it was easy to invent late deadlines to explain his absences, not that Annie apparently noticed.

'It's such a relief to be able to talk about this. The men at work... Well, they'd rip me to pieces for caring about her so much and tell me to find a mistress. Honestly, you've been an absolute lifeline.'

Margarete patted his hand, keeping her nails carefully sheathed. She didn't take hold of his fingers – she imagined he would buck like a frightened horse if she did. She'd known within half an hour of accepting a light that Harry was the last man on earth who would take his colleagues' advice and find solace in another woman's bed.

But Annie doesn't need to know that.

Margarete sipped her gin and made soothing noises. Annie was a puzzle, and puzzles were a problem. Her ties to the intelligence services were a potential problem too. Harry had made it clear that she no longer worked for them, but he'd also made it clear that Annie was bored. And Annie, even on brief acquaintance, was too bright to be bored.

Which means I either do what her father would thank me for doing and bring her back to the cause. Or – if that's not a path she'll easily go down – I'll be forced to break her, and use her, before she goes after me.

The more Margarete considered the option of bringing Annie into the fold – however it had to happen – the more she liked it. 'I'm more interested in whether you've wiped Bormann away from your history too, or if you're still a faithful Party member' had definitely carried a challenge. Margarete wasn't unhappy about that – she was hardly someone who shied from a fight. She wasn't unhappy either that she wouldn't have to seduce Harry. He was too earnest. He would end up falling in love with her, which was always a nuisance. So not his lover, but she could be his friend. She could make sure this version of her that he'd met was seen sharing confidences with him in discreetly public places. She could let gossip do its work. Because what Harry didn't understand was that adultery wasn't the issue: he'd already begun to break his wife's heart.

Margarete barely knew Annie, but she recognised her type. She sensed she was the kind of woman who believed loyalty lay as much in the mind as the body. That she'd never forgive Harry for opening his heart to another woman, even if that heart was full of her. Which meant photographs from a seedy hotel bedroom weren't necessary. Photographs of him pouring his heart out to a pretty woman hanging on his every word would do the trick instead. As to what she'd use the pictures for? Margarete hadn't decided yet. Perhaps to blackmail him, perhaps to blackmail her; perhaps to blackmail them both. She'd learned from Goebbels, the master of manipulation and propaganda, that the point was to collect the evidence first and decide what to do with it later. Making sure the targets did her bidding was what mattered the most.

Harry had finally stopped talking; he was waiting for Margarete to speak. She had no idea what he'd said. She leaned forward, patted his hand again and blinked as if he'd talked her to tears. Which in a way he had.

'You poor thing, what a mess. Why don't you tell me more about Annie – who sounds lovely by the way – and let's see if we can't fix this together?'

He beamed and sighed and thanked her. He started all over again.

CHAPTER TWENTY-ONE

JULY 1947

Annie had become two creatures; on some days she was three. And each of the worlds she lived in had become harder to hold within its own boundaries.

'Can I talk to you, Dad? You see I've been thinking, and it strikes me you might be right about some of the evidence I had to handle at Nuremberg. We weren't always told where the photos had come from or who'd made the films. So it's possible that some of it could have been manufactured, the way you said. I wondered about it at the time, but, well, the men I worked with weren't the kind of people you could say things like that to. And I know I was angry with you when you brought the possibility up. But I've been confused since I came home, and I've been worrying whether I did the right thing over there. The way you asked me to do when you talked about good men.'

Annie's stomach had almost leapt through her throat as she'd poured that out in a rush to Sid. She hadn't been sure she could hide her hatred of him deep enough to do it. She'd expected him to question her sudden change of heart and trip her up. Instead, he hadn't questioned anything. He'd been so eager to have her back on his side, he'd swallowed her declaration with all the ease of a pint of his favourite Eagle Stout. The relief had momentarily made her forget what a dangerous and deluded liar he was, and what exactly she was walking back into.

Annie had gone to meet her father as he walked home to Arnold Circus from one of his meetings – something she'd never done before – in order to find a way back into his world, and his trust. It was the last thing she wanted to do, but she had no choice – despite how useful she'd promised the 43 Group she could be as their agent, in reality she was a long way out of the fold. Sid talked about Mosley constantly but his eulogies focused on the past: he was guarded about specific details when it came to the man's future plans. And he wasn't a fool. Annie knew he'd grow suspicious very quickly if she suddenly began to visit more often when he was at home, or professed an ardent belief in his politics after distancing herself from them for so long. He hadn't forgiven her for running away from Earl's Court in 1939, never mind for serving at Nuremberg. He wasn't a man who gave up his grudges lightly.

But I've got him now. And once I've got what the 43 Group need, I'll play him again and get to the truth about my mother.

She'd certainly caught him off guard this time. Choosing a spring evening and persuading him to walk up to the bandstand with her to watch the sun setting in a coral-tinged glow the way she'd loved to do as a child had softened his edges. He'd become almost gentle as the sunset turned the clouds into fields of lavender and she'd reminded him that he used to tell her stories up there about his own childhood. Once she'd shared her doubts about the trials with him, he'd dropped a hand onto her shoulder that didn't feel like its usual deadening weight. That had been unnerving. As unpleasant in its way as the lecture he then treated her to about how sorry he'd felt for the soldiers 'who'd lost their lives in a war that should never have been fought, to save people who shouldn't have been saved'. And about the 'brave SS warriors who have thankfully gone free, who are Hitler's natural successors'. His relish at that possibility had made her shiver far more than the cooling evening breeze. As had his plans for her, even though they offered the way in she wanted.

'You need to shed the misinformation that dreadful job fed you with. I'll arrange for you to join one of the fortnightly book groups we've set up to discuss Mosley's writings and his latest ideas. That will give you a better understanding of what this post-war world needs.'

Unfortunately, that was as far as she was able to push him.

'What is that though, Dad? What's Mosley going to do given the British Union's been banned for years now? Is he going to start a new party and run for election?'

His soft edges had solidified then. 'Why so keen all of a sudden? Why the sudden interest in information that's not for you? You've caused me problems with your attitude in the past, don't forget, and I'm not going to stand for a repeat of that. Smaller steps will do. Let's see how you do with a book club or two. Let's see you prove yourself. Then maybe I'll let you attend a dinner with the great man himself, if you're really serious about playing a part.'

It was a repeat of the days when he'd told her which rallies she could and couldn't attend, and he was no easier to budge on the rules he set up for her now than he had been ten years earlier. The small steps he wanted led nowhere but frustration. Annie had no idea how long he would keep her at arm's-length. She had little stomach left for his company. She couldn't get close to Margarete. She could see her mother fading further away as Sid colonised the flat, but there was nothing she could do to unseat him. Most of the policemen in the East End were his friends and his political allies – they'd laugh her out of the station if she took her accusations there. And then they'd take her tale-telling to Sid, and God knows where she – or Peggy –

would be left then. And the whole time she was juggling how to keep her father on side, the 43 Group was waiting for her intelligence-gathering to bear fruit and growing equally as paranoid as the Blackshirts.

The Group guarded its workings as closely as the fascists did. Membership lists didn't exist. Each of its sectors operated as independent fighting units and were organised with a military precision that would have impressed Mosley. Their ability to fundraise would have impressed him too. Their slogan, *There's Still a War On*, drew thousands of pounds in support from the Jewish shopkeepers, factory owners and businessmen whose families had been torn up by Hitler's murderous war machine. There were no lists of the donors either. And Annie knew almost nobody involved in the operation except Gerry and Morris, whose trust she knew would ebb away if she couldn't deliver anything more concrete than what they already knew. That as spring slipped into summer, Mosley was mobilising.

The whole East End knew that. The two camps started circling each other as the days grew longer, baring their fists and their teeth on street corners. Waiting as the sun started to heat up the pavements for an explosion that hadn't yet revealed its shape, despite the attempts each side made to infiltrate the other which extended beyond Annie's manoeuvrings. An explosion nobody wanted to stop; whose coming collided her two hidden worlds with her third.

'Where have you been?'

Harry was already sitting at the table in the sitting room's nook as Annie rushed in, his hat and coat flung over the sofa. He was an hour earlier than he said he'd be. Which meant he was early enough to realise that there were no cooking smells waiting to greet him. That the kitchen surfaces were as undisturbed as the rest of the flat. That the only thing out of place was the sound of his fingers drumming against the veneered table top.

'Book club.' The answer was out of Annie's mouth as quickly as the copy of Daphne du Maurier's *The King's General* appeared out of her handbag. 'I didn't expect you home so soon, so I stayed chatting when we were done.'

That was true. Even if the actual book she'd spent the last two hours discussing was a first print of Mosley's *The Alternative*, a description of his vision of a united Europe that had made her brain scream. And her post-meeting conversation had been a fruitless attempt to ferret out which synagogues were on the hit list for the slogan painters on the following Friday night.

She bustled into the kitchen as Harry muttered something about how busy she was for a woman who was always complaining she had nothing to do. She pushed the door shut to drown him out and sank onto a chair.

How did we get to this point?

She might as well have asked herself how many times a week that thought tripped her up. *This point* was him waiting for a meal as if it was his right and acting as if he was her guardian. It was her carrying props to hide her life behind. It was him coming home early when he said he'd be late, as if he was trying to catch her out.

Perhaps because he thinks you might be having an affair. The same way you think he might be having one.

She had to hold on to the table to steady herself. She couldn't remember how to breathe. All the doubts which had been buzzing around her head for the last few weeks suddenly swarmed into a dark cloud and bit. She was certain about her own fidelity, but there were questions hanging over his.

'I saw Harry having dinner in Rules last Tuesday with a woman who was the spit of that American actress, Veronica

Lake. Does he have some glamorous sister hidden away you've never mentioned?'

'I saw Harry coming up Tottenham Court Road the other day with the most stunning woman. Does she work at the paper as a secretary or something? I'll be keeping my Gerald on a tighter rein if she does – nobody needs bombshells like that turning their heads.'

It was poison of course – Annie kept telling herself that. Malicious jabs from the wives of colleagues Harry had beaten to a promotion or a front-page headline. Annie had brushed them off and continued with the dull dinner parties where the gossip was served up with each course as if nothing had bothered her. But she hadn't mentioned the woman to Harry. She couldn't. Not after she'd matched up the date of the dinner at Rules with the night he'd come home particularly late, trailing the ghost of a perfume Annie didn't wear. Not when she'd caught the same lingering scent on his coat a week later. Not when the thought of confronting him, of catching the wrong look in his eyes, of hearing a too-long hesitation while he groped for an answer was impossible to contemplate.

And now here we are, at this horrible point. Keeping secrets from each other and digging a hole that will swallow us if we don't mend it.

Annie had almost lost count of all the things she kept hidden. She hadn't said a word about the 43 Group to Harry. She hadn't mentioned Margarete since he'd dismissed her as unimportant. She hadn't told him she was attending Mosleyite meetings again as a spy. Or that she was burning to confront Sid and Margarete about Peggy and terrified of the consequences. Once she hadn't mentioned one thing, it had become harder to mention the other. Now her life was slipping so far away from Harry's, it was if they inhabited separate planets. And that, she realised as she gazed at the closed door between them, wasn't a situation she wanted at all. She needed him; she was battling so many fronts on her own. Their marriage wasn't within a mile of perfect – both of them knew that. They'd fallen into roles that – if she was honest with herself, never mind him – Annie doubted made Harry any happier than they made her. But he'd been her first love, and he still was. And when their defences were down long enough for her to properly see him, she knew that he loved her too. Which meant the perfume had to be nothing, a chance brushing against someone in a bar. And the affair she was imagining him caught up in had to be as mythical as the one he was imagining for her.

So this has to be fixable. If I trust him. If I tell him the truth. If nothing else, he's a newspaper man and the 43 Group is an incredible story. Even he must see that.

The Group believed her suspicions about a reinvigorated fascist campaign with new money at the bottom of it, even if she hadn't as yet found the proof. And Gerry and Morris were exservicemen like Harry. He'd listen to them; he might even be able to persuade Morris to give him an interview about Mosley's reawakened threat to the East End and beyond. That had to be a scoop worth having.

And working on it together could be the adventure we promised ourselves. A new version of the story we planned to uncover in 1939. And that would be a stepping stone to Margarete's, the first one we need to get justice for my mother.

'Harry, can we talk? Can we properly talk?'

Annie wiped her face and pulled herself together. She ran back into the sitting room, ready to rediscover her husband and her marriage. But Harry's hat and coat were gone. And so was he.

CHAPTER TWENTY-TWO
SEPTEMBER 1947

'No man's left behind, same as in the war. Remember that. Whatever happens, no matter how hard they come at us, we look after our own.'

The streets which had begun to heat up in the middle of June were at boiling point by the end of August. And the centre of the storm every weekend could be found at Ridley Road. The market there dated back to the 1880s and had been one of the East End's liveliest melting pots for as long as Annie could remember. The long, straight street ran down the side of a smoke-belching railway cutting. On Saturdays, its soot-grimed and one-storeyed shops were joined by dozens of stalls whose owners were as likely to speak Yiddish as cockney. And from 5 p.m. onwards – when the stalls closed and the political groups competing for the community's soul could claim their street-corner pitches ready for Sunday morning – Ridley Road prepared for battle.

The meetings had begun to descend into brawls from the first sunny weekend. Annie slipped away to monitor the situation there on as many Sundays as she could, although it wasn't an easy manoeuvre. Sundays for the combined families were firmly about Sunday lunch and that was firmly about 'refusing to buckle under once again to the Germans', as some of the more excitable newspapers put it. Rationing hadn't ended with the war; if anything, it had got worse, as part of Britain's food stocks continued to be diverted to feed Germany's far hungrier population. But Sundays were sacrosanct and patriotic, and the meal – which involved endless favour-swapping with the butcher to secure any bit of meat that wasn't corned beef or horse – moved between Dolly and Annie on a revolving basis.

There were no lunches hosted at Arnold Circus, which was one relief: Peggy wasn't up to it, and Sid wanted no more to do with Dolly and Jim than they wanted with him and never went to their house, or to his daughter's. Which meant that once a fortnight, when she was in control of the day from her little kitchen at Eleanor Road, Annie was able to disappear.

'Why don't you go for a pint?' released Jim and Harry from the house once the syrup-soaked suet pudding and custard was cleared away. 'Why don't you both have another little drop of port and relax while I wash up?' set the two mothers napping. If Annie timed everything right, she could carve herself out a couple of hours when nobody noticed she was missing. And two hours in Ridley Road was more than enough to see which way the wind was blowing.

The weapons had worsened. That was the first thing Annie noticed as Morris sent his fighting contingent out from the back room of the Robin Hood pub on Shacklewell Lane. In June, the men had come armed with knuckledusters and anger. Now it was early September, and those men had tangled with Mosley's men so many times, they were Ridley Road veterans. They carried broken light bulbs in their pockets and coshes made of lead or copper piping concealed in their sleeves. They brought razor blades wrapped in wads of paper. They'd learned the art of the 'flying wedge' – a triangular formation which could shape up and slam through a crowd before the crowd saw it coming. And their anger had flamed into a blind fury against the black-shirted thugs the police refused to arrest, although they had no problem sweeping up Jews, as the numbers needing bail money on a Sunday night proved.

Annie wasn't allowed to fight – none of the women who supported the group were. But she followed the brigade towards the market anyway. The first stops were always at the corners where the exhausted men who'd been holding meetings throughout the night to keep their pitches safe from the fascists – who would seize them the second the spots were left empty — were slumped against the walls waiting to be replaced by fresher muscles. Nobody pretended to discuss the finer points of politics; slogans and insults were all that mattered. 'Down with Mosley!' rose in a tidal wave and crashed into the answering bellow from his supporters, who were already filling the narrow streets, calling on their leader to 'Save England from its plague of Jews!' Each cry added more flames to the pyre. Violence filled the air. The crowds swelled in number, swelled again with their rage. Faces merged, became a blur of burning eyes and screaming mouths and hatred.

I could get trampled here. I could disappear.

Ridley Road was even more dangerous than Cable Street had been – the men facing up to each other had come to inflict injuries; some of them were wild enough to do worse. There was nothing she could do except get in the way. Annie dropped back, looking for a side street with less teeth to watch the struggle from.

'He won't come. No matter how loudly they shout for or against him. This is all a bit... animalistic for him.'

Annie whirled round. Margarete was standing behind her, dressed in an immaculate powder-blue suit, smiling at the fists flying in front of her as if she was a guest at a garden party.

Annie hadn't seen her in months. She was so startled by the encounter, she couldn't gather her scattering thoughts.

'Who won't?'

Margarete's laugh grated across her whole body. 'Oh, Annie, really? What a silly question. I expected better from you, especially after all Sid's glowing reports about your newly discovered devotion. Mosley of course. He's not going to cheapen himself by attempting to shout over this rabble. That's hardly going well for him over there, is it?'

Annie followed Margarete's nod to the pitch nearest to where she thought she'd found shelter. Jeffrey Hamm, one of Mosley's key lieutenants, was perched on top of the armoured car everyone knew as 'the Elephant', shouting through a megaphone at the top of his lungs. Nobody could hear him. His words dropped into the baying crowd at his feet and were lost.

Margarete sniffed. 'It's hardly dignified is it, this street brawling? It may break a Jewish bone or two, which is all to the good, but it's not the way to spread the message to the right people that we're back and ready for leadership.'

Disdain dripped from her voice. Annie – who didn't know if Margarete had followed her on purpose and didn't believe in coincidences – kept her tone neutral.

'And which right people are they?'

Margarete smiled as if she was watching Annie carefully making her way through an exam paper. 'That's a more interesting question, but then you're an interesting person, aren't you? One minute you're in Nuremberg weeping over the Jews and wondering how your father could still put on a black shirt. And the next? You're trotting back home so enamoured of the cause again, Sid's been singing your praises. When he was wavering last Christmas – when you didn't turn up at the party and made a fool of him – I offered to help bring you back into the fold, but I'm not needed now apparently. You've seen the light on your own. Even Mosley's stopped questioning your loyalty – and Sid's by default.' She paused and looked out at the street and its flying fists again. 'And yet here you are, apparently flip-flopping again. Keeping company with the wrong people. Skulking in alleyways. Trying not to be seen. And here I am, wondering what you're doing.'

She let the menace hang. Her threat was unspoken. It was as light as the whisper of autumn scenting the breeze, but as surely as autumn, it was coming.

She knows I've been working with the 43 Group. She's setting a trap for me.

Annie's stomach was a nest of butterflies. It didn't matter how Margarete knew she'd been living a double life; it only mattered that she did.

And if she scents blood, I'm finished. I won't survive my fall.

Annie linked her hands behind her back to stop them shaking and ignored her dancing stomach.

'And what if I'm wondering the same about you? You're hiding in an alleyway too.'

Margarete took a long pull on a cigarette that she'd managed perfectly efficiently to light herself before she answered. She let the menacing tone drop.

'You're a tough one, I'll give you that. All right, why don't I throw you a little something and then perhaps you'll do the same. I'm here to watch him, among others.' She nodded to the platform and Hamm, but she looked back at Annie on the word *others*. 'I'm weighing people up, assessing their skills, or their lack of them. I'm deciding who's useful and who's simply taking up space.' She left a short pause Annie wasn't foolish enough to fill. 'And yes, I'm watching you too, which is the question you wanted to ask. And I have so many questions myself.' Her smile was almost flirtatious, it made Annie's skin crawl. 'But I think we should meet and continue getting to know each other in better surroundings than this. Over tea perhaps, or a drink, which could be fun. Why don't I find us somewhere lovely and send a message via your father. I'm sure he'll be pleased we're growing closer, even if he seems to think – foolish man – that he can manage his affairs without me.'

Margarete didn't wait for Annie to answer. She stamped out her cigarette under her Cuban heel and moved away through a crowd that – despite the chaos – instinctively parted for her.

Foolish man. I'm deciding who's useful. I'm watching you too.

Margarete's words had too many layers for Annie to unpick in an alley surrounded by shouting and breaking glass. They carried the past and the present and the future in them, and a promise that Margarete was in charge of all three. That was frightening in itself. But that wasn't what flew Annie's hand to her mouth.

She's shifted her appearance again. It's not just me she's watching or meeting. She's dragged him into her games too.

She groped her way to an abandoned vegetable crate and sank down onto it as her legs started shaking. Annie had been listening not looking when Margarete appeared. It was only now that the woman had walked away that she registered anything beyond the impossibly out-of-place pastel suit. Margarete was wearing a new hairstyle: a wave of curls that tumbled over one eye, exactly like Veronica Lake. And with that realisation, Annie's other senses woke up and everything else about Margarete came properly into focus. It wasn't only her hair that had changed. The faint scent Annie had detected wandering through the air when she appeared wasn't the promise of autumn.

She did that on purpose too. Kept it light so I wouldn't place it straight away. So it became more of a game.

She closed her eyes and breathed deeply, and there it was, the scent, unravelling. Jasmine and roses. Beneath them the richer notes of sandalwood. The perfume she'd last smelled lingering like a lover's kiss on her husband's overcoat.

CHAPTER TWENTY-THREE
SEPTEMBER 1947

The Savoy Hotel was a London landmark, famous for its luxurious rooms and legendary parties, and the watchword for discretion when discretion was needed. Margarete had slipped into it like a second skin, which was why she'd chosen it as a venue for her meeting with Annie.

Bless her, how hard she's tried. And how utterly out of place she is.

Annie's forest-green fitted coat had sharp shoulders and a bow at the hip. Her flower-sprigged dress had a similar drape at the neck. She was wearing rose-pink gloves and a matching petal-covered cap which Margarete suspected from its less than pristine edges that she'd trimmed herself. It was all perfectly nice. It was probably the height of fashion in the East End, but there was something about it that was a little... Margarete hunted for the right word and finally landed on *provincial*. It certainly wasn't good enough for the Savoy.

Nobody who frequented the hotel's restaurants and bars wore the narrow cuts Annie's budget clearly restricted her to. Unlike the drab and fashion-deprived women who Margarete blamed for making London so dreary, the Savoy's female guests lived in a world entirely free of coupons and constraints. Their coats and jackets were spun from curves and peplums and soft shoulders and hugged rather than encased the body. Their skirts swung like church bells from cinched-in waists. The women who frequented the Savoy were used to being showered with gifts and attention. Which was why the hotel suited Margarete far more than it would ever suit Annie.

She fluffed out her full skirt as she watched Annie taking her in. Her outfit had been as carefully chosen as Annie's East End ensemble. Her lemon-coloured hat circled her face like a halo. Her matching nipped-in jacket was paired with a navy blue circle skirt in a light and dark copy of Christian Dior's wonderful Bar Suit. She'd positioned herself so the soft cream walls and gold-and-powder-blue chairs had become her personal backdrop. So that the room's antique mirrors perfectly reflected her elegance. The effect was intended to make Annie wilt. It was even more entertaining when she didn't.

She's got backbone; she's an exact match for the role I intend her to play. It's a shame she doesn't have sisters.

It was equally as amusing when Annie took a tight breath and adopted the look of disdain women who coveted but couldn't afford Dior's New Look always took refuge in before they declared its excessive use of material was unpatriotic. Margarete saved her the effort.

'Here you are and looking so charming. Simplicity does so suit you English roses. Do come and have a seat. I've ordered you a cocktail.' She pushed a frosted glass towards Annie as she sat down. 'It's a gimlet. I've ordered it the way I drink it. Gin and lime and no syrup.'

To her credit, Annie managed not to wince beyond a slight narrowing of her eyes as she took a sip of the sour liquid. But she didn't speak either, beyond a polite, 'Thank you.'

Margarete – who'd decided to give Annie a little rein – leaned forward as if they were about to share a confidence and continued with her cheerful tone. 'Isn't this a lovely place? It's my favourite haunt in the city – always so many interesting men to flirt with. But not today of course; today will be about you and me and what a treat that is. So many questions, so much to learn about each other. Where shall we start? Shall we trade one piece of information for another? Shall we play swaps?'

Margarete imagined her tone must sound grating – it was certainly grating on her. But however Annie felt about it, she didn't react. And hers remained far more pleasant than her words.

'We could do that. Or I could ask the questions and you could answer, and we could stop this pretence that we're friends.'

It was hard not to clap. Margarete had to give Annie credit again. She missed nothing – including the telltale perfume, if her slight sniff was anything to go by – which was the reason why Margarete had leaned forward. She raised an eyebrow as if to say, 'All right then, why don't you?' and waited for Harry to be the opening gambit – or Peggy. And Annie impressed her again when she took a completely different tack.

'What are you doing in England? Why have you involved yourself with Mosley again? What's your plan?'

The directness was the afternoon's second surprise. Margarete hadn't expected to hear Mosley's name so quickly or any mention of a plan. She took a sip of her drink and considered her response. It wasn't time to take the gloves off, but it was time to stop dancing around. She waved to the waiter to freshen their glasses while Annie sat back. She could afford to let the fool have a little rope.

'How wonderfully precise. I didn't know anybody in England was capable of going straight to the heart of the matter. All right, if you're in the mood for plain speaking, why don't we turn this around? Why don't you tell me all the theories you've been storing up about me? I imagine there's a few of them.'

Margarete re-draped her skirt as she spoke, smiling to herself as Annie unconsciously mirrored her movements. Sipping her own drink, smoothing down her narrow dress. Smiling as if she was the one holding the power. Behaving exactly as Margarete knew she would in her eagerness to show off whatever story she'd concocted – too grateful she had someone willing to listen to take care.

'If that's what you want, fine. I don't have all the pieces, so I won't pretend that I do – I don't know anything about your family or how you ended up working for Bormann, or why you stayed in the bunker for as long as you did. But I can hazard some guesses.'

She paused as if she was asking for permission. Margarete pushed her on with a nod.

'I assume your father – like mine – always had strong leanings towards fascism and towards Hitler. There were a lot of links between the British Union of Fascists and the Nazi Party before the war, and I know – from the letters I've seen between you and my father – you were one of them. After that?' Annie's shrug was an attempt at nonchalance that told Margarete she'd barely progressed beyond broad strokes. 'You must have been a trusted Party member to stay in the bunker to the end, even if the account you gave in your testimony was too bland to tell us anything useful.'

'And this is all history and rather dull to be honest.' Margarete plucked the slice of lime from her drink and bit out its centre. 'Don't you have anything better?'

Annie's poise slipped, which was Margarete's intention. She switched from certainties to speculation and onto her back foot. And, without realising it, started to sail closer than Margarete expected she would to the truth.

'All right. I think you were under orders to come here and make contact with Mosley, or whoever might have replaced him. I think you brought funds or instructions, or both, out of Germany for him.'

Something – perhaps Margarete's complete lack of response, which she suddenly realised could be damning – stiffened Annie's courage, and her voice grew stronger.

'Reinventing yourself as a newspaper patron plays into that – it gives you access to influence, and you're a better public face to deal with than Mosley. People who don't want to be seen talking to him could use you as a conduit. Nobody would think twice about them keeping company with a pretty, rich woman. That's why you hate the thugs who gravitate to him and the street battles. You don't like the image it creates; it's presumably not the one Hitler would have wanted. Oh my God.'

Annie stopped and sucked in a deep breath. She didn't give Margarete a chance to marshal herself or jump a step ahead.

'Seeds scatter everywhere – they get carried by the wind. You're not the only one, are you? You're not his only agent. I bet there's Germans like you worming your way into positions of influence everywhere. Keeping the flame alive. Waiting for the next depression, the next economic collapse or disaster that'll lead to chaos. That'll let you leap into the empty spaces where governments have failed and left behind people frightened and vulnerable to your poison.'

Annie's eyes were wild. It was as if she could see fields of soldiers ready to be cropped like wheat the moment they were needed. Waiting to be sewn and resewn until the battle for control of hearts and minds was done.

And she's horrified at the prospect; she's not one of ours at all. Which will make things harder for her, not for me.

Margarete broke into a round of applause and snapped Annie out of her trance.

'Bravo, that was quite a performance. We'll need to revisit *poison*, but you've put more of the pieces together than I expected you would. And your understanding of how women fit into this? That's helpful – that's something for you to remember.'

Whatever response Annie had been expecting, it clearly wasn't praise. She looked drained, although she ignored the drink Margarete pushed towards her.

'But why?'

Margarete knew what Annie meant, but she wasn't about to make anything easier. Not after *poison.*

'Why what?'

'Why this path? Why fascism when you know the horrors it's led to? Why would you want to keep such a destructive force alive?'

Destructive. Horrors. Margarete sighed. She'd had enough. Annie was as tiresome as she was clever, and she needed pulling back into place.

'How disappointed your father would be if he could hear the nonsense spilling out of your mouth. How badly it would reflect on him. Fascism isn't a *destructive force.* It's a cleansing one; it's a power for good. Why do I have to explain that to you? And of course there's loss, but what of it? Rebirth can't happen until the dead wood is gone. Pure blood can't flourish until the parasites are purged. Weren't you brought up to know that?'

She sighed again as Annie grimaced and began arguing, but it was better to let her have her say and hack out her dead wood too.

'I wasn't *brought up;* I was bullied. Why don't you say what you mean? Not *purged* but murder, something you know plenty about. It's what you tried to do to my mother.'

Annie picked up her drink and drained it in one gulp, clearly waiting for Margarete to contradict her. She didn't – it was far more pleasurable to say nothing. Which Annie couldn't do.

'There's the truth, in your silence. Fascism can't exist without violence, can it? That's the true heart of your creed.

Eliminating opposition, eliminating "other". That's what my mother was to you. That's what the camps and the ghettoes were about. That's why the thugs you pretend you want rid of matter as much as the rich men and the politicians. You need the disenchanted and the bitter to join you because you need an army fashioned from hate.'

Margarete sat back and drew out a cigarette, although she waved away the waiter who sprang forward to light it. Clicking the flame gave her something to do. Re-educating lost disciples wasn't her job, although she was determined now to cure her boredom by teaching Annie a hard lesson.

'Goodness, what a speech. Your mother wasn't a problem for me, you silly girl. She was a problem for your father. He'd have been happy with her dead, but then he'd have set his sights on me, and that was frankly disgusting. I pushed her, yes, but I saved her life. You should be thanking me.'

The air oozed out of Annie in a shuddering breath that spread her limply across the chair. Margarete gave herself a second or two to enjoy her victory, and then she pressed home the knife.

'You never worked that out because you don't have a clue about the real world. All this concern about the camps and the ghettoes… If only your government had cared half as much. They knew about our plans for the Jews – and how well-oiled the machinery was – by the end of 1942. Our intelligence proved it. But what did they do? Did they bomb Auschwitz and Belsen? Did they mount rescue campaigns? No. Your parliament stood up like the brave men they were and observed a moment's thoughtful silence. Goodness, how that made Hitler shiver.'

It was interesting watching Annie try to rally; it proved she had a spine. Not that Margarete was about to indulge her. 'Don't argue with me – I don't care what you believe. You've surely realised nobody wants to talk about the camps anymore, that everyone would rather forget they existed. As for our *army fashioned from hate*, as you so melodramatically put it...' She shrugged. 'You're right. They're useful, but they're not the only way to power. They're certainly not the best one. People like me – and you – are.'

You pushed some life back into Annie's body; it alerted her that a blow was coming. So Margarete took the gloves off.

'The street fighting has served its purpose. It's spread fear. It's spotlit the communities who have no part to play in our new England. But now it's time for the next phase. The chaos you're talking about. That requires a helping hand, which will be supplied. And when it comes? Then we'll need men with vision and money, leaders with the power to build better nations where right-minded people thrive. And we'll need ambassadors, not thugs, to build on that success.'

Annie stiffened. She clenched her fists as if she was trying to fight the future. Margarete let her have her illusions, for a minute. She let her make her little speech. Annie's voice was hoarse; Margarete suspected it was choked with tears for her mother and for her father's duplicity that she refused to let fall.

'Leaders? What, like Hitler and Goebbels? Like Göring and Himmler? Men who brought your country to its knees and took refuge in suicide instead of facing up to their terrible crimes? You want more men like them to persuade people that fascism works? Good luck with that.'

Margarete folded her hands to stop herself slapping the insults out of Annie's mouth.

'You're very fond of words like *terrible*, aren't you? Especially when you don't know what you're talking about. The Führer was the bravest man in the world. Please God we do find men like him and Goebbels again – they understood how the world should be run. Which is a lesson you clearly still need to learn. And you will when I'm your teacher.'

How things had developed wasn't ideal. Margarete would

have preferred delight and co-operation from the start, although she'd guessed before Ridley Road that Annie had been playing a double game and the odds were stacked against that outcome. Instead, she was going to have to break Annie to her will. It wasn't a perfect scenario, but it could be done. And she had the girl now. Annie's cheeks had lost their roses. *Teacher* had shackled her.

'What are you talking about? What are you going to teach me?'

'The value of loyalty for one. Something that will reap huge rewards when you stop resisting what you were brought up to do and start working with us.' Margarete shook her head as Annie tried to speak again. 'Enough. I don't need to hear what you won't do. Or how committed you are to the 43 Group, who, yes, I know about. You'll betray them quick enough when I tell you to do it, which I will. It's time to see sense, Annie. You're never going to rise through their ranks, are you? And you want to rise somewhere; you want to be noticed. We both know that. This life you've ended up with isn't worthy of you. A girl who was bright enough to go from a factory to a ringside seat at Nuremberg, stuck tending house with no prospects? That's such a waste, and what comes after it? A heap of babies and watching your life disappear?'

That's such a waste had been perfectly judged, despite Annie's confusion. It had hit a nerve and made her tense up. Margarete had guessed it would be the right sore to pick at. She'd also guessed it would reignite Annie's fight, so she let that flare one last time.

'No. I won't listen to this. My life mightn't be perfect, but I'm not one of you. I'm not a fascist, and I'm finished with pretending I can stomach any more of this. You're evil. You can't make me do anything; you can't make me betray anyone. Don't contact me again, do you hear? Don't think you can involve me in your twisted schemes.'

Annie started to get up. Margarete stopped her with a claw-like grip on her arm and a savage, 'Sit down now, or you'll be sorry.

'That's better. You'll stay until I say otherwise, and you'll listen. You were right about why I'm here; you were right about a lot of things – I came to England at the Führer's command, to carry out his orders. Orders that mean more to me than my life or anyone else's. And I'll use whatever resources I can to fulfil them. Which is all you are to me, Annie: a resource.'

Annie froze.

Margarete released her grip. 'Do you think I'd put up with your insolence if I didn't have some use for you? You have a pedigree that makes you valuable, Annie my dear, although it needs quite a polish. Our people are under surveillance and under attack, and they, quite rightly, trust nobody outside a tightly defined circle. Which you're not only part of by reason of your father, you've also been pushing yourself back into it so you could play the spy.' She nodded as Annie's face fell. 'You didn't think of that, did you? That by putting yourself back at the heart of the movement, you'd be considered as a girl with a bright future again? Well, you are now. Which is good news for me. And as for your little indiscretion with the Jews? That will be wiped away by a narrative that makes you into our spy, not theirs.'

'No. Don't do that, please.'

Margarete shrugged. 'It's already done; they'll never let you inside their meetings again.'

She paused as Annie curled in on herself and decided to take a slightly softer tack when the girl rubbed her reddening eyes and asked – in a far less prickly voice – what was meant by 'resource'. Her fight was gone, which should mean she was open to coaching.

Margarete remembered to smile. 'The best kind. Men will fill the leading roles as they always do, but as you've already learned, pretty women can hold so much power. Doors open to us if we know how to manipulate the men holding them. If I've one criticism of the Reich it's that almost nobody realised that fact – women were kept in the background, and that was a mistake I won't be repeating. Our new leaders will have wives who aren't simply decorative; they'll be politically astute, soaked in our ideology, trained in diplomatic skills, fluent in more than one language. Partners capable of winning trust and finding out secrets, not well-dressed hangers-on.' She stopped as a face floated back from the past. 'If you'd ever had the privilege of meeting Magda Goebbels, you'd know exactly what I mean. She could have been so much more than she was allowed to be.'

'What has any of this got to do with me?'

Margarete had to give herself a shake. She'd been so wrapped up in outlining her blueprint for the future – one not even Mosley knew about, although he had a crucial role to play in it – she'd almost forgotten Annie was there. It was irritating to have to spell the connection out; she'd hoped Annie would see the logic for herself.

'Everything. You're going to be one of those wives.'

Annie's instant, 'You're out of your mind,' was rude, but Margarete chose to put it down to shock and let it go. The girl would come round one way or another. Margarete was, after all, holding all the cards. She stopped the rest of Annie's tirade as it reached, 'And never mind the rest of the madness, I'm already married.'

'Are you though?'

That shut Annie up.

'I mean technically you are, but are you really committed to it? Is he? You're definitely wavering, and he's not as trustworthy as you thought, is he? It's a lingering scent this one, not my first choice but effective. So you know I have him dangling. Oh, and your father too – obviously he's in my control given the little secret about dear Peggy we share. I'm pulling the strings here,

Annie. One way or another, your marriage will end, and you'll do what I tell you. It's important you understand that. Do you?'

Annie shook her head. She was as white as the walls, as small as a child. Her hands were clawing at each other as if wasps filled them.

Margarete leaned forward again and let her perfume lap round the two of them. 'Then let me be clear. I can break relationships as easily as I can break bones. Nobody is safe if you say no to me. Not Harry. Not Sid. Not your mother, but you already know that. You've seen me in action.' She paused and let that image sink in. 'I can get to anyone, and nobody can get to me. You don't have an ally, Annie. You don't have anyone in your corner. So it's best to do the sensible thing and listen.' She'd won – that was obvious from Annie's barely hidden sob. But she pressed the point home anyway. 'Do I need to draw up a bigger list than the names I've mentioned? I can. There are a lot of lives I can ruin if you say no. But you're not going to say no, are you?'

Annie's eyes filled her face. Her hands went limp.

Margarete patted her arm as she slowly shook her head. 'Good girl. That's much better.'

She got to her feet and waved for the cheque.

'I'd sit here for a bit if I was you. I imagine this has come as a shock – it's quite a change in your fortunes after all, but I'm sure you'll see the sense, and the pleasure, in it once you've had time to adjust to the idea. And you will adjust. I'm certain of that. I'll be in touch shortly – there's a lot of arrangements to be made, and someone I want you to meet. You'll be riding high, my dear, trust me on that. Even Vivien won't be able to compete in the new hierarchy, not now she's got herself engaged to a man who's spectacularly dull. In the meantime, be sensible, won't you? Don't tell anybody about our conversation – don't think I won't know if you do. And don't ignore my next summons. We've got work to do.'

She waited for Annie to nod before she picked up her hand-bag. It had all gone better than she'd expected in the end, and it was essential to keep things that way. The last thing she needed was Annie fooling herself she had any other choice except to follow orders.

'Perfect. It would be such a shame if you slipped up and crossed me and I had to teach you another lesson. It would be very unfair on poor Harry.'

CHAPTER TWENTY-FOUR

SEPTEMBER 1947

'Come with us. Get into the car. Don't make a fuss. Don't draw attention.'

More orders, more *don't*s firing across her like bullets. Annie was barely a dozen steps outside the Savoy when she was swept up. The two men – one silent and one talking – were dark-suited and unremarkable and appeared out of nowhere. They fell into place one on each side of her, tucking hands under her elbows that were very far from protective, their bodies forming a wall. They didn't identify themselves, not that they needed to. Annie had spent enough time around intelligence officers to know how they carried themselves when a prisoner needed moving – as if they operated inside an invisible cordon of power. And she did as she was told because she'd also seen the alternative. The quick pinch to the sides of the neck. The swift jab to the temple. The victim unconscious before they had a chance to open their mouth and dropped into the waiting car or cell as if they were ill or drunk. Nobody ever noticing – or not enough to intervene.

She sat between them in the back seat of the car unable to see past their bulk and out of the windows. Neither man spoke again. Annie knew better than to ask questions. She also knew where she was going even if she didn't know why, and that events there would play out along a timescale she couldn't influence. She focused instead on her breathing, trying to lower her speeding heart rate. Trying to stay in the present and not think backward, to where images of Harry and Margarete had formed like a frieze in her mind, or forward to whatever was coming. Trying not to lose herself inside the madness that was *You're going to be one of those wives.*

One of her minders leaned forward to speak to the driver as they sped into the interrogation centre at Kensington Palace Gardens, allowing Annie a glimpse of the white terrace but nothing else that she recognised. The car pulled up alongside an anonymous grey door round the back of the furthest building, a long way from the street. It wasn't until she was bundled out of the car and into one of the windowless basement rooms that she fully understood where she was. Although knowing that didn't help. 'Sit on that side of the desk,' put her into the prisoners' camp and completely altered the air.

You've done nothing wrong. They've no reason to hold you.

That didn't help either. Annie had been on the interrogators' side of the desk too many times to be fooled by notions of innocent and guilty: she knew how elastic those concepts could be. She readied herself as much as she was able. She folded her hands in her lap to stop them shaking. She hooked one foot round the other to steady her knees. She waited for the circling to begin, for the traps to reveal themselves a second too late. But the man who sat opposite her, holding a folder bearing her name, got straight to the heart of the matter.

'How long have you been working with Margarete Fleiss?'

The question was half expected, but Annie had presumed the verb would be *known* not *working with.* She forced her face to stay blank; she held her hands tight – she had no intention of reacting to those words or to any others. She'd seen outbursts of emotion go badly wrong before.

She resisted the urge to swallow and shook her head. 'I'm not working with her.'

She might as well not have spoken.

'Did the relationship resume when she was brought to the Palace of Justice, or when you visited her Nuremberg lodgings?'

It was one thing to hold her face still; it was another to slow down her pulse. Annie's mind began racing, trying to sift through all the things she'd done that could have been misconstrued, but she kept stalling at *resume*. She swallowed hard this time – she couldn't stop herself – and hoped he wouldn't spot the white lie.

'I never met her at either of those places. She'd left the city before I went to the Guest House.'

Her words floated away again as he turned to the next page.

'How have you kept up the relationship with her which, according to your report, began in 1934?'

Her report had been read, but now it was being used as a weapon against her. Annie wondered why she'd expected anything else.

'I haven't kept it up because nothing began then. I barely knew her; I was a child. We met briefly for a few hours. And I only knew her as Grete, the au pair.'

Yet another page turned as Annie began scrabbling round her life, wondering how much of it had been scrutinised. A considerable amount, it seemed.

'But your father knew her, which suggests a deeper family connection. They met at a number of Anglo-German Fellowship dinners in London between 1935 and 1939, some of which were presided over by Sir Oswald Mosley, and they kept up a regular correspondence.'

Annie briefly considered telling him what she'd learned about Sid and Margarete's relationship, but she knew he wouldn't believe her. She stayed silent as he started removing papers from the folder and pushing them towards her.

'This is a record of you meeting with Fräulein Fleiss at a party on the fourth of December 1946. This is a record of you meeting with her in an alleyway off Ridley Road on the seventh of September this year. You met her again today at The Savoy. Which is why I'm going to ask you the question again. When did you start working with her?'

His tone hadn't shifted from bland but – despite how powerless she was supposed to feel – Annie's blood began boiling. Nothing about her situation was fair. She'd done everything she could to warn MI6 about Margarete, but their first response was to get the facts wrong. Langley had dismissed her concerns; so had Harry. And yet here she was, her not Margarete, sat on the wrong side of the table and being accused of working with a Nazi based on two encounters she hadn't asked for and a meeting she hadn't wanted to attend. The injustice of it was an insult, and she'd had enough of staying quiet while other people misused their power.

'I'm not working with her; I hate her. One of those times she came to London, she attacked my mother, which I bet isn't in your file about her because it was my father who ordered it. You're looking for a pattern that doesn't exist. I had no idea she would be at the party; she surprised me at Ridley Road. I met her today under duress. So forgive me if I fail to see how three meetings in ten months adds up to me working with her, especially when I've been trying to do the complete opposite and keep my distance or bring her to book. The same as I have with the rest of Mosley's men. My father included.'

Her voice bounced round the room – she'd made no attempt to soften it. And it made no more impression on her interrogator than anything else she'd said.

'We suspect there have been more meetings than these three. You have attended Mosleyite book club sessions – which are political gatherings in everything but name – on a regular basis. Fräulein Fleiss attended those too.'

Annie was about to protest that she'd never seen Margarete there, when he reached into the folder again and pulled out a photograph.

'And when she wasn't meeting with you, she was meeting with your husband. Given what we've observed, I'll assume that was not with your blessing.'

Annie's fight drained away as she stared at the picture. She thought she was going to be sick. This was far worse than a lingering perfume and Margarete's taunts. This was proof that she'd lost him. The picture was a grainy shot, snapped across a bar, but the couple bathed in candlelight were clearly Harry and Margarete. She was leaning towards him, her hair tumbling like a waterfall. He was leaning towards her, one hand stretched out across the tabletop. Nobody would have seen the image and captioned it as colleagues.

Her interrogator passed over a second picture. 'In case you aren't sure.' Their hands had met in this one; they were looking straight into each other's eyes.

'There are more, if you'd like to see them.'

Annie had to dig her nails into her palms to stop them clawing his face. Whatever this was, she was done with it.

'I don't know what you want from me; if it's tears or outrage, you'll be disappointed. This is what Margarete does – it's what she's best at. She traps people, and then she uses them. That's what she's been doing with me; I assume it's what she's doing with Harry. And she's quite mad, if you haven't already worked that out. She's working on a plan to rebuild Hitler's failed Reich and establish it all across Europe, including here and apparently – even though I'm not a fascist and never could be – she's planning to turn me into a perfect Nazi wife to help her with her scheme. Which wouldn't be that hard to believe I imagine, given my background, and I have to agree to go along with it even though it's insane, or she's going to destroy my family. She's also going to do that if I tell anyone and – given that she seems to know everything I do – I probably already condemned everyone I love the instant I walked in here.'

Annie ran out of breath and words. She stared blindly at the photographs, her eyes burning. Her edges dissolved as all the months trying to find a purpose, of trying to straddle different worlds, of thinking she could beat Margarete, came crashing down.

And why would he believe me any more than anyone else has? Whichever way you slice it, I'll be the one who pays.

She rubbed her face; her shoulders slumped. She pushed the pictures away.

'I've nothing more to say. I've told you the truth. I've been doing that all along – trying to explain that we won the war but we didn't beat fascism. That it's alive and well because of fanatics like Margarete. Trying to get justice for my mother when no one cares what happened to her. And maybe you've finally woken up to the idea that Margarete is dangerous if you're asking questions about her, so that's something. But I'm not *with her*, whatever you're trying to prove.'

'I know. I'm sorry, Mrs Garnet. We had to treat you like a suspect – we couldn't take any chances. But I believe you, and it's done and time to get you out of here. I apologise for the distress I've caused you.'

His sudden shift from a blank face to an almost-smile and a certainly softer tone took Annie so much by surprise, he had to repeat, 'It's done,' a second time.

He hurried round the table and offered her an arm as she got shakily to her feet. She didn't take it – the impulse to scratch his eyes out hadn't gone. She did allow him to guide her through a second door at the back of the room, up a spiral staircase and into an office with a thickly carpeted floor and a pair of cushioned chairs. She accepted his offer of tea and biscuits, although she didn't stand when he left and a second man entered. When he introduced himself as Alan and asked if he could call her by her first name, Annie shook her head. She'd had her fill of being polite.

'I understand, and I'll add my apologies, which I hope you'll accept as sincere. My officer is satisfied you're telling the truth, as am I, but I will confess, Mrs Garnet, you're not an easy woman to pigeonhole. As I'm sure you've now realised, we've been watching you as part of our investigations into Mosley and his associates and your activities lately – hopping from one side to the other – have been, shall we say, rather blurred. They've caused us some doubts about your loyalties we didn't want to have. Can you shed a bit more light on what you've been doing?'

Annie could, but she had her own questions to ask first. 'Yes. As long as you can assure me that you're taking Margarete seriously. That I'm not wasting my time here. Because the lack of interest in my report before now suggests that I am.'

'Which is something else I need to apologise for.' Alan picked up one of the folders from a desk that was far tidier than Langley's. 'This is what you're talking about, I think. The one from eighteen months ago, which took far too long to reach the right person.' He opened the folder and pointed to one of the many comments written in red pen across the typed pages. 'Here, this was what sparked one of our clerks into flagging it up: Hitler sneaking into England in 1934. The idea sounded so absurd, I'm afraid that put everything else you'd written into question. But apparently a woman in the village had also reported seeing him at the time – she'd been out very early walking her dogs and caught a glimpse of him through a car window. That wasn't followed up either – for the same reason I assume – but the clerk who was eventually passed your report remembered an older colleague mentioning it as a strange story, and he went digging.'

'I thought it had been ignored.' Annie passed the folder

back and closed her eyes briefly as she remembered all the doors she'd shut by writing it. 'I had to reveal who my father was to get the story out. I lost my job because of it.'

Alan coughed and – for the first time since Annie had sat down in his office – he looked less sure of himself.

'Which was unfortunate. We could have used your talents on any number of projects. We could certainly use them now.'

Annie put her cup down before she spilled tea on his expensive-looking orange-and-blue rug. She knew what he was about to ask, which meant he needed to know what had already gone badly.

'You asked me what I've been doing, why I seem to have been "flip-flopping" as someone else put it. I was trying to help the 43 Group get intelligence to use in the fight against Mosley. I didn't do the best job of it. Margarete's already identified some of them, and I'll struggle to keep the rest of the names back from her. I may not have the skills you think I have.'

Alan passed her a pad of paper and a pen. 'If you write down who you're most concerned about, I'll see what protection we can put in place, although I can't promise it will help. The Group hasn't got a lot of faith in British intelligence, which is on us.'

Annie wrote down the names, hoping she was doing the right thing. She doubted Morris and Gerry would thank her, but she couldn't leave them and their loved ones to Margarete's whim. And it wasn't as if she would be welcomed back at their meetings.

'You want me to really work with her, don't you?' She shuddered as Alan nodded, although she wasn't surprised. 'Then I suppose it will help that so does she, although she had a very different plan in mind for me. Maybe it's time I told you about that.'

Annie ran through everything Margarete had told her and added Peggy's story as proof of how serious the woman's threats were. It took Alan a moment to gather himself when he heard the whole story. When he did, Annie, who was now utterly exhausted, let him talk without interruption.

'There will be justice for your mother, I promise you, although that can't be our priority yet. As for Margarete's plan, it's deluded in the extreme. I can't see how it'll get further than her imagination. However, that doesn't make the danger to you and your family any less real, and I won't ignore that, I promise you that too. But we need you, Annie, in the real world, not in her fantasy one. We know Mosley is planning some kind of a relaunch, but we can't get anyone close enough on the inside to find out the scale of it, which is what's worrying me. What you've told me ties in with other rumours we've picked up – that there's Nazis crawling out of the woodwork all over Europe, and it seems Mosley, presumably with Margarete as his guide, is helping to form a network that would stretch too wide for any one country to police. We need the names of these contacts, and we need to stop the network forming. Which is where you come in.'

Annie stared around the room, at the portraits of Prime Minister Atlee and King George and wondered how soon it would be before they were forced to put the country on a war footing again. It was both unthinkable and all too possible if people like Margarete got their way and began rebuilding armies.

Or maybe there won't be a war; maybe that won't be needed. Maybe there'll be a gradual takeover instead that we sleepwalk into.

That was unthinkable too – and even more possible.

'I was convinced in Nuremberg that she'd brought funding and instructions with her out of the bunker to pay for this operation. Nothing has happened to change my mind about that, and when I suggested the idea to her, she didn't deny it. But I still can't prove it's true.'

Alan's face – which Annie wouldn't have been able to describe as young or old – grew grey and weary.

'We can't either. But Captain Collins – Doug – who is hopefully now a much wiser man, has admitted she likely came to England with the means to leave him almost at once. He confirmed she had a small velvet bag she wouldn't be parted from or let him see. But it's all supposition.' He pinched the bridge of his nose and shook his head, as if he was coming to a decision. His sigh told her it wasn't a good one. 'I'd like to say you have a choice in this, but that's not true if you want her stopped, and I think you know it. Arresting Margarete now wouldn't keep your family safe. It would leave so many trailing leads and carry so little chance of a conviction, I'd never get clearance to do it. Leaving her be is the worst option, but it's our only one. We'll have eyes on you; we'll pull you out if things get too rough. But we'll be putting you back into the middle of a nasty crowd, one that's hurt you, one you've done your best to separate yourself from. I'm truly sorry about that.'

Annie was sorry about that too. The thought of associating with Mosley and his supporters on a closer level than she already had made her skin crawl. Sid's friends had worsened since the war – they dragged their anger round like chains. The language they used to describe the East End's Jewish communities had grown even nastier. The language the men and women at the book club used was the same. Their faces turned thick with hatred the instant the word *Jew* was mentioned, and they used that like a signpost to turn down some very dark alleyways. And now that she knew what he'd planned with Margarete...

'It is horrible, you're right, but I'll do it. I'll do whatever's needed to bring her and my father and the rest of them down. But we can't underestimate Margarete again. She's cold and cruel, and so fanatically dedicated to the cause, she could carry armies on the back of her beliefs.' Annie stopped, looking for the right word to describe the woman, but only one word would do. 'She's dangerous, Alan. She's really dangerous. And whatever Mosley's planning, I guarantee she's planning worse. I can feel it.'

Alan nodded, but he paused before he answered. The pain Annie had been pushing away since she saw the photographs came flooding back when he did.

'I know that now. I'm glad you do too. Please God it will help keep you safe. But what about your husband? Does he have any idea who she is? Does he understand the mess he's caught up in?'

He didn't. That became clear from the fight they fell into when Annie finally stumbled exhausted through the front door and Harry stormed out of the sitting room to shout at her.

'Where have you been? It's almost midnight; I've been imagining all sorts. What in God's name have you been doing till this time?'

All Annie wanted to do was to fall into bed, but Harry had worked himself up into a state that, if she was honest, her disappearance had justified, in terms of his worry at least, but not the level of his rage. He didn't give her a chance to speak – he looked at the outfit she'd chosen hours ago for the Savoy and exploded.

'Okay, I get it. I'm the fool here. Who is he? Who have you been meeting all tricked up like that? I knew you were up to something, but an affair? That's low, Annie. That's really low.'

Annie put a hand on the banister to steady herself. She'd been running on adrenaline all day. Holding her emotions in check, pushing away fear. Facing blackmail and threats. Spinning between the certainty that she was in danger and the possibility that danger might be worth the risk.

And looking at pictures of you staring into the eyes of another woman and throwing our lives away.

'Don't you dare.'

Her humiliation and her fear and her rage at the day distilled into a single burning point. It was no surprise Harry took a step back.

'Don't. You. Dare.'

The repetition, the deliberate snap of its syllables and the pauses between them pushed him another step further away. Annie removed her hand from the wood before her fingernails scored it.

'You're accusing me of having an affair? Oh, that's rich, that's poetic. When you're the one coming home smelling of a perfume that's definitely not mine. When you're the one holding hands in public with another woman.'

He blanched then. He started fumbling over denials she had no interest in.

'Don't lie; don't humiliate us both. Two of your colleagues' wives saw you with her. I've seen photographs of you with her. But that's not the worst of it.' She stared at his white face and wondered if she could ever love him in the same way again. 'You don't know who your new "friend" is, do you? You've no idea.'

She'd wrong-footed him – he'd been expecting more accusations. He slowly shook his head.

'Do you remember Countess Kalnoky, the fake Austrian widow paying Lord Beaverbrook for access to his ear? The woman I told you after the Christmas party was actually the Nazi Margarete Fleiss?' She swore as he frowned and muttered something about not seeing the woman that night. 'But you could have been more wary, couldn't you? You could have thought twice if a strange woman approached you. I told you she was good at reinventing herself, and now she's done it again. She's changed her hairstyle and changed her perfume, and she's made a puppet of you. It's *Miss Dior* by the way, the perfume, if you're tempted to buy her a bottle. Although you've probably got plenty on your coat she could use if she runs out.'

Harry leapt in the second Annie stopped to draw breath. His voice was shakier than hers.

'Annie, for God's sake slow down. What's this got to do with the countess? What's Miss Dior got to do with anything? You're not making sense.'

'Really? That's your response? When I'm the only one who's been making sense all along, but nobody's been listening!'

She started shouting so loudly the next-door neighbours began banging on the wall – and stopped as quickly when she screamed at them to shut up.

'I'm talking about you and Margarete Fleiss! The Nazi from the bunker who's the same woman as the fake countess and the German au pair from Moseley's house. The woman who's seduced you. Who's used you to blackmail me. And if you don't believe me, ask the intelligence services. They're the ones with the photos – that's who showed them to me.'

Harry slumped so fast his shoulders hit the wall. He shook his head. He kept shaking it while he spoke. He sounded as if he was talking to himself.

'No, no. That can't be right. Her name's not Margarete; it's Alina. She's Polish, not Austrian or German. She's a singer so she can't possibly be a countess – that would be ridiculous. And she'd never blackmail anyone; she wouldn't have that in her.'

'What an angel she sounds. No wonder your head was so easily turned.'

Harry stared up at Annie as if he'd forgotten it was her he was talking to. He didn't seem able to focus.

Annie pushed past him. Her legs were too tired to hold her; her heart was too bruised to look at him. When he finally pulled himself together and followed her into the sitting room, sinking into the chair furthest from the one she'd chosen, Annie could barely speak again without shouting.

'You do admit to meeting her then?'

He nodded. If Annie had had any credit left in her, she would have given it to him for not denying it.

'Yes, but I had no idea who she really was. I met her for lunches – and drinks. For dinner once. But that was all, Annie. I swear it. She didn't seduce me; there's been nothing like that.'

If he'd hoped that information would help, he'd never understood his wife, or not as well as Margarete did. *Nothing like that* meant very little to Annie.

'But you talked to her, didn't you? You discussed me and our marriage with her?'

She heard him take a breath and say a slow *yes*; she heard him understand. She'd stopped trying to look at him.

'I am so sorry. I was flattered, that's the truth. We got talking one night in a pub, and she seemed to care about the problems I was having, so I told her we were struggling. And I told her that I'd pushed you into marriage and you'd—' He stopped as Annie's head came up. He finally started to think. 'I told her things I had no right to say. That's the real truth. I opened what should have been private. I thought I wasn't betraying you because we never slept together. I didn't realise how wrong that was.'

He stopped, but Annie's skin was so thin she couldn't speak; she was sure it would tear if she tried. Harry wiped his palms on his trouser legs and started again, his voice growing shakier as the truth continued to dawn.

'What have I done? Why is she blackmailing you? Why did she go after me in the first place?'

Annie closed her eyes, wishing she could leap forward to the point where Margarete was in prison and Mosley was finished and she and Harry were...

What? Over and done? Mended? Trying to put things right?

She had no idea which of those options she wanted, but she knew she couldn't fight everybody. She forced herself to look at him, to look for the husband she'd loved. Unfortunately, that Harry seemed a long way away.

'You asked what I'd been doing, so I'll tell you. But you'd better believe me this time.'

She led him through the maze of the last few months, starting with the slogans and the 43 Group and ending with her interrogation. She included Margarete's plans. She didn't allow him to ask, 'Why didn't you tell me before now?' although he tried. She didn't have the space in her to let him feel betrayed. She refused to accept his certainty that Margarete could never control or destroy their marriage.

'She thinks she can, which is the issue, and you helped her get to that point. She targeted you to get a hold over me, and for the fun of it of course.' It was hard for Annie to keep the contempt out of her voice, so she didn't try; she felt a little better when he shrank from it. 'She collects men – none of you can resist her; you jump the second she clicks her fingers. She knew you'd be as stupid over her as the rest.'

She paused to rub her stinging eyes. But then she stopped blinking and let the tears flow. If Harry understood nothing else, he needed to see how deeply he'd hurt her. And how much danger he'd put them both in.

'Annie.'

He stayed where he was. If he'd moved to her side and tried to touch her, Annie would have left the room. He said it again, attached to a desperate *please* before she could find the strength to look up. There was some comfort in the fact that his face was as tear-streaked as hers.

'I'm so sorry. I wish there was a better way to say it, but I am. I've been full of my own importance. I've done everything wrong. I didn't listen when you told me how much your job mattered, or how you weren't ready to get married. I didn't listen about Margarete. I never guessed for a second that a stupid flirtation would lead us here...' He stopped. Rubbed his hands together and swallowed. Reached out towards her; thought better of it. 'I didn't think at all. I was afraid you'd leave me if you had other options, and that's a terrible thing to admit. I should have walked away when she first approached me; I should never have discussed you.'

He paused. Annie said nothing: everything he'd said was true.

'And I can't tell you not to do what this Alan wants, can I? I can't tell you it's too dangerous and ask you to step back?' He nodded to himself as she shook her head. 'And I can't keep saying sorry if there's nothing solid behind it.'

There were so many accusations Annie wanted to hurl at him; there was so much pain of her own she longed to release by inflicting pain onto him. It was when she held back, when she stayed silent, she knew she still loved him. But trusting him was a different matter, and Harry knew that too.

'We've been working against each other, and that's my fault, Annie. I fell in love with a clever woman who was full of dreams, but I stopped seeing them, and I stopped listening. Maybe that was the war's doing, and maybe it's also time to stop using that excuse. I do know—' He stopped and drew a deep breath that steadied his voice. 'I do know it felt safe being that man who wanted a carefully held-together life, but the trouble is I don't think I like him very much. He's been afraid of the world since he stepped into a lifeboat, and that won't work for us, will it? Me trying to fence myself – and you – in. That'll end us. And I know I've no right to ask you anything, but could you help me find a way back to being the old Harry you married, do you think? And could you let me be on your side? Could you let me help you, as a sounding board if nothing else, while you work out a way to beat Margarete? No promises more than that? The rest kept for another day?'

He meant it – Annie had no doubt about that. She also knew there was a fight coming, for her safety and for his. For tolerance and compassion. For a better world than the one which had been plunged into darkness by a creed that couldn't be allowed to regather its strength.

And I'm only a small cog in the battle, but a small cog can help a big machine work, especially if it's not working alone.

She let herself look properly at Harry. *No promises more than that.* He wasn't waiting to pull her into his arms; he wasn't expecting that to happen. He was asking for small steps, and those she could manage. And as much as she could face Margarete alone if she had to, she didn't want to act in secrecy anymore. She nodded. Margarete had told her there was no one in her corner, but that didn't have to be true.

'I could do that, I think. I'd like you on my side. I'd like there to be honesty. And for us to be equals.'

His nod was a bridge that allowed her to reach for his hand. His, 'I'd like that too,' stopped her letting go of it. And told her that, although they were a very long way from mended, they weren't completely broken yet.

CHAPTER TWENTY-FIVE
DECEMBER 1947

'It's been a long time, Margarete. And yet you haven't said you missed me at all, not even the tiniest bit. Are you trying to break my heart?'

'Not that I'm aware. That I'd broken it, or that I missed you.'

It was the answer Hans expected her to give, which was why Margarete had obliged him. It wasn't strictly true. She hadn't seen him since the last days in the bunker, but she'd thought about him. She wasn't made of stone – the welcome she'd given him in her bed should have told him whatever he needed to know. But it wasn't as a lover she'd missed him the most.

You'll find each other when it's time.

'What are you smiling at? Are you secretly delighted I'm here?'

He was teasing her again, and she didn't like it; she didn't like games of any sort, unless she was the one playing them. Hans, it was clear, was going to require careful managing. She had no intention of letting him think he held any kind of a hold over her. Or assuming that – because he was a man – he could step in and take charge when she told him her plans. She had no need of a hero.

But I need his support, so I can't risk alienating him either.

Hans was stubborn. He didn't like being told what to do, especially by women. He'd expected a level of deference from the moment he'd received his first Iron Cross, and he'd always responded best to flattery. Margarete had ignored all that in the past – her indifference to his almost mythical status was one of the reasons he'd kept coming back to her. But it wouldn't hurt to sweeten him a little now.

'Maybe I am pleased. Would that be so strange? We were meant to meet up again after all, and I was never unhappy at the prospect of that.'

She matched his teasing tone, although it pained her to use it. Not that Hans noticed – he'd turned back to his breakfast at *pleased.* Margarete carried on complimenting him – and herself.

'That's actually what I was remembering and smiling about. The last days when everything seemed lost, but the Führer still had the courage to look to the future. When he told me there would be a network of us out in the world, carrying the flame, and that we'd find each other when the time was right. And now here we are, in England together. Reunited.'

Hans finally put his knife and fork down. 'And that time is now, is that what you're saying? Is that why Mosley's started shaking trees across Europe?'

Margarete stopped herself from pointing out that she was the one who'd suggested shaking the trees, even if Mosley had put his name to it. It was important the man kept some credibility, given what she was about to say next.

'Yes, that's it, or so Mosley believes. But I have to confess, I do wonder if he's seeing what he wants to see and not what's really there.'

That was all it needed, a little seed of doubt. She hid her smile in her coffee cup as Hans frowned.

'What's wrong? Are you starting to doubt Mosley's abilities? Do you think he's not up to the job?'

He was where she needed him to be. Now all she had to do was reel him in.

'That rather depends on the actual job. I think he's the right figurehead for the movement – he's certainly its best-known face. He's also an aristocrat, which counts for a lot here. He speaks the same language as the upper classes, and the lower ones jump when men like him tell them to jump. And he was the Führer's choice of course, but...'

Hans filled in the blanks the second she left them there for him.

'But that could have been because there wasn't anyone else. He always had his reservations about Mosley's character – you know that. And things are very different now than they were in the 1930s, which he couldn't have foreseen. So you're not being disloyal if you have concerns about whether Mosley is the right man now, if that's what's worrying you.'

Margarete ever being disloyal was such a ridiculous concept, she briefly wondered if Hans was yet another wrong man. She took a deep breath, found a smile that would have to stand in for the *thank you* he was clearly expecting and carried on.

'There are differences, yes, but it's what's stayed the same that's the issue for me when it comes to Mosley. I'm not convinced the timing is ever right with him. I'm never sure he's as close to the heart of things as he pretends to be.' She had her example ready when Hans frowned again. 'I was there when he came to Berlin in 1936 to get married. At the reception afterwards, he promised the Führer that he would be able to deliver the English King's support. He acted as if Edward VIII was his close friend and swore that he would also be Germany's staunchest ally, that he'd bring the two countries into a partnership. Hitler believed him – he had no reason not to. But barely two months after that, Edward abdicated, which Mosley obviously had no idea was on the cards. Hitler was warier of his promises after that. That's why he didn't share his war plans with him when Mosley couldn't get the English to rise up for peace in big enough numbers in 1939. Which is another reason why I don't think he's a man who delivers. And that's what's worrying me.'

Hans picked up the coffee pot and poured them both another cup. 'Does anyone else feel the same way? His latest letter talked about a new party he's planning to launch – what's it called, the Union Movement? He wrote as if there was a huge swell of support behind him.'

'And what did you, and your contacts, think of that?'

Margarete wasn't interested in what anybody else thought about it, but she wanted to know what Hans had heard. She was careful not to react as he told her.

'That it seems interesting. The letter contained a copy of the speech he made last month, and I have to say I found it pretty impressive. He didn't pull any punches. Promising that a fascist British government would deport Jews. Condemning the hangings at Nuremberg as contemptible and the alleged crimes at the camps as unproven propaganda. There must have been a lot of excitement in the room when he spoke.'

There had been excitement, but not from Margarete. The supporters gathered inside Farringdon Memorial Hall had cheered and applauded and saluted Mosley exactly as they'd always done. And Mosley had promised them a glorious new future, exactly as he'd always done too. And that was the problem. Margarete swallowed the rest of her coffee without tasting it. It was time to lead Hans to the final stop.

'I suppose it was. We always loved a rally, didn't we? We always had fun after those.' She let him take her hand as the memories she'd been hinting at lit up his eyes, but she sighed rather than moving into the embrace he was angling for. 'But, as much as I wish he was, Mosley's not the Führer. He's a good speaker, but he doesn't have Hitler's power or reach, or a Goebbels behind him. His speeches are empty words: they never call for specific action. His new party is one more variation of the old. And yes, he can whip up an army of thugs and get a handful of streets closed and a few heads broken, but that's all it is – localised street riots. Nobody's worried about Mosley outside the East End. And – if we really want to change the future – they have to be.'

Hans looked at her as if he was weighing her up, which he rarely did. They rarely looked at each other at all once they were outside the bedroom.

'It's not just Mosley's leadership qualities that's the problem, is it? England is an issue as well. From what I've seen of it, it's recovering from the war a great deal faster than Germany. Which means it's perhaps not as ripe for a takeover as we thought.'

The question, and the observation, surprised her. Margarete had assumed Hans wasn't interested in the finer details of political manoeuvring. She'd assumed the only thing he had any knowledge about was flying. She glanced down at his hand wrapped round hers. She'd always enjoyed his touch; he'd always understood her body better than anyone else she'd shared it with. And he'd been the one person in her world who could make her laugh.

Perhaps we could do this together, the two of us leading the way. Perhaps we don't need a figurehead.

She held the idea for less than a minute before she let go of it. Her plan had been carefully thought out – it couldn't be changed on a whim because Hans had made a couple of astute comments. No matter how attractive he looked.

She slipped her hand from under his and nodded. 'You're right, it's not. There's no major economic collapse coming here. More foodstuffs are being taken off ration, there's plans for a free health service, men are getting back into employment. And Mosley doesn't understand that increasing stability is a brick wall for us. He doesn't see that he can launch his new party and pull in all the European connections who've been waiting for the call, but if the conditions don't change, the seeds will fall on stony ground. I've no desire to watch that happen. I don't want to see the Reich fail again. So the only option is to change things. We need to turn England on its head and make it afraid. We need to unleash chaos. That's how we'll sweep in.'

She'd used the right words. *Sweep in* had put Hans back into a plane, diving towards the next kill. And he didn't need her to explain what *chaos* meant or why it mattered. They'd been raised in the same faith; their loyalty had been fattened on the stories of how the Reich had terrified its citizens and purged its enemies.

'You've got a list, haven't you? One Mosley doesn't know about.'

She nodded. Writing the names down went against everything she'd been taught – Goebbels would have called her an idiot or worse. But reading through them at night was a comfort that soothed her frustrations with Mosley. The list had become one of her favourite possessions, along with the bag of diamonds.

'Who's on it?'

His eyes widened when she told him. He laughed at her emphatic, 'Oh yes they will,' when he asked if the Jews would get the blame once the killings began. Margarete couldn't help but grin back.

'They're so easy to bring down, honestly it's barely a challenge. There's a Jewish mob in the East End which calls itself the 43 Group. They've already got a reputation as hotheads with a penchant for violence, and they're permanently at war with the police, never mind Mosley's supporters. The cells round Ridley Road are packed with its members on a Sunday night. It's perfect. The authorities will race to find a scapegoat, and it won't be difficult to put them in the frame.'

Hans began tapping on the tablecloth as if he was running through a checklist. 'Well done. I like that a lot. But what about resources? Pulling these attacks off – especially the bribes we'll need if we're going to get close to the targets, never mind the means to carry them out – won't come cheap.'

'And that's all in hand too.'

Margarete sat back. She was enjoying herself now. Hans's obvious belief in her abilities had wiped away the sting of Annie's *You're out of your mind.* Margarete knew nothing was further from the truth, but the reaction had got under her skin. It was far nicer to bask in Hans's admiration, which was why she couldn't wait to reveal her last card.

'What did you leave the bunker with on your last day there, apart from another medal?'

Hans frowned. 'Hitler's thanks for my service. And his request that I continue in the faith and continue to uphold his legacy.' He suddenly sat forward as Margarete's smile widened and realisation dawned. 'Oh my God, that's why you're asking me, isn't it? Because the rumours are true. He gave messages to some people, and jewels, didn't he? Did he give those to you?'

It was impossible not to laugh, she was so pleased with herself.

'Yes. Yes, he did, and it was the proudest moment of my life. He gave me his final instructions, which involved getting to England and to Mosley, and a bag of diamonds to help me do that and fund the cause here. And I did what he asked. I gave Mosley some of the money I raised from the jewels that I sold straight away. But not all of it. Once I got his measure, I held a considerable sum back. There's enough money, and diamonds, left to cover all our needs, for quite a long time to come.'

Hans almost grabbed her then. He was so delighted with her cleverness, the plans almost took a detour to the bedroom.

But Margarete knew there was one more question he'd be forced to ask, so she held herself away and let him get it over with.

'And what about us? Surely we're going to lead this push to power together? I'll divorce Ursula; we'll marry. We'll bring England into the fold. We don't need Mosley for this.'

It wasn't unpleasant to hear *us* and *together*. It wasn't unpleasant to hear that he'd end his marriage for her or for the cause, which was what she needed him to do. But Margarete had already dismissed any thought of mixing their personal and their political destinies, and she wasn't about to change course now.

'As tempting as that sounds, it wouldn't work. We're German – there's no getting past that. We'll be the enemy for a long time here. We'd never be able to take power, no matter how much chaos we cause from behind the scenes. But that doesn't mean there aren't important roles for us both to play.' She smiled at him and reverted to the teasing tone he'd seemed to like. 'And I do have someone who'll make a far better wife for you than Ursula. Who'll be far better suited to your new position once we've got the regime in place.'

She'd expected the disappointment that clouded his face. At some point – once Annie was subdued and settled into her role as Hans's wife – she'd let him know they could pick up their affair. At some point before the wedding ring she was aiming for landed on her finger, she'd tell him she'd always been playing for higher stakes. Margarete hadn't decided when that point would be, but, for once, Hans was a step ahead.

'You're going after Mosley, aren't you? You're going to take Diana out of the picture and take him for yourself. He'll be the figurehead, but you'll be the power. The First Lady of the new Reich.'

Margarete nodded; it would have been an insult to them both to lie. She took his hand. But she wouldn't let him kiss her again, not that he tried. She'd moved past him now, and he saw it. He saw who she was meant to be. *The First Lady of the new Reich.* It was the nicest thing he'd ever said to her, better than any flowery protestations of love. He'd accepted her as his queen.

CHAPTER TWENTY-SIX
FEBRUARY 1948

'Well, this is quite the triumph; it's even better than it looked on paper. No more divisions, no more usurpers setting up their own parties and thinking they can steal our crown. He's pulled every fascist supporter in the country on side with him now. Which is one in the eye for the fools who said that he's yesterday's man.'

Sid glowed as he surveyed the packed hall. Every time he heard somebody whisper, 'That's Sid Kirson. He's one of Mosley's closest advisors; he's a good man to know,' his shoulders took up more space.

'Look at them, Annie.' He waved across the floor to where people were gathered in clumps, wearing badges she didn't recognise on their coats. 'The British League of Ex-Servicemen and Women, the British People's Party, all the little splinter groups that we've infiltrated and taken over. Cheering as loudly for Mosley as those of us who were here at the start and ready to fly our new flag. And wait till you hear his speech – he's not only speaking for England today; he's speaking for Europe. This is a great day, a truly great day. We're a force to be reckoned with now.'

Annie could take issue with *great*, but it was harder to argue with *force*. There was a sense of purpose in the hall that doubled when Mosley finally appeared and began speaking. After almost nine years of addressing his followers from the shadows, Mosley was firmly back on the stage. He was fifty-two now, and his black hair was threaded with grey, but the leading-man good looks which had captivated audiences – and a revolving door full of women – before the war hadn't faded. If anything, ill health had sharpened his cheekbones, and the months recuperating in the Mediterranean had given him a tan which darkened his eyes. The female stewards guiding the families in were fluttering and breathless. It was little wonder Diana rarely left his side.

A New Party, A New Hope

The slogan fluttering high above the stage had been adopted as a chant as soon as the hall filled, punctuated with shouts of *Mosley! Mosley!* They were also quickly accompanied by a raft of darker songs promising vengeance on the 'Yids'.

Annie tried to block the vile words out, but the noise made it impossible. Once again, the past and the present collided, as the Wilfred Street School in Victoria – the venue Mosley had chosen for the launch of his new party in a failed attempt to throw off the protestors – rang with the leader's name like a drumbeat. The cries turned ecstatic when he finally walked out onto the stage, and rose to a howl when he raised his arm in the familiar salute. The numbers were smaller this time – this was a specifically invited audience; a bigger rally was promised – but the fervour, and the hatred that it ran on, was the same.

'Europe is a nation that must speak with one voice. Now is the day we look to a new world order, when we will cause a new empire to rise.'

A forest of arms clad in black flew up to mirror Mosley's as the leader started his speech. Time slipped and slid around Annie.

We could be in Berlin in 1933. We could be at Earl's Court in 1939 or at any of the Nuremberg rallies. Everyone deaf to anything except the false promise of strength and rebirth. Everyone forgetting what the pursuit of those cost the world the last time.

The speech droned on. Mosley was talking in circles. Making meaningless references to pilots and motor-racing drivers who crashed because they couldn't pivot and make quick decisions. Inviting his followers to come with him and grab the opportunities which would be offered when 'Europe is remade the right way'. Promising untold wealth and prosperity for the winners of his 'historic and glorious crusade'. It was nonsense, but his audience lapped it up. Nothing Mosley said was new; nothing held any substance. But the emperor's new clothes were fitting better than ever, and the arms flew up and the voices roared and the crowd drank in his empty words as if they were nectar.

Smile and clap at whatever he says. Don't make excuses and try to leave – that will draw attention. You're our eyes and ears inside there, Annie. Stand outside yourself if you can.

Annie wrapped herself inside Alan's instructions and cheered as loudly as the rest. He'd played his part. He'd made good on his promise to provide eyes dedicated to keeping her safe, using nondescript female agents to trail her as Annie had suggested because they would be beneath Margarete's notice. But he hadn't been able to get another agent into the hall to watch over her there – every one of the delegates had been carefully vetted, and the ticketing system was a labyrinth only the organisers who'd designed it could crack. Annie had made the cut on Margarete's say-so, but – no matter how much he'd wanted to be at her side – there'd been no place for Harry. He was known because he was Sid's son-in-law, but he wasn't trusted. Quite the opposite, in fact. Trying to get him a ticket would have roused suspicions. Besides, Annie hadn't wanted him anywhere near – never mind Margarete or her father spotting him; he would have ended up in trouble before he made it into the hall once he saw how the protesters treated her. Wilfred Street was narrow. It was packed full of police and members of the 43 Group. There was very little chance of avoiding violence or avoiding being seen. She'd told him to go to work and pretend it was a normal night instead.

And thank God I did. If he'd heard what Morris shouted at me, I'd never have been able to pull him back.

The Group had seen her come in. They'd seen her walk into the school beside her father. The shock and the anger on their faces had hit her harder than a brick.

Margarete won't have to spread a story about me – none of them will ever trust me again anyway.

The memory of the way they'd jeered at her was one she'd never shake. Morris had been front and centre, leading the anti-fascists, his pockets no doubt full of stones. His clothes were splashed with the same white paint that had been used to paint the slogan, *Mosley Speaks Here, Insult to our Children,* in letters three feet high across the school's wall. He clearly didn't care that the paint would instantly mark him out to the police. But he cared when he saw her. He'd pointed her out to the rest of the crowd, who'd roared insults with him. He'd called her 'a traitorous bitch'.

Annie couldn't blame him. Mosley's men – emboldened by their leader's reappearance in their midst at the end of November and under Margarete's direction – had increased their attacks on the Group's headquarters in Bayswater Road, beating up men and women alike as they left. Annie knew Morris would soon start blaming her for that – the surge in the violence had coincided with her disappearance from their meetings. He'd seen the proof that she was firmly in the enemy's camp for himself now. And Sid – who believed Margarete's story that Annie had been bravely spying on the Jews – had only worsened her case. He'd hurled threats and abuse back at the protestors and hugged her as tightly on the way in as if she was precious metal. His touch was as sickening as the Group's anger.

Nothing I've done to break away from my upbringing matters. I'm the enemy now to the people who count. Margarete has already rewritten me.

Of all the hard blows the years since the war had brought, that was one of the hardest. To be numbered by good men among the antisemites and the haters. To be numbered amongst the doubters and the liars. Annie's skin snapped round her so tight, she couldn't bear the feel of herself.

'You're trembling.'

Sid's smile was so proud as he gazed down at her, Annie stopped trying to hold back her tears. She'd let him read her whichever way he wanted if it gave her a moment's release from all the hatred curled up at her core.

'It's a joy to have you back in the fold, sweetheart. Oh, and the future that's in your grasp now...' He backtracked as Annie frowned at him. 'And that's not mine for the telling. Stop crying now and go and fix up your face – there's a good girl. There's a party after this you need to look your best for. Polly will show you where the facilities are and bring you safely back.'

There was nothing to be gained by asking what he'd meant. Sid was back at his old weight and back in charge of the family. Peggy was a shadow who danced to whatever tune he told her to dance to. She'd forgotten a lot, but that pattern was knocked into her bones. Which left Annie clinging on to Alan's promise that there would be justice and doing everything she could to keep the peace.

'This way, please, Mrs Garnet. I'm afraid the bathrooms

aren't terribly fancy – it is a school after all – but I'm sure you can make do.'

Polly was all neat black skirt and stiff black shirt and a smile that didn't reach her eyes. She carried the air of a prison warden about her. She stood in the bathroom which smelled of mildew and chalk for the five minutes she allowed Annie to straighten her hair and her face. Then she led her back out, saying, 'It won't do to miss the end,' in a voice that could have been borrowed from a headmistress. Annie wondered if Polly had been told about her disappearing act from Earl's Court. She wondered how much she was really trusted and prayed the answer was the *not enough* that might get her out of Margarete's clutches. But Sid beamed and patted her arm when she returned to her seat as if she was a show pony, and *not enough* was a lifetime away.

The private dining room on the first floor of the Royal Court Hotel was awash with champagne and triumph. Mosley arrived with Diana curled across his arm, but his eyes rarely left Margarete. And Margarete acted throughout as if the party was hers, immediately dragging Annie away from Sid's side.

'Sit by me, darling. There's so many people I want you to meet.'

Annie sat down with the smile that was now her default around Margarete. There was nobody in the room she wanted to meet, but Alan would be interested in all of them, and – whatever else this day was – keeping Alan updated on the Union's activities was both her job and her lifeline. She gazed round at the guests, her brain automatically matching faces with files the way she'd been trained to do. It was an unpleasant task. The men sitting around drinking hadn't been at the public meeting, but their presence confirmed that Mosley's commitment to Europe wasn't only confined to the stage.

Annie stared as discreetly as she could at the entourage surrounding Margarete – and paying far more attention to her than to the Union Movement's leader. They were a roll call of European right-wing royalty; Annie would have had them all put in prison. When Margarete beckoned her over, she pretended the names being reeled off were new to her, but every one of them was on a British Intelligence watchlist. Which Annie knew meant they'd sneaked into the country, either with fake identities and fake passports, or by some secret route.

Giorgio Almirante, the head of Italy's newly reborn fascist party and the heir to Mussolini. Arthur Erhardt, Hitler's former expert on anti-partisan warfare. Werner Naumann, who'd been State Secretary in Goebbels' Ministry of Propaganda and – with Margarete – one of the last Nazis in the bunker. Each of them had blood on their hands; each of them swaggered round the room as if they had nothing to be ashamed of. By the time Margarete introduced Annie to her 'absolute favourite' – the German fighter pilot Hans-Ulrich Rudel, who was as famous in Britain for his courage as he had been in his own country – her palm was itching for soap. And she wasn't in the mood to be Margarete's lapdog.

'Goodness, Margarete, what a cosmopolitan crowd you've gathered. MI6 would implode if they knew who you'd squirrelled in here.'

It was a daring thing to say, but Annie delivered the lines with a grin and a wink that had the men roaring and even brought a thin smile to Margarete's lips.

'I'm sure you're right, so it's a good thing that they don't. One of the joys of my new home is the private airfield close by. It's such a delightful way to bring in my friends.'

'A new home? How lovely. Is it in London, or have you moved?'

Annie slipped on an innocent smile, but it was Diana's reaction to the answer that captured her attention even more than Margarete's response. The woman's face was as blank as ever, but her eyes were lightning bolts. And Margarete had noticed that too.

'Moved out of London? Good gracious no. Where else could I possibly live? But it's nice to have a little bolthole too, so I'm renting Savehay Farm. You remember it, don't you, Annie? It's where we met. It's where Sir Oswald used to live.' She turned to Diana with a light-bulb smile that wasn't returned. 'But of course you sold it, didn't you, dear? What a wrench that must have been, but needs must I suppose when the purse strings bite. And what could I do when it came up for rent except grab it? I've such happy memories of my time there, especially the hours I spent in the Rose Garden and wandering through the Lilac Walk. The little nooks and crannies they hid were always so full of surprises.'

Mosley laughed loudest at Margarete's raised eyebrow; Diana barely managed a smile. Annie stopped paying attention to Herr Rudel's over-intrusive claims on her attention and concentrated on Margarete and Mosley. Whatever had happened in the gardens all those years ago – and it wasn't difficult to guess – the memory had rubbed the shine off Diana. The power balance was shifting – Diana could feel it and so could Annie, which was another nugget for filing away. Margarete was playing very publicly with Mosley. She'd added him to her list of tame men, and he was clearly happy to indulge her. Annie could almost see the electricity pulling them closer together.

She's going to take him from Diana; she's firing the warning shots. And Diana won't go down without a fight.

There had to be a reason why Margarete was playing for such high stakes, but Annie couldn't take the time she needed to puzzle it out. Rudel was in her ear again, asking her if she'd ever wanted to travel, and his attentions were becoming uncomfortable. The man was handsome enough if rather sharply cut, but he had little conversation beyond his beloved planes and his flying exploits, and he was monopolising her in a way that felt increasingly claustrophobic. He was also a Nazi, which was by far his worst crime. It was a relief when he excused himself – even if he promised to hurry back – and Sid slipped into his place.

'He's quite the charmer, our pilot, isn't he?'

Annie had no polite way to respond to that so she said nothing and let Sid carry on. It seemed he was far more besotted with Rudel than she was.

'He had quite the war too. Did Margarete tell you that? He's the most decorated man any of us have ever met, a genuine hero. He won Germany's highest medal for bravery five times, which is an incredible feat when you think about it. Most fighter pilots would be lucky to win that once – the death toll among those young men was a tragedy. But Rudel flew over two thousand bombing missions. He even blew up a Russian battleship.'

Sid sat back, rubbing his hands together. Annie managed not to tell him that she didn't care. But she wasn't prepared for what he said next.

'Do you like him?'

It was such an odd question. Sid had never asked her if she liked Harry; he'd certainly never praised him. He never asked about her feelings at all, although he was perfectly happy to tell her what they should be. Annie nodded because she had to give him some sort of an answer; she could hardly tell the truth and say *no*.

'Excellent, that's excellent.'

Sid folded his hands over his stomach and beamed at Rudel, who'd returned to the room but was currently hovering on its edges, watching Annie and her father with an intensity that was out of place.

Why is he hanging back like that? Why's he looking at my father and me like a nervous suitor?

The penny dropped with the word *suitor*. She froze as Sid patted her arm and left his hand on her sleeve like a warning.

'You were very young when you got married, and I didn't give you the right guidance. I'd like a chance to remedy that. Harry's a pleasant-enough chap, and he's set you both up nicely, but he's not one of us. He's not what my daughter deserves.'

The room was alive with laughter and toasts, glasses clinking against each other and spilling champagne. Men were shouting to each other across tables, swapping stories and telling jokes as their wives sipped their drinks and looked on. It may as well have been silent. Annie couldn't hear it. She was back in the Savoy. Listening to Margarete explain how women would have a very different place in the new Reich and how important they – including Annie – would be. Listening to herself telling Margarete that she was out of her mind. But now it seemed that the madness had spread.

'What are you talking about?'

She asked her father the question calmly, to buy herself time, although she had no idea what that time might be for. Sid patted her arm again.

'How life can change if you have the right partner. Something I wish I'd given more thought to.'

Annie's stomach lurched. He had given it plenty of thought; he'd given permission for his wife to be killed.

He knows about Margarete's plan. He's embraced it. He'd have no more problem removing Harry from my life than she would.

And he couldn't know that she'd guessed where his ambitions, and his delusions, lay. Annie took a deep breath and found him a smile her mouth hated.

'I'm sorry you feel that way about Harry, but I'm happy with him, Dad, and isn't that the main thing?'

It was true. That they'd started making their way back to each other with far more success than she'd believed would be possible in September. And – even though she'd insisted he had to carry on meeting Margarete so she wouldn't get suspicious, which he loathed doing – trust was beginning to flower again. Now she needed to hold on to him.

'And I appreciate you looking out for my interests, but I'm a married woman and – whatever you think might be better for me – nothing's going to change that fact. So I think maybe it's best I went home too, before anything more awkward gets said.'

'No, it's not. It's far better that you stay here.'

She'd forgotten Margarete was sitting so close by. Her hand clamped Annie's wrist in a vice before she was halfway out of her seat. Her voice was as light as Sid's, but there was poison inside the honey.

'You should listen to your father, Annie. He knows your marriage isn't happy, so there's no need to put a brave face on things, not when we're here to help. Poor Hans is unhappily married too, and he deserves a partner who'll help him rise in the world, same as you do. He's a wonderful man, and it's perfect timing for you both. You want to do good for your country, like we talked about, don't you? Well, this way you can. And you can also have a little fun in the process.'

She gave Sid one of her prettiest smiles as she explained the transaction to Annie. It was clear from his response that he'd already signed off on it.

'And why not have some fun, eh? Balls and parties and travelling round the world on the arm of a handsome husband – what girl doesn't want that? Herr and Frau Rudel, the ambassador and his beautiful wife. It's the position I raised you for, my dear, and the possibilities are endless.' He raised his glass in a toast to himself as he sketched out Annie's perfect future. 'Argentina, Berlin, Rome, and England of course – who knows where this journey will take you? My elegant daughter spreading our word, balancing out the violence that too many dissenters associate with us. The perfect heiress – along with Margarete naturally – to the lovely Magda Goebbels.'

He'd been well coached. The Sid Annie had grown up with would never have spoken like that. He was perfectly happy to win arguments with violence – he had no time for fancy rhetoric or women with opinions. As for Magda Goebbels... It was on the tip of Annie's tongue to ask if he expected her to murder her children if this Reich failed as disastrously as the last one. She held that back. But she might as well have not said, 'It's a ludicrous idea, and I won't do it,' either. Rudel – who'd come in to close the circle around her while Sid was talking – smiled as if she was a child needing coaxing out of a tantrum. Sid tutted in a similar fashion. But it was Margarete who shot the bolt home.

'But you will, once we've made the arrangements and you've adjusted to the idea. Because you're a good girl, aren't you? And you want the best for yourself and your family.'

She leaned in to Annie as the two men congratulated each other over her head. Her lips were close enough to touch Annie's ear.

'I own them all, remember. Harry, who thinks he's in love with me. Your father, who thinks it's his future I'm protecting. Your mother, who will hate our plan but won't have the courage to stop it after what happened to her the last time. Do I need to go on?'

Annie eyed the knife lying in front of her; she felt her hand twitch. Margarete moved it away with a, 'Don't be a fool,' that whispered ice through Annie's blood.

This is insanity; it can't happen. I'll tell her Harry knows the truth. I'll tell Harry she's involved my father and we need to get help. I'll tell Alan who was here and make him arrest her straight away. I won't dance to her mad tune anymore.

Except she had no proof. There was no guest list, no

photographs. Nothing more than her words, which would carry no weight. And Margarete was three paces ahead. Her butterfly lips flew back to Annie's ear.

'I know you were pulled in by intelligence, Annie; I know everything. I'm hoping you weren't foolish enough to give me away. And I have my own people in there now, so one word to any of the contacts clicking through your head about this party or my plan and I start picking your family off immediately. Do you understand?'

Annie nodded as if she did, but she didn't. She'd forgotten to hide her feelings. Hatred lit up her eyes; defiance blazed through her face. She didn't realise her mistake until Margarete jerked back as if she'd been scalded. And by then it was far too late.

CHAPTER TWENTY-SEVEN
FEBRUARY 1948

'It came from nowhere. If someone hadn't pulled me back by my arm at the last minute... Well, I wouldn't be here now.'

Harry's words came slowly, floating on a sea of pain medication. Annie sat by his bedside in the London Hospital, holding a hand which had barely any grip, knowing her stupidity had put him there. Every time she thought about the Royal Court, she felt sick. She'd been too clever from the start. Trying to act as if she held as much power as Margarete by making misplaced jokes. Saying, 'I won't do it,' as if her voice would be heard. Failing to hide her true feelings.

Margarete hadn't given Annie a chance to atone for the defiance she'd stupidly let show. The car which hit Harry had been despatched the same night, timed to race down the street precisely as he left his office. He hadn't been killed – which Annie assumed had been the intention – but Margarete couldn't have made her message any clearer. *I have eyes everywhere; I know every inch of your lives.* She'd underscored the point anyway – in case Annie was still foolish enough to think they were playing from equal positions or that the collision had been an accident. She'd sent a wreath of white lilies to the house the next day.

Annie burned the flowers, but that was her last independent task. She'd moved back into Arnold Circus at Sid's insistence, knowing Margarete was behind the summons. Peggy was an empty presence again, sleepy and sedated, suffering, or so Sid said, from another attack of her nerves. Sid ruled the flat and Annie's life from the minute she stepped back through its door. He accompanied her to the hospital where Harry – who'd sustained two broken legs and a severe concussion – had drifted in and out of consciousness for the first three days after he was admitted and everyone told her how lucky he was. There was a minder to walk her there or home again if her father was busy. On one of the rare occasions when she was left in the flat alone, she telephoned Alan on his private number and told him about Harry's accident. She kept the call short and told him nothing about it being deliberate or about who had attended the party. If Margarete could embed a spy inside Kensington Gardens, she had to assume there could also be someone listening in at the telephone exchange. For the rest of the time, she sat in the flat, wondering how her father had become her jailer, wondering how her mother had become a ghost. And acting as an audience for Margarete, who was delighted to explain in more detail how her plan would play out.

Hans would get a divorce and so would Annie, not that she had to do anything to facilitate that. Her petition would cite adultery against Harry, using the photographs Margarete had staged and one or two more using a stand-in nobody would look too closely at once they'd viewed the first pictures. Harry's signature would be forged; Annie would be instructed where to sign or hers would be forged too. The judge presiding would be sympathetic to the cause, as many of them apparently were. Two months from start to finish to get everything done, perhaps three, or so Margarete promised. After that, a wedding to plan and a bright, shiny new future.

Annie had smiled at each briefing. She smiled at everything; she rarely spoke. Except to Harry, who was struggling with his memory in a dreadful echo of Peggy and had weeks of treatment and hospital stays to come and no idea of the chaos breaking around them. Annie couldn't talk to him about the mess they were in – she had to assume there were spies in the hospital too. She wove stories for him – and for herself – instead. She drew a new life for them, out of London, away from the influence of Margarete and Mosley. A fresh start with a job on a regional newspaper for him and a pretty house in the country and maybe even a child or two. She didn't weave her own dreams into the fairy tales. It was hard enough keeping hold of reality, never mind imagining a future where she had choices. She also didn't tell Harry that, outside the hospital, she was never alone. If it wasn't Sid or one of his cronies by her side, it was Margarete. Or Rudel, who came in and out of the country using a false passport and a false name. She didn't tell Harry a lot of things.

She said nothing about them being forced into a divorce. She kept quiet about her suspicions that Margarete was intending to replace Diana and become the next Lady Mosley. Or that she was convinced – from the snatched scraps of conversations in German Annie understood a lot better than the speakers guessed – that Margarete and Rudel were planning a far more dangerous campaign to speed up the Union's success than anything Mosley had in his arsenal. Or how hard she listened to every exchange between Margarete and her tamed men, digging for a nugget that would give her a weapon. Or how alone and desperate and frightened she felt, living in a world which resembled a twisted version of *Alice in Wonderland*. What could he do if she did? Except make himself sicker than he already was? So she kept silent, but inside she was screaming.

The attack on Harry hadn't frightened Annie in the way it had been intended to, or not after the immediate shock of it had faded. It had made her angry to a degree she didn't know she was capable of. Not hot but cold, filled with a white fury that seared through her. And that anger was the weapon she needed.

Annie had no idea yet how she could stop Margarete without flinging more danger across innocent lives. She didn't care about Sid – he deserved whatever punishment was coming to him. But she had no intention of seeing Peggy killed, because that was surely the next step, or Dolly or Jim in the same state as Harry. She also knew it might be impossible to prevent Harry suffering any more pain. If the divorce papers arrived before she came up with a plan, she would have to pretend it was her doing, that she hadn't forgiven him after all. That was unthinkable, but where would the truth lead except to more misery caused by Margarete and to more weeping beside a hospital bed?

Annie kissed Harry's hand as he slipped into sleep again. She didn't envy him the accident that had almost taken his life, but she envied him the peace the morphine brought with it.

Which we'll never have again if I don't act.

Annie closed her eyes along with Harry and forced her mind to stop racing. The method didn't matter – she'd find that because she had to. She wasn't going to fall into step with Margarete's plan; she'd never been going to do that.

But she thinks I will. She's so blinded by her own brilliance, she thinks she rules the whole world. And that's how I'll break her.

Her heart slowed; her brain stopped turning. Margarete had laid out her plans, assuming in her madness that she'd broken Annie. There was no need to panic, no need to rush into anything foolish because she'd told Annie exactly what she needed to know. That she had time to watch and learn and find the weakness. That she had two months to reattach the world to its axis, or perhaps three if she was lucky.

'Leave the shopping. Jackson will bring it upstairs.'

Margarete whirled past the doorman, who knew better than to correct her mistake, leaving a trail of beribboned boxes in her wake.

'Thank you, Mr Jenkins. There's really no need to hurry.'

Annie kept her voice to a whisper and raised her eyebrows in apology at the poker-faced man. His smile was a fleeting one, but it was another weapon to add to Annie's pile. Margarete paid very little attention to the people who ran around doing her bidding, and if she bothered to see them, she was rarely polite. It was Annie who learned names, who left tips and smiles. Who put into practice the lesson Peggy had instilled in her since childhood, that it never hurt to be kind. Annie was hoping it would do more than that.

She'd watched Margarete grow increasingly regal since she'd arrived in England. Taking Annie's lack of visible resistance to her schemes as assent to them was part of that pattern. And Annie had taken advantage of that mistake by turning herself into the perfect attendant, full of approval and flattery and there to do Margarete's bidding. Margarete didn't have friends – Annie doubted she knew or cared what the word meant – but she liked to think she was popular. She wanted other women's envy. And Annie was pretty enough to fit that role, so she let Annie step into it.

They became shopping companions, flitting between Derry and Toms and Swan and Edgar and Liberty as the mood struck Margarete's apparently bottomless purse. They became afternoon tea and evening cocktail companions. And on one or two particularly late nights – when the gin had filled Margarete's glass more often than Annie's and the dancing went on into the small hours – Annie had been allowed to stay at Margarete's flat in St George's Square. And those were the nights when Margarete grew careless.

Margarete was the type of drunk who grew nostalgic, who told stories, who forgot which year she was living in. Once she'd opened the Armagnac brandy that Hans brought with him from Germany to remind her of home, her accent slipped from the cut-glass tones she increasingly cultivated. She got tangled up in her memories. And she told Annie far more than the daytime Margarete ever did.

'My father was the most elegant man you could meet. He was never without his silver-topped cane or his pearl-grey gloves. He was clever too. When Germany fell apart in the twenties, he doubled his money and turned his steel business into Germany's best. That's why Hitler thought so highly of him. And he brought me up to be as sharp as him. Which is both good and bad. It's dull sleeping with men who can't match up to me.'

Once she'd dispensed with that complaint, she would start waxing lyrical about her beloved *Uncle Wolf*.

'He was the best of men too, such a sweetheart, so kind. Our cook in Bavaria made the most wonderful apple cake, and Wolf so loved to tease her – he swore she was trying to fatten him up every summer.'

Uncle Wolf. My darling Hitler. She filled the flat with the man as soon as she closed the front door. Annie's smile grew exhausted as Margarete sang the Führer's praises. Her patience wore down to the bone under the weight of his 'brave choices'. She forced herself to endure it because of what always came next.

'He'll never be forgotten. Not the man, not his legacy. Not while I have breath in my body.'

She made the same declaration every time she picked over the last days in the bunker, and the shift was immediate. Margarete's body stayed in the room, but she slipped into the past. Waiting for that moment was what kept Annie awake through the slurred monologues and kept her bitten lips shut.

'He trusted me more than anyone. He knew I'd bring everything safely out. That I'd pull his network together when the time was right.'

That was usually where the night ended, in the vagueness of *everything* and *network*. Annie would be forced to go to bed empty-handed and spend a sleepless night wondering how she could change the script. But tonight she didn't need to do it because Margarete did it for her and carried on talking.

'Hans really likes you; he couldn't take his eyes off you at the bar. Not that he cared one way or the other about that – he does whatever is right for the cause, and whatever I tell him. He would have married you whether you pleased him or not. But he'll be easier to manage this way. He can get a little tricky with people who bore him.'

Annie didn't want to know what *tricky* meant. Rudel wasn't a person to her; he was a Nazi who'd escaped justice. She pretended to take a sip from the overfull glass Margarete had poured for her – she'd been pretending to drink most of the night. Luckily, the head waiter at the American Bar, where their nights invariably finished, valued Annie's generous tips and was happy to ensure her cocktails were mostly made of water. She'd suspected for a while that Rudel was one of Margarete's conquests and it didn't surprise her – they were cut from the same cloth, both too in love with themselves to love anyone else. She imagined that neither of them planned to stop the affair whatever marriage plots they were spinning. She still wanted to hear that from Margarete.

'Were you and he ever...' She waved a hand as if she was overstepping. 'I'm sorry, that was intrusive. It's just that, well, you say he likes me, but I've seen him looking at you, and his eyes really do light up then. I hope I won't have a reason to be jealous.'

The flattery – and the pretence of bowing to Margarete's power over men – worked. Margarete as good as purred.

'They do, don't they? And of course you won't – I've other game in my sights. It's true we've had our little flings in the past, he and I, but Hans knows how the land lies now. He's made his peace with it.'

I hate her. I hate her smugness. I hate the way she thinks she's handed me a prize. I hate that I have to pretend I don't know what she did to my husband and the way she thinks we're on the same side now.

Annie hated everything about the situation she was in. But she pushed that aside and smiled.

'How does it lie, Margarete? You're such a tease. Is there someone else in your sights? Won't you tell me what you're hinting at?'

It was a risk. Any direct question around Margarete was a risk. The woman had the instincts of a leopard. Annie waited for Margarete to close the conversation down. When Margarete leaned forward instead and grinned, relief rushed through her like a shock of cold water.

'Shall I? Can't you guess?' She came as close as Margarete could come to giggling when Annie shook her head. 'Mosley of course. He's my big game. He's acting like an old man, and it's no good for anyone. Do you know how hard it was to persuade him to get back on the stage? He'd grown weak and slow, sitting in his study all day, churning out his endless pamphlets. He'd forgotten how much he loved being in the limelight. Well, he's remembered now, and I won't let him forget it.' She stopped and grinned at a memory Annie did not want her to share. 'He needed a burst of energy, that was all, and he'll never get that from Diana. The woman's got frost in her veins – she'd keep him locked up at her side if she could. She's no use to him for what's coming.'

Annie took a deep breath. It was no surprise that Margarete had designs on Mosley – Annie had suspected that for long enough. But to hear her admit it, boast about it, was deeply unpleasant – and troubling. The parallels with Lady Macbeth pushing and goading her husband leapt into her head, and it was all she could do to keep her tone light.

'Mosley? Goodness, but yes, that makes perfect sense. The two of you would be an amazing couple, and he's always carried a torch for you – anyone can see that. But what do you mean? What's coming?'

Her attempt to sound casual didn't fool Margarete.

'Oh, Annie, you're so funny; your eyes look as if they're about to fall out of your head. But it's not the time yet, my dear. You'll know everything when you're married to Hans and properly one of ours, with no lingering notions about Harry to distract you.'

She was too wrapped in her delusions to push further. Annie stood up with another forced smile as Margarete waved her towards the spare bedroom.

'Off you go and get your beauty sleep. We're standing on the edge of great times, Annie, but we're not quite there, and that's all you need to know. Except for how lucky you are.'

Annie went to bed with *lucky* ringing like a curse through her head, determined to get back up again as soon as Margarete was quiet. There were secrets hidden in the flat – she could sense them. Secrets that could reveal what *everything* and *network* meant. Proof that would put Margarete at the centre of the plot; that Annie could take to Kensington in exchange for her freedom.

Freedom. The word wrapped around her like Harry's arms. She couldn't remember the last time she'd felt that way, certainly not since she'd come back from Nuremberg and lost control of her life.

I'll bring her down. I'll bring them all down. I'll dig up the seeds and the plants she's nurtured, and I'll burn them until they are less than a memory. And then I'll rebuild my life in the ruins of hers.

It was an exhilarating thought.

Annie crept out of bed, although she wanted to leap. She mentally mapped out the cupboards and drawers in the flat that she intended to check through. She crossed to the door, preparing to comb through every inch of the flat until she found the key to that freedom. But Margarete was only as careless as she chose to be. There wasn't a sound from outside Annie's bedroom door. Not a step or a creak or a word. But the lock clicked shut before Annie could reach it and reminded her who was in charge.

CHAPTER TWENTY-NINE
MAY 1948

'It's not my place to pass judgement on the state of your marriage, Mrs Garnet, but I'm surprised to see you here, I must say. The poor man has no memory of signing those papers he received yesterday, and the shock of it has undone all our good work.'

It had been three days now since their confrontation, but Annie couldn't get the matron's pinched face out of her head. She couldn't push Harry's face away either, although she'd done everything she could to mitigate the shock that had – according to Matron – 'put the poor soul into a catatonic state'. The grooves despair had cut through him had cut the same scars into her.

She'd been outplayed; the timescales had speeded up. The divorce papers had arrived at Harry's convalescent home without warning and with the deed done. Annie had never wanted to murder anyone before, but she could have killed Margarete without blinking when she saw the broken mess the woman's cruelty had made out of Harry.

I never believed it would get this far. I thought I had time to stop her.

That was no comfort to her. She hadn't been able to offer it as an apology to Harry either – she couldn't be certain one of the hovering nurses wasn't in Margarete's pay. But she'd come close to spilling it all when he'd cried.

Annie had to stop and cling on to one of the trees bordering Pimlico Gardens. The air was warm with the first breath of spring, but she was as cold as December. Harry's memory had been shaky since the car hit him, and he didn't seem to have any recollection of what she'd told him about Margarete and the plot surrounding her before the accident. He kept falling back into the part of their marriage when they were strangers and a divorce wasn't unthinkable and got stuck there. His tears had slipped down his face in silent waves. They'd burned through her like acid.

But I made it right in the end. I made him remember; I must have.

She wiped her face and repeated the words to the sparrows hopping round her feet and the tulips nodding in the gardens. Hoping that, if she spread them widely enough, they'd sound true. Because she had to believe she'd got through to him. She had to believe Harry had been able to see her love shining through the lies.

This is Margarete's doing, like I warned you. We didn't sign anything; it's not what I wanted. I'll make it right, I promise.

Three lines. That was all she'd had time to scribble down when she excused herself and went to the bathroom. Three minutes was all Harry had to read the note before the nurse came back and she'd had to snatch it out of his hand. He'd read them, but Annie knew they'd made no sense, and she hadn't been able to help him with that. Every time he'd said, 'But I don't remember, I don't understand,' she'd had to cut him off with a quick, 'Wait till you're better,' for the nurse's benefit that had sliced him into pieces again.

But he stopped crying in the end. And he squeezed my hand

when I left him. And I will make this right today, whatever the consequences.

Annie's plan was so full of risks and elements that were out of her control it was barely a plan. But it was an opportunity, and she'd had too few of those to waste this one.

She was alone for the first time since February, which felt like a miracle. A May Day rally was due to start in Dalston in half an hour, and it was widely expected Mosley's speech would draw crowds bent on violence. Sid would be tied up for the whole day, along with her revolving circle of minders.

And if there's any justice, a club or a hammer will find him.

As for Margarete, she was at Savehay Farm for the weekend, on business whose details she hadn't shared with Annie. Hans had also disappeared again – which Annie presumed was connected to Margarete's sudden urge to visit the country. There was nobody to supervise her, and she had only one goal: to search Margarete's apartment. As long as she could cross the first hurdle and get in.

'Mr Jenkins, how are you? And how are your grandchildren? Do you have any up-to-date photos of them? I'm so sorry to be bothering you, but the countess is away for the weekend and she's asked me to take care of some correspondence while she's gone. The trouble is I can't find the key she gave me. I don't suppose you could save my life and let me in, could you? You know how she gets when things aren't done to her liking.'

It was a gamble, but the whole day was a gamble, and the doorman felt like the safest bet. Mr Jenkins huffed and puffed about protocols, as she expected him to do, but his hastily swallowed smile at *you know how she gets* was a promising start. By the time she'd oohed and aahed over his granddaughters, he was easily persuaded to lend her the spare key that was kept for emergencies. And he softened his, 'Let's hope neither of us gets into trouble for this with her ladyship,' with a wink.

The first step was done. She'd got the maids' schedule right and the flat was empty. Annie closed the door behind her and took her first proper breath. The apartment was a beautiful place, a shrine to Art Deco elegance, from the black-and-white tiles in the hall to the organza curtains blurring the windows. It might as well have been a stage set for all its sophistication. There wasn't a personal picture or memento to be seen. But there were cupboards and there were drawers, and Annie was determined to search all of them.

She moved quickly, aware that Mr Jenkins could have a pang of conscience and a change of heart. There was nothing to explore in the hallway, so she ran to the inlaid writing desk that sat in a curve of the windows facing St George's Square's central garden and worked quickly through its drawers, moving the contents as little as possible, making sure everything was put back into place. There was nothing of interest inside it or hidden in the polished walnut cocktail cabinet. There was nothing to be found in the kitchen either, and Annie had already checked the spare room. The enterprise began to feel hopeless, and Annie couldn't live with that.

Stop racing and think. Where would Margarete keep her most precious items? Where would she hide a small velvet bag?

The answer was obvious as soon as she gave herself a chance to find it. Her bedroom. Annie started with the bedside cabinet, instantly dropping the well-thumbed copy of *Mein Kampf* she found there. Then she turned to the dressing table, and her heart began thudding. There it was, the place she would have hidden something valuable herself if she had it. In amongst the crystal perfume atomisers and the powder puffs and jewelled lipstick cases neatly arranged on the top was a square mahogany jewellery box big enough to hold a dozen velvet bags.

Annie ran to it, her fingers shaking. She opened the lid and lifted out the earring tray, which was filled with button- and bow-shaped clip-ons in a rainbow of colours she instinctively knew weren't made out of paste. The bags fashioned to hold bracelets and necklaces were lined up below that. Annie steadied herself and pulled them out, making sure to lay them in the correct order on the dressing table's glass top before she began to go carefully through their contents. One contained a double row of pearls set with an amethyst cluster. Others contained crystal pendants fashioned into butterflies and bees. Annie had seen most of the pieces before, draped across Margarete. But she'd never seen anything like the contents of the fourth bag.

Half a dozen diamonds fell out when she shook it and landed in her palm like pieces of light chipped from a star. Annie couldn't breathe; she couldn't begin to calculate their value. They certainly explained Margarete's lavish lifestyle. They would be enough to support Mosley, and her, for years.

I've found it. I've found what I need to take to Alan.

Except she hadn't. Annie dropped the stones back into their pouch and stowed that in her jacket pocket, telling herself it was a good start even as her heart sank. The diamonds were evidence, but they weren't enough: Margarete could invent any story she chose to explain them away, and simply possessing the jewels wasn't illegal. She returned the rest of the bags to the box and willed herself to start again. Not just funds, there were surely orders too. They had to be here somewhere.

She went back to the rest of the flat. She checked every drawer she'd already checked through. There was nothing else to be found.

What if the diamonds are all there is? What if there's nothing I can do to stop her?

Annie returned to the bedroom and sank down on the bed. She'd never seriously imagined Margarete's mad scheme coming to fruition, but now she couldn't stop picturing it. Scenes flew through her mind in a sickening slide show. Margarete with a syringe of some drug that would calm but not completely sedate her. Sid walking her down the aisle like a sleepwalker towards where Rudel was waiting, dressed in a black SS uniform. A marriage made without her consent, a life lived out as a prisoner. It was absurd and impossible, but sitting there in Margarete's room, with her marriage legally ended and no visible means to stop the plan's progression, it also felt horribly real.

It can't be. It won't be. I'll kill her first. I'll kill them all if I have to.

And that wasn't possible either. Annie shook herself out of one trance and refused to fall into another. She didn't know how to fire a gun or wield a knife; she couldn't take a life. She'd seen enough evidence of what murder and cruelty could do to know the act was beyond her.

She got up slowly, straightening the crumpled bedspread as if finding that out of place would be the thing that annoyed Margarete. There was more to find; there had to be. *He trusted me... He knew I'd bring everything safely out* had confirmed that.

And why have two hiding places if one would do?

Annie blinked away the image of Rudel in his uniform. She forced herself to move slowly, to keep her hopes in check for fear of making a mistake that might betray her. She went back to the dressing table and opened the jewellery box. She took out the tray and all of the bags. She ran her fingers round the felt lining. She could have sobbed with relief when she picked at a corner and it gave way, revealing a set of papers folded carefully beneath.

My Political Testament, authorised by Adolf Hitler.

The first document she eased out was typed in German on six sheets of onionskin-thin paper. Annie scanned the pages, knowing they would need more careful scrutiny when she was in a safer place. They were a pool of bile and sordid lies that made for sickening reading. An echo of the past that had to be silenced before more fanatics like Margarete consumed them. And as for the final page…

Hitler had gone to his death in the firm belief that Germany would stay true to the path he'd set it on in 1933, despite the nightmare that had led to for the citizens he'd professed to love, never mind anyone else. The last paragraph was a call on his successors to maintain 'the pitiless resistance' against the Jews, 'the universal poisoner of all people'. And the very last words of all – scribbled in a shaking hand that had blotted the paper – were a personal call to Margarete that had lit a fire inside her Annie knew nothing would quench.

Finde unseren Mann in England und baue wieder auf.
Finde die Anderen. Bleib treu.

Annie read and reread the words, but the meaning didn't change. *Find our man in England and rebuild. Find the others. Stay true.*

She put the pages down, her head spinning. How many other copies of his testament had been circulated? How many more personal missions had the Führer set in motion? How many people had heard Hitler's unrepentant, hate-soaked voice since his death and embraced it? Thousands in Dalston today, via Mosley's speech. Thousands more probably in Glasgow and Birmingham and Liverpool, which had also now seen riots in favour of the fascists. No doubt thousands more again across the whole country once the summer got started. Questions flew like wasps through her head. But she didn't have to waste time finding an answer for the most urgent one – where will this all lead? The answer was there on the second folded sheet. The list contained in that was short, but it was no less terrifying for its brevity.

Targets, Group One:

- *Atlee, easiest during summer holiday in Nefyn,
  North Wales, first week in August*
- *Churchill, at Chartwell private residence*
- *Princess Margaret, use contact at 400 Club which
  she visits weekly*
- *Lewis W. Douglas, American Ambassador,
  frequents the Ritz without bodyguards*

Annie stared at the names and the notes beside them. It was unmistakably a hit list, compiled in Margarete's distinctively slanted handwriting. It was the promise of a series of catastrophes that would destabilise the government and the country, and impact on America too. That would create fear and panic if they were linked into a conspiracy and send the press screaming for a scapegoat Annie knew would be easily served up. That would let the men offering the meaningless lure of strong leadership and decisive action step into the void and take hold.

And make laws which will camouflage hatred under the guise of national interest before anyone realises their freedoms – or their lives – have gone.

'You're supposed to look happy when you read those.'

Annie hadn't heard the door's soft click. She hadn't heard Margarete's careful footsteps. She'd been too absorbed.

Or she's been prepared for this all along.

Annie had been fooled – she'd walked blindly into a trap. She saw that the instant she turned round. Margarete was standing in the doorway, leaning against its cream frame, nodding at the pages scattered over the bed. She did not look surprised to see Annie sitting there.

'You've read our Führer's final words, which is a privilege. You've seen his message to me, and no doubt you've worked out there were others he instructed in the same way. You've read the list, so I assume you also now understand how we're going to create the conditions under which Mosley – which actually means me and Hans, and your father if he carries on doing as he's told – will sweep in to power. You should be beaming with delight. But you're not, are you? You're horrified.'

Annie gathered the pages back up. *Horrified* didn't come close. She'd moved outside herself when she read the target list. She'd seen the bombs and the bullets and the shocked faces of the victims as if she was looking at a screen. But in the moment of reading their names, in the moment of making the link between the carnage and its intended consequences, Annie had lost her fear. The stakes were too high to waste time on that. She looked up at Margarete. The woman's hard face expected terror from her or pleading. But Annie's body was burning with a heat that was brighter than the poison filling Margarete, and the last thing she was about to do was beg.

'Of course I am – any decent person would be. And I feel sorry for you, I really do. Something inside you is broken. You've put your faith in madmen and grown mad yourself – or perhaps you were as twisted as them all along. It doesn't matter which. None of this will happen. You do know that, don't you? Or is your grip on reality completely gone? You might get close to one of your targets; you might hurt, or even kill, one of them. But one will be all. The intelligence services will swing into action, and Mosley will be a suspect. So will you. The authorities will close ranks to prevent a panic – the story will be rewritten as a lone wolf who the police have apprehended because they will catch you, and Mosley will give you up to save his own neck. You'll vanish then; they're very good at that. The victim – if there is one – will be remembered, but you and your cause will be buried and forgotten.'

Annie stopped. She hadn't expected to be allowed to say so much without interruption. She didn't understand why Margarete's expression had barely flickered.

'What a lovely speech. I assume you drew on your vast experience of the intelligence services to craft it. And perhaps it would be true, if I was the only link in the chain. But you know I'm not. And perhaps it would also be true if we didn't have supporters at every level of the police who know when to step back. But we do.' Margarete paused to let Annie take that in. 'Or if you were in a position to walk out of here with the evidence. But you're not. You're clever, Annie, I'll give you that. You're just not clever enough. I've never really trusted you; I never really trust anyone. All this time you've been watching me, and trying to learn how I work, but you didn't understand that. Which is your loss, not mine.'

Margarete's smile came slowly and widened. Annie couldn't stop herself shrinking back.

'You were too compliant – that was your mistake. You're a fighter; we both know that. You've never forgiven me for Peggy or Harry; we both know that too. And yet you crumbled so quickly, I assumed you still had a stunt to pull, and here you are. Following the breadcrumbs, taking the bait. Thinking I would tell you when I was out of town and give you free rein to rummage through my flat as if I would ever be such a fool. It's a shame really. I do think you could have made a life for yourself with Hans, but it's your choice. We'll both live with the disappointment. But not with the mess which you could cause us – that won't be helpful. So now I need to clean things up.'

She'd opened her bag while she was talking. The gun she pulled out was so small it looked like a theatre prop. Annie wasn't fooled. She knew that it would be loaded, that Margarete would use it, and find a way to clean that mess up too. She got to her feet before she was told to.

'Good girl. Now give me the papers, and the diamonds which I imagine are in your pocket, and let's go down past dear Jackson or Jennings or whatever he's called, without causing a fuss.'

There wasn't a moment in the lift when Annie could have wrenched away the gun. It was pressed too hard into her side. There wasn't a moment in the entrance hall either – she had no doubt Margarete would shoot the doorman she marched past without speaking to if she had to. But there was a second where Annie was able to wriggle her arm and drop the piece of paper concealed in her sleeve. The one she'd scribbled a message on in case Margarete had been playing her for a fool and set a trap. The one she had to pray Jenkins would find.

CHAPTER THIRTY
MAY 1948

'That way. Down towards the water. Hurry up.'

Margarete gripped Annie's arm in a vice as they left the apartment block, and she jabbed the gun harder against her ribs. There was no space in which Annie could twist and turn the tables. And there was no waiting car either. Margarete laughed her hollow laugh when she saw Annie glance around the street.

'You thought I'd take you to Savehay, didn't you? I bet you've left a note somewhere for the besotted doorman to find – or your handlers at Kensington. Does it start, *If I disappear, I'll be in the countryside with the nasty Nazi?* Oh bless you, Annie. You do keep trying. You really could have done well working with us.'

Annie stumbled – she couldn't help herself. Margarete's nails almost broke through her skin. But she had to keep Jenkins out of the story and keep her courage up.

'Of course I haven't. When would I have had time to do that? It wasn't as if I expected you to arrive in the flat. But they'll come looking anyway. You're not the only person with eyes on me.'

'Oh, but I am.'

Margarete half pushed and half dragged Annie across Grosvenor Road towards the Thames as she answered. The street was deserted although it wasn't yet dark. Annie had lost track of time, but the slight chill in the breeze as much as the lack of people told her that evening was drawing in. It had to be close to dinner time. Mothers would be gathering up their children and tending to their stoves. Fathers would be dawdling in their gardens, smoking and pretending to prune the roses. London life rolling along its spring patterns.

Which I'll never see again if she has her way.

Annie forced herself to listen to what Margarete was saying. Anything could be a clue, a way out of danger.

'The grey women have stopped trailing behind you, didn't you notice? Not that I can blame you if you didn't. Half the city looks as drab as they did – who can tell one from the other? Which I presume was the point.' She leaned in closer and twisted the gun. 'But here's the thing, you're not the only clever one in the game. You know what a good forger I am; I was certainly good enough to fool poor old Harry. I dropped a note in to your boss a couple of weeks ago. You explained in it how you thought I'd picked up on your minders and was growing suspicious. Which was true. And you told him to call off the little grey geese. So you're on your own, Annie dear. You don't have any protection. But I do.'

They were close to the water's edge now, only a partially rotted fence and a rusty chain's length away from the river. The Thames was swollen, not long past high tide. It flowed past Annie in a slate-coloured stream that was too cold to pick up the last blue drops from the sky. Annie turned her head away from its hypnotic tumble – it was too easy to imagine the push that would send her flying down into it. She focused on the pathway they were walking along instead, although the view was no more comforting there. The wharves had been gutted by the war. The warehouses that had once been filled to their rafters with coal and timber and Spanish oranges were a derelict mess of broken beams and weed-choked bomb craters. She wouldn't put her faith in anyone who might be lurking in them. All she could do was to try and understand how weighted the scales were against her.

'What do you mean, you've got protection? Is Rudel waiting? Are you going to hand me over to him?'

Margarete's laugh disturbed a row of musty smelling pigeons who whirled away in a smudge of dust-darkened feathers.

'Would you like it to be Hans? Have you come round to the idea of him?' She stopped suddenly and pulled Annie round to face her, pushing the gun hard into Annie's stomach. 'As if I'd insult him any more than I already have by thinking you were good enough to be his wife. Hans has gone back to Germany, for now. He'll come back when we strike. There's no more wedding, there are no more plans for you except what you see here.' She jerked her head towards the water while Annie tried not to shiver. 'I didn't intend to do this, but you've given me no choice. And don't get any ideas about fighting back, there's a good girl. I told you – I've put in an insurance policy.'

The woman's beautiful face, which was inches away from Annie's, was far colder than the slate-coloured water.

They could have flown in from Hollywood.

1934's Christmas party flew back faster than the pigeons had flown away. Two young girls staring at two elegant women whose beauty they hoped one day to share. The thought of comparing herself to them now made Annie feel sick. Margarete talked about Hitler as if he was a great hero, a man to be worshipped. Diana Mosley had clapped at a 'joke' at the Royal Court dinner about how the plans for the redevelopment of the East End should include an oven or two.

And I was supposed to be one of their coven. I'd rather pluck out my own tongue. Or theirs.

Blood surged through her veins. Her body stiffened as if it was ready to pounce.

Margarete felt it and nodded. 'There it is. The fire you love to hide. It's always been there, hasn't it? Bubbling away as you act like a nice girl while you plot. Don't try anything, Annie. I've a man at the hospital, watching your husband; if he doesn't get a call from me in the next hour, Harry won't be coming out of there alive. Jim's next on his list. Just imagine poor broken Dolly, left all alone, no husband, no son. What a legacy to leave them.' She waited while Annie turned the same pale grey as the clouds rolling past them and her body drooped. 'Good girl. Surrender to me and surrender to the water and this will be over nice and quick, and none of the little people will get hurt. That's a win, surely?'

Annie ignored *win*. She ignored all the ways Margarete had got in front of her. She might be beaten, but she couldn't stay quiet.

'But everyone on your hit list will be killed if you get your way and some of the people who'll get caught up in the riots you'll engineer next. And all those you'll target if you really do manage to propel Mosley and yourself into power. Where does this end, Margarete? With ghettoes and camps and execution pits again? Are we really back in that circle of hell?'

Margarete sighed. 'So dramatic, so tedious. I won't miss you one bit. All these *ifs*. They don't exist; there's only *when*. And this time it ends in glory. Now stop talking and walk; I'm bored with you. I can't bear another minute of your theatrics.'

Margarete shoved Annie back round and pushed her further along the cracked path. It was obvious where they were heading. There was a break in the chain a little further along, and the half-rotted remains of a pier. Annie knew that was destined to be her last stop. Seeing it pushed everything else out of her head. She sucked in a silent breath and ran through what was coming, trying to find a loophole. She imagined there would be another sharp shove, not a gunshot – the air was so still a gun's sharp retort would echo as far as Vauxhall Bridge and bring people running. The wood looked slippery enough for a push to work. Margarete had the advantage of both height and timing over Annie. She had the advantage of believing she'd be the one who stayed alive.

Panic began fluttering like balloons bobbing in the corners of Annie's eyes. She forced herself to look past them, to look away. If she let panic overwhelm her, the water might as well already be over her head, and there'd be no surviving that. The Thames had a notoriously strong current and – even if the shock of the cold and the weight of her clothes didn't immediately drag her down – Annie was a poor swimmer.

I never had two or three months to turn this around. And now I don't have two or three minutes.

They were on the pier. Annie's shoes slid the second she stepped onto its slimy surface. But so did Margarete's. Her grip fell away. Annie spun round, ducking as both women temporarily lost their balance.

Avoid the gun. Knock her out with a blow to her temple or her neck.

The moves flashed through Annie's head in the brief pause between Margarete slipping and righting herself, but the moves didn't land how they were meant to land. Margarete had no more intention of dying than Annie did. The shot rang out in the same moment Annie's elbow flew towards Margarete's head.

The bullet seared through Annie's left arm as her right collided with Margarete. They both screamed in pain and shock. But it was Margarete who teetered. Who'd spun round and lost her bearings. Who took one too many steps backward on the treacherous pier. Whose face crumpled in surprise as one foot and then the next couldn't find anything but splinters and air to step onto, and she fell backward and over the edge of the rotten wood. Down as gracefully as if she was flying into the endlessly moving grey water.

'I am so sorry. She played us all for fools, not that I need to tell you that. If I'd had any idea that it was her who wrote me the note calling off your protection... If I'd had any idea she had someone on the inside at the Gardens... If anything had happened to you on that pier... Have you any idea how lucky you've been?'

Alan's stiff upper lip had badly let him down when he appeared next to Annie's hospital bed the next day. Her injury wasn't a serious one – the bullet had passed through with less damage than the blood loss suggested – but he'd acted as if he'd inflicted the wound himself. His concern was kind, but all Annie wanted to talk about was Margarete.

'I didn't mean to knock her in. My plan – not that I had an actual plan, but my intention anyway – was to knock her out and tie her up and get the papers and the diamonds. I begged the policeman who came to start dragging the river for her straight away in case she swam for it. But he seemed to think I was making it all up, or I'd had a bang to the head. Until I forced him to call you and he finally listened.'

Everyone in the Brewer's Arms had thought Annie was

suffering from concussion, or worse, when she'd staggered into its gloomy depths, dripping with blood and demanding a telephone.

'I have to make a call; it's an emergency. My husband could die if I don't.'

Harry had been Annie's only thought as Margarete plunged into the water and disappeared. She had less than an hour to save him and no idea whether the man sent to watch over him would really wait that long. She'd run into a pub half a mile along the riverside – a battered-looking place which had once served a bustling dockland and was now as run-down as the warehouses where its few drinkers had once worked – as if she was intending to hold it at gunpoint. She'd been greeted as if she was deranged. The landlord had taken one look at the blood pouring from her arm and at her wild face and refused to let her anywhere near his precious telephone. He'd sent for the police instead. Annie had then refused any medical treatment until the horrified policeman – who was the comfortable local sort more used to clearing drunks from the alleyways they'd fallen asleep in – gave in to her pleading and called Alan.

She had little memory of what happened after that, apart from giving a very garbled statement to a confused man who'd just been informed that the bedraggled woman gulping down brandy was 'an essential intelligence asset'. The evening had become a blur of sirens and an ambulance and an oxygen mask, and somebody at some timeless point telling her that Harry and everyone else was safe. She'd insisted on giving a clearer statement the next morning once she was bandaged and propped up in bed. She'd been counting the minutes until Alan's arrival ever since.

'Have they found her?'

His face resumed its more formal shape. He nodded. 'Yes. Her body was recovered earlier this morning, not far from

Lambeth Bridge. The diamonds were in her pocket, but I'm afraid the papers were a sodden mess.'

Annie closed her eyes and pretended it was a wave of pain. All the evidence lost for the sake of a slippery pier. She was furious with herself, but Alan – who'd seen enough frustrated operatives to know how she felt – wasn't.

'It's better this way, I promise you. Nobody benefits from reading that man's last words. And as for the list... From what you've told me about Margarete, I'm surprised she wrote the names down in the first place. Perhaps it was a vanity thing – who knows? The point is, we've turned her flat and the Farm upside down, and there isn't another copy. Which serves us better too. There won't be an investigation; there won't be a conspiracy for the press to feed over. We won't report Margarete's death except as another unidentified suicide and unfortunately, there are too many of those for the papers to care about. She was never more than a ghost in a lot of people's lives. And now she'll be forgotten.'

Forgotten. How Margarete would hate that. How fitting it felt. Annie's body lost its tight edges.

'And the targets?'

Alan smiled the smile of a man satisfied with the way he'd done his job. 'They've been warned about a threat that's now dealt with; their security's been increased. Apparently the princess wasn't happy about having her evening excursions curbed, although that was the King's doing, not ours. I gather he was relieved to have an excuse to rein her in.' He permitted himself a twinkle as Annie laughed. 'The important thing is that everyone is safe, and you can take the credit for that. You stopped her.' He paused and his eyes grew serious again. 'You should also know that we pulled Mosley into the Gardens for questioning, as well as your father.'

Annie shot up – and winced with real pain this time. 'How far are they implicated?'

Alan shook his head. 'Not at all it seems in Mosley's case. He was horrified – the prospect, and the gravity, of the killings took the wind out of his sails, which is no bad thing. I've a feeling we might start seeing a little less of him soon. It was suggested that if he's such a passionate advocate of Europe, he might want to start spending a bit more time there. He seemed to be listening.'

That was news that eased her sore arm, but there was clearly a more difficult message coming.

'And what about my father? You said, *not in Mosley's case*.'

Alan's voice hardened. 'He's in it up to his neck. Margarete really had him under her spell. He wouldn't believe she was dead at first; I think he fancied himself in love with her. And... I'm sorry, Annie, but it's clear that he knew attacks were planned, although he was less clear on the targets. Given that and what happened to Peggy – which we'll get out of him, don't you worry – he's written himself a ticket for a long spell behind bars.'

Annie lay back against the pillows. Sid returned to prison, with his bitterness and his delusions and utterly undeserved sense of self-importance – it was everything he deserved. He was the author of his own misfortune; he'd tried to be the author of her whole life. He would have covered up his wife's murder if Peggy had died; he'd ruined her life when she'd lived. And now he was gone, and she – and more importantly, her mother – was free of him. That was a victory worth celebrating. And she wanted the same fate for the rest.

'There were others who were at the Royal Court who may have had access to the same instructions and wealth that Margarete had. I included their names in the statement I made this morning, and they'll be known to you. And I don't know how widely she'd discussed the plot, but I'm fairly certain Hans Rudel would be party to it. They've been lovers for years.'

It took Annie a while to tell Alan all about the Royal Court and how Sid had got involved with the plan to marry her off to Hans – she kept saying sorry for not contacting him sooner; he kept telling her she'd had no other choice.

'So there's more than one loose end left, although we'll leave Rudel and his cronies for another day. You're the one whose future I came to deal with.' Alan smiled with real warmth as Annie frowned at him. And then he began talking and reopened all the closed doors.

'Are you ready, Mrs Garnet? There's a very fancy black car waiting for us outside the front door.'

Mrs Garnet. How she loved the sound of that title now. It was all the more precious for losing it. Annie smiled down at her new rings as she pulled on her crimson suede gloves. A simple gold band, a solitaire sapphire. No diamonds. A small ceremony at Hackney Town Hall in front of their parents but no other guests. No borrowed dress, no hand-me-down engagement ring. No reluctance. All Annie had insisted on was that they waited until her arm was out of its cast, so she could properly embrace her new husband. And that his crutches were gone so they could run down the town hall steps together.

Alan's 'Have you any idea how lucky you've been?' at her bedside had taken on a lot more resonance since she'd been given her life back. Since the moment Alan had left and Harry had hobbled in, carrying a bunch of red roses and his heart.

'It's a fresh start for you, and for Harry too if you want to include him. We can make space for you both.'

Alan had been deliberately tactful and very clear that he

wasn't interested in rules about married women – he wanted Annie on his team however she chose to come. And he'd given her choices, which no one had done since Miss Carter had plucked her out of the typing pool. She would be forever grateful to him for that.

'Are you okay? You're not developing cold feet, are you?'

Harry wasn't serious. Annie shook her head and smiled at her husband – another word she'd grown far fonder of than when it had first entered her life. It was wonderful to be back in a place where they could tease each other. That had been a long time coming too.

'Not in the slightest, have you?'

His shrug that said *don't be ridiculous* made her laugh, but she was glad that he'd asked. That he'd checked. Their new commitment to honesty, whatever the circumstances, was proving to be a very successful development. All secrets had led to was vigils at hospital beds and a marriage neither of them had properly valued or nurtured until it was snatched away. They'd toasted this new version after their second wedding with a dusty bottle of champagne the pub landlord had been astonished to sell, and a set of vows intended to rewrite them both. No more closed minds or hearts. No more pieces of their lives tucked away. No more letting anyone but themselves steer their lives. They were brave promises; they stripped away layers and let vulnerability in. But they were also a burst of spring air, especially for Harry, who'd let go of his crutches in every sense.

'We're going on an adventure, Mrs Garnet, like we promised each other years ago that we would. How can I feel anything but happy that I'm doing this with you?'

He was as enamoured of *Mrs Garnet* and *wife* as she was enamoured of *husband*, but he understood there were many different shades to a marriage now. And she'd stopped seeing it as a trap. Annie laughed as she closed the front door and slipped the keys back through the letterbox, and the house on Eleanor Road that had never felt like hers stopped being hers to worry about. She knew Harry wouldn't miss it either. Alan's proposition had been a far more exciting prospect for them both than any ties to bricks and mortar.

'You were right in that report you wrote from Nuremberg. We won the war, but we didn't beat fascism. And perhaps the time for correcting that isn't now – we can't ignore the Russians; the Americans won't let us – but it will come, and we need to prepare for it. The dust is still settling from the war, but there'll be new questions once it does. New demands for justice against the men who got away. Different demands for a reckoning that will focus – as it should – on what was specifically done to the Jews, rather than counting all the numbers of the dead together. There's already rumblings to that end. We need people to start preparing the groundwork for when that happens, Annie. I need one of those people to be you.'

He'd handed her a cause. A crusade against the people who'd swallowed the same poison that had taken Margarete out of the bunker and onto a crusade of her own. He'd handed her the way to balance out her father and make amends to everyone who men like him had hurt. It was the best gift she'd ever been given.

'Come on. You can build your schemes on the plane.'

Harry was holding the car door open; he was holding out his hand. He also had a new job to go to if he wanted it – as German correspondent for *The Times*. But Harry had plans of his own too and was talking about writing a book, a novel looking back at the war through the eyes of the people it had tried to break. His future was beckoning bright, but Annie's future was...

Boundless.

She was going to Linz in Austria first, to meet with a man called Simon Wiesenthal, a Jewish survivor of Mauthausen concentration camp who'd founded an agency dedicated to tracking down escaped Nazis. And then to Hamburg and an office of her own to begin the same task, until the Soviet blockade of Berlin was broken and they could find a more permanent home there at the heart of the new Germany. 'A place to prepare for the hunt from,' as Alan had called it. 'A place where good people will come.'

Good people.

Annie knew plenty of them. Peggy had moved out of Arnold Circus and in with Dolly and Jim. Between the four of them, they'd make sure she never disappeared from her life again. Annie had begun to rebuild her connections with Gerry and Morris, who'd been reluctant to meet with her at first but were slowly coming round since Alan had spoken with them. She was confident that connection would hold and lead in turn to more, to men and women all over Europe who believed in justice as passionately as they did and would never give up the fight.

And together we'll sow the right seeds and weed out the bad ones. We'll chop Hitler's legacy down.

As for the bad ones, Sid would never leave prison – the warden at Brixton had confirmed that. He'd offered to lead Annie from his office to Sid's cell, but she'd had no need of a meeting. She'd seen the miserable state of the place – the smell of sweat and mould that permeated the air and the decades of dirt that had become one with the bricks and seeped through the whitewash like stale bruises. It was the right place to house him. She'd read his confession about Peggy; there was nothing more to say.

And maybe Margarete has gone, but Hans will be the first name on my list.

Annie put out her hand and clasped Harry's. She climbed into the car beside him without a backward glance. The sun was shining, softening the clouds and turning the leaves to gold against the autumn sky. It could have been pouring with rain for all Annie noticed. The shadows that had hung round her family for too long were gone. Her mother was safe. She had the husband she cherished at her side and a whole world of possibilities waiting to be picked.

She'd never been more in love with life.

A LETTER FROM CATHERINE

Dear Reader,

Thank you so much for choosing to read *The Girl Who Told the Truth*. If you enjoyed it, and want to keep up to date with what's coming next, just sign up at the following link. Your email address will never be shared, you can unsubscribe at any time and you'll get a free short story download, *The Last Casualty*, as a thank you!

www.bookouture.com/catherine-hokin

I often cite multiple inspirations when I'm writing a book, but this is an unusual one as a larger number of the characters than I normally include are real people, and Margarete's story was inspired by one. I'll come back to her in a minute.

I'm sure you recognise Mosley and Diana Mitford as well as Hitler's inner circle, but Hans-Ulrich Rudel was also the skilled pilot I portray him as and, given his well-documented activities after the Second World War, a very plausible accomplice for my fictional Margarete. On a pleasanter note, Gerry and Morris were real heroes of the 43 Group – I've included a wonderful book about them in the acknowledgements, and it was a privilege to spend time learning about them. As for the inspiration for Margarete, that's a curious tale...

Like all historical fiction writers, I'm always looking for the gap in the narrative, the seam where you can go mining for gold, and the story of Else Krüger was too good to be ignored. I first came across her via historian Mark Felton's YouTube video, which is well worth a watch. Frau Krüger is a writer's dream. She was Bormann's secretary, and she escaped from the Berlin bunker after Hitler's death, allegedly carrying a copy of his final testament and a bag of diamonds. She was arrested in Hamburg, taken to Nuremberg (where the real countess met her) and did marry her interrogator before she settled in England, where she passed herself off as a Danish war bride. It's an amazing story, but that's where it ends – unlike the other secretaries and survivors of the bunker, Else never wrote a memoir or discussed her experiences, and the truth about the documents and the diamonds died with her. My Margarete is, of course, fictional, but how could any writer walk away from a nugget like that?

Anyway, I'd love your thoughts on this story and anything that's gone into its building. There are lots of ways that you can get in touch, through my social media pages, Goodreads or my website. The details are all given below.

Thank you again.

Best wishes,

Catherine

www.catherinehokin.com

 instagram.com/cathokinauthor

 facebook.com/cathokin

wasn't even Elizabeth, and her harrowing story
begins long before Karen was born.

It's 1941 in Nazi-occupied Berlin, and a young
Jewish woman called Liese is being forced to wear
a yellow star...

**A beautiful and gripping wartime story about
family secrets and impossible choices in the face
of terrible hardship**. Perfect for fans of *The Tattooist of
Auschwitz, We Were the Lucky Ones* and *The Alice Network.*

A story to break your heart – if you read only one book this year, make it this one.

Germany, 1941. When **Inge** – all blonde curls and good manners – first locks eyes with **Felix**, she knows instinctively that he's off limits. Her staunchly proper parents will never approve of a working-class Jewish boy for their precious only daughter. But that doesn't make their first, shy kiss less significant, or the moment they're torn apart less shocking.

The next time they see each other, it will be across the packed courtyard of a Nazi concentration camp – Felix in the prisoners' ranks and Inge on the arm of her new, Nazi husband.

Inge never knew that her father's 'party loyalty' would extend to marrying her off to a cruel Nazi officer twice her age, who sees his new wife as just another thing to control. She has always been a good girl – a silent wife – **but when Inge sees Felix**

**that day – beaten, bloody and brave – she knows
she can't stay silent any longer.**

She must save him, whatever the cost, whatever her husband or
even her country might do to her later...

ACKNOWLEDGEMENTS

As always, so many books went into the writing of this one, but there are some specific sources I would like to acknowledge and recommend if you want to know more about the subjects that I've covered in *The Girl Who Told the Truth*.

There is a wealth of information for Oswald Mosley, but some of it, including Diana Mitford's autobiography, needs to be approached with caution as something of a cult seems to have developed around them. *Blackshirt* by Stephen Dorril is one I would recommend, and *We Fight Fascists* by Daniel Sonabend is an excellent guide to the 43 Group. *Austerity Britain* provided remarkable details for Britain after the war, as did *Our Street* by Gilda O'Neill for the East End. For accounts of the Berlin bunker's last days: *Until the Final Hour* by Traudl Junge is incredibly rich on the details of daily life, plus *He Was My Chief* by Christa Schroeder and *Inside Hitler's Bunker* by Joachim Fest. For post-war Germany: *Don't Let's Be Beastly to the Germans* by Daniel Cowling and *Darkness over Germany* by Amy Buller. For the trials: *Inside Nuremberg Prison* by Helen Fry and *Nuremberg Diary* by G.M. Gilbert, and the fascinating *The Guest House* by Countess Kalnoky.

And now to my personal thanks. To my editor Harriet for doing such a wonderfully collaborative job in editing my novels and for making the whole process such an enjoyable experience. To the Bookouture team who are rightly detailed in the following pages, especially Sally and Sarah. To my friends and family who haven't jumped ship yet. To Robert, who still manages to brim with enthusiasm for everything I do and is loving the research trips. To Claire and Daniel for all their love and cheerleading. And for Clive, a writer of great talent and a lovely man, who will be always missed. Much love to you all.

Proofreader
Laura Kincaid

Marketing
Alex Crow
Melanie Price
Occy Carr
Cíara Rosney
Martyna Młynarska

Operations and distribution
Marina Valles
Joe Morris

Production
Hannah Snetsinger
Mandy Kullar
Nadia Michael
Charlotte Hegley

Publicity
Kim Nash
Noelle Holten
Jess Readett
Sarah Hardy

Rights and contracts
Peta Nightingale
Richard King
Saidah Graham

Dear Reader,

We'd love your attention for one more page to tell you about the crisis in children's reading, and what we can all do.

Studies have shown that reading for fun is the **single biggest predictor of a child's future life chances** – more than family circumstance, parents' educational background or income. It improves academic results, mental health, wealth, communication skills, ambition and happiness.

The number of children reading for fun is in rapid decline. Young people have a lot of competition for their time, and a worryingly high number do not have a single book at home.

Hachette works extensively with schools, libraries and literacy charities, but here are some ways we can all raise more readers:

- Reading to children for just 10 minutes a day makes a difference
- Don't give up if children aren't regular readers – there will be books for them!

- Visit bookshops and libraries to get recommendations
- Encourage them to listen to audiobooks
- Support school libraries
- Give books as gifts

There's a lot more information about how to encourage children to read on our websites: **www.RaisingReaders.co.uk** and **www.JoinRaisingReaders.com**.

Thank you for reading.